DREAD TRIBUNAL of LAST RESORT

A NOVEL OF THE CIVIL WAR

Brian Kaufman

Black Rose Writing | Texas

ISBN: 978-1-68513-474-7
PUBLISHED BY BLACK ROSE WRITING
www.blackrosewriting.com

Printed in the United States of America
Suggested Retail Price (SRP) $24.95

Dread Tribunal of Last Resort is printed in Book Antiqua

*As a planet-friendly publisher, Black Rose Writing does its best to eliminate unnecessary waste to reduce paper usage and energy costs, while never compromising the reading experience. As a result, the final word count vs. page count may not meet common expectations.

PRAISE FOR
DREAD TRIBUNAL OF LAST RESORT

"Kaufman does an impressive job detailing the inner conflict of each character. The pace is quick and speedy... with a lot of lively secondary characters, there's a lot here for readers to enjoy. Recommended."
–Historical Novel Society

"*Dread Tribunal of Last Resort* creates a moving story that delves into the hearts and minds of those who are swept up in a war of ideals."
–D. Donovan, Senior Reviewer, *Midwest Book Review*

"A gripping read, *Dread Tribunal* reminds us not only of the agony of the Civil War but the torment inflicted on those who had to fight it. The pain lives on."
–Mark James Miller, author of *The White Cockade: A Novel of the American Revolution*

To my wife and children, born free.

DREAD TRIBUNAL
of LAST RESORT

CHAPTER ONE

Aquia Creek, Maryland, to Richmond, Virginia
April 1861

"I had reasoned this out in my mind; there was one of two things I had a right to, liberty, or death; if I could not have one, I would have the other. . . "
~Harriet Tubman

Decker Brown leaned out far enough to watch the train cars winding behind him. Some were house cars, like giant boxes on wheels. Others were flatcars, loaded and tied down for the journey. Most passengers rode the rear flatcar, which was only half-stocked with crates. The engine lurched, starting up an incline. The jolt sent a shudder through each trailing car. Decker leaned back, gripping the open doorframe of the house car. He glanced at his valise, which hadn't moved. Good. He didn't own much, but everything he had was in the bag. His mother's ring. Some clothing. And the illumination.

Everything else of value, he carried between his ears and in his heart. He smiled, and the smile became a laugh. Tonight, he would launch his future life. He and his father would begin crafting their rockets. He would celebrate the enterprise with the package in his valise. And he would claim Paula as his own, if she would still have him, and if her father would now consent to the union.

He'd spent the last two years working with his Uncle Oskar in Boston. Now, the *Richmond, Fredericksburg & Potomac* would take him into Richmond.

The train entered a denser part of the wilderness, slowing near the crest of a hill, creeping no faster than a man could walk. Tree branches brushed the sides of the house car as it passed, twigs and spring buds whispering across the wood. Decker draped his legs over the edge of the open doorway, resisting the urge to hop out and run alongside the train. Leaning out again, he looked at the engine, just two cars away. Black smoke, lit with sparks, billowed from the stack.

When he arrived in Richmond, he would hurry to his father's home. His father would be sure to open a bottle. Then, as soon as Decker could get away, he would call upon the Crane family. He imagined climbing the steps of their three-story home, knocking at the door and waiting, one hand on the Ionic columns that bracketed the entrance, the other hand holding his hat. A servant would answer — Henry Lee or Millie. If Millie answered the door, she would sneak a smile. If Henry Lee came instead, he'd scowl like an old blackbird and turn away, leaving Decker to cool his heels on the porch. Either way, Paula would come to the door, and he would need only a glance to answer his every question.

In revisiting his daydream, he found himself anxious. The trees were denser now, the canopy of branches blocking out the late afternoon sun. A chill made him back up into the house car and lean against a stack of crates. The air felt damper than before. He drummed his fingers on the car's wooden floor, glancing for the dozenth time at his valise. His hat had blown back into the car's recesses. He stood up with a mind to retrieve it when the trees parted, opening the view to a long slope down to the plains below, dotted with farms and buildings. In the distance sat the irregular shapes of a city, jutting like the upturned teeth of a lumber saw at the edge of the horizon. The sky had opened up as well, with tufts of cloud lit from below by a reddened sun.

Richmond. He was nearly home.

The rails ran to the edge of town. The train station was a flat brick building with a long deck for a platform. Decker stood, hat and valise in hand, waiting for the train to stop.

Preoccupied, he did not take notice of the small crowd waiting for the train's arrival. By happenstance, the train came to rest near the end of the platform, precisely in front of an old, Black man. Something in the man struck him as familiar — the bent head, as if his neck muscles had given out, leaving him stooped but defiant, and the wizened hands, knuckles the size of walnuts. He *knew* the man.

And he knew the woman stepping out from behind. Her auburn curls framed an angular face with dark eyes that were too large, too intelligent to be conventionally beautiful. Her skin was fine porcelain, more bone ash and alabaster than flesh. When she smiled, his knees went weak.

Decker leapt from the car onto the platform, valise and hat in hand. Henry Lee reached for the valise without a word, and Decker gave it up without thinking. "You're here. How did you know?"

"I didn't," she said.

"We done greeted every train into Richmond for the last three days," Henry Lee grumbled.

She nodded. The sun, low in the sky behind her, lit the red highlights in her hair.

Decker dropped his hat, his hands now uncertain. He wanted to take her in his arms, but there had been no formal agreement, and he did not want to embarrass her. Henry Lee moved closer — *damn him* — and Decker stood still, flummoxed, his hat at his feet.

She laughed.

He stepped to the side, whispering around Henry Lee's obvious efforts to intrude. "Tell me. Are you mine?"

"Forever. Until the mountains crumble and the seas boil." He stood close enough to feel the heat from her face as she blushed.

He reached out to Henry Lee to retrieve his valise and the ring inside. "Then I'm home."

$$\bullet \quad \bullet \quad \bullet$$

With Henry Lee to escort her, Paula returned to the Crane's house near the center of the city, having extracted a promise from him. Decker would come calling the very next day. In the meantime, he would go home to his father, who lived at the south end of town.

The modest, two-story brick building sat on the other side of the city, past the Capitol building and the Custom House. Like several of the neighboring houses, the entrance featured an overhanging roof bracketed by columns. A picket fence bordered the tiny front yard. Decker opened the gate and tried to latch it behind him — the latch was loose and would not hook to the tired wood. *Work to* do, he thought. When he reached the front door, he didn't bother to knock.

His father sat at a table, sharpening his beloved Bowie on an oiled stone. He took pains with each stroke before setting the knife on a muslin cloth. He looked up. "You're home."

Decker nodded. Like the gate latch, his father looked old and worn.

"Well, sit down then." George Brown stood up, wiping his hands on his pants. "Will you have a drink with me?"

Decker smiled. "Of course, Pops." He went to the table and sat, while George shuffled to the cupboard, fetching a bottle.

"Bark juice. Nothing fancy," he said.

"I don't need fancy."

"Good." Pops set two small glasses on the table and poured two fingers into each. Then he pushed the sharpening stone aside.

"I love that knife," Decker said.

"I know it." Pops picked up his glass. Decker stood, grabbing his own glass.

"To the future?" Decker asked.

His father's face sank, a subtle downturn of the mouth and softening of the eyes. "And all of its challenges."

They touched glasses and drank. Decker tossed his back in a single swallow. George sipped and set the glass back down on the table. "You've acquired a taste, then."

"Oskar is a drinking man."

Pops nodded and sat down. "How is my brother?"

"Oskar is Oskar," Decker said. He reached for the bottle and poured himself another drink. This one he would sip.

"Is he healthy?"

"He didn't stop coughing the whole time I was there." Decker laughed and then noticed his father's face. "He's a tough old buzzard. He may live forever."

His father seemed to relax. "Good. And how did you two get along?"

"I made no mistake small enough to escape criticism," Decker said, a smile on his face. "He is an exacting man. And I learned a great deal."

"Tell me."

"I can read French and Italian. I can't speak so well, but I can read. And he taught me to grapple and strike." George's eyebrows went up. "As I said, he's a tough old buzzard." Decker shook his head. "And I learned how to mix chemicals without blowing myself up."

"I'm glad of that."

Decker leaned forward. "The Italians know more about illuminations than I'd have ever guessed. Pops, there's no one in the South that will be able to produce what we can produce!"

Pops frowned. "How was your journey?"

Decker sat back. "Wonderful. I was anxious to come home, and once started, a journey always takes longer than one wishes, but this is beautiful country, and I saw astounding things."

"Tell me."

"I saw a locomotive the height of two men. I saw a herd of deer jumping the tracks in front of a train, barely slipping past. Donkeys pulling a canal boat like a horse pulls a plow. And factories. I saw machinery that could do the work of two dozen men!" He paused, taking a sip of his whiskey. The burn in his throat was welcome, tempering his emotions. "Someday, we'll own machinery like that. We'll manufacture for the whole of the South!"

His father looked away. "Pops?"

He shook his head. "It's a good thing to have dreams." Decker sat still.

"How is Paula Crane?"

Decker blushed. "She met me at the station. She couldn't wait to see me."

Pops smiled for the first time. He was missing a front tooth, and that wasn't the only sign he'd aged in Decker's absence. He'd lost a great deal of weight. Always a beefy man, he was lean now, but not the rawboned kind of lean—the wasted, shrunken kind of lean. His sharp cheekbones jutted out as if they might break the skin. A scab on his thinning hairline looked fresh and angry.

"Are you going to marry that girl?"

"Yes."

Pops nodded. "Good. There's nothing more important in a man's life than finding someone to share that life with. Nothing."

"You and Mom were together for a long time."

Pops smiled, but his eyes were wet, and his lip trembled. "Your mother was the love of my life."

Decker reached out and patted his father's hand. "I know she was." He looked around the room. "The house looks good."

A lie. His father was a terrible housekeeper. The center of the front room was clean, but every corner showed evidence of dust, dirt, and scraps. The walls were coated, as if he'd not bothered to wash the walls free of candle smudge for the two years Decker had been gone.

"I clean up after myself," Pops said, downing his drink and pouring himself another. "My mother did laundry for extra money. Never bothered her — doing the work of a servant. Did you know that?"

Decker shrugged. He'd heard the tales a hundred times. "Made you want to clean up your own messes, right?"

His father gave him a wry smile. "I repeat myself, do I?"

"That's all right, Pops. Good stories should be told and retold." He grabbed his glass and finished it. George took the bottle and poured another two fingers into Decker's glass. "I brought home a special illumination for you and Paula," Decker continued. "It's a double. One explosion, and then another."

"You can do that?"

"I can do better. The first is blue. The second is gold." Pops sat with his mouth open, dumbfounded.

"I can't wait for you to see it. We're invited to the Crane's home for supper tomorrow. When it's dark, I'll launch. I think you'll be amazed."

"I hope you can make good on a boast like that!"

Decker laughed. "If the cake doesn't fall, the cook's not bragging."

"Well, I'm sure you'll pass muster. I'm afraid I'll have to disappoint you about the visit tomorrow. I've been under the weather, and it's best I stay home and rest."

"What's wrong, Pops?" Decker glanced down at the man's glass. "Should you be drinking?"

"That's the only thing that's keeping the engine fired," he answered.

"How long have you been sick?"

"Not sick. Under the weather."

"You need to take care of yourself, Pops."

His father was silent for a long moment, scratching his chin as if wondering what to say next. "So, how did you make your way here? I got your letter, but I wondered how you traveled."

"Went some of the way on toll roads and a canal. The last leg was the best. I took the *RF & P* to the Richmond Depot. Took two hours, Pops. Seventeen miles!"

George shook his head. "Amazing."

"And now I'm home. So, when do we get started?"

"Started?"

"You know, with the business."

George shrank in his chair. His eyes took on a hard look, as if Decker had mis-stepped. "Pops? Has something changed? Bad financial times?"

"The world has changed, son."

Decker shifted in his seat. "How so?"

"Don't they have newspapers up in Boston? South Carolina seceded. Six other states, as well."

Decker knew about secession. He'd been assaulted with the news for weeks, and he'd studiously avoided thinking about the possibility of war. "Yes, Pops. They have papers. The North is completely civilized."

His father scowled. "Then you know that the time is not right for a new business. We'll be at war soon."

"Not possible." Decker emptied his glass. George grabbed his and did the same. As Pops refilled the glasses, Decker added, "We won't go to war."

"What makes you think so?"

"Because it would be stupid."

"Go on." His father's face hardened.

"So many people up north, Pops. Everywhere you turn. And they have a factory on every corner. Some battles can't be won. War with the North would be suicide."

He sat upright, downed his drink, and pushed the glass away. "A Virginian can take on ten Yankees."

"Two, maybe three. Ten? Someone's going to get off a lucky shot. The Yankees aren't squirrels, Pops."

"You don't sound like a patriot."

"I am, Pops. But I'm not a fool."

They stared at each other in silence. George Brown scratched his chin, a casual move belied by the fire in his eyes — part anger and part whiskey. His father was half Decker's size, but he was formidable when angry or fueled by drink. "What will you do when you find out you're wrong?"

Decker stood and walked the bottle back to the cupboard. When he returned, he said, "What will I do when I discover I'm wrong? I'll mark the moment. I might even note it in my journal. *No longer perfect. Tell Jesus Christ on his throne that his record is safe.*"

His father's eyes grew large as cartwheels, and he started to laugh. "Ha! His record is safe!" He laughed so hard he began to cough, and it took him almost a minute to settle down. Tears ran down his cheeks, and he wiped snot with the sleeve of his shirt. "No longer perfect! That's a rich one. By God, you're an arrogant little snipe. Glad you're home!"

"I love you, Pops," Decker said. "Am I sleeping upstairs?"

"Your room is just where you left it."

"Thanks," he said, adding, "But don't worry. I'm right. We won't be going to war."

CHAPTER TWO

Richmond, Virginia
April 1861

"Men love to wonder, and that is the seed of science."
~Ralph Waldo Emerson

William Crane owned the Crane Flour Mill on the northern edge of Richmond. He'd built the business using a modest inheritance from his father's estate. His brother, who'd received a like amount when their father died, invested his money in a proposed small gauge railroad west of Richmond. The project went bankrupt, which proved a basic principle of economics according to William — *travel is a luxury, and flour is a necessity.* Necessities, like foodstuffs and cotton, would never fail, whereas gadgets, particularly those produced in Northern factories, were risky investments at best.

"I might have made my fortune in King Cotton," William said, a glass of bourbon in one hand and a cane in the other, "but I was convinced otherwise by a simple thought experiment. I imagined myself trapped in a cell for two weeks. I asked the question, would I rather be clothed and hungry, or naked and well-fed?" He paused, a subtle smile on his lips, his bushy eyebrows twitching. "Naked as a jaybird, I tell you!"

Laughter greeted the punch line, as it had each of the twenty times Paula Crane had heard the story. Her mother feigned embarrassment, complete with a blush and a flutter of her fan, crying, "Scandalous! Simply scandalous!" A dozen guests chuckled with appreciation.

Paula turned to her right. At the edge of the room, Decker Brown leaned back against the wall, his attention on her father. He wore the same clothing he'd worn on the train, though he'd had the jacket brushed and cleaned. His hair caught the light from the late afternoon sun through the window. Round-faced and towheaded, he reminded her of the plates in her father's mythology books. Theseus. Jason. He was half again as large as any other man in the room. The sight of him made her swoon.

At the opposite edge of the room, Whitaker Hill, son of Jubal Hill, whose vast tobacco fields lay south of Richmond proper, stood ramrod straight, his shoulders pinned back by his tailored vest and coat, purchased in England. With his low-cut boots, polished to a sheen and trimmed goatee, the dashing young man was the embodiment of Sir Wilfred of Ivanhoe, both in looks and stubborn bearing.

He stared at her now, his punch glass in hand. Having caught her eye, he tilted his head and nodded.

Paula looked away, blushing. Whitaker had spent the better part of the day circling her father like a celestial body, careful to block Decker's clumsy attempts to share a private word with the man, eclipsing Decker's efforts with the smooth sort of charm that made Whitaker the delight of the unmarried women of Richmond.

Whitaker. Whit. *He has that, too.* Paula sighed. Her father had promised to give his permission to marry Decker, should her beloved finish his apprenticeship in Boston. She'd known her father made those assurances, believing that time and distance would cool her ardor. His own marriage had been a sound alliance based on financial realities. An alliance between the Cranes and the Hills would be equally advantageous. But money didn't interest Paula.

She shifted in her chair. She was thin enough not to wear tightlacing, but the layering demanded by fashion and modesty left her sweltering, cool spring air notwithstanding. Her crinolines were soaked in sweat. A glance to the side reminded her she was blessed. Dori Curtis, her friend since childhood, wore much the same ballroom outfit with the added disadvantage of hoops. Dori was fond of pastries and sweet tea, and in truth, most foods, from game to breads. Fashion did not fit the body—the body was meant to fit the fashion. Paula imagined Dori's corset, tight beyond breathing, was likely rubbing her raw. Summer would be here soon enough, and all Southern womanhood would suffer in silence.

Whitaker continued to stare, so she turned back to Decker, who was glaring across the room at Whitaker.

Encouraged by her father, Whit had visited the Crane house several times over the past year. She'd done her best to seem aloof. Tea in the drawing room. Bourbon on the porch at sunset. Stories and boasts. All the while, she smiled and thought of Decker Brown. Now, she worried over Decker's glares. She had not mentioned Whit in her letters. Why would she? But somehow, Decker could sense something was amiss.

Her mother announced the commencement of dinner, and the group made their way to the dining room. The table had been set with the finest linens, a sterling silver cruet set at the center. Saltcellars, pickle vases, and mustard jars were all in reach. Once the guests were seated, servants delivered bowls of gazpacho—soft biscuits topped with layers of fresh tomato, cucumbers, and onion, and finished with a juice made from stewed tomatoes and mustard. Paula took a few bites between stolen glances toward the end of the table. Whit and Decker sat next to each other, eating silently, both staring straight ahead.

Decker had a bit of tomato on his chin.

William Crane continued to entertain the party with stories while the servants delivered the second course—cod baked in a pepper-vinegar fish sauce. The flavor was too tart for Paula's taste, but she swallowed a single forkful. Nothing could go untasted, but a lady did not finish a serving. She glanced across the table. Dori mopped up sauce with her last forkful of fish. *Poor Dori! She eats when she's nervous.* Paula was nervous as well, and with cause.

The main course consisted of roast beef, served alongside stuffed squab. Stewed okra and tomatoes finished the presentation. Paula tried each, saving the beef for last. Squab was not a favorite. She preferred her fowl fried, not baked. The beef was tender and delicious, though, and she had to force herself to leave a portion untouched on the plate.

"So, young Brown," her father said from the head of the table. At the other end, Decker raised his head, chewing a mouthful of beef. William Crane smiled. "I understand you intend to found a business."

"Yes, sir. Illuminations."

"How charming," Paula's mother said. Elizabeth Crane was a shorter, stouter version of her daughter. She'd retained much of her beauty, though the sharper lines of her face had softened with age, and her graying hair had thinned. "I have always loved them, ever since I was a child."

"Am I correct in saying that you brought us a sample of your work?" Crane asked.

Decker nodded. "Just one rocket. But it's a good one."

Crane glanced at the window. "The sun is down. Perhaps after we finish here, we can retire to the porch and view your handiwork."

"It would be my honor, sir," Decker said.

The servants cleared plates and then served shortcake. Later, the party took drinks to the veranda at the rear of the Crane's home, settling in chairs and on the porch rail. Flower beds that were the envy of the neighbors decorated the yard. Decker carried his parcel to the center of the lot, accompanied by Paula. Glancing back, she discovered that Whit had followed.

Decker unwrapped the rocket—a small contraption, no more than knee-high. Earlier, Henry Lee had helped him pound a metal tube into the ground. The tube would guide the rocket the first few feet in its flight. The pipe had a cutaway at ground level for ignition.

"So, that's an illusion," Whit said.

"Illumination." Decker didn't look up.

"We'll see. Where is the stick? I thought these rockets had sticks."

"Congreve rockets have sticks. This is a Hale. The thrust is vectored."

"You need a longer tube, don't you? You might hit the house."

"It's not dangerous," Paula said. "That's right, isn't it, Decker?"

"This is filled with gunpowder," Decker said. He paused in his efforts and looked up at Whit. "You might want to get back on the porch. You'll be safer there."

Whit smiled, shaking his head. "I'll stay close by. You might catch fire."

Paula took a step back, beckoning. "Whit, why don't you come back to the veranda with me? Let Decker do what he needs to."

"All right then," Whit drawled.

Decker nudged the tube to ensure it was well anchored. Then he slipped the rocket in from the top. Paula backed away, step by step, until Whit followed her.

Decker had shown her the launch tube earlier in the day. After the first few feet, the canted exhaust holes would spin the rocket, keeping the flight straight and true. "Most illuminations are still made the old way, with a stick for guidance," he told her. "I spent weeks playing with this design, thinking of this night."

Paula waited for the launch from the steps of the veranda. Whit stood at her elbow, close as the damp evening air. Decker was a silhouette in the dark, lighting a stick of punk. When the punk had a steady glow, he looked up and waved. Paula stepped forward, out from under the eaves. She wanted a clear view of the display.

Decker knelt, and for long moments, nothing happened. Too far away to see what was transpiring, she had to wait in silence, while those behind her began to wonder.

"What's wrong?"

"A shame if it doesn't work!"

Whit hummed. "A shame if it explodes in the tube."

A whooshing sound accompanied by a flash of light announced the launch. A flame marked the progress of the rocket, straight into the night sky. Though the star field was glorious, the moon had not yet risen, and Paula could easily follow the rocket's path, higher and higher.

Then, a sudden flash of light sent streamers out from the center, blue as Virginia daylight, followed by the pop of an explosion. The sparkling light lasted a few long seconds, and then winked out. The guests behind her applauded, a soft patter accompanied by murmurs of approval.

A second explosion sent tendrils streaking across the sky — this time in gold. Paula stared in amazement as the sky flashed, illuminating the gray smoke trails from the first eruption and casting a gilded hue on the city below.

The display caused a minor sensation behind her. Her mother seemed quite amazed. "Oh, my! Wasn't that a wonder?"

Paula walked forward, alone this time. Decker stood waiting by the smoking tube, his hands on his hips. "I've never seen anything like that," she said when she reached him.

In the dark, his face was hard to read. "I sometimes . . ."

She took his arm, hoping to guide him back to the porch, but he resisted.

"I wanted to say . . ."

She stopped. "It was beautiful."

He leaned closer. "There are things I've wanted to tell you, but words don't always . . . come. If I were a poet . . ." He pointed up at the sky. "*That's* what I would say."

"Thank you," she whispered, and though the other guests had crossed the lawn to join them in congratulations, she felt as if they were alone for a few timeless seconds. She could not see his face, only his shape, but she knew he was smiling.

• • •

"Colors!" William Crane exclaimed. "I've never seen such a thing before. How did you manage?" The men had gathered in the drawing room for cigars and brandy. Paula stood near the doorway, watching and listening. Whit had provided the cigars, featuring tobacco from his father's plantation.

Decker had accepted a snifter of brandy but declined the offered cigar. "The colors are a matter of chemism. For example, the golden color came from lampblack."

"Really! Extraordinary."

Paula smiled at her father's exuberance. Perhaps he would warm to Decker at last. "Your toy flew straight," Whit said.

Decker did not seem huffed by the question. "The result of vectored thrust."

Whit tugged at his goatee. "Seems as if the design might have military applications." Decker shrugged.

"Yes, how about that?" William Crane asked. "Might the military be interested?"

"I don't know. My interest is scientific."

Whit picked up his brandy and took a small sip. "I'm surprised you haven't investigated that, what with war looming. Toy or not."

Colonel Lance, an old friend of the Cranes, spoke next. "Rockets have proven to be an effective deterrent against cavalry. The British used them extensively in India. Frightened their horses, they did."

"I've heard the British rockets were undependable." William held out his snifter for a refill. His cheeks were the color of catchfly—ruddy with the glow of liquor. "Difficulty in consistency, if I recall."

"True, true," Colonel Lance said, scratching at his white muttonchops. "All the more reason to advance a solution for the problem of directed flight."

"My rocket is based on the design of the Hale rocket," Decker said. "The Hale is an accurate weapon, with a range—"

"So, your design isn't actually your design?" Whit asked.

"I believe I mentioned Mr. Hale's name." Decker's voice had gone cold. He swallowed the remainder of his brandy and set the glass aside.

Dori came to the doorway at the rear of the room, pressing as close to Paula as her hoop skirt would allow. "Those boys need to behave," she whispered.

"Whit thinks he's being clever."

"I think he's being clever," Dori sighed.

Paula frowned. "I wish he'd stop." She laced her fingers to keep her hands still. Her father appeared to be warming to Decker, thanks to the rocket. Please, please, don't let anything go wrong now. *Let my father see Decker for who he is. And keep Whit quiet!*

"At a time like this, I think you'd want to apply your gifts to the coming war effort," Whit said.

"Hear, hear," Colonel Lance said.

"Yes, what about the coming storm, young Brown?" William Crane asked.

Decker looked at Paula, holding her gaze with an expression of misery. His down-turned mouth and wide eyes seemed to beg for rescue. The conversation had turned away from his moment of triumph, as every conversation had these past months, converging paths that led inexorably to war, always war.

"Rockets have applications other than battle," Decker said at last. "Ship-to-ship rescue, for instance. Two-stage Hale rockets have been used to launch ropes across a thousand yards."

"Rockets will never replace cannon," one of the other guests offered.

"Tredegar is the finest gun works in the world," Whit agreed. "I would take a single twelve-pounder from the Tredegar Iron Works over a dozen Yankee guns."

"The ratio sounds right," Decker muttered.

"We agree, then?" Whit cocked his head to the side, as if in surprise.

"Tredegar makes fine field artillery. And if war comes, the Yankees may well line up a dozen guns against our one to test your theory."

"You believe rockets would serve the South better?"

Decker snorted. "No. A Tredegar gun is accurate and deadly."

"What is your complaint, then?"

"I have none."

Colonel Lance raised his glass. "A toast, then. To Tredegar Iron Works."

A score of voices answered, "Tredegar Iron Works!" Having no glass to raise, Decker bowed and backed away from the other men.

Dori nudged Paula. "Your beau? I think he's coming over here."

Paula leaned against the doorjamb to be certain her posture was plumb straight. Between the heat from the crowded room and her rising anxiety, she was sure her face showed enough color. She took a deep breath and smiled.

Decker walked out of the room without a word. "Oh, my," Dori whispered.

Paula peered out into the hall, watching Decker stride to the front door and exit.

No! Don't go! Paula rushed to the door and paused. Dori had followed her halfway, hissing to catch Paula's attention. Paula turned back. Her friend shook her head as if to say, *don't do it!* Near tears, Paula pulled the door open and walked out into the entry.

Decker Brown stood a yard away from the bottom step, staring up with his hands in his pockets.

"Well! Were you intending to leave without saying goodbye?" He shrugged, which infuriated her. "I had great expectations for this evening, too," she said. "I'm sorry things didn't go as you wished. But really, Decker, the only thing people talk about these days is war. It was a miracle that everyone watched the launch."

He scowled.

"Do you have anything to say, or are you just going to stand there?" Nothing. "Does Whit worry you?"

"Not at all." His lip twitched.

"What then?"

Crickets and cicadas sounded out their spring lullaby, joined by the croak of a frog near the front gate. The touch of a breeze cooled her face. Paula waited. *Talk to me, Decker.*

"They think this will last forever."

When he didn't continue, she urged him on. "What, Decker?"

"This," he said, gesturing at the night. "The sounds, the smells."

"I don't understand."

"Evenings like this. Friends. Brandy. None of this will last."

"Why not?"

"Because if we go to war—"

The door opened behind them, and Henry Lee stepped out onto the porch. "Miss Paula? Your father is asking after you." The old man's gaze was narrow and foreboding. She'd grown up with that frown and knew no argument could be mounted against such a summons. Henry Lee stepped back under the eaves, squinting at them from the shadows.

"I should leave," Decker said.

Not yet. Not like this! "Will you be at Whit's party on Friday?"

"I hadn't thought about it."

"It's his father's party, really. They're going to roast a pig. I am going, so you *must* go." She set her jaw and waited for his answer.

Decker nodded. "All right, then." With nothing more to say—at least in Henry Lee's presence—Paula curtsied and went back inside the house.

CHAPTER THREE

Richmond, Virginia
April 1861

"The unrestricted exploitation of so-called free society is more oppressive to the laborer than domestic slavery."
~George Fitzhugh

Decker stood still, staring at the closed door. Henry Lee didn't move, as if guarding the entrance. The spring air had turned, and Decker shivered a little.

"Were you able to see my illumination, Henry Lee?"

"Yes suh."

"What did you think of it?"

The old man didn't move. He squinted, narrowing the whites of his eyes to the shape of almonds.

Decker leaned back against one of the columns that bracketed the steps. Even in the dark, he could see the brown stains on the whitewash, reminding him of tobacco. The smell of tobacco coated his clothes and drifted in the night air. Whit's tobacco. "I first came here three years ago, Henry Lee." Decker paused. "I came for dinner. Not so many guests as tonight, of course. So, I've had the pleasure of your acquaintance for some time. You have always struck me as an observant man, and I believe you have observed me well enough to have an idea of who I am." He pointed at the door. "The folks in there are very polite. But I wonder what *you* thought about the illumination."

Henry Lee tilted his head, still silent.

"It would be completely acceptable if you didn't think much of it."

Henry Lee spoke, his voice like pea gravel. "The illumination was pretty. Lights and color and sound. I liked your toy, suh."

"A pretty toy," Decker repeated. He shook his head. "I suppose that's *exactly* what I was aiming for." He turned to leave. "Good night, Henry Lee."

"Good night, suh."

Decker turned up his collar, keeping a brisk pace to stay warm. He walked the length of Grace Street, headed south to his father's neighborhood, hands jammed in his pockets, chin tucked into his chest. His thoughts jumped from subject to subject like moths in the night air. His pretty toy. Whit and war. Henry Lee. And slavery.

Somehow, Henry Lee's use of the word *toy* hadn't bothered him the way Whit's comment had. Perhaps because he'd solicited the opinion.

Decker thought back, recalling a conversation he'd had with an intense freed Black man in Boston. They'd spoken at a small gathering for no more than five minutes. He couldn't remember the man's name, but his eyes, dark as his skin and on fire, had burned their way into his memory.

Decker had attended the party in place of his uncle—an unremarkable evening, save for the guest list, which included a freed slave. Well-spoken and self-educated, the man was regarded favorably for the novelty of his presence. For Decker, the man was a revelation—he was clearly the intellectual superior of every person in the room, though that singular fact seemed to escape the others.

Unable to consider the brief conversation out of context, Decker spent many subsequent nights wondering at the meaning of those five minutes spent listening to such eloquence and fire.

The dark-eyed fellow was a *man*, worthy of Mr. Jefferson's life, liberty, and the pursuit of happiness. What of the servants and the field hands at home? Were they not men and women, too? Certainly not property. And yet the courts had decided as such. The question plagued him.

He began speaking to the freedmen working in his uncle's factory. When they responded at all, they did so in short, sullen bursts, always evading, as if he were a policeman, rather than an apprentice. With time, they responded more openly, although thinking now, he decided he'd never been any more than a curiosity to them—the young, earnest nephew of their boss, every bit as crazy as the old German who'd hired them.

Couldn't they see that he wanted only to pass the time with friendly words? In the case of Henry Lee, Decker had long thought the man's scowl and reserved disposition to be a sign of some hidden wisdom. If so, the man was not inclined to drop his guard. Not for Decker.

A puzzle, he decided. Worthy of more thought, to be sure. And he had time—the walk home, winding past the center of Richmond, north to his father's house, would take the better part of an hour.

• • •

The Hill plantation was a sprawling tract northwest of Richmond. Jubal Hill, Whit's father, had a reputation for fine tobacco. The smokehouses, where he hung hands of bright green tobacco leaves to be cured above smoldering fires of damp sawdust, lined the road on the way to the center of the plantation. There, Decker found a small community that comprised the plantation proper.

The Hill residence was an I-house, two stories tall, two rooms wide, divided down its length by a main hallway. The building was constructed from timber cut from the land. Chimney bricks had been fired by an on-site kiln, which stood to the rear of the house, though the days of firing brick had ended five decades earlier. The basic simplicity of the architecture had been masked by recent embellishments. A portico extended half the length of the house, featuring neoclassical columns added to the structure just four years earlier. The columns disrupted the view, which was not, Decker supposed, such a bad thing.

Slave housing stood across the small meadow that served as a courtyard, in clear view of the planter's house. The housing consisted of a series of roughly built, single room log cabins with crude stone chimneys. Trees offered some respite from the sun, though the finest copse of sourwoods sheltered the overseer's house — a tiny, two-story white building at the end of the row of cabins. Jubal Hill employed a white overseer named Edgar Cully, a choice that, though not rare, was unusual. Cully was a gimpy man with bad teeth and a worse disposition. Decker had not liked the man upon introductions. Now, two years later, Cully looked as if he'd aged a decade in Decker's absence. His hair had gone thin, and his bald pate had scabbed over in two places. He stood staring as Decker rode to the planter's house. *That man doesn't like me any more than I like him,* Decker thought. He urged his horse forward, past the smokehouse, the chapel, and the other dependencies that circled the meadow, stopping at the carriage house. There, a wizened old Black man took his horse, leaving him to walk past the cookhouse to the Hill home.

Paula was already there, smiling at him from between the columns, Whit at her hip like a holster. Jubal Hill stood smoking at the far end of the portico, talking to one of several men clustered together. Decker recognized Mr. Crane and Colonel Lance, but the other man was a stranger to him. Seeing Hill standing next to the stranger was a study in contrasts. Hill was a short, stout man with a protruding stomach that spoke to the skills of his cook. His teeth were brown, and his skin was tobacco stained and wrinkled, as if he himself had been hung on a pole and cured in one of the smokehouses. Only his dark hair, still thick, gave evidence of his real age.

The guest, by contrast, was tall, with a striking mane of white hair. Decker was reminded of the Vanderlyn portrait of Andrew Jackson he'd seen in Boston. The man's shoulders were narrow and stooped, though it was difficult to know if he'd purposely bent closer to better hear Hill, who was talking nonstop, waving his cigar for emphasis. Crane and Colonel Lance stood silent, listening to Hill's dissertation. When Decker climbed the steps, Hill paused, leaving a moment of silence to acknowledge Decker's arrival.

"Young Brown," William Crane said, nodding. "Come here, I want to introduce you to someone."

Decker reluctantly passed by Paula and joined the men.

"Decker Brown, allow me to introduce George Fitzhugh. George is a law clerk for the Attorney General, and a marvelous writer. You may have read some of his work." He turned to Fitzhugh. "Young Brown here is quite a reader." He turned back. "Have you read *Sociology for the South*?"

"I don't believe so," Decker said.

"You'd remember if you'd read it," Colonel Lance said, snorting.

William Crane nodded. "The esteemed Mr. Fitzhugh is an avid supporter of our peculiar institution. He argues the benefits to the Negro race so convincingly, that he would extend those benefits to the white race as well."

Fitzhugh nodded, tossing a strand of white hair. "Capitalism, the economic face of liberty, has been a catastrophic failure. The artisan class has been dismembered, leaving a class of wage slaves without protection or support. I was just explaining to Mr. Hill that the workers of the North are slaves in everything but name."

"How so? I've just spent two years in Boston—"

"A prime example. The worker unrest there is palpable."

Another man joined the discussion, tugging at his goatee as he spoke. Decker did not recognize him either, though the resemblance to Hill was enough to suspect the man was a relative. "Unrest, yes. To depend on a wage position is to give up the independence that we hold so dear here in the South. The resentment is directed at the factories that employ them, restricting them in every aspect."

"I understand some factories require their workers not to drink." William Crane took a sip of his brandy.

"And economy has replaced art in the production of everything from furniture to firearms," Colonel Lance said. "I'm told that they can take weapons apart and reassemble them, switching pieces at will."

"Horrific," Mr. Hill said, blowing smoke with the utterance of the word.

"Socialism, gentlemen." Fitzhugh's pronouncement stood like a statue on the veranda. "The failures of universal liberty have led to the revival of this most perfect form of economics." He pointed between the columns at the slave shacks across the meadow. "Food, shelter, medical attention. These are not worries to our slaves, whilst every factory worker in Boston agonizes over his pennies, wondering after that which any slave in the South takes for granted." As he spoke these last words, he turned to Decker, as if asking for a response.

"I didn't find it so," Decker said. "Wages up north are good. My uncle—"

"Yes, but the idea of white slaves—"

Fitzhugh waved away Mr. Hill's complaint. "This is not a matter of color. Why reserve the benefits of our peculiar institution to any one race? Socialism is slavery in all aspects but the master. The plantation model is a perfect form—"

"Plato," Crane interjected.

"Yes," Fitzhugh said, nodding with enthusiasm.

"But what of us? Myself, for example. How do we fit into your scheme?" Hill demanded.

"As I said, Mr. Hill. The plantation is a perfect form. There must be a governing force."

He turned to Crane. "You mentioned Plato. The plantation owner is the ideal model for government, the embodiment of the Platonic philosopher king." He turned back to Hill. "Your role would not be diminished, Mr. Hill. It would expand."

"Sounds more like Lincoln than Jefferson," the man with the goatee said.

"It is generally acknowledged that Mr. Jefferson's philosophies have failed," Fitzhugh answered. "Socialism requires the power of control, to protect the weak and helpless. It stands to reason that men like Mr. Hill would, by their nature, acquire and exercise that power."

Hill nodded thoughtfully.

"I am advocating a form of economic slavery for poor whites, as well as the Negros. Men of distinction, guided by a sense of morality, will eventually force others to agree, if only for the general good. That is my prediction."

"I am having trouble envisioning any of the political parties embracing your theories—" Fitzhugh shrugged. "I think the most broad-minded of the parties—the Democrats—might consider what is inevitable."

"I was a Whig for many years," Colonel Lance said. "I even supported Taylor, and had he lived, he might have done less harm than Fillmore."

"The Whigs are finished," William Crane said. "The Southern Whigs are becoming Democrats now, probably much to their dismay."

"True," Lance noted.

"And the Northern Whigs are all Republicans," Decker said.

Fitzhugh smiled. "You follow politics, then?"

"No, sir. But politics seem to follow me." The group chuckled. "By that, I mean politics are difficult to escape."

"A necessary evil," Colonel Lance pronounced.

"What is your take on the situation in the North, then, young man?" Fitzhugh asked. Decker pursed his lips. "I think that they are ready for war."

"They weren't ready for the last one," Colonel Lance said. He took a sure sip of his drink and brushed his mustache. "The South carried the water in Mexico."

A house servant approached with a tray, offering Decker a clear drink. He took a glass, nodding at the servant, and cradled the beverage without drinking. "I fear that their industrial capacity will be the deciding factor."

William Crane stared as if struck dumb. "Really? Astounding." Decker bit his cheek, silencing himself.

"I don't think the North is as united in its philosophies as you might imagine," Mr. Hill said. "The sheer number of fragment parties convinces me that at the first sign of trouble, they will desert Lincoln and the abolitionists. The Know Nothings, for example."

"The American Party benefited the Democrats here in the South. Stole away Whig votes," Fitzhugh said, agreeing with Hill.

"Lincoln's Republic hasn't got the stomach for a real fight," Hill finished. "I think one good thrashing in the field will suffice."

Crane stood with his back to the group, glancing at his daughter and Whit. She nodded at him and then at Decker, as if to urge her father in his direction. Decker took a deep breath. He'd come here to speak to the man. Might as well get it over with. Just as he stepped forward, however, the iron bell rang in the yard. Mrs. Hill approached from the front lawn, wearing a pink, high-necked dress with Bishop sleeves to protect her pale skin from the sun. "Jubal?" she called. "I believe it's time to let our guests eat instead of talking nasty old politics."

"Pork instead of politics," he agreed. Guests greeted the announcement enthusiastically.

A pig roast was a much-anticipated event, and Hill's roasts were legend.

The servants had dug a pit the night before and placed the pig meat-side down on hot coals fortified with hardwood. After flipping the carcass in the early afternoon, they'd used a broom to whisk off the ashes before dousing the pig in marinade. Because Hill's grandfather came from Charleston, the sauce had a healthy dose of mustard, and the pungent smell drifted across the yard, pulling the guests from the veranda to the serving table. There, they found cabbage slaw, bean soup, rice, and cornmeal hush puppies, along with an array of teas. Bottles of pepper sauce caught Decker's eye.

"Let the pickin' begin," Jubal Hill announced, and the guests edged closer to the pig, armed with forks and plates.

Decker drifted back, trying to position himself near William Crane. The man continued to chat with Fitzhugh. As Decker approached, Crane made a subtle turn to the left, showing his back. Decker stepped to Crane's side, waiting while Fitzhugh rhapsodized about the virtues of an ordered society. *The man never draws a breath.* Decker wanted to interrupt, but a breach of manners simply wouldn't do. Crane stood, hands behind his back, leaning forward as if braving a still breeze, though the air was hot and still as a sleeping cicada.

Fitzhugh paused to sip his sweet tea.

"Excuse my interruption, Mr. Fitzhugh," Decker said, bowing. He pivoted to his right, facing Paula's father. "Mr. Crane. Might I have a moment of your time?"

Crane flinched. "Yes, yes, of course, Young Brown. Perhaps after we dine?" He turned to Fitzhugh. "Great minds need to be fed, do they not, Mr. Fitzhugh?"

He nodded. "I'm partial to pork."

Leaving Decker behind, the two men made their way toward the pig.

Decker let out a breath he hadn't known he'd been holding. He glanced left and right, spotting Paula near the pit. Whit was busy filling a plate for her. *The man is obvious. I believe I'm going to have to say something to him.*

Paula frowned, her hands folded in front of her. Her eyes half-closed, her hair flattened by the humidity, she struck him suddenly as an image of sorrow — a visage shimmering in the heat rising from the pit. Servants tugged at the roasted pig, spilling fat into the fire. Wisps of smoke obscured her face for a moment. As Decker stood, hands thrust in his poor pockets, a sense of melancholy overtook him. *Her father intends to deny us.* The thought was not an accusation, but rather, a dour certainty.

His own father had often told him, "Once you know what you want, what you ought to do next will become clear." He'd added, "The problem is, most people don't have any idea what they want." *But I know. I want to marry her, build a small business, and have children. That is what I want.* A modest dream, but one that was now in doubt.

A gunshot cut short his thoughts. Across the meadow, a rider came pounding between two of the slave cabins, waving his gun in the air. A woman who'd been boiling some clothing in front of the cabin had to dodge to the side. Both man and horse were covered in dust.

Whit was quick to move, pushing Paula behind him and striding toward the rider, who pulled up short at Whit's approach. The man dismounted. Though Decker could not hear the conversation, Whit's body language said everything. He pointed at the rider's gun, and the rider, expression stricken, holstered the weapon.

"Apparently, the sound of the dinner bell traveled," Colonel Lance said. Crane and Fitzhugh chuckled with appreciation.

". . . dressed like a wharf rat. I certainly didn't invite him." Jubal Hill seemed outraged. He turned to several of the women guests. "Not to worry. My son seems to have things well in hand." Stepping back, he glanced toward the house. The man whom Decker had taken as a relative stood on the steps of the veranda, rifle at his side.

Whit, his back to the group, put both hands on his hips. The rider stood silent. Whit nodded, and turned back to the group, drawing the rider along with a curt wave of his hand. They approached the assembled guests with measured steps. The expression on Whit's face was grave, though Decker sensed there was a measure of anticipation as well.

Whit paused near the pit and held up a hand. "Ladies and gentlemen? We've received word that our friends in South Carolina fired on Fort Sumter early this morning. The battle rages as we speak. It seems—" He paused. "It seems that we will soon be at war."

CHAPTER FOUR

Richmond, Virginia
April 1861

*"I've always understood that we went to war on account of the thing
we quarreled with the north about. I've never heard of any other cause
of quarrel than slavery."*
~John S. Mosby

Having avoided him for the duration of the party, William Crane came to Decker once his guests had been served. "Young Brown, take a walk with me," he said, gesturing toward the trees across the meadow.

Decker followed without comment. Nervous, he kept his eyes on the slave cabins across the way. A group of slave children spread out from the row of cabins, playing some sort of game, apparently searching the grounds near the overseer's house. Several of them pulled up short, whispering to each other, afraid to venture ahead. One of the older children—a willowy girl with wild, spiraling hair—crept to the side of Cully's house. Shouting, she grabbed the branch of a tree and held it up. The other children scattered, screaming. The girl with the branch chased those children closest to her, striking them repeatedly. The screams drew Edgar Cully to the door. He pointed at the tall girl, and she froze, dropping the branch.

"What is that about?" Decker wondered aloud.

"They're playing *hide the switch*," Crane explained. "Whoever finds the branch earns the right to beat the others." He shook his head. "Children." As they walked, Cully strode out among the children, grabbing the tall girl by the hair, jerking her to her knees. Crane sighed. "The children have drawn Mr. Cully's ire."

"Mr. Cully's ire is easily drawn."

"Sadly so." Crane veered to the right, away from the drama. "You intend to ask me for my daughter's hand in marriage, is that not so?"

"I did so two years ago." Decker measured his words. "You asked me to wait until my apprenticeship was complete. I complied with your wishes."

"You showed great patience," Crane said. "And now, I must ask you to be patient once more."

Their walk had taken them past the overseer's house and down a path toward the tobacco fields. A junco trilled in the distance as they walked. Decker tried to keep calm, though his hands shook. "Why is that, sir?"

Crane cleared his throat. "I think the impending war might have something to do with it."

Decker scowled, despite his best efforts. "We are in love, and we plan to spend our lives together. What has war to do with that?"

Crane stopped, turning to face him. "I admire you, Decker. And I respect you. You deserve nothing less than my candor. I served in the Mexican conflict. I have an understanding of these things. An understanding earned through experience."

To Decker's knowledge, Crane had never seen battle. He'd been a supply officer during the war with Mexico. Instead, he'd been stationed in Washington, procuring Crane cotton for the war effort. "Go on, sir."

"Men die in war. I do not want my daughter to be a widow at seventeen. And if you truly care for her, you will agree."

Decker stood still, battling his desire to lash out. *Your objections have nothing to do with war. I am not a landowner. My father is a tradesman. You don't have the courage to tell me the truth.* He longed to say what was in his heart. He wanted to watch the man's face when confronted with the truth.

Except.

Crane might be right.

Decker nodded. "Your argument is persuasive."

Crane relaxed. He put a hand on Decker's shoulder.

Decker resisted the urge to shrug the hand away. "Perhaps the consensus is right about the duration of the war, sir. The North may find the cost of maintaining the Republic too dear. If so, I'll be back by summer's end. Paula will be eighteen years old." He stepped away. "Your daughter adores you. I hope that you will offer your blessing when we are married."

Silence. Decker wanted to turn and stride away—an exclamation mark for his small, angry speech. He resisted, gathering his reserves of grace and manners.

Crane seemed about to lose his temper. His face was red and sweat coated his face. Or perhaps the summer heat and a full stomach had put him off his best intentions. He straightened, tugged at the collar of his shirt, and nodded. "I admire your honesty, young Brown."

"And I yours," Decker said, though he feared he did not sound sincere. "Shall we return? I find myself coveting another plate of pig."

Crane seemed grateful for an amicable, if abrupt, end to the conversation.

• • •

Paula followed Decker to the stables when he went for his horse. "Are you leaving without saying anything?" she called.

He turned to face her. She met his gaze, and her shoulders sagged. "My father said no."

A statement, not a question.

"He said later." Decker walked forward to the front of the stable door, taking her by the elbows, his forearms against hers. "He's afraid you'll be a widow at seventeen."

"That's not—"

"Yes, it is. It *is* right. *He's* right." He bent down and stared into her eyes. "Let's not argue about this. Men die in war. I don't want your life to be over before it begins."

"You won't die—"

"I might. I can't promise I won't." Decker stopped when he saw her eyes well with tears.

He took her in his arms. "But I *won't* die. And I told your father that when I return, I intend to marry you, with or without his permission."

He waited. After a moment, she lay her face on his chest. "Yes," she said. "I'm glad you said so."

He smiled. "Four children, I think. Two boys and two girls."

"Will the boys be as stubborn as their father?"

"Perhaps. The girls will certainly be as smart and sassy as their mother." He started to pull away, but she clutched him tight. He wrapped his arms around her, pressing close.

"This is what I want for my life," she whispered.

After a moment, he felt her chest heave against him. "Are you crying?"

"No," she said into his chest. "I'm trying not to smell the barn."

Decker burst out laughing. "The smell is foul, isn't it? I suppose the servants shovel the stalls in the morning?"

"I believe so," she giggled. Grabbing him by the jacket lapels, she dragged him away from the stable door. "You are half a romantic, Decker Brown. The sun is setting, and you have a girl—"

"A beautiful girl—"

"—in your arms, but instead of lilacs or honeysuckle—"

"Horse apples?"

"Yes." She glanced back at the Hill house, sighing. "My father will send a search party soon."

"I expect so."

"Then use your time wisely," she said, standing on her tiptoes to kiss him.

· · ·

Decker had journeyed to the pig roast on a borrowed horse, belonging to a friend. The ride home was an exercise in frustration, despite the mild weather. His thoughts came much too quickly for comfort. He replayed his conversation with Paula's father several times, trying to imagine a more compelling dialogue—one that ended with the man's blessing and plans for an immediate wedding. But no such scene could erase what had happened or unmake Decker's own opinion.

Crane is right. I must wait. This war stands directly in the way of any possible happiness. Events have constructed a massive hurdle that I must overcome. Perhaps the war will end as soon as everyone seems to believe. Perhaps the South would even triumph.

No. The war would be long and bloody, and the South would fall. As the horse ambled on, Decker looked up at the night sky, trying very hard not to follow his line of thought to its logical conclusion. At any rate, he could not alter his situation now, riding a horse in the dark. In the morning, he would talk to Pops. Pops would say something Decker hadn't thought of. He would know what to do.

After delivering the horse to its owner on the north side of Richmond, Decker began the long walk home. Along the way, he passed *The Old Tavern* on Manchester. True to its name, the establishment had been in business for a very long time.

Tonight, the old wooden pub was full, and revelers spilled into the street. Someone a block away fired a small illumination, which arced up into the sky and popped to the shouts and cheers of gamblers and drunks.

"Death to Lincoln!"

"Three cheers and a tiger for Virginia!"

This last was greeted with growls and laughter from the women at the tavern door.

Decker shoved his hands into his pockets, head down. *Idiots. They're cheering for the death of everything they love.* He tried to circumvent the crowd, but men danced in his way, celebrating the advent of war. *And war will surely come. Virginia will secede now. We will all get uniforms and carry flags and be blasted to bits —*

He bumped into someone. Startled, he stepped back. "Sorry —"

The figure in front of him stood, arms folded. It took Decker a moment to realize two things. First, the contact hadn't been an accident. Second, he knew the man.

"Look who's here." Edgar Cully, the overseer from the Hill plantation, stood flanked on either side by two other men, each taller than Cully, but neither one the measure of Decker Brown. The man to Cully's left was slender, moving with a limp as he stepped forward. The other man, larger and uglier, had a wart over his right eye, and a patch of hair coming out of a mole on his cheek. All three men seemed flush with drink.

Decker took a deep breath. "I saw you at the plantation —"

"I rode here after you fine folks ate pig. I have a horse, you know." He sneered. "I see you're on foot."

"I am," Decker said. "And I have a distance to go, so if you'll excuse me —" He tried to sidestep, but the three men moved with him, a clumsy maneuver that gave away a certain level of intoxication.

"Where are you going?" Cully demanded. "Home so soon on a night such as this? Stay, and share a drink. We'll drink to war and Virginia."

"Thank you, but no."

Cully's gaze narrowed, though he managed a thin smile. In the dim light coming from the tavern lanterns hung near the entrance, his bad teeth looked nearly black. "No? You refuse to drink to Virginia?"

"You forget your place," Decker said. The man with the wart growled.

Cully nodded. "Oh, I know my place, and it's a damn sight finer place than yours." He squinted. "You don't own any land, Brown. You're the same as me, except I work for a gentleman."

"I'm nothing like you. Now, stand aside."

"No, I don't think so. You're going to apologize to Virginia, or—"

"You do not represent Virginia."

"I sure as hell don't. I was born and raised in Tennessee, and damned proud of it. Finest state in the South. But you Virginia boys, you don't even respect your own country—"

"Enough." Decker tried to shove his way past, but the man with the wart shoved back. *If this goes any further,* Decker thought, *we'll go to blows.* Decker squared up, eyeing the man who'd put hands on him. "You're drunk," he said. "Enjoy your celebration. Find you a fancy lady. Drink to the war you're so happy for. I'm a working man, headed for a night's sleep."

"Eh? Fancy lady? I seen *yours*—"

Decker's face reddened. "Pardon me?" Menace crept into his voice, and the man with the wart took a step back, his hands at his sides, ready to grapple.

Cully laughed. "Oh, I seen you both. Out by the stable. Kissy-kissy."

Decker's voice dropped, barely audible over the laughter behind them. "Step aside."

"I don't think so," Cully said, taking a breath that inflated his chest like a rooster ready to crow. "You insulted me, and you insulted Virginia. I expect an apology."

"I'm sorry. Sorry you're wallpapered."

Cully took a moment to register the affront. "Wall—" He sputtered, turning to his friends, and then back again. "By God, I demand satisfaction!"

Decker snorted. "You want a duel?"

"You heard me."

"Duels are for gentlemen. You're a thug who beats children for playing games."

Cully's expression grew wild. "You'll fight me! You'll fight me, by God, or I'll have you posted! Then everyone will know you're a coward, including that fast trick you were kissing by the stable—"

Decker held up a hand. "You're talking about your employer's daughter." He paused. "A time and place of my choice?"

Cully nodded.

"And weapon?"

Cully nodded again, a little slower this time, as if he'd had a moment to consider the consequences.

"All right," Decker said. "Here. Now. Fists."

Cully blinked. "You're alone. You don't have seconds—"

"Don't need seconds. *Here. Now. Fists.*" He stepped back, removing his jacket.

"Fists? That ain't a duel."

"And I'm not a slave girl. Let's begin."

"Show him something, Cully," the slender man with the limp said.

Decker held his jacket out. "Hold this for me." The request left the slender man dumbfounded. "Don't worry. I won't inconvenience you for long."

A crowd had begun to gather. Cully had friends in the tavern, and shouts drew more onlookers. Decker stretched, then backed away to touch his toes. A few men in the crowd laughed, and Cully seemed reassured. One of the tavern ladies brought Cully a small glass of whiskey, and he tossed it back as if drinking were a pre-fight ritual. "You ready then?" he called.

Decker didn't answer. Instead, he took an odd stance, half-turned, fists up as if to protect his face. Situated, he stood at the ready.

"What the hell?" Cully asked.

"You wanted satisfaction," Decker said. "Come and get some."

More laughter. Cully nodded enthusiastically. "Bully. Let me show you what a Tennessee boy can do." He rushed forward suddenly, swinging with both fists. Decker stood his ground, lashing out with a straight left punch at the last moment, popping Cully in the nose.

Cully stumbled back, stunned. "What the hell?" he repeated.

"Satisfied?"

Cully circled. Decker turned with him.

"Ain't you gonna fight?" Cully demanded.

Decker extended his left hand a few inches, slowly opening his fist. He wiggled his fingers, waving.

Cully bellowed and bull-rushed, arms extended. Decker slipped to the side, shoveling him over an extended leg, tripping him. Cully went down in a heap.

The gathering crowd laughed, which surprised Decker. They wanted blood, but they didn't seem particular about *whose* blood. Nonetheless, he found himself glancing over his shoulder, worried who might come to Cully's aid.

As if on cue, someone shouted, "Look out!" The man with the eye wart rushed forward. Decker had time to see the flash of a knife blade before the man was on him. Decker turned the man's knife hand with a circular, sweeping motion, followed by a crashing right to the side of the man's head, dropping him as if struck with an axe handle. Decker felt a stinging sensation. Glancing down, he found that the man had put a six-inch gash in his forearm.

Meanwhile, Cully was back on his feet, rushing him for a third time. Decker plunged forward himself, elbows up, crashing into Cully, knocking him to the dirt. Cully rolled onto his stomach, trying to regain his feet. Decker stepped on his hand. "Stay down," he growled, twisting his boot until the bones snapped.

Cully screamed.

Decker turned again. The thin man with the limp had dropped his jacket and was advancing, fists raised. Decker held up a hand, stopping him. "Don't be stupid. Pick up my jacket."

The thin man scowled, backing up a step.

"My jacket?"

The man bent to retrieve Decker's garment. Cully lay on the ground, moaning over his ruined hand. The man with the wart lay face down in the dirt, motionless.

Decker took a deep breath. The danger ended, a sense of exhilaration washed over him. "*I seen you*. I seen you before," a man from the crowd called out, pointing with a crooked finger. "You fought bare-knuckle in Norfolk." Decker shook his head. "Not me."

"You *was* bigger then. Taller." The man paused. "Maybe it weren't you."

Decker folded his jacket under his arm and crossed over to the lantern at the entrance to examine his arm. The wound was long, but not too deep. Blood soaked his shirtsleeve, but the wound was seeping rather than pumping. *I hope Pops is sober. I'm going to need him to stitch me up.*

"That was worth a drink," a woman in a bustier said. She smiled, but even by lantern light, he could see her pockmarked skin, and her breath made him wince.

"No thank you," he said.

She gave him a playful shove. "The drink is for me, silly."

The men gathered around them burst into laughter, clapping him on the back. One of them shoved a mug in his hand, then helped him spill it by bumping into him. "What's your name?" he asked with evident good cheer.

"Decker Brown."

"Three cheers for Decker Brown! Three cheers for Virginia!" Another illumination popped in the distance.

CHAPTER FIVE

Richmond, Virginia
April 1861

". . . that all efforts of the abolitionists or others made to induce congress to interfere with questions of slavery, or to take incipient steps in relation thereto, are calculated to lead to the most alarming and dangerous consequences . . ."
~Democratic Party Platform of 1852

George Brown stood at the side of Decker's bed, pitcher in hand. "Wake up, or I'll water you like a pumpkin."

"I'm awake, Pops." Decker rubbed his eyes with his good arm. The other arm rested under the pillow. His nightshirt was stained brown with blood.

"How did you sleep?"

"Not so well. My arm aches, and it keeps me awake."

He grunted. "Serves you well enough. Teach you to fight in the streets like a criminal."

Decker sat up. "You assume."

"I assume you ought to get yourself dressed. We have things to do."

Decker growled and slipped out from under his blanket. "Do we have time to eat?"

"No." Pops set the pitcher down on the nightstand. "Drink some water. It'll fill your stomach."

"Eggs and bacon. Biscuits. Butter and maple syrup."

"Water."

Decker stood up and fetched his trousers. "Where are we off to?"

"The Capitol building," he said. "No more questions."

As Decker dressed, he glanced at his father, surprised to see the beloved Bowie strapped to his leg. He pointed at the knife. "You expecting trouble, Pops?"

"Just want everyone to know I'm at the ready," he said. The firm set of his jaw and tight- lipped smile spoke of resolve.

Once out the door, they made their way toward the Capitol building. Decker slowed his steps to keep from outpacing the older man. Though early in the morning, the streets were unusually busy. Men walked in small groups, headed in the same direction as Decker and his father, laughing and talking in loud voices. Approaching the center of the city, the architecture of surrounding buildings took on a stately appearance, with firm brick and columns. The air was crisp and sweet, and Decker forgot about his injured arm. Richmond was a beautiful city.

Ahead, a wagon sat in front of a small shop. Three slaves rested on the wagon's buckboard, staring at a pallet full of supplies. As Decker and his father passed, one of the slaves lifted a bag of cornmeal from the pallet, pitched it into the wagon, and sat down again. The three men laughed, jostling each other. "Be done soon," another said, triggering a second round of laughter.

Decker asked, "Did you see that?"

"Lazy."

Decker snorted. "*That* is why slavery will never survive. You need an overseer to supervise those three. Better off hiring *one* man as buying three and *still* having to hire one. Stupid."

Pops stopped. "You sound like one of those damned abolitionists. What's wrong with you? Don't you care about your country?" His eyes were dark with fury. Decker started to walk on, but his father stood planted in the street. Men brushed past them, hurrying ahead.

"Pops? You've never been an apologist for slavery. What's bothering you?"

His father scowled. "For starters, I don't like hearing how you beat some little fellow with a limp. Heard it from our neighbor, first thing this morning."

Decker considered this for a moment. "Well, when you asked me for my side of the business, what did I say?"

Pops looked confused. "What do you mean?"

"What did I say happened?"

"You didn't." Confusion gave way to a sour expression. "I didn't ask."

"Exactly."

Pops closed his eyes. "All right. What's your story?"

"After I dropped off the horse I borrowed, I took the straight-line home, past *The Old Tavern*. Cully wanted me to drink with him. I wanted to go home. He took insult and challenged me to a duel."

"A *duel*?" Pops shook his head in disbelief. "He was drunk?"

"Wallpapered."

"Why didn't you just ignore him?"

"He said he'd have me posted." Decker paused. "And he questioned Paula's virtue." This last, he said in a lower voice, so passersby wouldn't overhear.

"So?"

"The choice of particulars was mine. I chose fists, and I chose not to delay." He pointed at his arm. "One of Cully's seconds came at me with a knife, and I put him down."

Pops squinted, as if to search Decker's face. "Why didn't you tell me this while I was stitching you up?"

"You taught me not to tell tales. I figured the matter was ended."

"You figured wrong," Pops said. "Cully's calling you out as a coward and a bully."

"I've never known you to put stock in the word of a man like Cully."

Pops folded his arms and thought for a moment. "Well. I guess that's right, then." He looked up at Decker. "Two of 'em, eh?"

"The third one decided not to get involved after the first two hit the ground."

Pops laughed and slapped his thigh. "Ha! Well, you're well suited for what's coming, I guess."

"What do you mean?"

"War, son. War."

Decker shook his head. "I've been thinking about that. I wonder if states like Virginia might broker a truce. We're not Deep South, Pops. Virginia has always been an enlightened state—"

"Too late for that." Pops grabbed his arm and dragged him along, trying to keep up with the men striding toward the center of Richmond. "This is Lincoln's war, now."

"Why is that?"

Pops stopped again. "You haven't heard, have you?" He reached to his back pocket, producing a crumpled newspaper page.

Decker unfolded it, then read the headline and a few paragraphs. He folded the article and handed it back to his father. "This is what has you fired up?"

His father snatched the paper from Decker's hands. "It by God surely does! Seventy-five thousand volunteers? It's tyranny, plain and simple. He means to force us to give up our rights as states, and he's building an army to do his bidding." He grabbed Decker's arm again, pulling him ahead. Decker tore his arm away.

"Pops! Virginia's been raising militia groups since Harpers Ferry. Jubal Hill financed his own little company and made his son a captain. The South is far ahead of the Republic when it comes to arming itself."

"There's no reason to call for volunteers, except to fight. And if that man wants a fight, he'll by God get one."

"So, what are we doing here?"

"We're *volunteering*." For a third time, he grabbed his son's arm, pulling Decker into the flow of men. The closer to the center of Richmond they ventured, the denser the crowds became. Coming in view of the Capitol building, they beheld an astounding sight. The street was jammed with men of every size and shape, with and without hats, wearing suits and homespun. The door to the Capitol was hopelessly packed. The murmurs of men joined and swelled, drowning out any attempt at conversation. Pops shouted something in Decker's ear, but he couldn't make out the words.

In front of the Capitol building, the stars and stripes slid down, pulled from below by an enthusiastic Virginian with an impressive set of muttonchops. A cheer went up from the crowd, thundering down the streets of Richmond.

"Pops!" Decker shouted. "Too many men! Let's go home!"

George Brown waved him off, and they waited. After being buffeted by the crowd for an hour, though, Decker felt the familiar grip on his elbow, dragging him back. "They aren't ready for us," he shouted.

"Not ready," Decker agreed. *Nor am I ready for this fool's errand.*

• • •

At home, Pops said, "We'll try later. They'll be better prepared for us in a day or two. Or a week. Doesn't matter. We'll find a company to take us."

Decker pushed at his plate of food, eating nothing. The beans and chunks of pork looked like fresh kill. He hung his head, eyes closed.

"You look like hell. Your arm hurting?"

"The arm is fine."

Pops wandered away for a moment, returning with a bottle. "Pour you a drink?"

"Not for me. It's early."

Pops sat down at the table. "You're not drinking. You're not eating, either. What's wrong, son?"

Decker shook his head. "Everything. This is all wrong. This war? It's not necessary. It can still be prevented."

His father frowned, filling a glass for himself.

"Virginia should stand firm. Take their grievances to the courts. The Supreme Court is filled with Southern Democrats, Pops. There is no need for war. The hotheads in South Carolina can't think that far ahead, so we are obliged to."

"Tell that to Lincoln. This is *his* war."

"Pops!" Decker grimaced, pain evident in his eyes. "What the hell would we be fighting for? Slavery? In all my years, I never heard you defend the institution. Not once! We don't own slaves. *I can, by God, dress myself.* How many times have you said that? You don't even *know* people who own slaves."

"You do," Pops said, glaring. His voice was low and even — a bad sign. "Your friends are well-invested in our peculiar institution."

Decker groaned. "Please, sir. You prove my point."

Pops scowled and tossed back the drink. "You don't have a choice, you know."

"I'm a free Virginian. I have choices."

His father snorted. "What? You gonna run off and fight with the Yankees?"

Decker sighed.

"That it? You want to take up arms against your friends and neighbors? Maybe put a round in your own Pops?"

"That's absurd —"

"It is? So, I'm absurd now?"

"At this moment, yes."

Pops reached full fury now, his face flushed red as a cabbage. Tendons stood out on his neck, and the blood vessel on his right temple throbbed. Spit flew through his missing tooth as he spoke. "You fight against Virginia, that's what will happen. Unless you head west and fight for strangers. Is that what you have in mind?"

"I don't have anything in mind, Pops." He tried to moderate his voice, but when his father poured himself another glass, Decker decided the effort was probably for naught. "I'm trying to figure out how to keep from turning my life completely upside down." He paused, wondering what to say next. The truth? "Paula's father wants us to wait to marry. Until the war is over. He doesn't want her to be a widow before her time."

Pops grumbled something, swallowing the words with another mouthful of whiskey.

Decker scowled. "So, no illuminations factory. No marriage. And you're angrier than Hell. All because Virginians want to keep their slaves —"

"We're talking about the encroachment of the Federal government on the rights of the States," Pops said, slapping the table with an open hand, spilling the second half of his drink.

"The right to turn men into property —"

"Damnation!" The word rose up out of his father like a Phoenix from hot ash, filling the room in a burst and leaving a simmering hole with the ensuing silence. "Will you kneel to tyranny?"

For a moment, father and son locked gazes. *We're cut from the same cloth. He won't budge. Nor will I.* Decker stood, pushing his plate away. "I'm going out to clear my head."

"You do that. Clear the webs out and come back the son I raised."

"I *am* the son you raised! I read the *Declaration of Independence* before I ever touched the *Bible*. In this house, the phrase 'life, liberty —'"

"Don't quote Jefferson at me! Thomas Jefferson was a Virginian, and he'd have stood by his country at a time like this."

"His country? Virginia or these United States?"

"Virginia. *Always* Virginia."

"Jefferson wasn't the President of Virginia."

Pops sat back, staring. "That may be the most damned-fool thing I've ever heard. One has nothing to do with the other." He refilled his glass, bottle shaking. He stared at the drink, and then at Decker. "You come back ready to be a man and fight for what's right. Or don't come back."

Decker nodded and left, lips pressed tight to keep from speaking. His father had changed in his absence. Was it age? Or had politics driven a hateful wedge between them?

• • •

By the time he reached the Crane house, the sun had started its descent. Henry Lee answered the door, a sour look on his face. "I need to speak to Paula, Henry Lee."

Paula's father appeared behind Henry Lee's shoulder, a drawn expression on his face. "Mr. Brown. What can we do for you?"

"I need to speak to Paula, sir." The words sounded dire, and Decker squared his shoulders, forcing a smile to his lips. "I haven't seen her since the barbecue. I'd hoped to catch up. A lot has happened."

"I've heard." Crane's voice was solemn, dark. He said no more.

Decker squirmed in place. "You may be referring to my run-in with Cully, and I assure you—"

"It's rather late, Mr. Brown."

"My conversation will be brief, sir. I will borrow your daughter for no more than a few minutes. Then I will leave. Thank you, sir."

Having steered the skirmish in his favor, Decker waited while a scowling William Crane called for his daughter.

Paula arrived at the door, wearing a simple house dress. Her hair hung flat around her face, and her eyes were wide and red. "Are you all right?" she asked. Both Henry Lee and her father hovered behind her, so her usual warmth seemed thin and distant.

"I'm fine," Decker said, forcing his smile to extend to his voice. "Come, walk with me for a moment." He held out his arm, and she took it without glancing back. They moved into the yard near the fence. Henry Lee stood in place, but William Crane shook his head and went inside the house.

"Are you all right?" she whispered, this time with urgency in her voice.

"I'm fine. You've been crying?"

She ignored the question. "We heard things about you and Cully. I knew *none* of it was true."

"Cully was drunk and wanted to duel. I hit him instead. His friend had a knife, but he didn't know how to use it."

Paula shuddered. "I *knew* it. I'm going to talk to Whit. Cully has to go—"

"No. Don't involve Whit. This is none of his business."

She looked into his eyes. "You don't like Whit."

"He likes you."

She tried to smile. "That's because I'm so charming."

Decker growled. "Let's not talk about Captain Hill."

"What shall we talk about?"

"Pops." Decker took a deep breath and shuddered. He'd tried to occupy himself on the walk over, staring at people passing by, listening to the birds, and humming old tunes. *Anything* to avoid thinking of his father's last words to him.

"Is he all right?"

"He dragged me down to the Capitol building to try to enlist. They weren't set up for it."

"I'm glad." She hugged him.

"I'm so happy to hear that," he said, relieved. "Everyone seems to want this war, and I can't figure it. What will we be fighting for? The end of the Union? The death of our founders' dreams?" He stepped back, kicking at the entry path stones. "We're not fighting for the sovereignty of Virginia. We're fighting for slavery."

"My father owns slaves—"

"Which makes him an anachronism. Industrialization has put slavery in the dustbin. The institution will wither of its own accord soon enough. Meanwhile, people are going to die, defending something that doesn't work. Why? Because the South's assets are tied up in *people*."

"Would you fight against Virginia, then?"

"Of course not. But I've come to a decision of sorts. I need to tell you my plan, since it involves our future. I *can't* support secession. If I must fight, I'll fight for the Union. But I *won't* fight my neighbors."

"You're going west."

"I won't fight against the Union. And I won't oppose friends and family. If we go to war, I'll follow the only path left to me."

"When will you leave?" Her voice was flat and emotionless, which surprised him.

"Virginia hasn't yet seceded. I hope Virginia seeks a compromise. I will pray for intercession." He paused. "But I don't expect it."

"Nor do I. Perhaps you should leave immediately."

Her voice had turned cold—a tone he'd never heard from her before. He felt his insides freeze. "You're angry." She did not answer. "You said you were glad I hadn't enlisted—"

"I'd hoped to have time with you before you went off to fight for Virginia." Her voice was soft and low, but her words had a certain finality to them.

"And now that you know?" He could barely squeeze the words from his throat. So much hung in the balance. She stood, hands folded in front of her, the last rays of the setting sun painting fire in her hair. Her expression was blank, but hints of a great struggle set her lips trembling. She would not meet his gaze, and when she blinked, a single tear rolled down her cheek.

"I am a patriot," she said at last. "I am my father's daughter."

Decker stood silent. Minutes passed without another word from either of them. The sun set, turning the top of the sky from blue to indigo. On the porch, Henry Lee stood guard, leaning against one of the pillars that bracketed the entryway.

"All right, then." Decker took a deep breath. "I suppose I will leave tonight. Will you wish me well?"

"Would you have me wish ill upon my friends and family?"

"I thought *we* were friends. I thought *we* were family."

"You made your choice," she said. Her voice had some steel to it, and Decker realized, his stomach sinking, that the conversation was over.

• • •

At home, he found his father at the table, a nearly empty bottle in front of him. He looked up, seemingly dazed, and pointed at a bundle, wrapped in a blanket and tied off with a leather strap. "Your things," he said, slurring.

Decker didn't touch the bundle. "I'm going west, Pops."

"I know it." He pointed again at the bundle. "Take your things and go." He gave his glass a baleful stare and grabbed for it, knocking it over, spilling the dregs of his drink on the table. He shook his head. "I never should have sent you to my brother. You came back a Yankee."

"I'm a Virginian. And I'm an American. I'm both."

"You can't be both. 'Tis one or the other."

"I'm a free man. I made my choice."

His father winced. "You . . ."

"What, Pops?"

His father shook his head. "Go ahead," Decker said.

"You go ahead. Get out."

"I love you, Pops."

Pops rocked back in his chair, meeting Decker's gaze. His lips pursed into a frown. "I have no son."

The words hung in the air like a death sentence. Decker reached for the bundle and tucked it under his arm. "Perhaps. But I have a father. Goodbye, Pops."

George Brown scowled and looked away. Decker waited for a moment, wondering if this was truly the end to the conversation. He glanced around the room, taking in every detail.

Remember this. You may never see this room, this man, again. You are not welcome here. After a moment, he turned to go, closing the door behind him.

Still on the steps, he heard the click of the door lock.

Walking to the street, with no plan beyond putting distance between himself and his beloved Richmond, he took a brief inventory of his thoughts. He felt a strange, angry sort of exhilaration at having chosen a path. Underneath was all sorrow, and he knew once his energy faded, misery would be his continual state. He'd lost his father and he'd lost the love of his life—the first two casualties of this abominable war. The thought stopped him in the street. He looked up at the sky. *Is this what you want for me? Am I to lose so much?* The stars hung like candles in a chandelier, flickering in silence.

He could always turn back, pound on the door, and beg Pops to let him in. He could enlist in a Virginia company. *The South is going to lose this war, with or without me.* Slavery was dead — killed with the first cannon shot at Fort Sumter. He could enlist, try to stay alive, and come home to Paula. He could help rebuild what was about to crumble.

No. That would be false. I made my decision.

As he stood thinking, a man and woman walked toward him from the end of the street — dark figures, little more than shadow, but he recognized them. Henry Lee and Paula.

Henry Lee stopped twenty feet away, leaning on a fence post. He looked tired. Paula continued forward, her hands folded in front of her. She'd changed into a hoop dress that covered her feet, and she seemed to float rather than pace, her shoulders still and her posture unbending. "I have something of yours," she said when she reached him.

She put the ring in his hand. He stared at it and then said, "Thank you. I appreciate it."

"So, you are gone then?"

"Yes."

She looked down. Her shoulders began to tremble, though no hint of emotion reached her face.

"There was no reason to return the ring tonight. I'd like to think you also came to say goodbye."

"No," she said. She looked up, her eyes wet. "I *can't* say goodbye to you. I can *never* say goodbye to you."

"Don't, then," he said. He wrapped his arms around her.

She sobbed in the dark, burying her face in his chest. "Do you have to do this?"

"I do," he said.

"Then, I'll wait for you."

He pulled free and grabbed her gloved hand, stuffing the ring into her palm. "Keep this. We'll need it someday."

She nodded.

"I know you don't understand," he said. "But I *have* to do this."

"I'm not going to tell anyone where you've gone."

"Are you ashamed?"

"No, but they wouldn't understand. *I don't understand.* If anyone asks, I'll tell them you couldn't wait to enlist. That you went west to fight for secession."

"They won't believe it."

"Yes, they will," she said, shaking her head. "Everyone's afraid the war will end before they get to kill a Yankee." She stifled a laugh and covered her face with her hands.

"Don't," he said, pulling her hands down. "I want to look at you. I want to freeze this moment so I can remember it."

"I'm a sight," she said. "Your timing is poor as always, sir." She tried to smile, falling well short.

"I have to go."

She nodded, lips trembling.

"I will write to you, but I don't think the mail will be reliable. If you don't hear from me, know that I'm thinking of you each and every moment I'm gone." He swept her into his arms again and kissed her, a kiss meant to stand in for the coming years.

With that, he turned and strode away. A block down the road, he looked back, but she was already gone, presumably headed home under Henry Lee's protection.

· · ·

Decker walked west until he left Richmond, until the city's meager lights were a faint glow in the distance. He found a tree to bed down under. Any excitement he'd felt at having taken a stand had been whittled away by the cold, a nagging hunger, and the sudden, devastating knowledge that he'd turned his back on everything he loved. Pops. Virginia. Paula.

He untied the bundle to see what his father had packed. A blanket. A single shirt and a pair of trousers. Socks. A half loaf of bread — which he began to eat. A tiny pouch jingled when he moved it. Inside were three gold pieces and some silver. Not much, but then, Pops didn't have much.

In the center of the bundle, he found a towel, wrapped around his father's beloved Bowie knife. Decker stared at it for a long time, tears welling in his eyes. "I love you, too, Pops," he whispered.

He lay down on the cold ground, wrapped in the wool blanket, and tried to sleep.

Sometime just before dawn, exhausted, he drifted off to the trill of the junco and wood thrush. The sun did not wake him until well past nine.

CHAPTER SIX

Richmond, Virginia
July 1861

"There stands Jackson like a stone wall! Rally behind the Virginians!"
~Brigadier General Barnard E. Bee

The carriage left Richmond proper behind, rolling onto the dirt road. An earlier rain made the air heavy and hot, and Paula could feel herself sweat, sitting still in the seat. Henry Lee rode in front, slumped forward, the reins loose in his hands. A horsefly buzzed past Paula's ear, and she brushed it away with a gloved hand, lest it settle on the cake in her lap. On her way out of the city, passersby were all smiles, but her own thoughts were jumbled. *Am I the only unhappy person in Virginia?*

News of the battle at Manassas Junction had taken Richmond like a song, accompanied by choral voices and brass, and illuminated from above by sunbeams. President Jefferson Davis was not in the city, of course, having ridden on horseback to the front lines to rally the troops in their time of need. But the rest of Richmond buzzed with the most delicious of all words—*victory*. No matter where she went, Paula heard the word over and over, as if, despite the bluster of the previous months, an undercurrent of doubt lurked, only to be banished by that glorious triumph. *Victory.*

The cake was her idea. She'd suggested that she deliver the confection to poor Whit, who lay at home, suffering a terrible battle wound. Paula's father was pleased by the idea, willing to part with the ingredients that had become scarce since the start of hostilities. Millie baked the small cake, spiced with apples and raisins and cinnamon. There were no eggs or milk to be had, yet the cake held together nicely. Millie had certain talents in the kitchen.

At first, Paula's father suggested a bourbon cake, but on reflection, agreed to supply the fruit rather than risk his supply of spirits. Paula understood his reluctance. The idea of parting with even a tiny portion of raisins gave her pause, whether or not Whit was a war hero.

Jubal Hill's company, a hundred men strong, fought on the front line at Manassas. McDowell, the Union general, had tried a series of flanking moves that were beyond the capabilities of his green troops, but the assault on the center of the Southern line was moderately successful, pushing the Confederate troops back to Henry House Hill, a gentle rise on the Hill estate. There, Whit and his company held position until the arrival of General Jackson, who made a courageous stand against the Union onslaught. When repeated charges against Jackson failed, the Union troops began to falter. Late arriving reinforcements sent the Yankees into full retreat, then rout, as panicked soldiers ran roughshod over civilians — onlookers who'd packed picnic baskets and spread blankets to watch the battle. A wagon overturned on Cub Run Bridge, holding up an entire regiment, putting the Union army into total disarray.

William Crane had delivered this account to his usual friends over dinner, along with sour commentary. "We were twenty-five miles from Washington! We should have pushed on and put a certain end to this war."

"It is over, isn't it?" Mrs. Hill asked. "That settles the matter?"

"I'm not so sure. But for Mr. Lincoln to win the war, he must conquer the entirety of the South, and he's learned just how difficult that proposition will be. That said, I rue the lost opportunity. I would have preferred General Beauregard run down the scoundrels and settled things once and for all."

Colonel Lance, who knew about such things, dismissed the idea of pursuing McDowell's army. "They had a sizable force in Centerville, and we were not prepared for the logistics of an invasion."

Paula had listened to the back and forth without comment, secretly wondering if her father's dinner talk was perhaps a little too smug. Victory came at a huge price, not evident in her father's smile and his brandy and cigar smoke. Casualty reports were horrific. Four hundred Southern boys had died in battle, with another sixteen hundred wounded — Whit among them. A shot struck bone in his right arm, shattering it, and the arm was amputated. His father had arranged for him to recover at home. The elder Hill suggested that a visit from Paula might cheer the boy up, and she agreed.

The carriage ride to the Hill plantation was not a brief one. July sun took the starch out of her dress and flattened her hair. Her appearance didn't matter so much — Whit could take her or leave her as she was. But she did worry over the condition of the cake, which had begun to weep in the summer heat. Henry Lee hit every rut and bump on the road to the Hill plantation, and all of Paula's powers of concentration focused on keeping the cake plate level. One perilous dip caused her to pitch forward, nearly losing the cake to the floorboards of the carriage. She started to berate Henry Lee for his carelessness, but a glance forward showed a road cluttered with ruts and tree limbs. The old man was steering the horse as best he could. With most of the men at war, there was no one to repair storm damage to the road.

Paula returned her attention to the cake. "Please Lord, let me arrive at the Hill's house with this cake intact. Don't let me spill." Having whispered the thought, she shook her head. Her prayer could have no significance to God today, burdened with the pleas of wounded soldiers. She felt ashamed, and for a moment, wondered if by pitching the cake over the side, she might free God to heal a Virginian. But that was silly—sillier than her prayer.

"There is a certain helplessness," she said, addressing Henry Lee, "in being a woman. The men are engaged in a fierce war, and there is precious little I can do to help. I am reduced to baking a cake." She waited a moment. He hadn't answered, but then, she'd not really asked a question. "Do you have an opinion about that, Henry Lee?"

He didn't turn around to answer. "It's a pretty cake, Miss Paula."

Indeed. I didn't even bake the cake. Millie did. She stared out the side of the carriage, watching the trees and bushes crawl past. "You think I'm being ridiculous, don't you?"

No answer. "Henry Lee?"

Again, he spoke without looking back. "I'm an old man. Love you like you was my own. Everybody crazy these days, though."

She sighed with frustration. There was no arguing his point.

When, at last, the carriage reached the Hill house, Paula steeled herself. She had never seen a man wounded in battle, and she worried she might be repulsed, and worse, that Whit might see it in her face. The heat had her stomach fluttering. What if she fell ill? What would he think?

Henry Lee held the cake while she stepped from the carriage. Whit's mother had run out to greet them, a frantic sort of relief in her face. "Oh, my dear, so *good* of you to come. Whitaker has not been himself and seeing you will be better than any medicine. I'm certain of it." She began to steer Paula toward the house.

"Henry Lee would appreciate a cold drink," Paula said, her eyes locked on the cake in her hands.

Mrs. Hill waved her handkerchief. "Of course. We'll see to the horse as well. But hurry, come inside."

Paula tried to keep up with Whit's mother, but the closer she came to the bedroom where Whit rested, the slower her feet moved. Having delivered her guest to the open bedroom door, Mrs. Hill disappeared. Inside, the curtains were shut, leaving the room in shadows. Paula could smell the faint odor of iodine and traces of vomit. As her eyes adjusted, she saw Whit propped up in his bed, his bandaged arm stump resting on a pillow. His dark hair was plastered to his head, wet with sweat. His beard was untrimmed, and he'd shriveled since she'd last seen him.

He groaned. "Are you coming in?"

She took a single step forward and held out the cake. "I brought you this," she said.

"It looks delicious, but I believe I'll have to wait until later. Food isn't staying down as it should." He gave her a tiny laugh. "You look lovely, my dear."

"And you look—." She stopped and tilted her head. "You look miserable, Whit. You've taken a terrible beating, haven't you?"

"It would seem so. I'm less than I was when last I saw you."

She crossed over and set the cake on his night table. "Nonsense. You're a hero, now." She struggled for a casual tone of voice. "Your face is thinner. It's a good look. Not so round."

"My face was never round. Now, I fear it's more skull than face."

"You're not *that* thin," she assured him. She took a deep breath. "Does your arm hurt?"

He raised his good arm. "This one's fine."

"The other one."

"The other one is no longer an arm." She stood silent. "I'm making you uncomfortable."

She gave him a hard look. "The sun is on the other side of the house. Why are your curtains closed?"

"The less you see, the better."

Paula grumbled and crossed over to the window, pulling back the curtains, lighting the room. "This is not a funeral parlor, and you are not a corpse."

"That's a fine way for a lady to talk—"

"Oh, shut up, Whit. We're old friends, and as your friend, I recommend sunshine and—" Turning, she got a closer look at his arm, amputated above the elbow. The bandages were colored brown and red—old and fresh blood spotting the linen. "That looks *horrible*," she said. "What are they giving you for the pain? It is painful, isn't it?"

"Yes, though my father has a *marvelous* selection of distilled spirits."

"Were you awake during the . . . surgery?"

"Yes, I was able to witness all. Would you like to hear about it?"

She pursed her lips. "No. But you may wish to tell me."

His face showed the hint of a smile, as if understanding a joke she had not yet grasped. "The surgeon cut the flesh and muscle first. They used a thin, single-sided blade. Hurt like a fury. It took three men to hold me still. Then, the surgeon pulled the arteries out with a hook so they could be tied off." Paula shuddered. "Finally, they cut the bone away with a saw. My surgeon was relatively new, and I believe he made something of a botch of things. The bone extends too far. Shall I unwrap and show you?"

Silence.

"The bandages are a bloody mess, aren't they?" he added.

"Do you have a reason for being cruel to me?" she asked.

He scowled. "You've done your good deed. Now, you can go home with a light heart. Wonderful to have seen you." He turned away, and she thought she saw his shoulders tremble.

"Whitaker Hill, you coward." Her voice hid the tears that threatened. The words seemed to shock him.

"You faced the Yankees in battle, and you didn't run, even when things were darkest. They say you and your men are responsible for holding the line until General Jackson could join the battle. You were wounded, and you suffered for your country. Virginia owes you a debt it can never repay." She paused. "And yet, here you are, afraid to face an old friend."

He waited a long time before answering. "I have faced other friends. Half of my company ended up dead or wounded. Some suffered injuries worse than mine. Many have come here—a parade of visitors. Some of them had pity in their eyes. Some were reminded of their own tribulations, and the reminder was unwelcome. Most were simply disgusted by my wound. I faced them all." He paused again. "But you? You are the one person whose disgust I couldn't bear."

She stepped to Whit's bedside. "Am I acting as if I'm disgusted?"

He stared at her. "I can't tell," he admitted.

"Well, I'm not. I admire what you did at Manassas, and I will never forget. And you have *always* been a handsome man, Whitaker Hill. But feeling sorry for yourself is *not* attractive."

He turned away. When he'd gathered himself again, he nodded at the cake. "Will you have some?"

"No. It was baked for you."

"*It was baked.*" He snorted. "Did *you* bake it?"

"I didn't say so." She smiled. "I simply allowed you to think it."

He laughed. Not the tiny, self-deprecating laugh, but a full-throated laugh that shook him, and then caused him to wince, though a rueful smile still graced his face. Paula glanced back and saw Mrs. Hill peering around the corner, beaming at the sound of her son's mirth.

Later, she took Paula by the arm, pressing her face into Paula's shoulder. "Thank you so much, my dear. You *must* come again. You put a smile on his face, and I feared I might never see one there again."

• • •

As the carriage pulled away, Paula found herself overcome with conflicting emotions, unable to sort them. Whit was in pieces, but somehow, he seemed nobler than before, as if the boy she'd known had been forged into a man in the space of a few weeks. And he was a hero for the Confederacy. For Virginia. If her father was right, and the war was truly over, Whit would be venerated for the rest of his life. That aside, he'd grown in her eyes, and she hated that he was in pain.

Then she thought of Decker. Decker the traitor. Decker, the love of her life.

The sun was lower in the sky, and the air had cooled. The wagon rocked to a slower beat, and the shuffle of the horse's hooves lulled her. Rain and a hot sun had coated the air with pollen, and the sweet smell might have been a blessing on some other evening.

What if Decker was fighting now, performing great heroics in the service of Lincoln and his Union armies? Worse, what if he lost an arm in battle? *How many poor Southerners will he kill? And what if he's killed himself?* Her thoughts were unbearable. How could she reconcile a love for her family, for her country, with her love for a man who fought against everything she believed in?

She began to cry. Softly, at first, and then huge, wracking sobs that she dared not release at home — not within hearing of her father and mother. Henry Lee drove the carriage into the sunset without comment. He kept his eyes forward, shoulders slumped. *Good. You never give me a straight answer, and you volunteer nothing. You're very fine at keeping a closed mouth, Henry Lee. I'm glad of it, now. I'm glad of it.*

CHAPTER SEVEN

Cairo, Illinois
September 1861

"I rise only to say that I do not intend to say anything. I thank you for your hearty welcomes and good cheers."
~Ulysses S. Grant, quoted from his "Perfect Speech"

Decker sat with the board braced against his knees, writing his letter home. Borrowed pencil, borrowed paper. He tried to keep his hand steady, but he was tired, and his penmanship suffered.

My Dearest Love,

I hope this letter finds you well. I have made my way west, as planned. Travel and terrible camp food have whittled me down like a stick. I have not had a meal worth eating since I left home.

Days are long here. We drill and drill some more. The first sergeant is an Irishman. He does not drink, and since spirits are the natural companion of an Irishman, he is an angry man. He provides some respite from the boredom.

I think of you every minute of every day. My feelings have not changed, nor will they ever change. Do not worry about me. I made a friend here, and together, we will keep our heads low.

Always, Decker

He dared not write the specifics of his journey west. He couldn't be certain who would read the letter.

The last line in the letter was telling. He'd made one friend—Mike Kelly, another Irishman. Mike was a short, thin-faced man with curly, dirt-blond hair, who'd not spoken a single word to him in the first few weeks in Cairo. Now, they were fast friends, thanks to First Sergeant McHenry.

The sergeant had taken an instant dislike to Decker. Walking a row of recruits on the first day in camp, cursing them for their slovenly, stupid faces, he'd paused in front of Decker and put his own face three inches away, jaw extended. "What do we have here?" he asked. His breath smelled like old teeth.

"Decker Brown."

"Decker Brown? Decker Brown? Prussian name. You a Prussian?" Decker did not answer. "I didn't hear an answer. Don't you know? Don't you know who your father was? Or maybe it's your mother who's the mystery?"

Decker kept his mouth shut. He'd been warned by other recruits against "back talk"—a punishable offense.

McHenry smiled, his lips pressed thin. There was no mirth in the expression. "You're a big one, aren't you Decker Brown? Head like a bag of spuds? You'll make a fine target for those Tennessee squirrel-hunting bastard sons of whores." He stepped back, addressing the rest of the troop. "Anybody smart will steer clear of this one when the fighting starts. Half the bullets that fly will be aimed at this big, dumb Prussian. Like shooting an ox."

In drills, Sergeant McHenry reserved special ire for Decker. Not a day passed without a new invective:

"You round-faced, dim-witted stook."

"Sausage-eating chicken-fucker."

Decker faced the onslaught in silence, which was why his accent did not immediately give him away. After one exchange, however, Sergeant McHenry stepped back to stare at Decker, as if considering him. "Say that again, Prussian." Decker was silent. McHenry waited a few silent moments before nodding and moving on.

The next day, when the men lined up for inspection, McHenry stopped in front of Decker and asked—his voice booming—"You have a lot of butter in your voice, Brown. Where are you from?"

Decker had considered the question in advance. He could hardly admit to Richmond.

Instead, he settled on a town in northern Illinois he'd seen on a post office map during his travels. "Buda, Sergeant. Buda, Illinois."

The answer seemed to surprise McHenry. "Buda? What the hell is Buda?"

Mike Kelly, standing a few men further down the line, spoke up. "Buda, Sergeant. Used to be French Grove, but they changed the name."

McHenry slid down the line, incredulous. "Buda? Is that where you're from, Kelly?"

"Yes Sir."

"What the hell kind of Godforsaken name for a town is that?" McHenry walked down the row, stopping in front of Kelly. "Don't lie to me, boyo. Do you know this Prussian, meat-faced bastard?"

"No, Sergeant."

McHenry started to back away, a furious grin on his face, but Kelly wasn't done. "I seen him before, but I don't know him. We ain't spoke."

McHenry froze. For a moment, the way he tugged at his lip with his teeth made Decker think he might lose his temper completely. Then, his shoulders squared, and he let out a deep breath he'd clearly been holding in. "Well, Kelly, if you say so, then there's no doubting it." He strolled back to Decker, malice in his smile. "But you talk like a secessionist, Prussian. Maybe you had some Tennessee boy's pecker in your mouth when you were younger. Is that what happened?"

Decker did not answer.

"You have a glad eye for sausage, don't you? Go on, admit it. No one will hold it against you."

Decker was silent, but a few men to the left of him had to swallow laughter. McHenry could not countenance laughter. He lurched to the side, screaming in one soldier's face, spitting his words. "Am I funny? Am I amusing you?"

"No, Sergeant," the man answered, his voice trembling.

McHenry could not countenance fear, either. Punishments were sure to follow.

Later, when the troop had marched for hours under a hot sun, and the laughing soldiers had been put to work, hauling the water cask and ladle to the rest of the men, Decker sought out the soldier who'd spoken up for him. Mike Kelly stood, hands on his hips, sweat turning his uniform blues a darker shade. His mouth hung open like a man ready to vomit. Kelly glanced up, his gray eyes dull and unfocused.

"Hello," Decker said. Kelly stood silent, his mouth still open. After a moment, he waved a small greeting. Decker cleared his throat. "I wanted to say thanks." Kelly shrugged, looking away. "You don't say much."

"You neither."

Decker bit the inside of his lip. How should he proceed? Pretend they were old friends? Engage him in casual conversation about Buda, plying him for information, in case McHenry decided to dig deeper? *No.* He took a deep breath. "I'm not from Buda."

"I know," he said, adding, "But I know how to mind my own beeswax."

"Just the same. Thank you."

Kelly took a ragged breath. "Don't have to thank me. I hate that sergeant."

The soldiers with the water came by. The chunky one, soaked with sweat, scowled at Decker, blaming him for punishment duty with the keg, but handed over a half-ladle of warm water. When Decker handed the ladle back, the soldier backed away, ignoring Kelly.

"Hey. What about him?" Decker asked, pointing to Kelly.

"I'm not serving no stupid mick."

Decker snorted. "He doesn't strike me as stupid," he said. "As for you, you've got one hand around a cask and another holding a ladle, and you're insulting a man with two free hands. Who's stupid?"

The soldier's eyes narrowed. He nodded at his partner. "I got a friend here."

"So does he," Decker said.

The chunky soldier took off his cap and mopped his forehead with his uniform sleeve. He glanced back at his partner, paused, and turned back. "Well," he said. "I guess it ain't worth a scrape."

"Give him the water." Decker's voice was stern.

"Ain't thirsty," Kelly said.

Decker looked to him, but Kelly wouldn't meet his gaze. "Suit yourself." The chunky soldier moved away.

After the water bearers had gone, Kelly looked up, seeing a question in Decker's eyes. "Like the man said. It weren't worth a scrape."

Later, after a dinner consisting of a chunk of salt pork, potato, a hunk of bread, and coffee, Decker stood at the camp's edge, away from the rows of tents and the low murmur of tired recruits. He didn't have sentry duty that night, and he found himself anxious for the *lights out* bugle call. The sun would set soon, and the air was already cool enough for sleep. Staring back at the camp, Decker spotted Kelly, making his way over, his little jaw set firm like a pit bull.

Kelly stopped ten feet away and spoke. "I told my Daddy I'd keep my head down. He says that's the only way to survive a war. And I stuck my neck out once today. That's why I didn't fight that Polack."

"That beefy fellah's Polish?" Kelly nodded. "Well," Decker said. "Thanks for spending your once-a-day on me."

The next morning, Sergeant McHenry ran his charges through a bayonet drill. Soldiers began in a basic guard position, bayonets fixed and rifles extended, with the stock of the rifle at the hip. The soldiers attacked with a two-handed *lunge*, or a fully extended, single arm thrust called the *lunge out*. The *thrust* was a shorter move, meant for close-in combat. The rest of the drill consisted of a variety of parrying moves. Decker was slow to catch on, and McHenry let him know. "Are you a man or a cow?" he screamed, his face as red as corned beef. "Look at your friend, damn you. Look at how an Irishman fights!"

Kelly seemed a natural with the bayonet, lunging and flipping the rifle back into position like a juggler. His quick, fluid moves had real power behind them.

That night, Decker wandered the perimeter of the camp, musket in hand, looking for Kelly. He found him at the crest of a small hill overlooking the town. "Hey," he called.

"Hey yourself."

Decker set the butt of the rifle on the ground, gripping the barrel. "I thought I'd get some practice," he said.

Kelly nodded.

"Care to give me a pointer?"

Kelly shrugged. "Comes natural to me." He looked away, as if the conversation were over, and then turned back. "I'm a farm boy. Spent many an hour with a pitchfork in my hand. Bayonet practice ain't nothing but sticking and pitching."

"Seems like a two-hand lunge is a little different from using a pitchfork."

Kelly scowled. "I won't do that lunge business in a battle. Too easy to parry. One good smack and a fool will lose his rifle. Meanwhile . . ." He paused before finishing. "I'll be pitching hay."

"Well, I should practice anyway. Tired of McHenry riding me. Got any advice?"

"Practice, I guess."

"I figured that much out already."

Kelly fished in his pocket and pulled out a penny—the old, larger kind. "Here," he said, flipping the penny to Decker. "This'll help. It's magic."

Decker caught the coin and glanced at it. "I don't believe that."

Kelly shrugged. "Well, in case it ain't magic, you best practice." Decker saw a slight tug at the corners of his mouth and wondered if Kelly might actually break into a smile someday.

The following evening, Kelly had sentry duty, and Decker kept him company, repeating the moves again and again. Kelly watched, commenting if he saw something wrong, silent if he saw something right. The extra work helped, and Decker's movements became faster.

"You're plenty good after you get something down, ain't you?"

Decker smiled. "I can fight with my fists. I can shoot. I can handle a knife. Even a sword. But this is new, and I don't do much of *anything* naturally." He thrust the rifle out, then pulled back as if to parry. "But I'll figure this out, too."

"Anxious to kill you a rebel?"

Decker shook his head. "I figure the difference between surviving and not surviving is on my shoulders. I can fight as well as anyone I know. When we see the elephant, I'm going to be ready."

"My daddy says the key to surviving is to keep your head low."

"I believe you mentioned that." Decker thrust again, a sudden movement that caused Kelly to flinch. Decker pulled back and set the rifle down.

"Aren't you supposed to hold onto that?" a voice called.

Decker turned to stare at the man standing behind them. Though his jacket was unbuttoned, and he appeared disheveled, he was clearly an officer. He was short as Kelly, with the stub of a cigar dangling in his fingers. His voice had been clear, but casual.

Kelly snapped to attention. "I'm on duty, sir. My friend here is just getting in some extra practice."

"At ease," the officer said, waving the cigar. "Practice, eh? Not enough drilling for you, son?"

Decker gave him a sheepish smile. "Need to be better, sir."

The officer turned away, staring out at the town below. "Well, that's admirable." He took a pull from his cigar and blew smoke into the cool air. "Fighting will start here soon enough." He shook his head. "News from back east worry you boys?"

"No, sir," they both answered.

The officer gave them a small laugh. "Good, good. You are fine boys, and I know you'll do well in battle." He turned to leave.

"General?" Kelly asked, guessing. "You're him, aren't you?"

The general paused.

"Are we going to move soon?" Kelly paused, glancing at Decker. "I mean, we're anxious to lay boots to those secessionists."

The general nodded, his face dark with shadows. "I know." He sighed. "Learn what you can here. And hold fast to the Bible. Once this begins, there'll be no turning back. We will move ahead until the thing is accomplished." He nodded and walked off.

Kelly was silent until the general was long gone. "Was that really—"

"I believe so," Decker said. "I've heard he doesn't sleep much. Walks the camp at night, like he was one of us."

"Did he seem drunk to you?"

Decker considered the question. He'd heard rumors of General Grant's drinking problem, but the man didn't seem inebriated to him. "I don't think so," he answered. "He seemed tired, or maybe worried."

"That's not good," Kelly said.

• • •

Cairo was a boomtown, home to more than two thousand people—a population that increased fivefold with the arrival of recruits. Decker was stationed in Camp Smith—a collection of wedge tents strung up in the mud. Each tent was meant to sleep four. Decker's tent slept five, so that at night, the men were spooned together. When one turned, all five turned. When rains came, and they came often, closed flaps meant trapped air. Decker slept at one end, face to the canvas, which was more pleasant by measure than the odors coming from some of the men, cleanliness being an unevenly distributed habit.

Once he and Kelly began spending time together, Decker switched places with one of Kelly's tent mates, and they began sleeping together as well—a blessing, since Kelly bathed on a regular basis. "Daddy said we raise pigs. We don't have to live like them." Some nights, trapped in the mud and stink, Decker suspected that despite good intentions, they'd become more like livestock than men.

When off duty, the men in Kelly's tent played cards. Kelly was skilled at cribbage. Decker disliked games of chance and abstained, and because the usual game featured two against two, Decker was the willing odd man out. Instead, he passed the time listening to insults and complaints while poring through the occasional book that passed from tent to tent. When books were unavailable, Decker read religious tracts, which were plentiful.

At night, the tents were dark, leaving smoking and conversation as the only options.

Kelly smoked only occasionally, and did not seem to enjoy it, though everyone enjoyed talking about home. Decker did not smoke, nor did he talk of home, and one of his tent mates took him to task for his silence. "Why are you always so quiet? You and Kelly come from the same town, right?"

"He talks enough for both of us," Decker said, which elicited a snort from Kelly.

One exception to his usual reticence came when Joshua, a recruit from Cincinnati, began talking about his fiancée. "Beth is her name. She's got hair the color of corn silk, a sweet face, and bigger titties than either of her sisters. Most of my pay goes to her on allotment whenever the paymaster comes around. We're not married—not yet—but we will be. When this war is over, I'm going to have me a bride and a pile of money waiting for me. Beth is a God-fearing girl, and she'll save every penny."

David, a thin, dour man from Chicago, asked, "Is she in church every Sunday?"

"She sure is," Joshua said. "Never misses a Sunday."

"Well," David said, "don't be surprised if she marries the preacher while you're gone. Women are like that."

"Not my Beth." Joshua's face went pale, lips pressed thin. "And what do you know anyway?" He searched for a comeback, before saying, "Everybody knows you're a beat."

"The hell you say." David's voice carried some small sense of outrage, but the others would have none of it.

"I've been waiting on that dollar from home for about two weeks, now."

"Two dollars for me."

"If that letter ever arrives, we're going to empty it for you."

David pursed his lips. "The letter's coming. Blame the post."

Joshua shook his head. "Forget you, anyway. I was talking about my Beth." He drew on his pipe and exhaled, filling the tent. His glance fell on Decker. "What about you, Brown? You got you a Prussian girlfriend?"

Decker didn't answer at first. When he spoke, his voice was low enough to cause the others in the tent to go silent, lest they miss a word. "English. Her family came over before the Revolution. Her granddad fought at Yorktown."

The men considered this for a moment. "Is she pretty?"

Decker's voice went lower still. "Some might say she's too thin. Others say her eyes are too large, and she's a little too smart for her own good. Her hair has a natural curl that becomes unruly on a damp day." He paused. "But without her, I could not breathe."

David broke the silence that followed. "What Joshua wants to know is, how big are her titties?"

Guffaws erupted as Kelly gave David a playful shove, and Joshua shouted out denials.

Decker shook his head, his rueful smile giving way to shared laughter.

Laughter had no place during the daytime. The men's duty hours belonged to Sergeant McHenry. "It's biscuits to a bear, training you rumbly bastards. Tighten up those ranks, damn you! I'll march you until the Devil makes splinters of your legs! Hay-foot, straw-foot, hay-foot, straw-foot!"

Decker listened to McHenry's voice, losing all meaning to the rhythm of the rant. Left, right, left, right, halt and begin again. Wipe the sweat from your eyes when at ease—otherwise let it run like a river from the bill of your cap to your chin. Keep the ranks straight over uneven ground, slogging through mud, tripping on rocks and fallen branches. "Tighten it up, Brown, you farkin' *arschgeburt*."

When the bugle sounded fatigue duty, the men fanned out over the campground, policing the grounds. Decker drew more than his share of stable duty—cleaning up the area under the picket rope, where the horses were tied off. Later, that duty was reserved for punishment, something of which McHenry was quite fond.

Wood detail, the rapid deforesting of the area around Camp Smith, gave birth to its own punishment. The men came to blows often, to be expected with recruits billeted like crackers in a tin. McHenry forced combatants to carry a log with them for the remainder of the day. Decker wondered at the mild punishment until a misstep in drills earned him his own log. By the day's end, his shoulders ached, and the pain stayed with him for days.

One day, David went missing from drills. He'd gotten drunk on popskull and had been bucked and gagged—a particularly harsh punishment for intoxication. His hands and feet were bound together, and a gag inserted in his mouth, which interfered with his natural inclination to vomit up his hangover. When he returned to the tent, he was the worse for wear. The other men were outraged. "McHenry can't drink, so nobody else can," Joshua groused. "David's a beat, but he didn't do no harm. We drill and drill, and clean and shovel. What's a man to do? What's the harm in a little homemade headache?"

The next day, two men from the neighboring tent went to blows, and wound up in the sweatbox.

All of which set Decker to thinking.

His opportunity to do something about the problem came two days later, when McHenry sent him on a message run to Colonel Morgan. Captain Williams had ordered an early march south of town, and McHenry was obliged to inform the company commander of the orders in writing. At first, Decker was angered by the errand. *McHenry's sun never sets. Damn the man.* But then, he realized he had the perfect opportunity to suggest his idea.

Colonel Morgan was a man of social standing. From his trim goatee to his quiet, detached airs, he reminded Decker of Whitaker Hill. Putting that unpleasant association aside, Decker entered the colonel's tent, saluted, delivered his message, and waited for the colonel to respond, which he did with a quick wave of the hand.

"Sir?"

The colonel looked up, surprised.

"I have an idea, sir. The men are bored—"

Colonel Morgan frowned, an incredulous look on his face. "Pardon?"

"The men are bored—"

Colonel Morgan sat back behind his wooden table and held up a finger. He sat silent for a moment and then addressed the other officer in the tent. "Captain? It seems that the men are bored. Can you arrange some light entertainment, please? Might I suggest that you bring in a Negro and his banjo, and perhaps a wagonload of town girls?"

Captain Williams—the officer who'd ordered McHenry's morning march, necessitating Decker's message—closed his eyes and smiled.

Decker tried again. "Nothing so fancy, sir. It's just that, being away from home and out of danger such as we are, well, that's a recipe for boredom. I'm suggesting a distraction."

Captain Williams opened his eyes and stared. "Pray, continue," Colonel Morgan said.

"Before the war, I apprenticed in Boston to make illuminations. The camp has everything I need to make a fine show. I could fire up a few rockets at dusk. Perhaps the men would like the colors."

Colonel Morgan shook his head. "Did you discuss this with your sergeant?"

"Sergeant McHenry is a busy man. He has his hands full with recruits."

The colonel snorted. "Really! And do I strike you as a man with time on my hands?"

"No, sir. But the sergeant would have to clear the idea with the captain, and then with you. This way, I've only inconvenienced one man—the man who can say yea or nay." Decker bit the inside of his lip and waited. A sideways glance at the captain noted that the officer was trying very hard not to laugh.

Colonel Morgan tented his fingers and nodded, as if considering the request. "And what materials would you need?"

Decker listed his requirements. "Lampblack? What's that about?"

"Lends color to the explosion, sir."

Colonel Morgan turned to the captain. "What is your opinion of this venture?"

The captain turned to Decker. "When would you construct these illuminations, Private?"

"Off-duty hours, sir. It will keep my hands busy."

The captain turned back to the colonel. "I see no harm."

Colonel Morgan pulled at his goatee. "Well, then. You have my permission."

"Thank you, sir." Decker saluted and turned to go.

"Private?"

Decker turned back. "Don't blow yourself up."

"No, sir," he promised.

CHAPTER EIGHT

Cairo, Illinois
October 1861

*"The Confederacy sought to overthrow our constitutional
government. When the Confederates fired on Fort Sumter in
Charleston Harbor, they were not merely firing at 'Federals' or the
Union army. They were firing at the United States Army and the
U.S. flag."*
~Frank Scaturro

Crafting the nonflammable portion of his illuminations gave
Decker something to do in the evenings, while his tent mates
rambled on about home, good food, and politics. Weeks into
training, the romance of war was long gone. What remained
was mud and McHenry's voice.

"I swear, that man's voice is like a bone saw," Joshua said.

"Like the whine of a mosquito," David added. "A five-foot-
tall mosquito." Decker chuckled as he worked.

"A funny one, huh Brown?" Decker nodded.

"What the hell is that thing in your hands?"

"A surprise."

David frowned and leaned forward. "McHenry know about
this?"

Decker stopped and looked up. "Right about now,
McHenry's probably got a surprise of his own in hand."

"Or maybe he's saving it for you." Decker nodded, undisturbed.

"He rides you like a donkey. Don't it bother you?"

Decker stopped working on the rocket tube and set it aside. "David, he's trying to get us ready for the real thing. I've been in scrapes before. But I've never seen *real* war." He paused, thinking of the brawl with Edgar Cully outside *The Old Tavern*. "What we learn here will help us when our time comes." He smiled, leaning back against the tent wall. "Besides, I'm the biggest fellah in the company. Why pick on a little guy? That won't impress anyone."

"You telling me you don't take him personal?" Joshua asked.

"Of course, he does," Kelly said.

Of course, I do. But I'll never admit it. Decker kept his gaze on Joshua. "Comes time for battle, you'll be glad he was such a hard case."

Kelly snorted. "You give the man too much credit."

"What do you mean?"

"He doesn't give a damn about us. He's just mean. He'd be a better man if he was scuttered. We ought to buy him a bottle."

"Maybe so," Decker said after a long silence.

• • •

The following morning began with bayonet drills. The men lined up in two long rows, with plenty of distance between each soldier. Decker's spot had tufts of grass poking through the mud, which helped him maintain his footing. Crisp air kept the sweat from his eyes.

He performed the drill flawlessly — perfect, powerful thrusts and lunges. Some small part of him hoped for McHenry's recognition, even if the recognition came in the form of an insult. But McHenry seemed oblivious to the improvement, venting his usual ire on other men.

When the drill ended, the sergeant stood silent, rocking on his heels. He stared at Decker, and Decker stared back, holding his gaze a moment too long.

"What do you want, Prussian?" The sergeant's jaw thrust forward, face more flushed than usual.

"That was a useful drill, Sergeant." A statement, not a question. When McHenry did not answer back, Decker nodded and started to back away.

"You did better," McHenry said.

Decker could scarcely believe his ears. The smile that crossed his face was involuntary. "Wipe that grin off your stupid Prussian face," McHenry said, the tone of his voice unchanged. "What do you suppose that's worth in battle? Do you think I'll stand behind you, shouting *lunge* and *parry* while the army of Tennessee rolls up and presents itself to your bayonet? War is not a *game*, Prussian."

"Thank you, Sergeant," Decker said, but the man wasn't finished.

"Exactly what do you think is going to happen when we go to battle? You'll fire, and then they'll fire, and both sides will come together like the Grand March at a ball?"

Decker scowled.

"You have a puss on you now, don't you? You wanted rules and niceties. Shake hands, before and after? You're in for a shock. *There are no rules in war.* There's just living and dying. And you? You're going to die. Or you'll leg it out at the first shot."

"I can fight, Sergeant," Decker said, though as soon as the words were out of his mouth, he regretted them. He sounded like a child, arguing with a parent. Why did it matter, anyway? The sergeant wasn't Pops. He was a sour blowhard and expecting him to come around was a fool's errand.

"We'll see, won't we?" McHenry said. A smirk crossed his face, and Decker began to wonder. *Does he really think I'll waver in battle? Does he think I can't fight? By God, I can fight as well as any man here, including this son of an Irish whore!*

His expression, always open, never guarded, gave him away. McHenry smirked and turned on his heels, striding across a field of mud toward Camp Smith.

• • •

On the appointed night, the bugler sounded assembly — four simple lines of music that called the men from their tents. Grumbling could be heard across the camp, since resting and smoking and letters home had to be put aside to join ranks in the open space beyond the tents. Decker stood next to Colonel Morgan and Captain Williams, his illuminations in an array behind him.

Decker tried to spot Kelly, David, Joshua, and the others, but dusk came early, and he couldn't make them out among the ranks.

Colonel Morgan stepped forward and began speaking. His voice was deep and resonant, sounding out across the meadow like a cannon. Captain Williams stood, gloved hands folded, listening.

". . . and in recognition of your commitment and hard work, we have commissioned a brief entertainment. The display you are about to witness is a celebration of your efforts." Colonel Morgan turned and glared at Decker. "All right, Brown," he said, his voice lowered only a little. "Don't let us down."

Decker lit the first rocket. After a hiss and a pause, the illumination shot skyward. The fiery trail disappeared after a few moments, leaving an empty, black October sky. Decker heard the colonel sigh just before the charge detonated — shooting gold sparks across the heavens.

Some of the men gasped at the sight. He lit the second illumination. The fuse sputtered and seemed to go dead. Just as

Decker stepped forward, the rocket shot into the sky. This time, purple sparks.

The third illumination showered the sky with green flecks. Decker glanced back. The men stood gaping at the sky, silent, as if in contemplation.

The fourth and final rocket fired a double burst of green and gold. Less than two minutes had passed since the display began.

"Is that all?" Colonel Morgan asked.

"Yes, sir."

The colonel nodded. "Well done, then."

The men were dismissed. They returned to their tents, muttering. No one approached him as he gathered his materials. Glancing at the woods just a few yards away, Decker saw the glow of a firefly, a tiny flash of phosphorescent green. *It seems that nature wishes to compete with me.* Laughing and shaking his head, he stepped back, bumping into Captain Williams.

"Your illuminations fly straight."

Decker nodded. "Yes, sir."

"I'm surprised you're not in the artillery corps."

"Artillery is different, Captain."

"Yes, of course it is. I'm just surprised to see a man of your talents in the infantry." Decker didn't know how to respond, so he stood silent. "Well, carry on, Private."

His tent mates were considerably warmer in their appraisals. Kelly gave him a solemn nod. "You did good."

"Angel trails in the sky," Joshua said. "Best illuminations I ever seen."

Tom, the smallest of the men in the tent, agreed. "I didn't know you could make something so beautiful."

David lay back, propping his head up on one arm. "Wasn't what I expected, but it was nice enough."

"What did you expect?"

David shrugged. "Thought it might last longer. It was too short."

Joshua started to laugh, but Kelly cut him off. "Don't say it, Joshua. It's too damned easy."

"What?" David asked, startled. "What?"

· · ·

Sergeant McHenry had seen the display as well, which he made clear during drills the following morning. Marching, the men slogged through the mud, out of step, half-awake. Angrier than usual, McHenry launched his own display of invectives, cursing the men, their families, and God for having vexed him with their presence.

When the time came for bayonet drill, the sergeant called the various moves, and then, in an apparent fit of pique, turned and stomped away, leaving the men waiting. The morning sun was pleasantly warm, and the flies seemed on holiday, so standing still was a blessing.

When McHenry returned, he stood in front of the ranks, silent for a long minute. He swayed in place, as if the anger was too much for him to contain. When he spoke, his voice was lower and somehow more menacing. "This is not a *game.*"

Then he waited for another minute. Some of the men, still at attention, began to glance at one another, wondering.

"Brown." McHenry held out a hand and waved Decker forward. "Come up here, Brown."

Decker stepped out, wondering.

McHenry stood silent again, leaving Decker in the lurch for another long minute. "You're very good with toys, Prussian. But war is not a game." He stepped back, rifle in hand, his own bayonet fixed. "Come at me." Decker stood silent, stunned.

"Come at me," McHenry said. "Don't stand there all boss-eyed. This is your chance. Stick me!"

"No, Sergeant."

Incredulous, McHenry shouted, "You will come at me, Brown, or you'll carry a log for a week, by God." The sergeant's face flushed hot, and his eyes grew wide and wild. "Come on! Come at me!"

Decker gripped the rifle, taking the basic guard stance. "I don't want to hurt you, Sergeant." His stomach rolled. *This man is crazy, and he wants to kill me.*

McHenry gave him a twisted, painful smile. "Oh, you won't hurt me. Come on then." His voice had gone low again. He took a basic guard stance that was too casual, too sloppy, as if to invite an attack.

Decker stood back, shouldering the rifle. "I believe I'll take the log," he said.

McHenry shook his head. "Too late for that, Private. You will attack me, or I'll attack *you*."

Decker couldn't believe his ears. He glanced around, desperately searching for someone who might intervene. There were no officers present. The men behind him stood at attention. "I came to fight rebels, Sergeant."

"You won't see the battlefield if you don't come at me now. You won't see —" The sergeant stopped short, and laughed, shaking his head.

Drunk. He's drunk.

"Last chance, Brown. I'm ordering you to come at me."

Anger surging through him, Decker lowered the rifle, taking his stance again. He tilted his head as if considering the attack and took a tentative step forward. McHenry waited.

Decker closed the distance between them, beginning the lunge move. McHenry locked his legs, ready to parry. In midmotion, Decker dropped low, kicking the sergeant's front leg out from under him, spilling the man into the mud. Before McHenry could right himself, Decker stood over him, rifle in hand, bayonet pointed at the sergeant's throat. For a moment, neither man moved.

"You were supposed to use your bayonet!" McHenry sputtered.

"*There are no rules in war, Sergeant.*" Decker's voice was a hiss and a whisper. He kept the point of the bayonet at McHenry's throat for another second or two and then stepped back. The men stood, mouths gaping.

"The sergeant is right," Decker said, freezing everyone with his voice. "This isn't a game. *And we are not ready.*" He turned to McHenry. "Thank you, Sergeant." He slipped back into the ranks, standing at attention, and began to pray silently.

McHenry stood, his face red as a rose, his uniform splattered with mud. His mouth opened to speak, but Kelly interrupted, shouting, "*Three Cheers for the Union!*" On cue, the men began to sing:

Farewell then, beloved one, take courage and trust –
Our promise to win may not prove a vain boast.
And, oh, if we die in battle on the field,
It is to our maker alone that we yield.

Sergeant McHenry waited while they sang, squinting at the ranks, his head cocked. When the verse ended, he scowled and took a deep breath. "Well. Let's begin again."

Later, when the day's drilling had ended, and Decker returned to his tent, drained like a well bucket, Kelly tapped him on the shoulder and whispered, "You need to be careful. That man wants to kill you now."

• • •

My Dearest Love,
I write to you with a heavy heart. I am afflicted with a profound nostalgia for home and for you. I am unable to sleep, and food has lost

its limited appeal – though now, the thought of a biscuit from home tells me that my mouth can still water and my stomach can still growl!

I daydream of tiny moments, each as precious as a gemstone. Most of all, I think of the day I came home to you from Boston. There on the railway platform, you made me a promise. I am so far from home, and our circumstances so dire – I would not blame you for changing your position. Obligations can have no part in our future.

As for myself, my feelings will never change. Should the war whittle me into pieces, I will remain –

Always yours, Decker

Mailing letters had become a problem. Since Grant took the town of Paducah without a shot fired, rebel scouts were less likely to roam the banks of the Mississippi. Each night at dusk, Decker ventured out to a favored spot and waited. On the third night, he saw a familiar face, beard, and butternut uniform. Waving, Decker stepped out on the riverbank, holding a pouch of tobacco and a letter.

The rebel stared long enough to be sure he recognized Decker, and then crept forward, cautious. The river was low, up to the shins, and he made his way past the rounded rocks and bits of driftwood until he stood a few yards away. "I'm a-hopin' you has somethin' for me." His voice had more bounce than butter, with a touch of country twang.

"Another letter?"

"Another letter." Decker said, stepping into the river.

"How are you boys?"

"Ready to stomp y'all, that's for sure." The rebel took the tobacco and letter. Decker glanced upriver, startled to see another rebel scout.

"Don't worry 'bout him," the rebel in butternut said. "He's a friendly sort."

The man in the distance stood, staring, his rifle at his side. He was smallish, without much meat on his bones. "You boys aren't eating too well, are you?" Decker asked.

"Seems like you shrunk a little since I first seen you."

Decker gave him a nervous chuckle, still glancing upriver. "Army food. Haven't had a good meal since I left home." He started to back away. "Say . . . I never got your name."

The rebel squinted and shook his head. "You don't want to know my name."

Decker sighed. "Enjoy the tobacco." He backed away, water tugging at his pants, one eye still on the other scout. The butternut rebel backed away too, one careful step after the other. The sun was setting, and he seemed as much shadow as man. Just before reaching the bank, he called out—

"Jamison. Jamison Harding."

Decker stopped, his heart suddenly bursting. In a few weeks, maybe days, he might be firing at this man. *What a tragedy! To fight against my own countrymen!* But for now, for just this moment, they could be friends.

"Decker. Decker Brown," he shouted, waving.

CHAPTER NINE

Richmond, Virginia
February 1862

"If society will not admit of woman's free development, then society must be remodeled."
~Elizabeth Blackwell

Paula waited while Whitaker Hill stepped down from the carriage. Wavering in place for a moment, he paused to rearrange his uniform, smoothing the wrinkles, and then circled the rig to offer her a hand down. She exited the carriage with considerably less difficulty than her escort, her hand extended to his for appearances. She released him the moment her feet touched ground.

He offered his arm, but she pretended not to see and headed off down the street, calling back, "I'll finish in an hour or so. Meet me at the carriage?"

He raced to catch her. "Your father asked me to escort you into town. He worries over your safety."

"Nonsense. Henry Lee usually takes me into town, and he waits in the carriage, just like he's waiting now."

"You're being unreasonable." She could hear him trying to keep up. The loss of an arm had weakened him. She slowed her pace, much against her will, and allowed him to take her elbow.

"Some of my errands are best accomplished alone," she said.

"I don't mind waiting."

"Some of my errands are inappropriate to the male species."

Whit sighed. "What sort of errand would that be?" he demanded.

Paula stopped. "You can hardly expect me to reveal the secrets of my sex, Whitaker Hill." She softened the rebuke with a tiny smile.

Whit stood puffing, his one good hand across his chest. "I've been tasked with your safety, mademoiselle."

Paula glanced around her. The street was populated with women and slaves, many of them headed to Rocketts Landing to see what the blockade runners had to offer in the way of goods. The few men in sight were graybeards, servants, or the occasional soldier. "I'm not in danger, sir."

Whit stood back, clearly exasperated. "You confound me. How am I to satisfy your father's wishes when you are so clearly set on disobeying them?"

Paula's face went blank, hiding the anger flaring inside. "Men seem anxious to protect women from the dangers that men themselves present." She tried to smile. "I'm safe, Whit. Please go back to the carriage and wait for me. I won't be long."

He stood motionless for a moment, and then nodded. "Of course." Stepping back, he bowed. Then she was off, alone and free. Though it was cold, the docks held some attraction. The family needed cloth, and what she wouldn't give for a cask of brandy for her father! But at the end of her errands, she would go to the post office and look for a letter from Decker. His missives were short, but they never failed to deliver some small but important comfort. Like Decker, the sentiments were direct and true.

She ignored the temptation to go to the post office first. Instead, she went to Rocketts Landing. The *James River Squadron* sat in the canal like fishing boats, moored for the winter. Soldiers bustled around the dock, unloading pig iron and coal, vapor billowing from their mouths. Blockade runners focused on the raw goods of manufacturing. Though shortages of food and cloth seemed impossible, given the South's cotton production, her father had explained that both were in short supply *because* of cotton. "We grow cotton and ship it to the English textile industry. In turn, they make the cloth we use. Because of the war, we've had to turn fields over to growing food, and we can't ship our cotton anywhere." When she'd expressed concern, he'd reassured her. "Don't worry your head, Paula. The British can't do without our cotton. They'll intercede soon, and the war will be over."

She wasn't so sure. The South was scrambling for materials, and the pig iron stacked on the dock wouldn't become cannon and swords by magic. *The war is exactly as Decker said it would be.* The thought of Decker being right infuriated her. How was that possible? How could she be angry with him and long so desperately for his letters at the same time?

Paula took a moment to brush her dress and jacket flat and compose herself. She had to believe the South would solve the struggle for supplies, and in fact, Whit Hill was part of the solution. His father had secured a position for Whit in the Ordnance Bureau, working directly with Josiah Gorgas. Major Gorgas was not a Virginian—he came from Pennsylvania—but Whit had nothing but praise for the man and his ability to procure raw materials. During dinner at the Crane's, he told her father, "The man is a genius. We're making saltpeter for gunpowder out of—" He continued in a hushed voice, likely in deference to her, but she heard him mention bat guano and chamber pots. She assumed the major was an expert at finding alternative resources for the war effort. *Good. Southern ingenuity will prevail in the end.*

Stymied in her search for cloth at the docks, she wandered the storefronts on the way to the post office. Loath to return empty-handed, she stopped at the mercantile and purchased a short length of wool and a spool of thread. She paid for the goods in silver coins. Confederate currency was viewed with suspicion, and given shortages and the prices being charged, the suspicion was well-founded. Her father had converted a fair portion of the family's assets to gold and silver, something he was clearly proud of, given his boasting. When she asked why he'd done so, he gave his cigar a tap and said, "Just looking after the family, my dear," which was no explanation at all. *Men are blowhards*, she decided, a judgment that did not include Decker Brown, who had indeed sent her a letter. She tucked the precious envelope into the sleeve of her jacket and left the post office.

Whit waited on the steps outside.

"What are you doing here?" she asked, her face flushing.

"Watching over your safety."

"I thought we'd agreed that wasn't necessary."

"You came to that conclusion," Whit drawled. "However, I had a prior agreement with your father."

"You are maddening, Whitaker Hill." He was also very charming, and that infuriated her, too.

He tilted his head and smiled. "May I assume you received the correspondence you hoped for? Mr. Brown, perhaps?"

Her face drained. Charm only went so far. "Why? Are you also charged with reporting my comings and goings?"

His smile disappeared. "I would not do that."

"Really? Seems you've already been quite the spy."

He offered his arm. "The carriage is just down the street." She walked past him in the direction he'd indicated.

"We are friends," he called.

She stopped and turned. "Are we?"

"Yes."

"Prove it." Her voice seethed with anger.

He'd caught up to her, and his face showed his surprise. "What would you have me do?"

Her gaze narrowed, and she flashed him a thin smile. "Teach me how to shoot."

He laughed. "That, mademoiselle, is the last thing I could have expected you to say."

"Why? Because I'm a woman?"

He gave her a bemused smile. "Frankly, yes, because you're a woman."

She poked him in the chest with her finger—surprising him again. "When the Yankees come, and they will come, I'm not going to face them unarmed. And if that amuses you, Whitaker Hill, then you'd do well to reconsider. Don't you read the papers? Fort Henry? Gone. Fort Donelson? Gone. Nashville may be next. Do you think Lincoln and his armies don't want Richmond?" He started to answer, but she continued, cutting him off. "Men started this war, but both men and women must endure. So, if we're friends, truly friends, you will show me how to shoot a pistol."

Whit shrugged, his hand extended, palm up. "If you want to learn to shoot, why not ask your father?"

"Because he's against it, of course. He says I don't have to worry because *he'll protect me.*"

"A sensible response," Whit said. "And I will be there at his side."

"You are an idiot. What good can you do against a division of Yankees?"

He smiled and tapped his goatee with his index finger, as if he'd trapped her. "You make my argument. What good would your one pistol do if ours are inadequate?"

"Every woman I know believes in liberty just as strongly as the men—perhaps more so, having witnessed freedom's uneven distribution. If the women of Richmond greeted the Yankees, armed and imbued with the true Southern spirit, they would think twice about what it means to invade someone else's home." Having said her piece, she folded her arms across her chest and glared at him.

Whit stood, wavering in place, his face red and his lips pressed thin. He appeared ready to speak, but no words would come. When Paula walked to the carriage, he followed, silent.

They'd traveled for no more than ten minutes, rolling through the center of Richmond, pausing for soldiers moving to and from the government buildings, when he turned to her. "All right. I'll teach you to shoot." He glanced at Henry Lee, who drove on in silence.

"Are you listening, Henry Lee?" Paula called.

"No, ma'am."

Paula smiled and said, "Go on."

"I will pick you up at your father's house. You may tell him we are going for an afternoon ride. That will please him."

She considered his plan and then smiled, nodding. "Will you really?"

"Yes," he groused. "How can I refuse someone such as you?"

"And what about your report to my father?"

"Friends don't inform on friends."

"All right, then," she said. "Let us be friends."

• • •

Paula waited until she was in her room, alone and away from prying eyes, to open the letter. Sitting on the four-post bed, sinking into the peach-colored duvet, she carefully opened the sealed flap, and began to read. Decker was brief—too brief— but as always, he professed his love in a straightforward, unassuming manner. So unlike Whit, who needed a dash of something in every expression, verbal and otherwise. Whit was all frosting and no cake.

Focused as she was on the letter, she did not hear her servant girl enter the room. When Millie cleared her throat, Paula jumped.

"You scared me!"

"I'm sorry —"

"Don't do that!" She tucked the letter behind her, blushing furiously. Millie stood still, her hands at her side, a wide-eyed expression on her face. Paula searched the girl's face, wondering if she understood why Paula was acting so secretively. She decided that Millie knew perfectly well, which made things much worse. "A person must be allowed to read their mail in private, without being crept up on." The words sounded petulant, and her trembling lip only made matters worse.

"I didn't see nothing," Millie said.

"Of course, you did," Paula sighed. She reached behind her and grabbed the letter, holding it out. "Did you want to read this, too?" Her voice dripped with sarcasm.

Millie seemed to shrink in place.

Paula dropped the letter into her lap. "This is a letter from Decker Brown. He's somewhere out west, fighting in the war. He is my very dear friend, but my father doesn't like him, and I don't want to cause trouble by announcing the letter."

"You don't want to stir a full pot," Millie said.

Paula considered this. "Yes, that's a wonderful way of putting things." She took a deep breath. "I have to ask you not to say anything, Millie."

"I won't, ma'am."

"I mean it, Millie."

"I know, ma'am."

Paula sighed. "You can't imagine how difficult it is, caring about someone who doesn't have your father's approval. A woman's life is a series of duties, and my father imagines that marriage is one of them. Well, he is mistaken. I will have a say in my own future." She glanced down at the letter. *Will I ever really marry him? For that matter, will I ever see him again?* She glanced up at Millie, whose face had gone blank. "What's wrong, Millie?"

"Nothing, ma'am," she mumbled.

Paula's expression wilted. *Oh, my! How stupid of me!* "Why, Millie. You understand what I mean perfectly well." Paula sat back on the bed. Any privations she suffered must be doubled for her servant. "I'm sorry, Millie."

"It's all right, Miss Paula. I don't mind. I have a nice home, here."

Paula searched the girl's face and decided she didn't believe a word. "How old are you, Millie? Seventeen?"

"Yes," she said.

"Why, I'm only a year older than you!" She gave a moment's thought to her exchange with Whit. *Every woman I know believes in liberty just as strongly as the men*, she'd said. What about Millie? Paula sat forward. "Tell me something, Millie. Have you ever been in love?"

Millie didn't answer, but something about the way her eyes shone in the late afternoon sun, and the way her hands, still clenched at her sides, suddenly relaxed, gave Paula all the answer she needed. "You're in love now, aren't you, Millie!"

The girl's expression blossomed like wildflowers — all buttercup and wild ginger — the most beautiful smile Paula had ever seen.

Paula beamed. "Who is he, Millie? Is he someone I know?"

Millie froze, as if considering something for the first time. A dark, open-mouthed expression of horror crept across her face. Her hands flew up, and she stepped back, away from Paula.

"No, Millie! Don't look like that! Love is a wonderful thing! Not something to bring you pain —" She stopped short, thinking of Decker, five hundred miles away. "Love is . . ." Her voice faded, and the room was silent.

Millie waited, hands still at her face. "Millie," she said, her voice low. "I do so wish we could have been friends."

Millie relaxed — a little — and tried to smile. "Yes, ma'am."

"Your secret is safe, Millie. Is mine?"

"Yes, Miss Paula." Millie's expression flattened, becoming almost stern. She curtsied before leaving the room.

Paula flopped back on the bed, overwhelmed. Her trip into town netted little benefit. Her father's stern opinions and restrictions left her angry. Was there room for women in the promise of liberty? She thought of Whit, and of Decker Brown. *Poor Millie. Her prospects as a servant are so much worse than mine!* She paused, wincing. *Not servant. Slave. I must call her what she is.*

Paula stood and walked to her dressing table. Like clothing and food, writing paper was scarce. She had two sheets left. She would use one of them now.

My Fine Sir,

I received your kind letter today, and due to events here in Richmond, am determined to write you now and fully express my thoughts and feelings. I had a discussion with Millie, our slave girl who is my age, and might be myself if not for an act of Providence or an accident of fate. She admitted to me that she is in love, but when I asked her who the lucky recipient of her affections was, she reacted with great horror. I do not know why, though a number of possibilities have crossed my mind.

Perhaps she fears that the object of her affections might be sold and shipped away, never to be seen again. Or perhaps she will find herself with child, caring for a baby that looks like someone known to the family. Don't be shocked — I am well aware that sort of thing occurs.

I wished out loud that we might have been friends, she and I, but of course, friends don't own their friends.

I have often reflected on your opinion of our peculiar institution, reciting the arguments for and against, but never before have I felt the very meaning of slavery. I feel that meaning now, marrow deep. Millie's life is a tragedy, and in different circumstances, I might have enjoyed the company of her friendship. Like you, I am feeling nostalgic.

I honor you for having done what you thought was right. Justice demands that I tell you so. I pray that you will honor my decision in the same spirit. There must be a way to alter our country's course. If Virginia could divest herself of slavery, would not the rest of the South follow? When this war is over, I will put my every effort toward that end.

I am going to send this letter your way, though I don't know how. Should my letter arrive, rest assured that it contains my love and affection, as well as these few poor words.

Forever yours, Paula

PostScript: I am learning how to fire a pistol. Woe to any Yankee who comes to my door.

CHAPTER TEN

Pittsburg Landing, Tennessee
March 1862

"Well, Grant, we've had the devil's own day, haven't we?"
~General William T. Sherman

Decker Brown marches forward, men at each shoulder. Tree trunks, stripped of their leaves and bark by Minié balls, grape and canister, block the path of the advancing Union soldiers, causing them to jog left and right as the situation demands. Rows of soldiers break and reform as they move across the uneven field toward the rebel lines. Decker's stomach clenches, threatening to double him over. He forces himself to stay more or less in line, though the desire to rush ahead battles with the desire to turn and run. He must do one or the other, and he cannot do either.

A day earlier, the rebel army crashed into Grant's troops at Pittsburg Landing, catching them unprepared, driving them back toward the Tennessee River and the bordering swamp. Decker and his tent mates were ordered to march but were too far away to join in the first day's battle. Rumors flew through the ranks, and none of them sounded encouraging.

The army is on the verge of collapse. Grant was drunk again.
Buell's men took the wrong road and got lost.

Sergeant McHenry controlled the situation by demanding silence, shutting down conversation, pushing the march. At night, it began to rain, and this morning, his men are wet, tired, and miserable, and none have yet seen battle.

To his left, Joshua marches, his rifle at his shoulder, bayonet fixed, his lips twisted. His face has gone pale, the color of gypsum. His eyes seem unfocused, and he is muttering something. On Decker's right, Mike Kelly tries to move ahead without stumbling. Rocks, ruts, and tree roots are treacherous, but as they approach the rebel line, the bodies of men killed in the previous day's action provide an additional, grizzly hazard. Ahead, Decker sees only the shoulders and caps of a hundred other men, jammed together in the advance.

The Union assault is consists of more men than Decker has ever seen in one place — doubling his memory of the crowd that had gathered in Richmond to enlist. The juggernaut moves in a single block. They hear muskets firing — a continuous rattle that sounds like canvas tearing. The closer they come to the enemy lines, the more corpses he finds underfoot. Decker is forced to look down to avoid tripping. Most of the bodies are dressed in blue. Their eyes are open and cloudy in death. Stepping over another stack, he realizes one of the men dressed in red-spattered gray is still alive. His mouth is open and moving, though no sounds come out. Decker tries to stop and help, but the rows move on, pushing him forward.

"Hay-foot, straw-foot!" Sergeant McHenry's voice booms above the sound of muskets and cannon.

To Decker's left, a pond. The water looks crimson, surely a trick of the morning light.

Staring, Decker stumbles, catching the crook of a corpse's elbow with his shoe. He falls forward, and the man in front pushes back. Kelly grabs Decker's arm, helping to right him. The advancing rows have slowed, climbing over bodies piled to the shins.

"Hay-foot, straw-foot!"

Thousands of men funnel their way toward the rebel line, weapons shouldered, waiting for the coming volley. Blood drums in his ears, drowning out the sounds of battle. All he can hear is McHenry's cadence, a dour, insistent call that cuts through everything, and Decker understands. Bayonet maneuvers will be meaningless in this tangle of bodies and blood. Target practice is pointless when massed armies clash in a space the size of a single cornfield. His quest for excellence has been wasted. *I am meat for the grinder.*

Months of training have had one aim — to teach him to listen to the sergeant. "Hay-foot, straw-foot," McHenry calls, and the men respond, moving ever forward. Without the sergeant, they would turn and run. Decker feels a sudden love for McHenry, a swelling burst of warmth. Without him, they would all be utterly and completely lost.

Decker can't yet see the rebel lines, but the pop of muskets seems closer. Abruptly, the man in front of him pitches back, bouncing off Decker's chest and dropping to the ground, and now Decker can see everything. The two front rows of the assault are gone, wiped away by a single volley. The rebel line is obscured by smoke. When a cold morning breeze thins the cloud, he sees a line of gray and butternut uniforms, furiously reloading. *Twenty seconds. It takes twenty seconds to reload.* Without another thought, Decker begins to run forward, hopping over corpses as quickly as he can, trying to close the gap before another volley ends him. Kelly runs with him, as does Joshua, screaming at the top of his lungs. They do not look back to see if the others are following.

Decker starts to stumble but regains his stride. A mud road lies ahead. The rebels crouch behind the far side of the road, using tree limbs and boxes for cover when possible. They are reloading much too quickly, and Decker races on, heedless of the corpses beneath him. *If I fall, I will die.*

Some of the rebels have finished reloading. They fire quick shots into the oncoming troops. Joshua, who has kept pace with Decker, jerks in midair. Part of his head blows back with his cap, though his body drives forward before dropping to the ground. Decker is screaming like a fury now, his musket to the front, bayonet at the ready. Just before he reaches the rebel line, some of the Southerners turn to run, not quite reloaded, unnerved by the headlong assault.

The front row of the Union line crashes into the rebels with a deafening sound, like a dozen wagons driving off a cliff. Decker rams his bayonet into a man so hard that he lifts him off the ground. He tries to pull free, but the man jerks forward — the blade is stuck in the rebel's spine. Decker plants a shoe on the dead man's stomach and pulls the bayonet free. As the body drops, Decker swings to the left, blindly striking out. He catches a second rebel in the side, crumpling him.

Now he glances right. The Union line has blasted through the rebel defenses. But the remaining Southerners have already been in battle, and they are changed. They don't panic. A cluster of rebels fire while backing away. One raises a musket and aims it at Decker. A puff of smoke is followed by the sting of a hornet at Decker's ear. He raises a hand to the side of his head. When he lowers it again, his fingers are covered in blood.

He has no time to consider the wound. An attack from his left nearly catches him. He parries the bayonet and lunges out — the answering parry nearly knocks the musket from his hands. Both men step back. Decker blinks in surprise, and then fires his musket. At point-blank range, he does not miss.

He looks around and realizes the Union charge has won. The remaining rebels retreat to the rise behind them. A wild triumph surges through him, and he shouts until his throat is raw. The sound of a fieldpiece drowns out the sound, and a cannon shot cuts a swath through the massed Union ranks.

Rebel cannon line the small hill, while the retreating rebels reform behind the big guns.

"What are ye waiting for?" McHenry bellows, and the men start through the trees toward the new line. "Hurry now, boys, and kill those Tennessee sons of whores."

Decker winds around a tree stump that is pocked with shot. Wood chips carpet the ground around the stump, along with a few broken branches. Once a tree, now chopped to pieces.

Cannon fire thunders ahead, blasting the remnants of what was once a forest, leaving piles of Union dead and dying. Decker wishes he'd had time to reload, but they must drive the rebels away from the big guns. He climbs as fast as he can, weaving around the rocks and wood shards. Some of the rebels are trying to break the guns down for transport, but there is no time for that. Others are reloading, and once again, the clock is Decker's foe. He must reach the top of the hill before another round of canister butchers him.

A thin row of soldiers fires a volley of muskets, and Decker hears the *zip* of a Minié ball passing by his left ear. He has no time to consider how lucky he's been as he crests the hill and lashes out at the nearest infantryman. Decker's bayonet cuts a slice in the man's side. The rebel howls, knocking Decker's musket to the ground with his parry. The rebel stops to stare at the blood spreading across the torn cloth of his uniform, and the pause is all Decker needs. He pulls the Bowie knife from its sheath and plunges it into the rebel's shoulder. The rebel screams again as he tumbles back, but the sound is drowned out by the fieldpiece five yards to the right. The blast deafens him. The rest of the battle sounds slip away. He turns right, staring at the gaping hole in the Union line where cannon shot cleared a path through the ranks. He leaps forward, knife in hand, plunging the blade into one of the cannon crew. The rest are overwhelmed as the attack swarms the rebel line, capturing the cannon.

Mike Kelly jabbers at his side, but Decker can't hear the words. Union soldiers struggle to turn the cannon, in the event that the rebels counterattack. The loss of cannon is grievous and can't go unanswered. Decker and Kelly struggle with the wheels while McHenry directs. Decker sees the sergeant's sudden dance from the corner of his eye. McHenry spins and then flies back, tumbling against the cannon axle as he falls.

A wave of rebels comes crashing forward through the ring of trees. Though the Union soldiers outnumber the attackers, they are not prepared to receive an assault.

Decker realizes his musket is on the ground. He races to grab it. As he bends down, he gazes into the eyes of the rebel he cut down with the Bowie. The man grimaces — still alive. Decker stands up, musket in hand, barrel and bayonet pointed down. "Stay down," he says. His own voice sounds far away. The rebel closes his eyes.

The musket is not loaded, but if the rebels reach the guns, he will use the bayonet. He grabs at the sheath for the Bowie. It's gone. *Pops's Bowie! Where did I put it?* There is no time. The rebels are nearly on them.

Kelly fires into the oncoming surge. The cannon is not yet reloaded, but the piece fifteen yards to the right is ready. The ensuing blast tosses a third of the rebels back into the trees, and the others stop, turning back.

Decker stands over McHenry, bayonet at the ready. "Don't worry, Sergeant," he calls, though he can't hear himself speak over the ringing in his ears. "We'll hold here and then get you to a field hospital."

Kelly races to reload the cannon. If a second assault comes, he wants to be ready. Decker steps back and begins to reload his musket, casting alternate glances at the trees and Sergeant McHenry. When he finishes, and the musket is ready, he feels an immense sense of relief, however foolish. With relief comes fatigue. *How long have we been fighting? Hours?* He glances up at the sun. Still morning.

He turns back, staring down the hill. Blue uniforms litter the field. Some of the bodies are moving. He imagines they are calling out, crying for help, but he can't hear them. The smell of powder, dirt, and death is overwhelming.

Then, he remembers his wound. He pats his ear, suddenly sore. Blood runs down the side of his cheek.

Kelly shouts at him. He watches his friend's lips. "Are you all right?"

Decker nods and then points at McHenry. "He needs a doctor." As soon as the words leave his mouth, he feels foolish. The field is littered with men who need attention.

Kelly gestures at the men strewn behind them. "Yes. They all need help."

Captain Williams has joined them, walking his horse up the hill, flanked by several other officers—a sure sign the new position has been safely taken. Kelly approaches him, pointing at McHenry, and then at the men on the hill. Captain Williams says something to his adjutant, who shouts down the hill at a group of approaching soldiers. One of them is the division's medical officer.

Kelly returns, slinging his musket over his shoulder by the strap. He bends down and grabs McHenry's feet. Decker nods, and having slung his own musket, grabs McHenry under the armpits. His ears still ring, so he's unaware of the sergeant's curses.

• • •

Seven long days would pass before the wounded were fully evacuated by boat to hospitals upriver. Union and Confederate soldiers alike lay on straw near the landing, hoping for aid. Decker did what he could to run meals and water to the wounded. The mass of Union deserters waiting by the Landing, shivering and miserable, showed little interest in helping.

On the first night, Decker managed a small measure of whiskey for the sergeant, who drank without comment. After the sergeant was gone, headed downriver on a boat, Decker continued to cook, change bedding, and do other tasks while the army tried to reorganize. When he wasn't helping the wounded, he and Kelly scoured the battlefield, looking for more survivors.

On the second evening, Decker and Kelly worked until after sunset. Rain clouds rolled in, blotting out the moon and stars, leaving a profound darkness. With nothing more to accomplish, and ready to return to their tent, they noticed a strange, phosphorescent glow on the field of battle. Some of the men, chilled by rain and left to die, had open wounds that glowed.

"You see this?" Kelly asked.

"I do." Decker's ears still hummed, but he could make out conversation.

"Good. Thought I was seeing something crazy." Kelly stared at the field, spotting patches of light everywhere.

"Ghosts?"

"Lot of dead men here." Kelly shivered.

They heard a cry for help and followed the broken ground to one such patch of light. A poor Tennessee boy lay gashed from wrist to elbow, and the full length of the wound glowed blue. The rebel had a shattered leg as well and had been trying to crawl for help. "I'm glowin' like an angel," he said. "Don't kill me."

Decker and Kelly carried the boy to the camp, where he was treated by the division surgeon.

Later, when running food to the wounded, Decker noticed the boy's arm wound was healing nicely. "You *were* touched by an angel," he said.

"Well," the Tennessee boy answered, "my leg is killing me. Wish the angel would have touched me there, too."

CHAPTER ELEVEN

Pittsburg Landing, Tennessee
March 1862

"War is a ghost that haunts you from the moment it exists until the moment you don't."
~Johan Steele, Lt. Colonel

The days following the battle seemed fragmented, like the bits of bone and iron littering the grounds around Shiloh Church. Decker couldn't sleep. Pictures of what he'd seen raced through his mind — a macabre gallery of images that would not end. He tossed his way through the night hours, unable to lie still in his tent. David complained until Kelly pointed out that there was more space to move inside the tent with Joshua gone. For his part, Decker *tried* to lay still, though his body betrayed him whenever, drifting near sleep, he jerked awake, startled by another memory, fresh and raw.

David had suffered a wound of sorts — he'd tripped and bashed his head against a tree stump, leaving him with a knot the size of a peach and the beginnings of an epic tale of war that would fascinate his grandchildren, should he live to have any.

Decker's earlobe had been notched where a Minié ball clipped him. He had to lay on his left side for the first week, owing to the soreness in his right ear. The other men in the tent considered themselves lucky to have escaped unscathed. Some tents in Camp Smith were completely empty now.

The absence of McHenry left the men to their own devices for several days. Decker and Kelly divided their time between searching for wounded among the corpses and tending to the wounded that had already been found. When searching the battlefield stopped yielding results, they shifted their efforts to burial detail. Officers, stunned by the carnage, seemed unable to proceed, as evidenced by an almost complete lack of direction. Decker and his tent mates went ahead anyway, grateful for the distraction of an unending series of duties.

The rebel dead presented a problem. Decker hated to bury them en masse — had the battle outcome been reversed, he'd hope that someone would take the time to identify him and say a few words to usher him on his journey from the land of the living. But the sheer number of corpses prevented any such care. Any special consideration for the men they'd so recently fought seemed too much to ask of his tent mates, given the overwhelming task of tending to the Union dead.

Approaching each corpse, Decker first made certain the man was dead — quick work in some cases. Men's insides had been torn out and their faces blasted away. Death left them cold as a wet Tennessee morning. Next, he searched pockets for some clue to the identity of the corpse. The Union soldiers were buried in shallow, individual graves, wrapped in blankets when possible. The rebels were dumped in piles and covered with dirt. In both cases, if Decker could identify names, he did so.

Negroes did much of the work, helping the soldiers that pitched in. When Decker stopped to say a few words over a fresh grave, the Negroes stood silent, hats over their chests.

Halfway through the second day of heavy digging, David became cross with Decker. "Why do you go on like that? Talking to dead men? This will take forever."

"A man shouldn't leave this world without notice," Decker said. He stood, arms folded in front of him, covered in mud to the shins. A light rain kept his face wet. The ground smelled of vegetation and rot. "Men deserve a moment and a word when they pass."

They'd only been able to procure two shovels. The men took turns digging holes until their arms and backs cried for a break and then passed the shovels on. Kelly stood to the side now, a shovel in hand and a somber look on his face. "There will be more battles," he said. "In the end, we'll just be burying meat."

Despite a sudden flash of anger, Decker wouldn't answer back. Kelly was right—he'd said as much himself—but no one wanted to hear the truth right now. Decker needed Kelly's support. Burial detail was an ugly duty, and every moment of it made his skin crawl. If Kelly got mad and quit, he'd want to do the same.

"The man's name was E. Cook," Decker said. "Can you cut that into the marker?" A tall Negro stood a few yards away, a stake in his hand. Thus far, he'd been shoveling.

"You can spell, can you?" David called.

The man frowned. "I know my letters." His voice was soft for such a huge man. He'd been following Decker's group all morning, and didn't seem to mind the job, though David said that anyone built like an ox ought to stick to the shovel.

Decker said his words—most of the comfort lost in the repetition—and moved on. They'd climbed the hill above the mud road, where cannon had nearly ended the Union assault. His tent mates hadn't questioned Decker's choice. Secretly, he hoped he might find his father's Bowie, lost somewhere on the crest of the hill. He knew chances were slim—a quality knife would be a good battlefield find for anyone. Still, he kept his eyes open.

Decker had a second motive as well. He wanted to find at least one of the men he'd killed, in order to give the man a proper Christian burial. He found one man who looked familiar, but he'd been shot in the back of the head—not Decker's victim. Working the crest of the hill, Decker had difficulty even identifying the spots on which he'd fought. Covered in mud and corpses, nothing looked familiar.

"I don't want to do this anymore," David announced.

Decker bit his lip. "I know."

"Most of these are rebel dead. I say, let them rot."

"I understand." Decker cut into the mud with his shovel, stomping down with his shoe, which had cracked on the bottom. His feet were wet. He turned the shovel and pitched the dirt to the side.

"To hell with your understanding," David said. "This ain't white man's work."

Decker stopped. His back hurt, and he flexed, trying to stave off the cramp that was sure to come. "The bodies need attention."

"They're cold, and they're wet. And they stink." David seemed near tears.

"They were our countrymen once."

David pointed at the body at Decker's feet. "That fellow tried to kill us. You act like a damned preacher. You don't give a damn which side you tend to, and you mutter your words, and—" He scowled, and stomped off down the hill. "I ain't doing this no more!"

The rest of the men followed David, all except for Mike Kelly and the big Negro. Kelly's face was drawn and angry, his mouth turned down, and his lower teeth showing. "I'm staying. But I don't like it. Don't like it at all."

Decker turned to the Negro. The man had the darkest skin he'd ever seen. His ears stuck out from his head like window shutters. "Can you dig again?" he asked.

The man sighed and stepped forward, grabbing the shovel. He glared at Decker and whispered, "I don't like it either."

"We're in agreement," Decker said.

. . .

After the third day, the bodies on the field began to swell, bloating to nearly double their normal size, squeezing out of their uniforms. Blood foam formed at the mouths and noses, smeared by the rain. The stench of sulfur permeated everything. Moving corpses became a problem—the outer layers of skin hung loose, and any exposed organs had already started to putrefy. Decker and Kelly began to dig next to each corpse, so they could roll the body directly into the fresh hole. If the ground was too rocky to dig, they moved on to a more promising corpse.

. . .

Returning to the tent after five days of burial detail, they found a corporal waiting for them. "You Private Brown?" he asked. Decker nodded. "Captain Williams wants to see you." He turned to Kelly. "And you're Kelly, right? You as well."

Decker considered this. In the absence of Sergeant McHenry, someone had to take over the unit. Perhaps they were being promoted. Or perhaps, their behavior after the battle had been noticed, and the captain wished to commend them. They followed the corporal to Captain Williams's tent, where the officer gave instructions to his subordinates. His voice, raw and hoarse, revealed his fatigue and irritation. The men around him stared at the ground with sullen frowns. "We stand to lose as many men to disease as battle if we don't dispose of the dead," Captain Williams said. "What is the problem? We're at a standstill."

"There's a thousand stragglers at the Landing," a lieutenant said. "Why aren't they digging?"

Williams pointed at the lieutenant. "Go organize them."

"They're not my men," the lieutenant said, disdain in his voice.

"By God," Williams shouted. His gaunt face had turned red. "You will have a detail on the field tomorrow, burying bodies, or you'll be out there yourself with a shovel in your hands."

"I'm an officer —"

"That could change, Lieutenant!" Williams roared. Like a child who'd been scolded and switched, the lieutenant's face fell. "You will follow my orders, and I'll be watching to see you do. If you don't want to carry a log for the rest of the war, you'll do as I say."

Decker glanced at Kelly and nodded.

When the officers dispersed, Williams turned to Kelly and Decker, still fuming. "I can't get the battlefield cleared," he muttered.

"We've been out there," Kelly said.

"Have you? Well done, then."

So much for commendations.

Captain Williams turned to Kelly. "McHenry says you're the man. He says you're a good Irish boy, and you know what you're doing."

Kelly stood silent. Williams handed him two sets of chevron stripes, one for each sleeve. "Can you handle sewing these on?" Williams asked. "We'll get you a proper uniform when the dead are buried and we're a little better organized."

Kelly took the stripes in hand, as if holding dog waste. His face was hard, his eyes unfocused.

"Well, then." Williams turned to Decker, surprised, as if just now seeing him. "Private Brown?"

"Sir."

Captain Williams returned to his tent for a moment, emerging with a paper in hand. "You're heading east, Brown. Here are your orders."

Decker stared at the paper. The same expression he'd seen on Kelly's face crossed his own. "East?"

"The New York Rocket Battalion, under Major Thomas Lion. My cousin serves in the War Department. I wrote him and mentioned your display — particularly how straight your rockets flew. He arranged the transfer." Williams paused, cocking his head. He pulled at his mustache. "You seem hesitant, Private."

"I appreciate the consideration, sir, but I'd prefer not. I want to stay with the other men."

Captain Williams snorted. "We're at war, Private. I don't give a *damn* about your preferences. Grab your things. You're heading out on the next ferry. That's an order."

Decker saluted and backed away. *East, the place I want least to be.* He did not want to kill Virginians. He could not, particularly now that he'd seen what this war would be.

But then again, he might not need to fight. He might simply work on rocket designs — a comforting thought for all of five seconds.

Would he be designing signal rockets? Not likely. He would be crafting weapons. His rockets would kill Virginians.

Pops, what can I do? There's no right path!

He walked back to the tent, stride for stride with his friend Mike Kelly. He would gather his things and be gone. The thought brought tears to his eyes, and the emotions he'd kept hidden for days in the wake of the battle threatened to break loose.

Kelly ducked into the tent and pitched his stripes into the corner. He looked back in Decker's direction. "Come on, then. Let's pack your bag."

"What's happening?" David demanded.

"Decker's going east," Kelly said. "He's going to make rockets. Help him gather his things and say goodbye."

Decker felt a lump in his throat he couldn't swallow away. Grateful that Kelly had made explanations for him, he grabbed his belongings and rolled them up in his blanket.

"If you happen to come across my father's Bowie knife—"

"I'll save it for you," Kelly said.

"No, you keep it. It's good luck."

"I'll save it for you."

David fished some hardtack from his pocket. "Here," he said, offering the cracker. "It's all I have."

"Thank you, David."

"I'm walking him to the Landing," Kelly said. He took a last look around the tent and ducked out.

Decker waited a moment, meeting each man's gaze. "God bless you, boys." For the second time that day, Decker felt near tears. He looked away, unable to speak.

Decker and Kelly made the hike to the Landing in silence, watching the sun set as they walked. Men who'd either deserted the battle or been unable to face combat packed the area.

Some had tents, but most suffered the days of rain in the open. Campfires lit the grounds, and the low murmur of voices drowned out the sound of insects. The evening was as damp as Decker's mood.

As they approached the banks of the Landing, where the flat-bottomed paddleboats waited, Decker began to worry that silence would mark their goodbye. When Kelly spoke, the words were a relief.

"If I'd known you were leaving, I wouldn't have been so huffy these last few days."

Decker nodded. "If I'd known, I wouldn't have spent the days burying the dead."

Kelly gave him a sharp glance. "Yes, you would've."

Decker shrugged. "I'd have worked slower."

"As if *that* was possible. You and your words."

Decker laughed. "I wish we had a bottle. I'd drink to you, Michael Kelly."

Kelly stopped. "This war is peeled. Broken all to hell."

"Yes."

"I'm *glad* you're going east. I hope you ride out the war in an office somewhere. I hope you spend every night like this in a pub, with a little dolly on your lap." He paused, staring off into the night. "My daddy was right. Only way to survive this war is to lay low."

"Give those sergeant stripes to David," Decker said.

"Can't. He'd take 'em."

Decker laughed, and Kelly managed a smile. Decker put a hand on Kelly's shoulder. "Here's where you turn around, friend. I can find my way from here." Kelly started to argue, but Decker shushed him. "It's a fair walk back to the tent in the dark, and until you return, there won't be a sensible mind inside the flaps." He stepped forward and hugged his friend. "After the war, you come visit me."

"I will."

Decker stepped away. "In Richmond. I come from Richmond."

"I figured," Kelly said. "Had to be somewhere south."

Decker wanted to keep talking, but there was too much to say, and both men's throats were thick. "Stay low, Kelly."

Kelly nodded and turned away.

Decker made it five paces before the tears started. He knew he looked the fool, stumbling through the camp on the banks, weeping like a child. He thought of Kelly and his tent mates; of poor Joshua, who would never go home to his girl; of the five men he'd killed on the field, every one of them a good Southern boy; of his father, who would never welcome him home again; and of the lost Bowie knife, no doubt wrapped in someone's blanket. Now he would go east and fight his neighbors, a two-day journey away from the woman he loved. The woman whose cherished values he betrayed with every step he took.

He stopped, staring up at the sky. *Lord, please tell me what you want from me. I don't know what I'm supposed to do.*

"Whatcha lookin' at, boy? Stars?" A soldier gave him a drunken nudge, a bottle dangling from his fingertips. Decker stared at the little man, red beard and gaps in his teeth. The man offered him a drink. "Popskull?" he asked.

"No thank you," Decker said.

"Well! Ain't you a polite one?"

• • •

His boat stopped in Evansville to take on fuel and supplies. With a few hours to kill, Decker visited the hospital, which cared for many of the Shiloh wounded, and that was where he found Sergeant McHenry.

The hospital, a huge brick building, housed more than seven hundred. Outside, overflow patients lay on piles of straw, waiting for a bed. Inside, cots were jammed into rows like church pews, each one filled with the living and the dying. An overpowering blend of ether, chloroform, urine, and rot permeated the interior. With help from guards, who kept order and assisted the nurses, Decker found the sergeant at the rear of the first floor. McHenry slept, his right arm draped across his chest. His left arm had been amputated.

As Decker approached the foot of the bed, the sergeant popped open one eye, staring warily. He mumbled something, but Decker couldn't make it out.

"Hello, Sergeant. I came to see how you were faring."

The sergeant closed his eye again, silent. A single nurse scuttled by, wiping her hands on her bib apron. She had a chubby, cheerful face, but her clothing was rumpled, and patches of blood marred her apron.

"Seems like they know what they're doing here," Decker said. He didn't think any such thing, but he didn't want to discourage McHenry. The hospital was filthy and cold. High ceilings and large windows made for drafty rooms. The patients did not have enough blankets.

"This place is a sty," McHenry slurred. "The food is slop and there's too little of it. Comes time for dinner, they pass me by like I didn't have a mouth on me." Decker chuckled.

"You think that's funny, do you?"

Decker froze. "I thought you were telling a joke."

"The only joke here is you, Prussian. I see you're still alive. You think that means anything? There will be a dozen battles like the one you just survived. Think you'll live through them all? Untouched?"

Decker flicked his sore ear. "Took a Minié ball to the ear."

"Pity the aim," McHenry said. "I *know* who you are, you Prussian secessionist son of a bitch. Buda, Illinois, my arse."

Decker struggled not to show a surge of anger. Certain his face had flushed, he managed to keep his voice even. "I stood over you on the battlefield. I protected you."

"I know who you are. You're a sausage-eating mongrel whore who came to see his sergeant all whittled down." McHenry rose up on his straw mattress, wincing with the pain of having moved. His voice rose. "When I recover, I'll be in the field again, and I'll sort you out, by God! That stunt you pulled in drills . . . did you think I'd forget?"

Drawn by the shouts, the nurse scurried back, a frown knitted to her face. "Now then, what's going on here?" She leaned down to adjust McHenry's blanket, but he waved her off, pointing at Decker.

"Is this man bothering you?" she asked, casting Decker an angry glance.

"This man's a *Southerner*."

She stared up at Decker's uniform. The guard at the front of the room began to make his way over to McHenry's bed.

"I saved your life at Shiloh," Decker said. His soft, sure words seemed to convince the nurse, who turned back to McHenry and reached to check his forehead for fever.

"Take your hands from me, Goddamn it!"

"Now! I'll not be talked to in that manner." The nurse motioned with one hand, stopping the guard. Cheery and docile at first glance, she clearly held sway over the ward. "You need to shut your gob. You're sick as a small hospital, and I won't have you disturbin' the others."

McHenry sagged back onto the mattress. "You're *Irish*."

"I was born in Adare, and you're making a stook of yourself."

Decker stepped back. "I'll take my leave."

McHenry tried to sit up again, but the nurse pushed him back down. He settled for a threat. "I'll see you again, Prussian."

Decker shook his head. "No, you won't. But I hope you get well. You're a bag of pus. The Union army needs men like you." He pivoted on his heel, just as the sergeant's drills had taught him, and walked down the corridor, past the beds filled with misery, past the guard at the door, and out into the courtyard and beyond, where a boat waited to take him east.

CHAPTER TWELVE

Camp Congreve, Washington, D.C.
April 1862

*"A certain combination of incompetence and indifference can cause
almost as much suffering as the most acute malevolence."*
~Bruce Catton, Civil War Historian

Decker made much of the journey by train, marveling at the power of the Union locomotives. Small towns and wide expanses of countryside whipped past his window at unheard of speed, putting the trains in Virginia to shame. Once in a while, he slept in his seat, trusting the rocking motion and the click of the rails to lull him. Most of the other passengers were soldiers. Some sat together, laughing and pointing at the landscape. Others huddled in their seats, quiet and alone. At night, Decker sat awake, trying to forget Pittsburg Landing.

When he arrived in Washington, he left the train station on foot, heading through the streets of the capital. Though summer was weeks away, the weather was already hot and humid. A sewage canal ran some distance from the Capitol building, filling the air with a variety of noxious odors, from chemical waste to feces. Along the way, Decker passed hospital after hospital, housing the wounded from battles in the east. He stopped counting after a dozen such establishments.

Washington was loud and boisterous. Soldiers and citizens filled the streets, talking loud enough for the whole town to hear, many bumping into Decker as he walked. No pleasantries, no apologies. Decker shook his head in disgust, feeling a long, long way from home.

The streets teemed with Negros as well, some of them openly celebrating with song and some with drink, though it wasn't clear what good news had prompted such rejoicing. General McClellan's siege of Yorktown had stalled, and the casualties in the west had horrified the nation.

On his arrival at Camp Congreve, he presented his orders and was assigned a tent.

Curious, he asked what was going on in the capital.

"Congress freed the slaves," the camp adjutant told him, spitting the words.

"All of them?" Decker asked, surprised.

"Just the ones in the capital. Three thousand of them, I hear. Republicans used war powers to accomplish that bit of foolishness."

"You don't approve?"

The officer glared. "They'll be dead or dead drunk by morning."

Decker considered the news. What sort of celebration would result when the South was defeated? The thought disturbed him, and his hands began to shake.

Camp Congreve was a small town of wedge tents on the outside of the capital, housing one-hundred sixty men. The grounds consisted of mud on top of mud, which made the camp seem familiar, almost home, after the streets of Washington. Decker stowed his meager belongings and headed to the mess tent. After a hasty meal, the first food he'd eaten in a day, Decker tried to locate the rocket workshop. He was interested in the level of technology being used, and a bit nervous that knowledge of rocketry had somehow passed him by in the year since he'd left Boston. He was a quick study, and once learned, he could embrace most any advance. But he did not relish seeming foolish or backward to his new commander.

In his journey east, he'd spent many of the long hours reading. In Ohio, he chanced across a recent edition of *Scientific American*, which carried an article on a breech-loading rocket gun. The article touted the sheer ferocity of the new development. *A rocket gun? Amazing! But won't such a contraption recoil like a cannon?*

Unable to locate a workshop, he presented himself to Captain Ransom, who escorted Decker to Major Lion's quarters just as the commander sat down for supper. Lion offered him a small plate of chicken and canned fruit, and since Decker was still hungry, he gratefully accepted.

Lion was a short man, with a thick mustache and dark, unruly hair. His British accent and the cane at his side gave him a slightly superior air. He introduced himself and launched into his personal history, which included an apprenticeship with Hale, the inventor of the vectored thrust rocket. "I added my own innovations to Mr. Hale's designs, of course. And he approved—yes indeed—as one would expect him to. A man dedicated to the sciences will always welcome suggestions. That is how innovation is maximized. In posing an answer to the conundrum of accuracy, I've put my efforts into designing a custom launcher. My launchers are open-ended, featuring spiral rods, reinforced by metal bands, that accentuate the spin of the rocket. Spin results in accuracy. Do you understand the concept?"

"I do," Decker said, stuffing food into his mouth. He glanced around the tent. Lion had decorated his table with knickknacks from South America and covered the canvas behind him with the pelt of an animal Decker didn't recognize.

"I've also considered experimenting with vectored thrust."

Decker stopped eating. "I've worked on that concept myself—"

"Well, then. You are in a most opportune place if I dare say so. Unfortunately, our resources are limited. We don't have the machinery necessary to manufacture here at the camp."

"I wondered. So, you haven't been able to set up a workshop yet?"

"No, no, not yet," Lion said. He bit down on a chicken leg and dabbed the corners of his mouth with a napkin. "This is all theoretical. The launcher, however, is an actuality."

Decker sat back on his stool. "Very exciting. You've gone far beyond anything I've seen."

Lion ran fingers through his hair, which caused it to stand straight up. "Be patient, my boy. You will learn a great deal in the coming days."

"I look forward to it, sir."

"I understand you developed some accuracy when building your toys." Lion brushed grease from his mustache, cleaning his fingers on a napkin.

"Yes, sir. You mentioned the angle of vectoring—"

"Yes, of course. At the moment, however, we are currently using rockets of previous manufacture. We had a number of weapons left over from the Mexican conflict. We received our modified launchers yesterday and intend to test them tomorrow or the next day. We'll fire them across the Potomac. You will accompany us."

"New launchers? The ones you described?"

"No. A revised design, meant for combat."

"Revised how?" Decker worried his inquiry might be too direct, but the major seemed enchanted with the discussion.

"The spiral rods did not strike command as durable, though they did add to accuracy. That is why I was anxious for you to observe a test. The new tubes are certainly stronger. We used wrought-iron construction, perforated at set intervals. Gasses can escape, the tubes are lighter, and cooling is accelerated. Comments?"

"None," Decker said. "I look forward to the test." He paused, staring at a bit of chicken stuck to Lion's mustache. "Will the new launchers enhance the accuracy, as you intended?"

Lion shrugged. "We'll see, shan't we? They *disregarded* my spin rods." He wiped his mustache again, dislodging the last bit of chicken.

Oh, no. This isn't good. Aware his expression might have changed, Decker scrambled for a question to ask. "What sort of cargo will the rockets deliver?"

Lion shrugged and clutched his cane. "Pellets, meant to disperse on impact. Effective against a cavalry assault. Eventually, I expect to deliver explosive charges."

Decker sat back, considering this.

"Well. If you're going to work at my side, you'll need a commission." He nodded toward Captain Ransom, who sat in the corner of the tent. "The captain's second lieutenant . . . Toddy?"

"Hoddy," Captain Ransom said.

"Hoddy," Lion agreed. "The man took ill and will not likely be ready for duty any time soon. We will offer you a lieutenant's commission, serving directly under Captain Ransom, though you will make yourself available to me as needed. Is that satisfactory?"

"Yes, sir. That's . . . that's quite unexpected."

"You seem to know your business," Lion said, "and I'm tired of trying to explain myself to men who don't know a rocket from a rooster." He leaned forward. "Have you any questions?"

Decker glanced at Captain Ransom. The man's face held no hint for him. At a loss, he settled on a matter of personal interest. "Does the promotion come with an increase in pay?"

"Little or no," Lion answered, without a hint of a smile.

• • •

Two days later, Decker followed Lion to the banks of the Potomac River to observe a test of the launchers and rockets. The launch site featured a huge rock outcropping, complete with a tree growing from the base. Across the river, buildings and factories rode the riverbank. The Alexandria Aqueduct—a massive bridge for canal boats, built with granite icebreakers to defend the piers against the Potomac's ice floes—stretched across the river to the left. In the middle of the river, a flatboat sat still in the water, hoisting an army blanket stretched across a frame as a target for Lion's rockets.

Major Lion stood to Decker's left, flanked by General Barry from Ordnance and several other Washington officials. The rockets being fired carried no cargo that might endanger the ship. Another flatboat waited downriver, in case an accident required an emergency rescue.

Decker had an opportunity to inspect the rockets in advance, and what he saw disturbed him. The rockets were early Hale designs, kept in storage for at least fifteen years. Two inches in diameter, the rockets looked small and old and would not likely be accurate. The Hale design had been much improved over the years—information Decker passed on to Captain Ransom.

"I expected as much," Ransom muttered.

"Sir?"

"I have served under Major Lion for six months, and rocketry is an imperfect science. My hopes are tempered." The captain's expression had not changed.

The blanket on the ship looked like a postage stamp in the distance. The first launch was greeted with cheers that cut short when the rocket took a sudden dive, scudding across the water like a skipped rock, and then dove beneath the choppy Potomac waters.

A second launch flew straight . . . at first. Decker stepped forward, hands stretched to his side, entranced with the moment. The rocket dipped down into the water before reaching the boat, jumped up, and struck the framework holding the blanket, bouncing back as if it had hit solid stone.

Decker glanced to his left. The ordnance officer stared at Major Lion, who stood red- faced and angry.

A third launch began straight, and then suddenly tumbled, fizzling into the river.

A fourth launch flew straight, spending its thrust before striking the boat just below the rail. The projectile flipped into the air and then tumbled into the river.

"If that rocket had a charge . . ." Lion said. The others in his party were silent.

A final rocket dove into the Potomac's waters, then shot out at a right angle, speeding past the flatboat stationed for emergencies.

General Barry left immediately after the failure of the fifth rocket, taking his ordnance officers with him. Lion stood on the banks of the Potomac, fuming. Captain Ransom stood to the side, overseeing the effort to load the remaining rockets into the wagon that had delivered them.

• • •

Captain Ransom announced the change of orders to the assembled battalion in Major Lion's absence. General Burnside required light artillery, so the New York Rocket Battalion exchanged its store of faulty Hale rockets for six-pounder cannons. The battalion would move south to North Carolina, with Major Lion still in command.

The news came like a hammer blow to Decker. He sought out Captain Ransom after the men were dismissed, prepared to beg for reassignment. *Burnside will end up fighting Virginians. I can't do that. They must send me back west.*

Ransom greeted the request with his customary reserve. He stared back at Camp Congreve as the men began to disassemble their tents. In a flat voice, he said, "I can't reassign you."

"Sir, respectfully — "

"You've already been reassigned. Find Captain Ross at the War Department. Someone has need of your services." He met Decker's gaze for the first time. "I never took you as someone with connections." So saying, he strode off, leaving Decker with nothing but questions.

The War Department was located in a pillared, plantation-style building to the west of the White House. Decker had not yet had time to be fitted for a proper uniform. He carried his shoulder straps — red, bordered in gold — in his pocket. Wallowing in the mud of Camp Congreve, he'd felt at ease in his old uniform. Now, meeting still another new commanding officer, Decker felt underdressed and out of place. *This meeting is too important. I look like a bumpkin.*

Finding Captain Ross took some time, as no one appeared to know the man. Decker located the right office in the farthest reaches of the building. He paused before reaching his destination, stopping to lean against the wall. The floor shifted beneath him. *What the hell is wrong with me?* The low ceilings and dingy walls of the hallway seemed to add to his discomfort. *I can't breathe.*

A young soldier in blue stomped past, papers in hand. Decker forced himself to stand straight, his shoulders back. With hat in hand, he walked the last few steps to the captain's office.

The captain was a slender man with a fine mustache and a dashing wave to his blond hair. Something in his aspect looked vaguely familiar, but then most officers in the Union army were cut from a similar cloth. Decker knocked on the doorframe — the office had no door — and introduced himself.

"I expected you yesterday," Captain Ross said, without looking up.

"Captain Ransom gave me my orders an hour ago, sir." Decker stood in the hallway, outside the closet-sized room. With no place for a desk, the captain had to make do with a tiny stool and table, cluttered with stacked papers and a single gas lamp.

"Well, then. You are here on the recommendation of my cousin, Captain Robert Williams. Do you recall him, Lieutenant?"

"Yes, sir," Decker said. Decker fingered his wounded ear, hoping. Might he duck yet another bullet?

"We've been in contact with a Mr. Joshua Burrows Hyde," Captain Ross continued. "Hyde was Hale's representative during the Mexican conflict. He's approached us with a plan for an improved rocket. More accurate, he says. Captain Dahlgren seems quite taken with him." Captain Ross shared certain facial similarities to Captain Williams, from the lean, chiseled face to the quizzical expression. Decker found himself warming to the man, despite his acquired lack of respect for officers.

"Has he described how his design is improved?"

Captain Ross shook his head, apparently disgusted. "No, he is unable to articulate the particulars of his advances." He pulled at his mustache, squinting at Decker. "He told Dahlgren that accuracy is related to the spin."

"Anyone who's fired a rifled musket knows that," Decker said, keeping his voice flat, to avoid sounding critical.

Captain Ross snorted and sat back. He seemed to study Decker. "I like you, Brown. Why is that?"

Decker was silent.

"There seems to be no foolishness about you. My cousin said as much. I can't say the same for the other *rocket men* I've encountered. I leave every conversation patting my wallet to make certain it's still in my pocket." He sat back as far as the wall behind him would allow and continued. "I have requests for working rockets from officers in the field, but so far, we built nothing substantive we can use in battle. Captain Dahlgren thinks Hyde is the real thing."

"And you, sir?"

Captain Ross frowned, a downturn of the mouth that mirrored the wrinkles on his forehead. "Our President is convinced all avenues of scientific advancement must be explored. The *Monitor* fought at Hampton Roads *before* your arrival in Washington, did it not?"

"Yes, sir."

"Iron ships in battle!" The captain shook his head. "This war will change the world. The sciences advance so quickly, our generals can scarcely keep pace. We have rifled muskets that can kill at a thousand feet, and rifled cannon that can hit a target a mile away. Yet we heard our boys into close ranks and march them against defensive positions, as if this were still the Revolution."

Decker shuddered, thinking of Pittsburgh Landing.

"You understand exactly what I'm saying, don't you, Brown?"

"Yes, sir. I was with Grant in Tennessee."

"Was it . . . was it as horrible as they say?"

Decker tried to speak but couldn't.

Captain Ross scowled. "I have spoken to my *superiors* repeatedly on this very subject. A frontal assault is murder, pure and simple. Yet, none of the great minds in this fine building can fathom—"

He stopped short, seeming to think better of his rant. "At any rate, Mr. Lincoln embraces scientific possibilities, entertaining all, from the genuine visionaries to the charlatans."

"And Mr. Hyde? Which is he?"

Captain Ross smiled, a thin-lipped grimace that answered Decker's question completely. "You will tell me, of course. You will be my eyes and ears. He will arrive in Washington next month. You will be our liaison. Until then, I'll send you on various errands—nothing too strenuous. Perhaps you can use the time to rest." At this last, his gaze narrowed. "You will report to me on a regular basis. Is that acceptable?"

Decker nodded. He felt his knees wobble. "Are you well, Lieutenant?"

"Yes, sir," Decker said.

"Well, be careful. Washington is a cesspool. More men will die from typhoid than from rebel shot."

"Yes, sir." Decker paused. "Washington *is* a different sort of city." Captain Ross nodded in apparent sympathy.

Outside, Decker had to remember to breathe, one hand to an entrance pillar for support.

For weeks, he'd been horrified by the possibility—the certainty—that he would have to fight Virginians. He had even contemplated the possibility of desertion. For the moment, he was safe from that unhappy fate. Miraculously, his new commanding officer seemed to be a man of sense.

But how long would his good fortune last?

Chapter Thirteen

Navy Yard, Washington, D.C.
November 1862

"In war, science has proven itself an evil genius; it has made war more terrible than it ever was before."
~William Jennings Bryan

The evening before the demonstration, Decker visited the dock. The launcher was set up in advance. Because of the size of the anticipated audience, Decker was charged with erecting a small bleacher with a clear view of the launch. "Erect the stands here," Mr. Hyde ordered. "I want the President to get a sense of the sheer power of rocketry."

Decker had no intention of following the man's orders. He instructed the dockworkers and the two privates at his disposal to build the stands as far away from the launchers as he could manage without compromising the angle of view. Disregarding Hyde's directions only bought him an additional forty feet. Decker hoped the extra distance would not be necessary.

Joshua Burrows Hyde, the man behind the latest rocketry project, had the open, empty smile of a peddler. When he spoke, Hyde seemed to be attentive, but his gaze angled too high, as if he were searching Decker's forehead, and his quick answers never quite connected with the question asked. At first, Decker dismissed the man's eccentricities as part and parcel of a busy schedule, but as the months ticked by, Decker realized the man *always* appeared busy, giving rise to the suspicion that the herky-jerky hand motions and the darting gaze were a means of avoiding a conversation.

The suspicion was confirmed when Decker was granted a look at Hyde's "new and improved" Hale rocket. Whenever Decker asked to see a prototype, Hyde rushed to assure him that his opinion *mattered.* Hyde *welcomed* outside recommendations, leaning heavily on the word *outside*, as if Decker were an interloper. The assurances never included an appointment to view the actual rocket. When Decker insisted, Hyde acquiesced immediately. His smile became businesslike, and his hands were at rest.

Hyde then began cancelling a series of appointments, owing to his "incredibly busy schedule."

When the first rockets of the new design were delivered, and Decker's inspection could no longer be avoided, Hyde invited him to the warehouse that served as his workshop to see the finished product. Hyde met him at the door, steering his every step, past a machine press and a lathe, to the worktable running the full length of the rear wall. The workers scurried around the room. None met his gaze.

The sample rocket, encased in iron, resembled Hale's designs. Hyde's rocket had a single, large gas hole at the bottom of the rocket. "The expansion of gasses as they leave the gas hole exerts pressure on the vanes, causing rotation," Hyde said. "Thus, my rocket has significantly more spin, which will increase accuracy."

"I'm familiar with the theory. I've wondered if using three smaller gas holes might directly influence the corresponding vanes without losing basic thrust. My illuminations use that sort of design."

Hyde let out a snort. "Well, I'm certain that works well for toys." He patted Decker's shoulder. "The thrust from one of these rockets is far, far greater than you've worked with, I assure you. And by concentrating thrust from a single aperture, my rockets can travel significantly farther."

Decker set the rocket on its side. "What are these, then?" he asked, pointing to holes on the rocket's side.

"Angled gas holes to accentuate the rocket's spin," Hyde said. "The launcher provides the initial direction, but during flight, additional spin is required."

"Then the rear gas hole isn't a single aperture."

Hyde frowned. "There is a significant difference between the spin holes and the main thrust aperture. Size, for example." His frown deepened. "Am I correct in guessing your direct experience with rocketry is limited to the manufacture of illuminations?"

"You are correct," Decker said with a smile. "That is why I have so many questions for you."

Hyde's smile returned. "Well, then. You'll be interested in this." He tapped the rear assembly of the rocket. "This is a wonderful innovation. The tailpiece and vanes are a single cast-iron unit that can be screwed onto the rocket's base. The rocket can be loaded with powder just prior to firing, rather than being primed and stored for long periods of time."

Decker glanced to the side. Hyde's assistants stood grouped around a machine press.

Hyde saw him staring at the machine, and with evident pride said, "That is a hydrostatic press, which provides a much more consistent gunpowder density. The design is one of my own, based on Mr. Hale's original press."

Decker nodded. "Fine piece of machinery. I'm interested in all aspects of your processes. What alterations to standard gunpowder do you use?"

Hyde blushed a little, waving his hand. "The Union army's standard issue powder is a remarkably consistent product—"

"No alteration to the saltpeter or charcoal ratios?"

Hyde frowned.

Decker moved to the table holding the finished rocket and began unscrewing the bottom piece. Afraid Hyde would object, he said, "You are quite right. This bottom piece is a remarkable advance." He cranked the bottom piece faster as he spoke. "The thread is quite gradual. Unscrewing the piece is an achievement of its own!" He laughed as he cranked away at the bottom, removing it before Hyde could intervene.

Inside, powder filled the rocket, flush with the back end.

"Interesting," Decker said. "I notice you've dispensed with the conical hole one might find in the propellant."

"Drilling a cone into compressed powder is risky, don't you think?" Hyde said. "And the additional powder gives additional thrust."

"What does your rocket use as a combustion chamber?" Decker asked.

Hyde was silent and blank-faced for a moment. "You do indeed ask a great number of questions, Lieutenant," he said at last, a rueful smile returning to his face. "One would think that you yourself worked with Mr. Hale for the last two decades, not I."

Decker nodded. "As I said, I'm curious, sir."

Hyde's fingers began to dance, and he summoned one of his workers to issue a series of orders, none of which seemed to merit the sudden urgency in his voice. When he returned to Decker, he explained he had several matters to attend to. "I did not expect your visit to last as long as it has. You will excuse me, sir? So much to attend to!" He moved over to the press, which was inactive, giving a flurry of instructions. Decker waited for several minutes, wondering if his refusal to leave would result in an extension of the conversation, but that was not to be.

• • •

Captain Ross had been sent west a month earlier. Before leaving, he arranged for Decker to continue his association with

Mr. Hyde's project by assigning him to Captain Dahlgren, also of Ordnance, and the current head of the Washington Navy Yard. "But he's Navy," Decker protested.

"And you're technically a lieutenant in the artillery," Captain Ross said. "Dahlgren is in charge of Mr. Hyde's project, so you will assist him as long as he requires." Leaning forward, he'd added, "Which allows you to continue with the Ordnance Department as an expert on rockets."

Dahlgren was well regarded in the War Department, in part because of his design for the navy gun bearing his name. The Dahlgren gun was a bottle-shaped, cast-iron cannon that provided accurate fire, along with additional support at the rear of the cannon, where explosions often resulted in the death of gunners.

Dahlgren had a reputation for charm, but Decker found him considerably less engaging than Ross. Some of his brusque nature was understandable, owing to his schedule. He had a bigger office than Ross, being stationed at Building One, just off the Navy Yard's main road. The brick, two-story building featured wraparound verandas that reminded Decker of home. Most of the office space was taken up by officers of the 71st New York Regiment, courtesy of the captain, who was known for accommodating others in the name of cooperation. The man was clearly worth the admiration the President was rumored to have for him — Lincoln made frequent visits to the Navy Yard — but that value did not translate into cordiality regarding Decker Brown.

"I do not believe Mr. Hyde knows anything about rockets beyond selling them," Decker said, after having inspected Hyde's rocket.

"Really?" One-word answers were to be expected, befitting Dahlgren's dour face and bushy sideburns.

"I'll be more specific," Decker said. Captain Ross appreciated blunt language. Perhaps Dahlgren would share that appreciation. "His design will not increase accuracy. I would hazard a guess that his rockets will fare worse than the ones we've seen so far. The use of spin apertures—"

"Pardon?"

"Hyde's rocket uses spin apertures as well as a single rear gas hole—"

"And that is important for what reason?"

"The rocket will spend a third of its thrust in the spin. Worse, Hyde's design does not include a combustion chamber. A combustion chamber is necessary—"

"I understand the concept, Lieutenant. I studied French rockets before the Mexican affair."

"There's nowhere for the ignited gases to expand," Decker finished.

Captain Dahlgren gave him a sour nod. "Well, we shall see. We've arranged a demonstration—"

"I wouldn't."

The captain scowled. "Allow me to finish my thought, Lieutenant. The President is quite anxious to see the new design in action. Members of the President's cabinet will also be in attendance."

"Sir."

Captain Dahlgren waited.

"I don't think the rockets are safe."

Dahlgren stared at him, as if evaluating a number of invisible criteria, his gaze settling on Decker's lieutenant bars. "Thank you for your input, Lieutenant. I will inspect Mr. Hyde's designs." He glanced once again at Decker's bars. "I imagine you are anxious to return to your unit. You will make yourself available at the demonstration. After, we'll decide how best to use your talents."

I'm going to the front lines. Decker slumped in his chair. *Damn my mouth.*

• • •

President Lincoln arrived the morning of the 15th, accompanied by Secretary of State William Seward and Secretary of the Treasury Salmon Chase and several aides. The group came by carriage, through the high brick walls that encircled the yard and past the warehouses and factories bordering the docks. Though the morning was young, the sound of steam machines filled the air.

Hyde arrived moments later with Captain Dahlgren and immediately began to complain about the placement of the seating. "I specifically gave orders to construct the bleacher here," he said, indicating the spot he'd designated the day before. He looked up, and upon spotting Decker, pointed at him. "That man has been a burden since you assigned him to me, Captain."

Captain Dahlgren was attired in full dress, as befitted the occasion. His long face and dark uniform gave him the appearance of a mortician. He waved Decker closer with a curt motion of the hand. "Was there a reason for moving the bleachers?" he asked, his voice like the far-off rumble of an impending storm.

"I had the President's safety in mind."

"Do I understand—"

Hyde interrupted. "The President and his cabinet are in no danger—"

Captain Dahlgren held up a hand. "Stop." He glanced at Decker. "We'll discuss this later." Turning to Hyde, he said, "Do you wish to move your launcher?"

Hyde sighed. "No. It was placed with certain scientific contingencies in mind." He pointed across the water to the grassy expanse on the far side, where a wooden platform had been erected. "The launcher has been calibrated to deliver a rocket to the designated target."

"Shall we dismantle the bleachers, then?"

"No, no, that would take too long."

"Proceed then," Dahlgren said.

Hyde sputtered for a few moments. Decker retreated to the end of the bleachers and waited. The President, his cabinet, and other aides took a seat. Lincoln was a tall man, gangly and odd-looking. His shoulders slumped, and his chest seemed caved in at the middle, as if he'd been punched and never recovered. *That is an ugly man. A cross between a flagpole and a scarecrow.* Only his whiskers gave his face any sense of gravity.

Then, Lincoln turned, staring straight at Decker, and smiled. The man's dark eyes seemed to take him in entirely, the clarity of his perception softened by crow's feet and the corners of his mouth. In his singular countenance, Decker imagined a kindness and a deep sense of humility. He felt drawn to that face—at once plain and plainly intelligent. Decker snapped to attention and saluted. The President's smile grew broader, friendlier, and he nodded in turn.

Then Hyde began to speak, ending the moment. "Allow me to welcome you to a demonstration of what will be the most powerful weapon in the Union arsenal. The Hale rocket has proven itself in battle, from the Mexican conflict to the distant mountains of India. We are here to witness a newer, improved version of Mr. Hale's great design. But before we begin, a word about how we came to be here, in the great Washington Navy Yard on this fine November morning—"

The President glanced at Secretary Seward, frowning. Captain Dahlgren cast an apologetic smile in Lincoln's direction and then glared at Hyde.

"Ah, indeed," Hyde said. "There will be time afterward for discussion." He motioned to one of his assistants, who hurried over to the rocket, already nestled in the launcher. The assistant bent to light the fuse, backed up a step, checking to ensure the fuse was indeed burning, and then retreated from the launcher.

Nothing.

Hyde waved at the assistant, pointing to the launcher with a stricken expression. The man crept forward like a hunter closing in on wounded game. He knelt, and then motioned Hyde forward. They consulted for a moment before Hyde returned to the bleachers. "A slight delay," he announced.

The fuse was reset, while Hyde explained that, as with cannon, occasional misfires were "normal." When the assistant nodded, Hyde clapped his hands and turned to watch.

A sudden blast startled everyone. Smoke obscured all, and a thundering roar echoed out into the harbor. Decker dropped flat to the ground, patting himself for a weapon. A piece of the launcher struck the bleachers to his left and tumbled away. Then the wind cleared the smoke, and—

—the President and his cabinet members sat, startled but unharmed. Seward had extended his arms in front of Lincoln, shielding the President. Chase huddled against the bleacher seats, shaking. Captain Dahlgren frantically checked everyone, white-faced, making certain no one had been injured by the explosion. Then he pivoted, meeting Decker's gaze. His face was unreadable.

Decker crossed the dock to check on Hyde and his assistant. Hyde seemed stunned, and he spoke in a series of half-sentences, none of which made sense. He saw Decker's approach and grabbed him by the forearms. "Rockets sometimes misfire!" he blurted.

"They do, sir. New technology never progresses without hiccups." The caveat was meant as a comfort.

Hyde growled, his face an angry sneer.

"The President is fine, sir," Decker said. Hyde glanced at the bleachers, and relaxed, apparently relieved.

From across the dock, Dahlgren stood transfixed, his eyes locked on Decker.

. . .

Decker sat in Dahlgren's office, late at night, a lantern providing illumination. The captain poured brandy into two snifters and offered one to Decker before taking a sip from the other. Clearing his throat, Dahlgren asked, "Do you know why I designed the gun that is presently named after me?"

"No, sir," Decker said.

Dahlgren closed his eyes. The captain's office had a different aspect at night — the soft yellow glow of the lantern transformed the plaster walls and perfunctory furniture into a comfortable setting — warm and secluded. Other officers were either asleep or in the city. They drank alone. The brandy was fine, and the cold night air could not penetrate the building's walls.

"Late in the forties, we were testing a thirty-two-pounder. The back end of the gun shredded, cutting the gunner to pieces. He didn't die in battle. He died testing a piece of equipment. Unforgivable. I vowed to build a safer gun, one that could be used to deliver both solid shot and shells. And I did." He took another sip of brandy.

Decker did the same.

"I didn't examine Mr. Hyde's design before the demonstration. I have many duties, from ordnance procurement to running the yard, to advising our President. These are not excuses, Lieutenant. These are explanations." He took another sip, then swirled the brandy in the snifter, as if studying the amber liquid. "You saved the President's life."

Decker frowned. He was uncomfortable with praise, and he shook his head as if to deny. "The world will never know. They don't give medals for the placement of bleacher seats."

Decker waited.

"But you and I will know." Dahlgren raised his glass. "If you had not performed your little subversion, the President might well be dead, and I would be reduced to designing the *Dahlgren Launcher,* with the safety of rocketeers in mind." He set his snifter on the desk in front of him and met Decker's gaze. "Thank you."

Decker mumbled. Dahlgren took a deep breath. Both men averted their gazes for a moment.

Dahlgren broke the ensuing silence. "Burnside will be marching to Richmond within the month."

"I wish him well."

"He can do no worse than Pope or McClellan. At least we took New Orleans." Dahlgren sighed.

"I thought McClellan did well at Antietam. He stopped the invasion."

Dahlgren shook his head. "I can't be specific, but I assure you, we had Bobby Lee in our hands, and we let him get away. This war should be over." He scowled. "Well, that's water beneath a rickety bridge. What now for you, Lieutenant? I imagined sending you back to Lion's battalion, but that seems a waste of your talents. Hyde intends another test, but I am confident the second launch will end much as the first. Even if he's successful, I won't send his rockets to the field of battle." He paused. "I wonder, Lieutenant. Given your obvious understanding of the mechanics of rocket flight, why haven't you proposed a project of your own?"

"There's no point," Decker said. "A rifled cannon is a fearsome weapon. Rockets will never compete with a cannon's accuracy or a shell's destructive force."

"Someday, perhaps," Dahlgren said.

Decker closed his eyes. The brandy and the buttery light of the lantern made him sleepy. "I am still fielding requests for rockets and launchers from some field commanders. The portability of launchers makes them a sensible choice when the terrain makes it impossible to move artillery into place."

"Swamps," Decker said. "Explosions from rockets might startle someone, and as you noted, launchers are portable. Other than that, I don't see the point."

CHAPTER FOURTEEN

Richmond, Virginia
April 1863

"The need of the immaterial is the most deeply rooted of all needs. One must have bread; but before bread, one must have the ideal."
~Victor Hugo

Henry Lee drove Paula into the center of Richmond with a carriage full of bread loaves. A day earlier, her father brought flour home from the mill, and Millie helped her bake the loaves. After delivering the food to the Baptist Church, the food would be distributed to those most needy.

Richmond was starving. Bacon sold for ten dollars a pound. The price of coffee had increased forty-fold since the start of the war — an unaffordable luxury. The government tried to intervene, placing price controls, but farmers responded by holding on to their crops, waiting out a fair price for their harvest. Soldiers in the battlefield received the best of the available goods, and what remained in the city came with a huge price tag.

In January, her father's silver had run out, and the family met ends through barter, parting with the treasures that made their house a home. The return on her trades left her horrified. Fine china hardly purchased the makings of a meal.

The government seemed unaware of the deprivations. At the end of March, President Davis called for a day of "fasting and prayer" for the cause. The request came on the heels of a devastating winter storm and an explosion at the ordnance plant that killed forty-five women working there. "The President is an imbecile," William Crane complained. "He would have us fast in the midst of famine."

In truth, William Crane's flour mills kept his family from the threat of starvation. The family's most basic needs being temporarily secured, Paula focused her concern on the people of Richmond. "If you can, Father, bring home flour. More flour. Millie and I will bake. I must do something, and baking will make a difference." The thought of the women of Richmond quietly supporting the cause with empty pantries and hungry children tortured her.

William promised to try. The army had demands that superseded his daughter's requests. "You have to do better than *try*," she told him. "You bring home flour for the household."

Crane was responsible for two house servant and thirty slaves at the mill. With so many to feed, he'd already committed to a certain amount of flour each month. Would a little more be so difficult?

Crane agreed, and Paula began her project, baking with Millie all day. On the following morning, she had the carriage loaded and accompanied Henry Lee to the Belvidere Baptist Church. Pastor Sheldon would know which families needed the most help.

But when Henry Lee rolled the carriage to the front steps, the church appeared deserted. After Henry Lee helped her down from the carriage, she went inside. The nave was empty. "Hello?" she called, her voice a faint echo in the rafters. In all her years, she'd never seen the church unoccupied. The sight gave her a chill.

She wandered back to the entrance. On the street below, Henry Lee stood talking to the minister. Pastor Sheldon was a stodgy man, made distinctive by his unfortunate hair. Having lost most of it, he'd decided to compensate by letting the tufts circumscribing his head just above the ears run loose in the style of untrimmed shrubbery. His wife spoke admiringly of the thatch, saying it invoked the image of St. Francis.

Pastor Sheldon utilized two distinct speaking voices. The first was a soft, Southern drawl full of honey and homily. Like any minister, he depended on the generosity of the flock for his living. He could be quite charming, though his banter—heavy on compliments—bordered on fawning. The second voice, his pulpit voice, was a sharper tone that cut to the bone. "The Lord's truth needs no varnish," he would explain, should someone's feelings be hurt by the minister's pronouncements.

Today, though, he spoke in a different, almost sardonic tone, with his eyebrow arched, and the hint of a smile. "You are too late, Miss Crane," he said.

"I'm sorry, Pastor. I didn't know you were expecting me."

"As I told your man, here, the women left more than an hour ago."

"I'm afraid I don't understand."

"Perhaps you slept in."

Paula couldn't be certain, but an accusation seemed hidden in the minister's words. "I was up with the sun, sir, as I am every morning. But again, I am at a loss—"

"The women didn't include you in their plans?" His hinted smile disappeared, and a hard look narrowed his gaze. "An oversight, perhaps." His gaze became a glare. "And perhaps not."

Paula took a breath before speaking again. Clearly, she'd done something to upset Pastor Sheldon. But what could it be? "I repeat myself, sir. Of which event are you speaking?"

"The women of Richmond have joined hands to demand food, Miss Crane. Plans were formulated yesterday, here in this very church. Families are starving." He closed his eyes, as if mustering patience for a slow-witted child. "The city's shelves are empty, and the women have marched to confront Governor Letcher. Food must be made available."

"Food goes to the armies first—"

"Food is a basic right, Miss Crane. Our government is unwilling to address that simple fact of nature."

Paula stared at the minister, blushing. He was clearly angry, and a portion of his anger was directed at her. She glanced to the side. Henry Lee stood, hands clasped and head down.

"Certain families don't share the burden of worry, of course," Pastor Sheldon continued. "You are blessed with a sufficient number of servants, allowing your father to avoid service. Thus, you have a head of household present to worry over details like eating. It must be gratifying to have poor families wage war on behalf of your continued prosperity."

The *Twenty Slave Law*, passed the previous year, exempted one male from conscription for each twenty slaves owned on a Confederate plantation. Otherwise, Paula's father would have already been pressed into service. Whit Hill's father had been exempted by the same law, allowing him to evade an officer's commission.

The law embittered many of the women at the Baptist Church. The minister's wife, a modest, frugal woman who seemed to notice every difference between her own circumstances and the circumstances of others, declared the law proof that the rebellion was "a rich man's war." For the first time, Paula had an inkling that Pastor Sheldon might be the source of his wife's ire.

"My father is much needed at home," Paula said. A cold note crept into her voice. "Someone must organize and direct the efforts of our slaves." From the corner of her eye, she watched Henry Lee. He did not move.

"Why does it not surprise me that the daughter of William Crane would be such an ardent defender of our peculiar institution?" The minister's thin-lipped, satisfied smile had returned.

"You mistake me, sir. Our country's capital is tied up in slaves. If no one remains on the home front to ensure production, our economy will shut down." *The man is an idiot. Does he expect slaves to work to protect the institutions that keep them in bondage?* She stopped, her eyes no longer focused on Pastor Sheldon. The conscription law wasn't about the rich or the poor. Rather, the law was a stark admission of failure. The failure of the South's economy. The failure of slavery. *Decker was right. He was right all along.*

"What good is an economy that will not meet the basic needs of its citizens?" the minister demanded.

"But sir, I brought bread," Paula answered.

Pastor Sheldon stepped closer to the carriage. "How many loaves have you?"

"Twenty-five."

He turned, his face stern. When he spoke, he did so with his minister's voice, thundering out into the street. "*Hundreds* of women joined the march. Perhaps *thousands*. Twenty-five loaves? Did you imagine you could recreate the miracle of the loaves and fishes?"

Her face went pale. "I imagined nothing. I baked loaves. Millie and I baked loaves. Real loaves of bread, unlike the imaginary bread that you demand as your *right*." Her voice had the raw edge of someone near tears, someone too angry to be silent. "And when you demand goods as a right, you are demanding someone provide those goods at your behest. Is that not the very essence of the slavery you claim to decry?" She stepped back, shaking. "I did what I could. That is what *your* sermons have taught me, sir. First and foremost — do what you *can*." She curtsied and headed to the carriage.

Pastor Sheldon burst into a coughing fit behind her. When he spoke again, he'd managed to soften his voice a bit. "Wait. What will you do now, child?"

"I will hand out bread," she said.

Henry Lee climbed in the carriage, picked up the reins, and released the brake. "Perhaps you should not. I would avoid — "

"You have already done so, sir. You did not speak against the war before it began. You and men like you forged this country and its institutions. Women did not have a say. This war has reduced them to marching in the streets while you guard your church. You have avoided *all*, sir." Paula did not glance back as the carriage rolled away.

Almost immediately, she began recounting the confrontation with the minister. She had glimpsed something important, but the words were slipping away, lost in the agitation and the clack of carriage wheels.

Henry Lee waited until they were several blocks away before speaking. "You shouldn't have spoken like that to Pastor Sheldon. He's a man of God."

Paula stared at the back of Henry Lee's head, surprised. After a while, she said, "Perhaps you're right." She would give him his say. She wiped an angry tear from the corner of her eye. "Let us find these women and hand out our bread." Ahead, they could hear shouting. "You missed your turn, Henry Lee."

"No, ma'am."

"Pardon me?"

Henry Lee shook his head. "I promised your father and Mr. Whitaker to keep you out of trouble. Since you bound and determined to dive into it, I'm taking you past his office."

"Promised Whit? When was this?"

"That morning, when you all came into Richmond, and you ran off on your own. Ought not to have done that, Miss Paula."

He gave the reins a shake, moving the horse along. "His office is just around the corner, and we're going there."

"I don't need Whitaker Hill—" Her voice cut short as they rounded a corner into another world. Henry Lee pulled back on the reins and brought the carriage to a stop. Ahead, they saw the Capitol building. Women filled the plaza, shouting curses and shaking fists. The street leading to the plaza was littered with glass from broken shop windows. Women climbed from the window frames, arms filled with cans or bolts of cloth—any goods they could strip from a shelf. Shop owners stood still in front of locked doors, watching as rioters ransacked their businesses.

A handful of soldiers guarded the perimeter of the plaza, unable to intervene. *What can they do? They can't fire on the women, for God's sake! They're helpless.*

Paula stood in the carriage, waving her arms. "Stop! I have bread!" Her voice did not carry over the roaring crowd, but a few women stopped, staring at the rich woman in the carriage with a loaf in her hand. One of them carried a knife—another an axe handle.

Several wandered over, some with full arms. One woman with a small ham under her arm shouted, "Bread?"

"I have bread!"

"Give it over," the woman with the ham said, rushing forward. Within a moment, the carriage was surrounded. Paula's efforts to disperse the loaves were not fast enough. Women climbed into the carriage, grabbing bread. The carriage rocked, and Paula tumbled to the side, spilling out into the street. Her head struck the wheel just as her body hit pavement, and for a moment, she blacked out. When she came to her senses, she saw the horse being dragged away. Henry Lee was gone. The legs of dozens of women raced past, and more than one kicked her or stepped on her arms in passing.

Someone grabbed her from behind, pulling her legs out from under the carriage. A firm arm wrapped around her midsection, whisking her away from the mob. In a moment, she found herself in the doorway of a brick building, sheltered from the women in the street by a man in uniform.

Whit.

He stood guard while Henry Lee fumbled with the door. In a moment, they were inside, the door closed behind them. "You're safe now," Whit said. "Are you all right?" He touched her forehead, and she winced. She could feel a knot forming.

"I must be a sight —"

"It doesn't matter. You're safe. That's all that matters." He brushed her hair into place.

A captain and his adjutant stared at the crowd from the hallway. The shouts and demands of the rioters sounded through the open windows. The captain was hunched and ancient, with a gray beard hanging to the middle of his chest. "They've called out the City Battalion."

The adjutant, a boy in his teens, said, "They mean to fire on the women." He wiped his nose with the sleeve of his uniform.

"Can you make it up the stairs?" Whit asked Paula.

"Of course. I'm fine, really."

They climbed the stairway to the second floor. Whit led her to a small balcony overlooking the edge of the plaza. Below, the mayor and the governor made their way up Mayo Street, bracketed by soldiers. The mayor tried to speak, shouting to the crowd with his arms extended. They drowned him out with their calls. Someone in the back of the crowd threw a rock, missing the mayor by a foot. "An ugly situation," Whit said.

Paula stood behind him, staring over his shoulder. This was not a Virginia she recognized. These women were not anyone she could understand.

As if reading her mind, Whit turned back, his face bearing a sadness she'd never seen before. "They're hungry," he explained. "This is who we have become."

"I can't believe that. There are good men and women fighting for the cause."

"They seem few and far away to me now."

"*You* are a good man, Whit."

Governor Letcher, a bald man with spectacles, stepped in front of the mayor, and for a moment, the crowd noise dropped. "The City Battalion is arriving now. I implore you! Ladies, if you do not disperse, they will open fire!"

Whit leaned out over the balcony rail, staring off to his right. "What is it?" Paula asked.

"Cannon. The city troops are rolling cannon into the side streets."

This can't be happening! She leaned forward, straining to see.

"Ladies, please!" The women of the mob answered Governor Letcher with a screeching roar, chanting "Bread or blood! Bread or blood!" Letcher shook his head and stepped aside.

Whit leaned over the rail again, staring for long moments. When he ducked back again, meeting her gaze, he simply said, "The President."

Paula stepped forward. Led by a cordon of troops, President Davis moved to the spot vacated by the mayor and governor. His arms out, hands clutching Confederate currency, he called to the crowd. "Please! Ladies of Richmond!" He began. "You say you're hungry and you have no money? Here is all I have. Take it. It is not much, but it's *all I have*." He emptied his pockets, and a few women scurried away, clutching bills.

"No more starvation!" a woman shouted, and the mob roared. The woman was as tall as any man, wearing a hat with a white feather standing straight up from the top. She pointed at President Davis. "Bread! Or blood!" The women around her began to chant again.

Governor Letcher stepped forward. "You have five minutes to vacate! In five minutes, we will open fire!"

Whit turned away from the balcony, moving Paula back into the room. "We must step away from the window now," he said, leading her to an office in the center of the second floor.

As they walked, he explained, "This may end in gunfire, and I don't want you to take a stray ball."

For a while, they sat in the tiny office, bracketed by shelves stuffed with papers. The room was filthy. Mud coated the floor, probably tracked in during the previous week's snowstorm. A rolltop desk that had seen the nicks and scratches of two decades sat in the corner. Dust covered the top like dirt over a grave.

Paula's thoughts, dark and unfettered, drifted back to the previous week. Each morning, she trudged with Millie to the well in Capitol Square for fresh water. In the harsh winter weather, the city's waterworks had failed. One warmer morning, when the sun had turned a foot of snow into a miserable slush, she'd been accosted three different times by men in groups, laughing and catcalling. No one offered to help them with their loads. Richmond had become a city of strangers. *We are going to lose the war. We have already lost.*

The old, gray-bearded officer poked his head inside the door and announced, "The crowd dispersed. No shots were fired." Henry Lee waited in the hallway.

Whit stood up from his stool, one hand across his chest and his empty sleeve pinned and hanging. "You are safe now," he said. His dark eyes matched his hair and goatee. He looked both solemn and gallant. "I will try to find a horse to get you home."

CHAPTER FIFTEEN

Boston, Massachusetts
July 1863

"The minute you understand racism, you're responsible for being racist. It's like eating from the tree of knowledge."
~Lynda Barry

In the middle of summer, the heat in Washington, D.C. took its toll on Decker Brown. The stench of the canal and the relentless assault of insects made him weak with a longing for home.

By the end of June, he contracted a fever. His commander granted him a furlough, with the accompanying suggestion that he might better recover his health outside of the city. Though he could not go home to Richmond, Decker decided to visit his Uncle Oskar in Boston. He'd been happy during his two-year apprenticeship there, and his uncle might enjoy a visit. Decker could inquire after his father. He wondered if Pops was still angry with him. *I'll bet he is. He's a stubborn, stubborn man.* Decker commandeered a horse and made the long journey against the doctor's advice. By the time he arrived in Boston, his fever had spiked again.

Oskar Brown was a squat, middle-aged man with the chiseled look that came from a lifetime of physical labor. Years of eating and drinking what he pleased put soft rings around his belly, and dark ones under his eyes, but there was no mistaking the muscle and bone underneath. He spoke like a hard man as well, firing short bursts of words with a hint of guttural German underneath his Boston accent.

"You are sick," he declared when Decker arrived at his doorstep.

"Cold out here." Decker had stabled the horse three blocks away, and the walk to Beacon Hill drained the last of his resolve. He shivered, despite the midsummer sun.

"Come in, then. I'll put you to bed. Follow me." He led Decker up the stairs, practically carrying him the last few steps.

Oskar Brown lived in a modest, two-story row house on the flat of the hill, at the edge of the north slope. Below, the free Negro community kept up a noisy bustle of activity. Laying in his old bed, in his old room, Decker listened to the sounds through the open window. Carts and wagons. The call of vendors. And above all, laughter. *Boston is a noisy town. Richmond is quieter. I miss home.*

Everything Uncle Oskar said about Boston was true. "The streets are clean. People walk. They don't run. In New York, people run." The restful dignity of the red brick buildings seemed almost European. But the Richmond in his mind sounded soft and low, like sinking into a comforter until the spinning stopped, soothing his fever. When an east wind tossed the bedroom curtains, Decker imagined the smell of the James River, and he was asleep.

When he woke again, his fever had broken. A day and a night had passed.

• • •

"It's time you were awake," Oskar said, setting the tray of eggs and sausages on the table next to the bed. "I didn't know whether to call a doctor or a mortician. I did not call either one." He squinted at Decker, no hint of a smile on his face. "You are hungry, no?"

"You know I don't like sausages," Decker said, rubbing his eyes.

"Try them. Your tastes may have changed."

Decker sat up and pushed back the covers. He was still in uniform. "I have to use a bathroom."

"Can you make it down the stairs?" Oskar asked. Decker nodded. "It's summer, so you can take a bath in the tub."

"No. A toilet will be enough."

"Good. I didn't want to change the bathwater."

Decker took the stairs down to Oskar's flush toilet, grateful for the convenience. When he'd finished, he tried the stairs again, and found them much more difficult going up than down. Oskar sat waiting for him in the bedroom. He'd already eaten one of Decker's three sausages. He looked up, his cheek pouched, and shrugged. "You said you didn't like them."

"Go on, eat up," Decker said, climbing back into bed.

"You have not heard the news." Oskar took another bite of sausage. Decker waited for him to chew and swallow. "Meade stopped Lee in Pennsylvania. The rebel army—what's left of it—is headed back to Virginia." He took another bite, this time with some eggs. "And," he added, his mouth full, "Grant took Vicksburg."

Decker sat up. "Vicksburg?"

Oskar nodded. "The Mississippi River belongs to the Union, from one end to the other." Decker sat back. "Well."

"I think we'll win, now. I wasn't so sure."

"Who could blame you after Fredericksburg? Chancellorsville? Each battle costlier than the last." Decker shook his head. "Lincoln's generals."

"Baboons."

"How can they not understand the idiocy of attacking fixed positions with today's weapons?" Decker asked. "An impossible task. Do you know the functional range of a rifled cannon?"

"*Ja,* better than Burnside does. Fredericksburg was murder. Plain and simple."

Decker scratched his chest, and then each arm in turn. His uniform smelled of fever sweat. "So, Meade was the one to stop Lee. How did he do it?"

"Lee attacked cannon in a fixed position. Lost a third of his army."

Oh, no. How many friends and neighbors did I lose? Decker sank back into his pillow and stared at the ceiling.

"You don't seem happy. The war may be ending."

"People I know may have died." He shook his head as if to dismiss the notion. "Have you heard from my father?"

"Serving with Lee, under Pickett," he said. "He's written to me three times, and each letter is more strident than the one before."

"He's a stubborn man," Decker said. "Is he still angry with me?"

"*Ja.* As you said, he is stubborn."

"Did you think of enlisting, Uncle?"

"Your father is too old for the army. And I am five years older than your father." He shifted in his seat and pointed at Decker's uniform. "I see you are a lieutenant now. How is it you're not in Pennsylvania?"

"I'm stationed with Ordnance in Washington." Oskar's eyebrows rose.

"What do you do there?"

"The army brought me east to work on rockets."

Oskar slapped his leg and leaned forward. "Wonderful! And so?"

"I was assigned to various projects, but the people in charge of them knew nothing about rockets. Later, new proposals were funneled through my office, and I had to evaluate whether they were useful or not. None were." He smiled at his uncle. "You know more about rockets than anyone I've met through the army." Oskar shrugged. "To fill my time," Decker continued, "I've done some research."

Oskar waited.

"I've spent a great deal of time studying propellant. Black powder has too many problems. Pockets of air. Poor thrust, and the thrust impulse is all at the front end. Sustainable thrust—"

"Stages."

"That's one solution," Decker said, suddenly animated. His face flushed, washing away his pale, almost cadaver-like appearance. His hands jumped in his lap as he talked. "Another involves alternate fuels." His voice took on a passionate edge. "You've heard of guncotton?"

"Ja. Too unstable for guns."

"You're right. But the idea of nitrocellulose-based propellant is intriguing for a rocket. And while I was in Washington, I saw an alternative proposal that looked promising as well." Decker paused and bit his lip. "You've heard of flour mills that burned down because the flour combusted—"

"Ja. Tiny particles in the air."

"The particulate is so fine that it combines with oxygen in a flash. Just a spark will blow up a mill to bits. Now, imagine if instead, the fuel was something naturally flammable, like paraffin. The trick is to combine fuel with a more usable source of oxygen to accelerate the oxygenation." He paused, his face growing hot. "Doctors have been using nitrous oxide for two decades. Imagine using—"

"Liquid gas?" His voice betrayed him. Oskar the stoic had given way to Oskar the curious.

"I know, the chemism—"

"Chemism?"

"The study of the chemicals involved. Is that the wrong word? I thought it was *your* word, Uncle." Oskar listened without comment. "No matter. Liquid gas seems like a radical solution, but this war has accelerated the sciences, and I think—"

"So, you are not really fighting."

Decker sat back. "I was at Pittsburg Landing."

Oskar's face fell, stricken by what he'd seemed to imply. "I'm sorry. I am told the battle was a doorway to *die Hölle.*" He patted Decker's leg. "I cannot even imagine." Then he leaned over to put a fork on the third sausage. Decker waved him off.

"I think I'm hungry. You might let me eat that one. You cooked them for me, didn't you, Uncle?"

Oskar seemed surprised. "I did, but you said you didn't want them."

"They smell good. Maybe you learned to cook."

Oskar sat back, hands on his knees. "*Red keinen Scheiß!*"

Decker laughed. He didn't understand all of it, but he recognized the word for *shit.* "I missed you, Uncle."

Oskar stood to leave and gave him a small smile. "I missed you. It is good to see you alive. And now I'm going to work. You can sleep." He pointed at the sausage. "But first, eat that. Or I will."

. . .

Decker slept. On the fifth morning, Oskar came into Decker's room with a briar pipe and no food. He straddled the chair next to Decker's bed and lit a bowl. His cheeks puffed, and he let out a little ring of smoke, and then sucked it back in as quickly as it appeared. Having performed one of his two smoke tricks, he drew in again and blew rings. "Would you like a pipe?" he asked after filling the room with smoke.

"I don't smoke."

"Oh." Oskar seemed to contemplate the answer. "I hope the pipe doesn't bother you." Decker smothered a cough. "So."

Oskar said. "Laziness is good for the bones, but you have been sleeping for a week."

"Not quite a week, I think." Oskar frowned.

Decker sat up, pulling the blanket in place. His uniform, cleaned and brushed, sat on the dresser. He felt somewhat ill at ease, being in a state of undress, but he'd left Washington without a change of clothes, and he hadn't left his bed other than to dine or use the indoor toilet. "Any war news?" he asked.

"None of note." Oskar puffed for a moment and blew another cloud into the room. "What have you been doing with your time while I'm out working?"

"Reading and thinking."

"Reading and thinking." Oskar repeated.

Decker pointed at the stacked paper on the nightstand. "*Traité des feux d'artifice pour le spectacle.* Brushing up on my French."

"No military applications there."

"I have enough of the military in my life," Decker said. "Frézier's treatise reminds me that rockets can be more than a weapon."

"And how did you fare with the language? You learned French and Italian while you were here the first time."

"I learned much more than that. As for the reading, my French is rusty. *Grouille ou rouille.*"

Oskar snorted. "Well, what else have you done besides raid my rocketry papers? Have you practiced your grappling? Your strikes?"

"No, I've been in bed," Decker said. "But I've become quite skilled at fighting. I think a few days off won't hurt. As I said, I've been thinking." He waited a moment to see if Oskar would let the subject rest, but his uncle sank down into his chair and took another deep draw from the pipe, as if settling in for a long wait. "I think the war will drag on," Decker continued. "I know my countrymen. They won't give up without a struggle. But the outcome may already be decided." He closed his eyes. "I thought it would be over by now."

"Southerners are stubborn. Think of my brother." He paused. "And so? Where does all this lead to?"

"I'm still thinking."

Oskar blew out another billow of tobacco smoke. "Fresh air might be good then. You should take a walk."

Eyes watering, Decker agreed.

• • •

Despite the heat, Decker found the walk to be just what he needed. The morning fog had taken a while to burn off. A pleasant haze and an overcast sky kept him from sweating too much, even in his blues. His legs ached, but that was to be expected. He'd not used them for days.

Passersby ignored him as he walked, leaving him to observe without engagement. Though the hectic pace he'd disliked in Washington was absent, there was still an edge to the people in the streets. Surly faces and sharp voices marked the conversations he overheard. As he walked on, a number of civilian men rushed past, racing to some unseen destination ahead. The farther he went, the more runners joined the previous ones.

Shouts several blocks away alerted him. Something unusual was happening. He tried to question a civilian, but the streets had become frantic in the space of moments. A soldier running in the opposite direction paused to yell at Decker. "Lieutenant! They're attacking the Copper Street Armory!"

Did Lee move on to Boston? Absurd! "Who is attacking the armory?"

The soldier motioned to the streets ahead. "The fucking Irish!"

Decker grabbed the soldier by the arm. "Slow down, Private. Tell me what's happening."

"They were delivering conscription notices on Prince Street, and the Micks aren't having it."

"Who is delivering notices?"

"Federal draft agents." The private tugged, as if to free himself. Decker gripped the man's sleeve harder. "Tell me what's *happening*."

The private, a gangly youth of no more than twenty years, mopped his face with the sleeve of his free arm. "Sorry, Lieutenant. But it's bad. Getting out of hand. The Irish women went to blows with the draft agents and pummeled them good. Then they marched on the armory. Hundreds of them. Men, too. And children. Started tearing bricks out of the sidewalk, they did, putting them through windows. I saw a woman holding a baby up, daring them to fire on her. They're animals!"

The unmistakable sound of a cannon interrupted them. "Let me loose," the private said, tugging his arm free. He backed away, arms extended. "If they come this way, they'll pummel you, too!" So saying, he turned and ran.

Decker stood frozen in place. For a moment, his heart threatened to run away from his chest. The sweat on his face turned cold. He stared at his hands—traitorous appendages that would not stay still. He clasped them together and clutched them to his chest.

Another man came racing past, away from the sounds of chaos. "They're coming this way," he shouted. "Don't let them catch you here—not in that uniform."

Decker stared at him.

"You're unarmed, you idiot!" the man called as he raced up the street, clutching his hat to his head.

Decker followed him, walking at first, and then running.

• • •

Oskar sat at the small table he used for meals. Accustomed to dining alone, he'd dragged a stool to the table for Decker. A plate of cheese biscuits sat next to a saucer of fresh butter. "I don't always eat this well," Oskar explained. "But you're my only family. You and that brother of mine." They took turns with the knife, painting tiny dollops of butter onto the biscuits. "Those sausages last week? Won't see those again for a while." He shoved a biscuit into his mouth and continued talking. "But you won't starve. A biscuit will carry a man." The bottle of rye whiskey was half empty, and both Oskar and Decker drained and refilled their glasses while they ate.

The newspaper sat folded next to Oskar. Night was falling, and the candle wasn't bright enough for reading, but Oskar had read the stories enough to memorize them. He tapped the paper and said, "It was a cannon you heard. With a riot just outside their door, the soldiers figured the best way to stop it was to put a round of shot through the armory door. And by Gott, they were right."

Decker remained silent.

"Foolishness, all of it. What was Lincoln thinking? You don't draft free men. If they want to fight, they'll fight. If they don't, they might fight you."

"Not much of a fight. Paper says the cannon killed a little boy."

"*Ja*, and that's a shame. Killed others, too. Serves *them* right." He shrugged. "Not the boy, though. That's a shame."

Oskar grabbed another biscuit. Time had not dampened the man's appetite. "The thing is, the Irish are an ugly, violent race."

"What's wrong with the Irish?"

"You can tell they aren't normal by the look of them. They are simian in appearance. I've seen many a Mick with his knuckles near to the ground, and a face that belongs in a tree. It makes them surly. And they are Catholic. We are a Protestant country, and we don't need foreign Catholics bringing their rituals over here." He leaned forward, his voice lowered. "I've heard the priests and nuns have relations with the dead."

"No," Decker scoffed.

"*Ja, ja*. Dead infants, I hear. I have it on good authority."

Decker emptied his glass and winced. After taking a breath, he said, "Your authority has had too much to drink."

Oskar pointed. "And there's that, too. They are imprudent with alcohol."

"I'm tipping a bottle myself," Decker said, refilling his glass.

"You are German. You can drink great amounts without effect. I share this ability." He poured himself another glass, splashing a little on his hand. "I much prefer Africans to the Irish. Their appearance intrigues me. The women are beautiful, with big bosoms and bottoms. Irish women, by contrast, are thick and spotty."

"Spotty?"

"Their skin is not good," Oskar said, frowning, as if the explanation were unnecessary. "And an African can *work*. They were bred for labor. An Irishman might work, or he might not. That is why I hire free Negros and won't hire a Mick." He took a long sip of rye and sat back. "So, did the walking and thinking do you any good, or do we need to break out the Bible and look for answers there?"

Decker sat back, his head spinning a little. "You know, Uncle, when you drink, your sentences get longer."

"See? Have another drink."

"Now you sound like Pops."

Oskar shrugged. "Of course. And so?"

Decker pursed his lips, considering what he could and couldn't say. When he spoke, his voice was soft and deliberate, with the enunciation of a man trying to hide his intoxication. "When the war began, I fought for an idea. Men—*all men*— should be the captains of their own lives. Liberty is worth fighting for. Worth dying for. And I've done more than my share. I fought at Pittsburg Landing."

"Yes."

"And I saved the President's life."

Oskar blinked twice. "Of course you did." He pulled the bottle away from Decker's side of the table. "You're not used to Boston rye."

Decker gave him a small wave. "No matter. I've done what I set out to do."

"*Ja.* You won the war. And now?"

Decker took a deep breath. "The war will end. The Union will win. But the fight will continue for a long time, and a lot more people will die. Men like my father won't quit. They will keep fighting."

"*Ja.* You have convinced me."

"Everything in life is a trade-off, Uncle. I fought for liberty, but I fought against my neighbors. Now, I'm thinking about what it will take to get back home. To Richmond."

"March in with the other soldiers."

"Be serious, Uncle."

Oskar nodded and poured himself another glass. "Go on, go on."

"My friends, my neighbors. They have a price to pay for this foolish war. And if I'm to live amongst them when the war ends, I need to make amends." Oskar stopped drinking and set his glass down. Decker added, "I must go south and join the rebel army."

"*What? Why?*"

"I owe a debt to Virginia. Much more of a debt than I can pay, I fear."

"Why would you go south now? The war is lost!"

"*Because* the war is lost."

Oskar shook his head. "You are not thinking this through. Too many men under the grass. The Union will make the South pay for starting this war. They will make them pay for slavery."

"Yes. And I must be there to accept my fair share."

"That is crazy. Who thinks like that?"

Decker shrugged.

Oskar scowled and scratched his belly. "You have heard me play the fiddle?"

"Don't threaten me with your music."

"Now it is *your* turn to be serious," Oskar said. "I make noise, no? What is it you say . . . I am untuned?"

"Out of tune."

"In the old country, I had a friend who was a fine musician. He could play the moon out of the sky. But he took an hour— no, two hours—just to tune his violin! As for me, I have a sorry old fiddle, so what is the point?" He grabbed his glass and emptied it, then went into a coughing spasm before continuing. "You are like my friend. The world is a broken instrument, and you would tune it to your fine sense of ethics. I ask again—*what is the point?*"

"I must do my duty, both to the Republic and to Virginia."

Oskar shook his head. "No, this is about the girl." He chuckled to himself, as if he'd solved a great mystery. "What is so special about this one? She must have plenty of wood in front of her shack."

Decker didn't answer.

"When did you last hear from her?"

"It's been a while," Decker said, his voice low. "But you're wrong. This isn't just about her. It's about Pops. It's about Mr. Crane. It's about everyone I know. I can't—"

"Damn those people! They keep men as property—"

"People are the same here, Uncle. Wherever I go, people are the same. That's something the war taught me." He paused to gather his thoughts. "Boston is proud of their freed Negros, are they not?"

"*Ja.* Boston is the heart of the abolition movement."

Decker took a deep breath. "And how do you treat the Irish? They volunteered for the war in droves here. True patriots—"

"That is what they say. But the numbers have been exaggerated—"

"Nonsense. They fight and they die, without waiting to be conscripted. And they are thanked with a cannon shot." Oskar started to argue, but Decker pressed on. "Uncle, we are all flawed. We all have sins to pay for. None of us is so righteous as to face God on Judgment Day without trembling."

Oskar gave him a wry smile. After a moment, he said, "Whiskey does fine things to *your* tongue as well."

Decker nodded and reached across the table for the bottle. He poured himself two fingers and continued. "My best friend out west was Irish. Michael Kelly was his name. He fought by my side and then helped me bury the dead when the battle was over. The finest, kindest man I know, besides you, Uncle." He glanced up. "And you would free the Africans and put the Irish in chains."

"I've said no such thing!"

"If I am wrong, then I have it wrong by degrees."

Oskar's face flushed and his fist closed tight around his glass, but as the seconds ticked past in silence, his face gained some composure, and even a measure of serenity. "You are young. You may mold a different world when it is your turn."

"My hands are already in the clay, sir, and the sculpture is a mess."

Oskar closed his eyes. "Will you leave soon?"

"I've witnessed enough incompetence to know the Union might yet achieve a defeat, despite their advantages. But when I'm *certain* the outcome is irreversible, I'll go south."

"Not so easy to go south. Both sides will want to shoot you."

"I only have to do it once," Decker said. "And then, I'll be home."

CHAPTER SIXTEEN

Boston, Massachusetts
December 1863

And in despair I bowed my head;
There is no peace on earth, I said;
For hate is strong,
And mocks the song
Of peace on earth, good-will to men!
~Henry Wadsworth Longfellow, from "Christmas Bells," 1863

Snow cannot be both ice and rain, Decker reasoned. *It must be one or the other.* A cold blast of wind sent him racing to the entry doors of the Washington Navy Yard, snow trickling into his exposed collar. Inside, he shook himself like a wet dog before heading to Rear Admiral Dahlgren's office. Dahlgren had been promoted to commander of the South Atlantic Blockading Squadron. At the start of the war, the navy assigned three ships to blockade duty. Now, over three hundred steamers and sailing ships patrolled fifteen hundred miles of the Confederate coast.

With the approach of Christmas, Dahlgren returned to Washington. Decker intended to keep the admiral abreast of his progress — or lack thereof. Decker had been north, in Maine, researching claims of an improved gunpowder. Written correspondence with the manufacturer was enough to convince him the journey would be a fool's errand, but he went anyway.

The would-be munitions provider knew considerably less about powder than Decker himself, and the demonstrations were a fizzling mess. "With sufficient financial backing," the man boasted, "I can make the finest gunpowder available. I only lack funds."

"With sufficient funding," Decker had said, his face expressionless, "I could make swine grow wings."

Now, at Dahlgren's office door, Decker saluted. "A merry Christmas to you and yours, Admiral."

"No merry Christmas for me," Dahlgren said, not looking up. "I've been waiting on the new Monitors, and I am weary of waiting." New ironclad ships meant a tighter blockade. He looked up. "Sit down, Lieutenant."

Decker took off his hat and sat in the chair near Dahlgren's desk. The new office was simple, as befitted the admiral's tastes. He smiled. "I wonder you didn't take the day off."

"Work, work, even for Christmas. Not tonight, though." Dahlgren met his gaze, a hint of a smile on his face. "My boys are in Washington, all on furlough."

"That's a happy circumstance."

"Very happy indeed. I wondered if we'd all be together again, given the war. Having them in one room makes one grateful."

"Your wife must be happy."

Dahlgren's face went blank. "Alas, my wife passed on eight years ago."

Decker's stomach dropped. "Admiral, I didn't know."

"Nor would you. I am not in the habit of sharing my personal life. Not proper to the rank." He cleared his throat and blushed a little, clearly uncomfortable. "But it's Christmas, so exceptions are in order. The boys and I will be feasting this evening. My cook managed to get a goose. Haven't eaten goose since the start of the war." He glanced over at Decker and blinked. "Would you like to join us, Lieutenant?"

"No, thank you, Admiral."

"I only ask because I mentioned goose, and your mouth dropped like a gangplank. Wipe your chin, son."

"Sorry," Decker laughed. "Roast goose sounds wonderful."

"Then join us."

"No, thank you. A gathering at Christmas is for family." An awkward silence followed, so he filled the void with a question. "Three boys, all in the army?"

"Three boys," Dahlgren said, seemingly enthusiastic at a chance to move the conversation ahead. "Charles, Ulric, and Paul. Charles is a captain in the Navy, though. Ulric and Paul serve in the Army."

"You are lucky to be reunited. What a wonderful holiday."

"Yes." Dahlgren pushed his paper aside. "So, how was the powder?"

Decker sighed. "Burned like sugar. All smoke and smell. No bang."

"I feared as much. So many wish to suckle at the government teat. Did you just arrive in town?"

"Yes."

"I thought so. The journey shows by your clothing."

"My apologies."

"No need. I appreciate your prompt report. Quite useless, of course." He frowned. "I wonder you haven't submitted a proposal yourself, Lieutenant. You know your business. I would imagine that any such proposition might make its way through channels."

Decker shook his head. "No, Admiral."

Dahlgren frowned and then looked away. "As you wish." He sat back, as if to regard Decker more closely. "Far from family for the holiday. You must be homesick. When were you home last?"

Decker swallowed and took a deep breath. "I visited Boston this summer."

"Fine city. Quite beautiful, I'm told."

Decker shrugged.

"What are your Christmas plans, then?"

"I'm spending the evening with a young lady," Decker said.

"Ah!" Dahlgren seemed surprised. "Excellent. I'll give you your leave, then, Lieutenant."

Decker replaced his cap and saluted. Before he exited the building, he pulled his cape tight across his chest and headed back into the icy wind.

• • •

My Dearest Love,

I am writing on the eve of Christmas to impart some important news. Sometime soon, I will be returning to Richmond. Perhaps my new unit will grant me a furlough, so that I can visit you. I long to see your face and hold you in my arms. God grant me the chance, sooner, rather than later.

The changing fortunes of war have altered my situation. I count the very minutes until again we meet. For now, I spend this holiday with only the memory of your face to make me merry.

Always, Decker

Decker pushed away from the table that served as a desk. His room in the three-story boardinghouse on Pennsylvania Avenue was tiny in the extreme, with barely enough room for his table and cot. The smell of paraffin made the windowless room stuffier than normal, so he snuffed the candle and sat in the dark.

From the floor below, he heard the clatter of pots. The kitchen had been busy with so many tenants staying in from the cold. Christmas dinner consisted of salted pork and dried toast, with even drier cake for dessert. Decker went without.

He eased himself onto the cot, facing the ceiling. Given his preference, he'd fall asleep and awaken with Christmas behind him, but the long Washington night was certain to have other plans for him. Rigid on his back, he was lucky to sleep half the hours he spent in his bed. The other half were given to worries over his job with the War Department, his health, his father, homesickness, and the war itself. Tonight, he worried over Paula—a worry so close to his heart that he didn't often dwell there, for fear of losing himself altogether.

Would she wait for him? Had she changed? Had he changed too much to resume the future they'd planned?

Switching sides would be dangerous. Would he survive the remainder of the war with a gray uniform on his back? He fingered his notched earlobe. How many battles could he endure?

His uncle's question came back to him—*what is the point*? Why switch sides now? Duty to Virginia was his answer. Since then, he'd drilled deeper, trying to understand. He'd fought for the North because he believed in the Union and liberty. He would not fight for the South because he did not support slavery. Both valid reasons. The same reason, really.

The same reason. He sat up on one elbow, staring into the darkened room. *If one believes in liberty, one must believe in liberty for all.* He'd never thought slavery to be tenable. Why had he not connected his love of liberty to his dislike for slavery until now? They were one and the same.

He lay back down, facing the ceiling. *Then why go south?*

He'd been raised to do his duty, and Virginia was his home. *You defend your home. That goes without question.* But here in his little room, he had nothing but questions.

This sin of slavery demanded expiation. Virginia was the fulcrum upon which the balance of the war rested. His family and friends would face the consequences. If he couldn't share their cause, he would share their punishment.

Noble nonsense, he thought. *You simply want to go home, and doing what's expected of you is the price you must pay.* He'd abandoned his father. Pops was ashamed of him. There was still time to redeem himself. *When this war is over, I want to live in Richmond. How can I face anyone if I don't share in the struggle? How can I face —*

— Paula. Was Oskar right? Was she the reason he was switching sides? He imagined arriving at her doorstep, dressed in gray. What would she think? *She would understand. She always understood.* Was that true? How could it be when he didn't really understand his own reasons?

He tried to conjure a picture that he carried in his mind — the evening in front of the stable at the Hill family barbecue. Nothing came to him. Instead, he saw a parade of victims at Pittsburg Landing, faces frozen in a timeless contortion. Explosions. The ripping sounds of gunfire. The smell of powder.

He clenched his fists and tried harder, drawing on a series of memories that he'd tucked away for nights like this. One by one, scenes came forth, blurred by time and circumstance. *This is a new cruelty. What does it mean when I cannot recall her face?*

Had something happened to her? Was she still alive?

He sat upright, suddenly unable to draw breath. *Stop this. Stop it now.* He felt his face flush hot. He was safe in a Washington boardinghouse, far from battle. Nothing had happened to her—God would not allow it. *Please, dear Lord, please. Watch over her. She's an innocent. She has nothing to do with this war.*

Though he still could not picture her, Paula's voice came, unbidden. He recalled his question on the train station platform—*Are you mine?*—and he heard her answer, clear and certain, as if she sat in the darkened room with him.

He drew a deep breath and held it. When he exhaled, he unclenched his fists and sank back into the cot.

• • •

In Richmond, Paula waited as her friend removed the soldier's bedpan.

"This is not the way to celebrate Christmas," Dori grumbled as she walked past, carrying the tin pan.

"This isn't how the men planned to spend Christmas either," Paula said. She meant the statement as a rebuke, but regretted her words the moment she spoke them. Dori flinched.

They'd been working since noon, and both women were hungry. "I'm sorry, Dori," she said. "When I'm tired, I turn into a harpy." She held out her hands, offering to take up the bedpan—atonement for her sharp words.

Dori gave up her burden without an argument. "You're not a harpy. You're the nicest person I know. Nobody feels very merry these days." Two years of deprivation had thinned Dori, leaving a whisper of the plump girl who'd been a frequent dinner guest at the Crane home before the war. Her blond hair, tied back in a severe bun, retained little of the sheen of which she'd been so proud. Her face remained roundish, though the puffy shape owed more to sleeplessness than regular meals.

Neither woman being married, they'd volunteered to cover shifts for those nurses with children, even if Santa would not be coming around this Christmas. Tilda, a matron with five little ones at home, explained to her children that "Santa couldn't make it through the blockade this year, my lovelies, and if he did, I'd shoot him, for I believe he's a Yankee." Tilda's tireless work with the Confederate sick and wounded made her a favorite among the patients and nurses. Paula and Dori managed to scrape together a packet of cakes and a little money for the children's stockings, a kindness that left Tilda in tears.

Paula stepped outside to dump the pan. Most days, the colored women, loaned out by their owners, would have done the job, but tonight, Dori and Paula were alone. The long walk to the trench was chilling. The day had been unexpectedly warm, but the sun was long gone, and the effects of a cold evening rain were worsened by the lack of food. Dori waited in the doorway behind her, a tiny shadow. Darkness spared Paula a glimpse inside the trench, but the smell made her gag. Once, she'd made the trek during the day, and spotted a severed hand poking up through the filth and fluids.

Back in the ward, Dori led the way. At night, each ward building that comprised Chimborazo Hospital was lit by a single candle. Walking from one end of the building to the other in the dark could be treacherous. Ten large windows graced each side of the wooden building. At night, only the thin white curtains kept the cold out.

The buildings were originally intended as soldiers' barracks, but the overwhelming need for medical attention, coupled with the expert direction of the surgeon-in-chief James B. McCaw, led to a miraculous transformation. Chimborazo became a hospital complex, complete with ninety ward buildings, bakehouses, kitchens, a stable, chapel, bathhouse, and various shops. At the far end of the camp, five buildings housed the dead before burial at Oakwood Cemetery.

Paula worked a sick ward, tending to those with a number of maladies, including pneumonia, typhoid, and dysentery. As a convalescent hospital, the wounded who arrived at Chimborazo had already faced the worst—field surgery, often leading to amputation—and been shipped to the hospital by rail or ambulance. Sick wards were more hazardous than the wards for the wounded, but Paula preferred them. Her usual duties included dispensing medicines, helping to feed the sick, and being a companion of sorts—writing letters for the soldiers and keeping them as comfortable as possible. The job title "matron" was well chosen. In many ways, they were a substitute mother for sick, frightened young boys.

Wards for the wounded were different. A gangrenous stench filled the buildings, overpowering even the smells of blood and body filth. The wounded suffered unrelenting pain. Paula tended the wound wards when absolutely necessary, but each shift left her sickened and empty.

As she made her way across the ward, a young private with pneumonia called to her. "Miss Crane? Is that you?"

She crossed to his bedside. "How are you, Jacob?"

He lay huddled under a single blanket on the cot, quivering. "I'm cold, ma'am. Cold to the bone."

She bent down and patted his knee. "I'll find you another blanket. Give me a moment." *He's as far from the woodstove as he could be, poor thing! Tomorrow, I'll get one of the men to switch beds for him. By then, someone will have died.* The thought brought her up short—not because death was so awful, but because it was so very commonplace.

"Do you know them all by name?" Dori asked. She often worked in one of the wound wards, but lately, she'd been riding up Chimborazo Hill in the carriage with Paula, driven by Henry Lee, allowing them to work together.

"Not all of them. But I know most of them."

"They advised me against that," Dori whispered. "The men might misunderstand." She glanced around before continuing. "My father still disapproves of my work here. He's been listening to his brother in South Carolina. *White women don't work in the Charlotte hospitals,* he says. *Not proper work for a lady,* he says."

"Yet here you are, dear," Paula said, patting Dori's shoulder. "These boys can't make all the sacrifices. We women must do our part."

"Well then. Where will you find an extra blanket?"

Paula's expression fell. "I don't know. But I will find one." An idle boast, yet, at the other end of the ward, she found an empty bed among the forty cots. She pulled the blanket loose and headed back to the private.

"That was lucky," Dori said. "You are charmed."

"Charmed and charming," Paula said, suppressing a grin. When she reached the private's cot, she spread the blanket over him.

He sighed, whispering. "Thank you, thank you."

"Did you have Christmas dinner?"

"Fresh pork," he said. Soldiers on either side slept and snored, so he kept his voice low. "Was hoping for a bird."

"You like poultry?"

"Wanted to send some to General Bragg."

Paula frowned. Grant's victory over Bragg at Lookout Mountain left the people of Richmond with a sense of impending doom. After Bragg's victory at Chickamauga, hopes had been high, but he refused to take advantage, and when Grant attacked, the entire left flank of the Confederate army collapsed. Now, seeing Paula's perplexed expression, the soldier added, "If they'd served bird tonight, I'd have sent Bragg a left wing."

From behind, Dori burst into a muffled laughter, smothering the sound with her hand.

The soldier to Paula's left groaned in his sleep. Paula gave Dori a scolding glance. Dori mouthed the word *sorry.* Turning back to the soldier, Paula said, "Jacob! That is a scandalous thing to say!" She tried and failed to suppress a wry smile.

"Wasn't my joke, ma'am. Wish it was, though. Your smile makes me glad to tell it."

Paula gave him a bigger smile, hoping he could see it. Smiles might warm him as much as the thin cotton blanket she'd brought him.

Dori ended the moment. "More bedpans, Paula."

Paula nodded. Together, they worked their way through the last few beds, trying to finish the unpleasant task as quickly and quietly as possible. A few of the men asked for assistance, from drinks of water to simple reassurances. "You're fine. I know you're sick, and it hurts, but you'll get through this. I heard the doctors say so. Yes, I heard them. I know they don't say a thing to you boys, but we hear them when they talk amongst themselves."

When the last bedpan was emptied, the men who could fall asleep had done so, and the ones still awake settled into silence, Paula and Dori moved to the front of the room, careful not to trip in the dark, far enough from the candle, stove, and cots to have a moment of privacy. Another nurse would come at midnight. Henry Lee would drive up the hill then, too, and they could go home to their beds.

"May I ask you something?" Dori's voice, so shrill and childlike before the war, had become the quiet, measured voice of a woman. Paula nodded. "Whatever became of your friend, Decker Brown?"

Paula leaned her head back against the wooden wall.

"Have you heard from him?"

"Not in some time." Paula was certain that the room was too dark to reveal her sudden tears. "How long?"

Paula mumbled.

Dori whispered louder. "I didn't hear you."

"A year. I haven't heard from him in more than a year."

"He's alive, isn't he? I mean, if he'd died, they'd have posted his name in the papers, wouldn't they? They posted his father's name after Gettysburg."

"I suppose they would," Paula said. *But he's a Yankee, and they don't list the Yankee dead in the Richmond papers.* She bit her lip. She couldn't have this conversation now.

Dori seemed to understand her short answers because she stopped asking questions. After a minute, she stepped closer and put her arms around Paula. "I'm sure he's fine. I'm sure he'll be home soon."

CHAPTER SEVENTEEN

Wilderness, Central Virginia
May 1864

"I propose to fight it out on this line if it takes all summer."
~General Ulysses S. Grant

The sign Decker had waited for, the sign the war would soon end, came in March, when President Lincoln promoted Ulysses S. Grant to Lieutenant General in command of all Union forces. The news ran through Washington, with strong opinions on either side. Grant was a genius or a drunk. A born fighter or a lucky dolt. Decker had served under him and had a different view than most. Grant was a pit bull, and when he latched on to Robert Lee, teeth to bone, he would not let go.

With Dahlgren at sea, he owed no one a goodbye. Decker applied for leave on the grounds that his Uncle Oskar was ill — a lie — and a month later, his request was granted. He had little or nothing to pack.

Decker had a vague plan in mind. He headed south, still wearing blue. Once he reached the wilderness area south of the Union lines, he would look for corpses. The battle around Chancellorsville yielded many dead on both sides. Perhaps he would find a uniform in his size.

Within hours, he found a suitable corpse, but the body had decomposed into the cloth, rendering the uniform useless. The stench reminded him of Pittsburg Landing.

The bulk of Grant's army was on the move, trying to cross the Rapidan River. Grant fared no better than Burnside had at moving across with speed. Scouts and snipers on both sides roamed the Wilderness—a dense, woodland area on the other side of the Rapidan. Thickets were cluttered with oaks and red maple, sweetgum and yellow poplar. Dogwood, red cedar, and sassafras choked off the sub-canopy. Hazelnut and blackberry shrubs filled the underbrush. The cluster of plant life made infantry and artillery maneuvers impossible. *This is where Lee will strike Grant. There is no advantage in numbers here.* Sporadic gunfire already echoed through the trees, though Decker saw nothing beyond a dozen yards, no matter which direction he looked.

When he came upon another, fresher corpse, he faced a choice. The dead man's uniform was small for his purposes, but he'd already decided he would not find the perfect fit. The further south he went, the more likely the chance of running into Southern troops. The moment he changed uniforms, he would become an enemy to the Union, and an object of suspicion to the Confederates. He wished the poor boy tangled in the underbrush had been taller. But Decker couldn't count on another opportunity. He glanced around, listening for any movement. Then he began to strip the corpse.

The smell was horrific. *Thank the Lord, he didn't foul himself when he died.*

The jacket was baggy enough to fit. The trousers were almost impossible to squeeze into. He managed by cutting a slit at the waistline, down to the middle of his hip. The shoes fit. *Thank you for your big feet,* he thought as he jammed himself into the clothing. The dead boy, a private, had a nearly empty cartridge box and a musket. Decker took them both.

He hid his blue uniform under a tangle of poison ivy some distance from the stripped corpse. Standing still, he held his arms out in front, palms turned up, and stared at his uniform. *Now, I'm a rebel.* A soft rain had dampened the underbrush, and the smell of lush, overgrown greenery somehow complemented the odor of decay emanating from his jacket. He shivered. No time to pause. No time to sort through the feelings he'd battled for so long—fear, regret, worry. He tucked them away. *I've done my part. I'm going home now. That is all that matters.*

He passed by the dead boy one last time, saluted his thanks, and made his way through the thicket. Having abandoned the Union, he was suddenly behind enemy lines. He would need to move quickly.

Hours passed without an encounter—thankfully. He made slow progress, stopping often to listen for movement. The longer he went without meeting men from either side, the better his chance to pull off the switch.

Early in the afternoon, he heard a number of men thrashing through the scrub, whispering. He couldn't make out the words. He crouched as they passed, praying. Blue uniforms. If they saw him, he was a dead man.

They moved slowly, testing Decker's nerve. When they stood abreast of him, no more than a dozen paces distant, they paused, and Decker stopped breathing. One of the soldiers stared in his direction and then turned away. *They can't see any better than I can.*

Five soldiers. They moved south, following a dry creek bed through the trees. Decker backed up as quietly as he could, and then ran south, parallel to the squad. If there were more Union soldiers here, he would encounter another patrol if he traveled east or west. His only chance was to move ahead as fast as he could manage.

After a few minutes, he reached a clearing. He hesitated at the edge. *If I cross here, I'm fair game to anyone who can shoot.*

Then he spotted Confederate officers at the other end of the clearing.

The small group of men sat on horseback, conversing. One of them, an elderly officer with a white beard, sat astride a gray American Saddlebred. *That's General Lee.* Decker did not think. He dropped his musket and ran into the clearing, waving his arms, but otherwise silent. Two of the party drew a quick bead on his approach but given that he wore gray and had no weapon in hand, they held fire.

"Move back, move back," Decker said, resisting the urge to shout. "Snipers, ten seconds behind me!"

One officer pointed to the rear. "General, follow me behind the tree line." General Lee seemed surprised, but calm. He followed the group into the trees. The two mounted soldiers stayed where they were, rifles trained on Decker.

Just as the officers reached the trees, Union soldiers emerged from the other side of the clearing and began firing. Decker heard the whine of a near miss. His old ear wound throbbed in anticipation. One of the mounted soldiers pitched back, unhorsed by a shot to the chest.

Decker ran forward, ducking down as he made his way to the tree line. Another shot struck the trunk of a tree as he passed. In seconds, he was among the officers and their horses.

"General, we need to move to the rear—"

The general stared down at Decker with cold eyes. "How many men?"

"Small patrol," Decker said. "But there may be more behind them."

"Yes, I would expect so," the general said. "Well, gentlemen, it appears we'll have a chance to see how the present idol of the North fares in the thickets." He scratched his chin whiskers and looked down from horseback at Decker. "I owe you my thanks, Private."

"I'm a Virginian, sir."

General Lee appeared amused. "Yes, so you are."

Another officer, on foot, grabbed Decker's arm and pulled him to the side. He stared at Decker's uniform and frowned. "What unit are you with, Private?"

The moment had arrived. Decker swallowed. "I'm on leave, sir. Borrowed the jacket and trousers. Mine were falling off."

"Borrowed?"

"Young man won't be needing them."

The captain squinted and frowned. His pencil mustache was damp, and his dark eyes were the same.

Decker counted the seconds before the captain spoke again.

"Ordnance provides gunpowder. Plenty of powder. But today, I'd trade a keg for a biscuit. Same thing for uniforms. Shoes."

"My shoes fit me," Decker said. "It's a miracle."

The captain nodded. "Where is your unit?"

"Mississippi," Decker said.

"What are you doing in Virginia?"

Decker swallowed. He had to tread carefully. "I'm from Richmond. Went west when I couldn't enlist right away. Too many volunteers."

The officer squinted again and then burst out laughing. "Well, that was a fine bit of thinking! Ha! Where in Richmond? I'm from there myself."

Decker tilted his head. The man looked vaguely familiar. *Could I be so lucky?*

"Time to move!" another officer called out. "If you're heading back to Richmond, Captain Jessup, you'd best be on your way. Things are going to heat up here in short order." General Lee pointed at Decker and said something to the officer, who nodded in turn. "Have your private run alongside. If you can find him a horse, he can escort you back to the capital. I'm afraid we have a battle on our hands."

Jessup stared at Decker. "You can ride, can't you?"

Decker snorted. "I'm a Virginian, sir." He followed the captain deeper into the thicket. Holding a branch aside, he noticed his hands were shaking. Had he pulled off a miracle? He thought back on his other chance encounters since the war had begun. He'd stood close to President Lincoln. Probably saved the man's life. But Lincoln's presence was tied to the rocket tests. Decker also met Grant, but the general wandered the ranks when he couldn't sleep. Half the men in Cairo had traded words with him. General Lee? That much was serendipity.

· · ·

The main Confederate lines were less than a half mile to the rear. There, Captain Jessup commandeered an aging horse from a chagrined lieutenant, who insisted the horse be returned to him after the journey. "I've grown fond of the animal. Never once shown a sign of fatigue," the lieutenant explained.

Decker had his doubts. The chestnut gelding, no more than twelve hands high, was all bones and skin, and moved with the urgency of a muddy creek. "I'm too big for this little bit of horse," Decker said.

"An officer appreciates a smaller horse," Captain Jessup said. "No use sitting tall in the saddle with snipers about."

Decker followed Jessup's mount, picking his way through the trees. In the distance, they heard the sound of muskets. "Won't be a lot of cannon fire," the captain predicted. "Too hard to move cannon through those woods. And their troops won't travel much faster than we're going now. But don't worry, Private. We'll encounter a road south, and we'll be in Richmond sooner than you think." He glanced over his shoulder. "I imagine you'll welcome a hot bath."

As they rode, Decker stared at the captain's back. He was a fine horseman if Decker was any judge. He rode with his back straight in the saddle, rolling with his mount's gait in easy balance. Reaching out to the side, the captain plucked an acorn from an oak and slipped it into his pocket. "I'll boil that later," he explained. He glanced back. "I expect you know all the tricks, having made your way east."

"Best trick of all is a generous neighbor."

The captain nodded. "So, what's your specialty, Private?"

"Rockets." The word leapt from his mouth before he could stop it.

"*Rockets*? Good Lord, I didn't think Johnston had rockets." He pulled on the reins, and his horse stopped. Looking back, he squinted and said, "Wait a moment. Rockets?" He nodded, as if a great mystery had been solved. "*Decker Brown*?"

The sound of his own name chilled him.

The captain laughed. "I remember now. We have a mutual friend, Brown. Major Whitaker Hill, in the Ordnance Department." Jessup ran a finger along his mustache. "I recall him bragging about your illuminations. Said they flew straighter than any rocket he'd ever seen." He nudged his horse and began to move. Decker, in turn, began to breathe again. "Tell me, Brown. Have you made any strides in perfecting your rockets?"

"No, sir."

Captain Jessup looked back, perplexed. "Is there more to the story than that?"

Decker stared ahead. He couldn't see more than a few dozen paces ahead. The trees and shrubs were too thick. "Rockets have inherent problems that make them a poor choice for war."

"How so?"

"As with cannon shot, thrust is limited to a single impulse. But a shot from a rifled cannon is more accurate, and the cannon tube does not follow the shot in its flight. All the weight is in the payload. The flight path of a rocket is not always predictable, and because the weight of the rocket and its propellant are part of the equation, rockets cannot yet carry a payload of substance."

"Yet?"

Decker stared down at his mount's head as the horse negotiated uneven ground, stepping over rocks and brambles. His legs clutched the horse's flanks. He forced himself to relax. He'd not been on a horse since before the war—since Whitaker Hill's barbecue. "I am out of practice on a horse," he admitted.

"Better than walking," Captain Jessup said. "So, tell me more about rockets."

Decker frowned. "I am not used to serious interest in the subject. The failure of rocketry generally leads to derision."

"Not at all," the captain said, still riding ahead. Decker wished he could see the man's face. Was he being dismissive, or perhaps fishing for a misstep? *I may have said too much already.*

Captain Jessup stopped again, plucking another acorn. "The President is interested in all schemes that might tip the balance of the war in our favor."

I've heard that before.

"You heard about our submersible in Charleston Harbor, no doubt."

"No, sir." The captain's questions seemed fraught with danger.

"Really?" Captain Jessup's face brightened. "Well, *there* is a story. Prepare to be amazed."

This man loves to talk, Decker thought.

"We built an underwater craft—the *H. L. Hunley.* Our fish boat sank the *Housatonic.* Blew it up and put it down, right there in Charleston Harbor. One less blockade ship."

"A submersible? Underwater?"

"Indeed."

Ducking under a low branch, the captain continued ahead. Decker's mount was slow to follow. "I'm sure that gave the blockade ships something to think about." He recalled Admiral Dahlgren and wondered what he thought about underwater attack ships.

"No doubt. The operation would have been a complete success had the *Hunley* survived the attack."

"It sank?"

"We assume so. The ship did not return to port." Captain Jessup stopped to allow Decker to catch up. A tiny brook snaked through the underbrush. Decker's mount ambled into the rock bed, pausing to take a drink. The thick tree canopy overhead blocked the late afternoon sun.

When the horse finished drinking, it ambled on, and Captain Jessup continued. "At any rate, the President is open, with good reason, to all weapon innovations." He pointed ahead. "That's the road I've been looking for. From here, we'll make better time."

Once they were on the muddy road, moving south, the captain resumed his questions. "What can be done to improve your rockets?"

Having decided Jessup was simply chatty, Decker felt more at ease with the conversation. "Two things might address the problem of limited thrust. Multiple stages allow sequential thrusting, each stage building on the previous stage's momentum. If the firing of a second stage could somehow disengage the rocket's casing, the problem of weight to thrust would be mitigated." He smiled. *Here is where I begin to sound like a madman.* "The biggest problem involves the limitations of black powder. A more powerful propellant would give a multistage rocket an additional burst. I have given thought to the idea of a liquid gas to facilitate oxidation—the burning process—allowing a more rapid, more powerful thrust."

"What kind of distance will your rocket attain? Our spies tell us the Yankees have a mortar that can lob a shell more than two miles. Could your rocket match that?"

Decker was taken aback for a moment. The captain was very free with his information. He considered his answer carefully. "If such a rocket could be built, it might travel many times that distance."

The two men rode side by side now. The captain turned left to face him, his eyes wide with apparent surprise. "You jest."

Decker shook his head. "I speak in terms of potentialities, sir. No such rocket has ever been built —"

"That would mean firing a rocket from one city to another. Richmond to Washington, for example."

"As I said —"

"But this is extraordinary! Whom have you discussed this with?"

"I've mentioned the idea before, but few take rocketry seriously."

Captain Jessup rode on, scratching his chin. Cannon sounded in the distance. Decker urged his horse to keep pace, but the horse had its own ideas. "If you're in a hurry, my poor old nag has a different notion."

"I *am* in a hurry." The slow gait of Jessup's horse argued otherwise. "What will you do in Richmond?"

Captain Jessup snorted. "I would hardly share that information with a private." He shook his head, as if Decker had asked a hopeless question. After a few moments, he traced a finger along his mustache and said, "All of this rocket talk begs a question, Brown. A man of your obvious talents — no less than Major Hill vouching for your skills — and yet you're only a private. How is that possible?"

Decker felt his face grow hot. *What is a safe answer?* Then, he remembered his friend in the west, Mike Kelly. "Just keeping my head down, sir."

"Keeping your head down?"

"Staying out of trouble."

Captain Jessup stopped and turned his horse to face Decker. "Tens of thousands of patriotic men have given their lives to the cause, Private. Families across the South are starving. No one has gone untouched. Perhaps it's time for you to stick your neck out a little." His face was as flushed as Decker imagined his own to be.

Decker's horse seemed pleased to stop in the middle of the road. A bird sounded in the trees to the right.

"Well, Private?"

"Begging your pardon, sir," Decker said. He bit the inside of his cheek, but the words came anyway. "You're in no position to judge me. I've given everything I had to this war. You'll forgive me if I don't jump into a grave to prove myself to you."

Captain Jessup gave him a slow nod, his eyes like slits. "Put a man on a horse, and he speaks like an officer." He kicked his horse and started out again. "Minus the sense, of course."

They rode on in silence. When evening fell, they bedded down in a small clearing. The captain shared a tin of coffee but had little more to say. Decker tried to strike up a conversation, asking questions about Richmond, but he tired of one-word answers and gave up. The warm day had given way to a cool evening, and Decker huddled against a tree without a blanket. *How is it I managed to go east without a bedroll? So much for my story. I'm an idiot. Jessup must know I'm crossing over.*

Jessup lay on his bedroll, ignoring him completely.

• • •

They met troops heading north at the outskirts of Richmond. Captain Jessup led his horse to the side of the road to allow the men to pass. Decker sat silent, regarding his beloved city. From a distance, little had changed. He tried to see home from the hilltop, but he was too far away. The sudden need to race down the slope to the outskirts left him agitated. His horse seemed to notice and began to shuffle in place.

"Lieutenant!" Captain Jessup addressed the first passing officer. The lieutenant walked over to the captain. "Sir?"

"You're on foot, Lieutenant."

"Lost my horse at Gettysburg, sir."

"Are you headed north?"

The lieutenant nodded.

Captain Jessup pointed a finger at Decker. "Private, give this man your horse." When Decker didn't move, Jessup added, "He's an officer. And you're leaving on foot." He turned to the lieutenant. "Private Brown will be joining your company."

"Sir?"

"I am sorry, Brown, but your leave is cancelled. Your country needs you."

Decker dismounted and handed the horse's reins to the lieutenant. He took a glance back at Richmond, and then a second glance at Captain Jessup.

"I'm going to share your ideas back at the War Department, Private Brown. Try to stay alive. If they choose to pursue this rocket idea of yours, they might offer you a nice, safe job in a laboratory. Until then."

Decker saluted, and the captain answered the salutation with a snappy motion of his own before turning his mount and heading down the road to Richmond.

CHAPTER EIGHTEEN

Spotsylvania Courthouse, Virginia
May 1864

*"We have met a man this time, who either does not know when he is
whipped, or who cares not if he loses his whole army."*
~One Southerner reflecting on the character of
General Ulysses S. Grant

News of a great Confederate victory in the Wilderness is
followed by warnings of a renewed assault to the east. Rather
than retreat to Fredericksburg and regroup, Grant sends his
army east to Spotsylvania—a crossing for the region's main
roads. Decker knows the town. *If Grant takes control of the town,
his army will be between Lee and Richmond, and Lee will have to
attack.*

Having marched for two days to join Lee's army in the
Wilderness, Decker's company changes direction, moving
instead to reinforce Confederate troops in Spotsylvania. Since
leaving Richmond, the column's progress has been slowed by
rain. The nights are cold and wet, and Decker sleeps very little.
Early on the morning of the 12th, the men are roused by officers
and hurried along the mud roads.

They pass the Spotsylvania courthouse just past noon.

As Decker marches, couriers arrive at regular intervals.
They are dour-faced boys, and judging by their expressions, the

news is bad and getting worse. Decker carries a musket and a full box of cartridges, taken from the field along the march. His bayonet is sturdy. Having spent an evening in the rain practicing his lunges, Decker is as prepared as his circumstances will allow.

The column hurries along Brock Road and then angles toward an open field, already littered with the dead. The lieutenant, riding his new mount, calls a halt and shouts down at yet another courier. Decker stands just a few feet away from the lieutenant but can barely hear the conversation over the roar of battle.

"Gordon's men pushed them back to the trenches, but he's spread thin," the courier shouts. "He needs help now!"

"Where? Which direction?" Smoke covers the field, obscuring the battle lines.

"Straight ahead. If you wait too long, the Yankees will come to *you*." The courier points. Tiny flashes of red pock the brown and gray cloud hovering over the wet grass.

The lieutenant hesitates. He leans forward, scanning the field, as if he can somehow stare his way through the smoke. In answer, rain starts again in earnest, tamping down the cloud. Two hundred yards ahead, men struggle in front of a log parapet. Satisfied, the lieutenant draws his sword and orders his men to advance.

Halfway across the field, Union soldiers scramble over the parapet, overwhelming the defenders in two spots. Decker breaks into a run. If he marches to the parapet, he will be too late.

His bayonet is fixed, and the musket is loaded, though Decker is not certain the musket will fire in the rain. The men at the parapet are engaged in hand-to-hand fighting, and they ignore his approach. He screams and his blood surges. Barrel extended, he thrusts his bayonet into a Union soldier, slamming him against the log wall, burying the tip of the blade in the wood. Decker pulls free, pushing the soldier off the blade with his foot.

The rest of the column arrives on his heels, firing as they run. This first volley drops men on both sides. The parapet is six feet high in some places. Decker pulls back the hammer and fires at a soldier trying to climb over the top. The soldier tumbles back behind the stacked logs.

A shallow trench backing the parapet on Decker's side is filled with corpses. Union soldiers hold their muskets over the top of the wall and fire blind. Decker crouches down to reload. There are enough Confederates at the wall to hold for a minute. Decker tears a paper cartridge with his teeth and tries to pour the gunpowder into the musket's barrel, but his hands are shaking, and he spills the powder into the mud. He grabs another cartridge from his pouch and, steadying his hand on the top of the barrel, pours the gunpowder home. He slides the Minié ball in, cone end up, and slams the ball home with his ramrod.

A Union soldier is over the wall, headed for him. Decker stands up out of the crouch, stepping to the side. The soldier in blue trips over a body, tumbling forward. Decker slams the butt of his musket into the soldier as he falls, and then stabs downward, planting the bayonet in the man's back. He screams, facedown, squirming in the mud, pinned by Decker's blade.

More men climb the wall. Decker steps back, cocking the hammer. The musket does not fire—there's no primer on the gun's nipple. With a surge of fear, he jumps forward, lunging at the top of the wall as another soldier climbs over. The bayonet skewers the man through the throat. Decker tugs to the side, and the body tumbles away, thrashing as it falls. Without pausing, Decker pulls back, spinning to the left, just in time to parry a thrust from a bayonet intended for him. He battles— thrust and parry, thrust and parry—expecting a blade in the back at any moment. Panicked, he bulls his way forward, overpowering his smaller opponent by sheer force, knocking him to the ground. One quick thrust and Decker whirls back, just as another Union soldier closes in on him.

Split seconds mean everything. Standing on a pile of the dead and dying, Decker lets fear drive him. His practiced moves become a frenzied dance. When the flow of Union soldiers abates, Decker slips a primer on the nipple of the musket, relieved to be reloaded.

No. The ramrod is still stuck fast in the barrel.

Lord please, please! He pulls the ramrod free, dropping it in the mud as a dozen Union soldiers pitch themselves over the log wall. With no time left, he cocks the hammer and fires point-blank.

There are too many! No time to reload. The rain falls in sheets now, washing blood into the mud, painting everything at his feet rust-red. He whirls and thrusts, back and forth across six feet of log parapet, and the Union soldiers fall.

From the other side, the Yankees fire another blind volley over the wall, sending rounds of lead into the copse of trees behind the Confederate line. The sound of groaning and a snap like a cannon shot is followed by the slow descent of a massive tree. Repeated shots have cut the trunk in two. Chips of wood — kindling for a thousand fires — litters the ground.

Less than half of Decker's company is still alive. The field behind the Confederate line is empty. No help coming. On the Union side, shouts, cries, and the clatter of muskets is deafening. The crack of thunder announces another surge as the Yankees try the top of the parapet again. Decker goes into his frenetic dance, cutting and slashing. One huge soldier — inches taller than Decker — shoves Decker to the ground. The man steps forward to plant his bayonet, but lurches to the side instead. He stares down, confused, as blood rolls from the hole in his temple. He looks down, meeting Decker's gaze, and then drops to the mud in a crumpled pile.

To his right, a soldier in gray stands with a musket, barrel smoking. His face is drawn, but otherwise blank.

We are all dead, here. No one survives this. The rain has soaked Decker through, and his clothing is as heavy as chains. Crouching, he strips his jacket off and reloads, taking a ramrod from a fallen soldier's musket. Twenty feet away, a Union soldier mounts the wall. His friends pass him loaded muskets, and he fires without pause. He's exposed to return fire, but seems fearless, dropping soldier after soldier on the Confederate side. Decker takes careful aim and blows the man off the wall.

As Decker tries to reload, a wave of muskets come flying over the top of the parapet like lances. The man closest to Decker takes a bayonet in the side. He screams and drops to the ground, joining the carpet of bodies. Another volley roars overhead. The whine sounds in Decker's ears. *How long before I'm cut down?* There are even fewer men on his side of the parapet now. As he watches, a blade slides between the logs, pointed his way. The Yankees are blindly stabbing through chinks in the logs.

Dark clouds grumble above, battering the men below with waves of cold rain that keep rhythm to the battle. The boom of cannon in the distance sounds like thunder—or does the thunder sound like cannon? Decker can't tell. With so much rain, he shouldn't be thirsty, but he is drier than he's ever been. His mouth tastes like paper and gunpowder.

He tries to reload again, but the barrel is fouled with burned powder. A ladle of water would clean it, but if he had water, he'd drink instead. He glances at the piles of dead, stacked on top of each other. *Should I grab a different musket?* The question leaves him momentarily befuddled. Instead, he holds on to what he has. The bayonet is the weapon of choice here, and the musket in his hands has served him well.

Another Union surge spills over the wall, and Decker launches himself into the melee. His arms are weary, but the men climbing the logs are just as weary. *They all die here. We all die here.* Each moment seems as if it will be his last. He hears the roar of an animal—a rabid beast—and realizes the guttural cry is coming from his own throat.

Then, in a moment's pause, he discovers he's nearly alone. There are not enough men left to defend the line—five or six soldiers for fifty feet of parapet. The man to his left stares at him, wild-eyed, mouth gaping. Decker looks down at his blood-covered hands. In front of him, the next wave of Yankees starts over the wall, like a pot bubbling over. *Now,* he thinks.

The high-pitched howl and yip behind him announces the arrival of reinforcements. A line of soldiers in gray race across the field. *Run, damn you, run!* Decker turns to face the Union onslaught.

When the volley cuts across the grass, Yankees spill from the top of the logs. His back to the volley, a Minié ball catches Decker behind the leg, blowing the kneecap out and spraying the log with blood and bone. Decker pitches forward, catching himself on the logs with his hands. A bayonet slides through from the other side, skewering his left hand. The pain is white hot. He pulls free, and stumbles back. A musket angles over the wall from the Union side and fires. He can feel the round strike bone in his left arm. He drops back, his shattered leg folding beneath him.

The pain begins immediately. At first, he cannot breathe. He anchors himself to the ground. Any movement is agony. *I've been shot! Dear God, I've been shot!* He tries to scream, but his throat will not respond. *Help me!* The bark of muskets and the cries of men continue on all sides. Someone steps on him, sending fresh spasms along his ruined leg.

I am going to die. This seems certain. *Lord, take me now. Take me into Heaven. Don't let me lay here. Take me home.* Someone discharges a musket just above him. The stench of smoke and butchered meat fills his nostrils.

Paula, I love you so much! Pops! He might be crying. The rain starts again. *My mouth is so dry.* He tries to open his lips, to let rain trickle in, but his lips press tight, and they won't part.

So tired. Weariness overtakes him, and he can feel himself slipping away. Like his pain, the sounds of battle are still there, but distanced. *I am going now.* Decker Brown shivers and closes his eyes.

. . .

The night sky yawns above him. The storm continues, both on the ground and in the sky. The fires of battle paint the cloud bottoms orange and red. Screams rise and fall — an arpeggio of misery. He is on his back. The pain begins again.

Stars shine through a crack in the clouds — pinpoints of white light, with colors dancing in the periphery, freckling the abyss. Vertigo seizes him. He feels as if he might detach from the earth and float into the void. Or perhaps he is staring into some unearthly well, ready to fall to its starry depths. What holds him in place is the weight of a corpse, sprawled across his midsection. He tries to move, but the resulting shock of pain convinces him to lie still.

"Hold on! Hold on!" Someone is shouting at him.

He can't answer. He fixes his gaze on the heavens again. The tiny circle of stars beckons to him. *There is Heaven,* he thinks. Then, fresh screams and the clash of steel on steel tells him that the battle still rages. *Impossible.* How could God allow such a crucible of pain? Dreaming, Decker imagines a hand sweeping away the bloody parapet and the men who cling to it like ants.

When someone steps on his ankle, he awakens, able to scream now.

There is no God.

The thought silences his scream, leaving him black and empty. *We are on our own. And this is how we are. This is what we do to each other.* Another body falls across his face, blocking the sky. He tries to shove the body away—pain be damned. *The sky! Let me see the sky!*

Miraculously, someone pulls the body away, letting him see the crack in the clouds, even as it telescopes closed, swallowed by the storm. *That is my home. Not Richmond. There in the sky.*

When the rain clouds seal the crack, leaving only a gray-scale world, he closes his eyes again. The battle continues.

• • •

Jonas Wesley shook his head, wiping his hands on his bloodied apron. "This one's dead already. I'm tired. I want to go home." Wesley was a physician, recruited from a nearby town to tend to the Confederate wounded. He'd set up shop in a farmhouse south of the battle lines the previous morning and had not rested since. Blood coated his arms and apron—some of it crusted, some thick and bright. Outside, soldiers pitched tents in the mud to house those that survived surgery.

The soldier on the table would *not* survive. Before the battle, Wesley had done nothing more gruesome than lancing a boil. Now, he stood with a bone saw in his hands. The hands shook. "We're nearly out of chloroform. I won't waste our supplies on lost causes."

His assistant, recruited by virtue of his experience in caring for horses, glanced back at the open door. "His friends insist. They say he's a hero."

"The arms and legs of heroes are piled at the side of the house." Wesley stared at the door. Outside, three tired, emaciated men stood, muskets cradled in their arms. A good gust of wind would clear the doorway, blowing them away like the dirt that covered them, but there was no wind. A charnel stench clung to everything and everyone.

"We have a lull. Let's see what we can do."

Wesley stared down at the boy on the table. *I should never have become a doctor. I would never have seen this day.* Wesley's arms dropped to his sides, and he nearly let go of the saw.

"Doctor?"

Wesley looked up. *Old Doc Wesley.* That's what they called him in town. He mixed elixirs, set children's bones, and helped the midwife with difficult deliveries. He eased the dying in their journey to the grave, providing what comfort he could. Today, he presided over an abattoir. "I am so tired."

"I know, sir. But let's do what we can. Perhaps God will make quick work of this one. He's almost bled out anyway."

Wesley peeled back the man's trousers. The sight of the knee, blown to pieces, set his stomach on edge. "It's a wonder the leg didn't drop off of its own accord."

"It seems they were very careful with him."

The doctor stared at the toolbox the regiment commander had provided him with. Amputation knives. Scalpels. Bullet extractors.

And the saws.

The house that served as his surgery room was little more than a cottage. The makeshift chandelier—a wagon wheel topped with candles—had come in handy overnight. Morning sun was in full evidence, now. Blood flecked the throw rug and the striped wallpaper. The dining room table bore the nicks and cuts of Wesley's blades. The woodstove was lit, smoldering behind him, but the room seemed forever cold.

"As you wish," he said, his voice flat with fatigue. "We'll take the leg above the knee."

"And the arm?"

Wesley glanced at the other wound and grimaced. "Yes. Take the arm, too."

CHAPTER NINETEEN

Richmond, Virginia
April 1865

*"We yelled, we cheered, we sang, we prayed, we wept.
We hugged each other and threw up our hats."*
~Frederick Chesson, 29th Connecticut Regiment,
upon entering Richmond

Paula sat on her bed, biting the inside of her cheek. She'd waited in her second-story bedroom for nearly twenty-four hours. The certainty she'd lingered too long left her shaking. What could she do? Her father was *not* coming home. Henry Lee and Millie were gone. She was alone in the house. Outside, shouts and angry laughter made her cringe. Half of the city had spilled into the streets, waiting for the Yankees. Her white lace curtains—the last finery not donated for bandages—glowed red and orange. Richmond was burning.

Paula was not surprised by the news from the battlefront. Throughout the eight-month siege of Petersburg, she'd waited for Lee to yield—for Richmond to fall. Her small traveling bag had been packed in advance with a change of clothes and other essentials. The bag sat at the foot of her bed like a dog, faithfully waiting on the darkest hour. Now that Richmond had fallen, she glared at the thing, with its fancy leather straps and wooden handle. Everything she had, under a single clasp. All else was lost.

She'd carried the bag to the train station the previous evening, accompanied by her father and ten slaves from his flour mill, chained together. William Crane demanded passage to Danville and was refused. With most of Richmond fleeing the Yankees, there was no room on the train for slaves. Crane would not abandon his property, and Paula would not abandon her father. The train pulled out of the station without them.

She should have gone. But how could she know the war's end would leave her so completely abandoned? The signs were as clear as the track warning sign at the train station, presumably now in flames.

After returning home, William Crane spent a fretful hour pacing the parlor floor by the light of a candle, his slaves huddled in the corner of the room. The mill foreman, a frightened little man who spoke in whispers, arrived, suffered a tirade from Crane, and then left. Though past midnight, her father announced that he must return to the mill, slaves in tow, ordering Paula to wait for him. She spent the night shivering in bed. Henry Lee and Millie greeted her in the morning with a small breakfast—a piece of dry toast—but by late afternoon, they were gone as well. Paula spent the day in her bedroom with her travel bag, praying for her father's return.

Her mother had passed on months before. In January, Mrs. Crane came down with smallpox. Paula bathed her, fed her, and sat by the bedside, reading to her from the Bible (the newspaper was simply too depressing). Her efforts were in vain. After two weeks, her mother succumbed to the disease. Her father buried his wife in the Shockoe Hill Cemetery.

What am I to do? The reality of her situation crept in with the evening shadows. She was a young woman on her own, and people were rioting. She could stay where she was and risk the privations of Union soldiers, or she could venture into the streets with no real destination and risk the mob. Either way, it seemed she must face a horrible tribulation.

The sea of flame, visible from her window, made her decision. She would leave the house and try to find a safe place. She grabbed her bag, and after giving her room a final glance, she headed into the hallway.

Fire scared her. Early that morning, an explosion at the south end of town rattled the windows. Henry Lee and Millie had no idea of the source of the blast. Smoke from the resulting blaze spread across the horizon, blanketing the sun. Had Confederate soldiers set fire to the town to leave a burned husk for the enemy? Had the Union army decided to punish Richmond for a war that cost them all so much? She didn't know.

She crept down the spiral stairway, trembling with each step. The foyer was dark as a funeral veil. She slid along the wall, bag in hand, careful not to fall. A rattling at the door froze her in place. She fumbled with the hasp and pulled a pistol from the bag. Cocking the hammer, she took another step down, pointing the weapon at the door.

The rattling came again.

The pistol was heavy, but she kept a steady aim. Whit taught her well enough. Someone knocked and jostled the doorknob.

Aim for the chest, she thought. *Shoot once, and then shoot again.*

The door burst open. A man tumbled in and stopped, straightening up at the sight of the gun leveled his way. "Don't shoot, my dear."

Whit, in the flesh. Paula's arm dropped to her side, the gun suddenly too heavy to lift.

She leaned back against the wall.

He rushed up the steps and wrapped his arm around her. "Come, I have a carriage outside."

"How — ?"

"Your man, Henry Lee." He helped her down the last few steps, taking the gun from her hand and returning it to her bag. "Resourceful fellow. He found us in the street, burning the last of the Ordnance Department records." She began to slump into his arm, and he whisked her toward the door. "I thought you were away from the city, safe. I thought you'd left on the train. It was a shock to learn you were still here."

"Father wouldn't leave without his slaves," she whispered. "He's at the mill now —" Whit stopped and turned her to face him directly. "I am sorry, dearest. The mill burned, as did most of the business district." He paused, his lips pursed. "I would spare you the details. Your father won't be coming home."

She nodded, her lip trembling. A moment passed before she could speak. "I thought not." There was nothing more to say. He ushered her through the doorway. Outside the fence, a carriage waited, guarded by two soldiers. Henry Lee stood on the flagstones leading to the gate.

Henry Lee. He hadn't abandoned her at all. He'd gone for Whit, just as he had during the bread riot. He'd saved her. Her heart, near breaking with the news of her father, swelled at the thought of the selfless old man who'd risked his safety for her. *I'm like a daughter to him. I'm sure of it.* Then, she thought, *He's free now. He can be done with us all.*

"These men will escort us safely out of town," Whit explained, pointing at the soldiers. "But we must hurry. The city no longer recognizes the rule of law."

Her breath fogged in the night air. "Come on, Henry Lee." The old Black man moved to the side, leaning back against the fence surrounding the Crane house.

Whit tightened his grip on her arm. "There's no room."

Paula shook her head, failing to understand. "But he came here with you —"

"And with you in the carriage, there will be no room for him." Whit shrugged. "He'll be fine. The Yankees are freeing the slaves, not killing them."

"But how will he eat?" Whit shrugged again.Paula fished in her bag, digging into the corners, past Decker's letters, retrieving a single silver coin. Taking a deep breath, she walked over to Henry Lee. Whit followed behind at a distance. "Thank you, Henry Lee. You saved me again. Thank you for your loyalty." She held out the coin.

Henry Lee took the silver and stared at it. His face, pitted like volcanic rock from Trimble Knob, bore no expression.

Paula cringed. "It's not much, Henry Lee. But it's all I have left."

Henry Lee looked up and met her gaze, his dark eyes softening at her apology. "I know, Miss Paula. And I thank you most kindly. It's just . . . I'm thinking of the difference."

"I don't understand."

Henry Lee tilted his head. Flames lit the city behind him, turning him into a silhouette. "The difference," he repeated. "Judas got thirty pieces of silver for betraying our Lord. I got one for my loyalty."

She could feel Whit stiffen, standing just behind her, and she reached back, putting a hand on his chest to hold him back. "Take care of Millie, Henry Lee," she said.

"Millie long gone," he answered. "She run off with her man. Plenty happy 'bout it, too."

"I'm glad," Paula said. After a short silence, Henry Lee bowed and turned to leave. He hobbled through the gate and down the street, away from the fire. Once in the carriage, they traveled in the same direction, passing him a block ahead. Paula waved, but he ignored her, seemingly intent on his journey.

The carriage moved northeast to Maddox Hill. They shared the road with others fleeing the city, but there were surprisingly few. Most of the city's displaced had traveled in the direction of Danville the previous day. Light from the fire cast soft, wavering shadows across the face of the hill, like the wisps of a dream expiring behind them.

"The bridges over the James have been burned," Whit said at last. "The Yankees are moving in from the west. We'll go north."

"What will you do?" she asked. Tears rolled down her face, and she made no attempt to hide them.

He didn't answer at first. They'd reached a flat spot near the top of the hill, and Whit paused the carriage. As he stepped down, he dismissed the two soldiers who'd accompanied them. "Try to cross the James at the Rockets," he said. "You might find someone there with a boat. Don't go west. I'm told the vanguard of the Union army is comprised of Black troops. They won't look kindly on us."

The soldiers glanced at each other, nodded, and hustled into the night, apparently relieved that their errand had been completed.

"Will they be all right?" Paula asked.

"I don't know." Whit stood straight, the sleeve of his missing arm pinned in place. "It doesn't matter, I suppose. This is the end of the war."

Paula stepped from the carriage, joining him. From this vantage, she could see the smoldering arc of fire blanketing the city in smoke. The underside of the sky glowed orange. Whit frowned, saying, "Quite beautiful, really. That is, if you're able to forget what's burning." His voice was steady, as if he were speaking of the price of tobacco.

"Can you see my father's house from here?"

"No."

"I hope it doesn't burn."

He shook his head. "We heard the Yankees began fighting the fire as soon as they arrived." He waved his hand across the horizon. "The damage looks widespread from here, but it hasn't crossed over into the center of the city yet."

She pointed. "Father's house must be north of the fire."

He looked down at her, frowning, and snatched her wrist, holding it aloft. The sleeve of her dress slid back, revealing a skeletal arm. His serene expression broke, a look of horror crossing his face. She tried to pull away, but he kept his grip. "My God!"

"Yes," she said, cringing. "I'm afraid there's not much left of me."

He closed his eyes, clutching her hand to his chest. A gust of wind rolled across the face of the hill, carrying the smell of smoke. She leaned closer to keep from tumbling away. "Where will you take me?" she asked.

"My aunt has a farmhouse northeast of here. She'll keep you safe. You'll like it there. She has four dogs, and they will all love you."

"And you? Where will you go?"

"Once you're safe, I'll go south and cross the James. From there, I'll travel west and join General Lee. I will share whatever fate has in store for us."

She shuddered. "We're lost."

He reached down and lifted her chin. "No."

His dark eyes reflected a hint of the fire. She'd never seen him so resolute, so certain. "We are defeated, but we are *not* lost. We will *never* be lost." He stepped away, gesturing to the fire. "Burn it all. We'll rebuild. Put us in chains, and we'll break free. We cannot be subjugated." Looking at her, he added, "You taught me that. Do you remember your first visit, after I lost my arm? You had no tears of pity for me. If you had, I might still be in bed."

She stared at him, beaten but unbroken, standing firm above her burning city.

"The South is more than buildings. The South is a spirit. A way of life. Look at you, Paula. You've wasted away to nothing, but when I come to rescue you, I found you with a gun in your hand, ready to blow me to hell."

"I thought you were—"

"I know what you thought. What a piece of work you are!" He laughed, shaking his head. "God help anyone who tries to stop you." His gaze narrowed. "And God help anyone who thinks we'll give in. The war may be ending, but I'll strike no tent. The Yankees will learn there's a difference between winning a war and winning a peace. We will resist them at every turn, and in the end, we will be triumphant. As for you, as long as you draw breath, the grace and beauty of the South can never die."

"I'm not beautiful anymore."

"Yes, you are," he said, stepping closer. "And now—" She tilted her head.

"I have a question to ask you."

CHAPTER TWENTY

Richmond, Virginia
May 1865

"You might as well appeal against the thunder-storm as against these terrible hardships of war."
~General William Tecumseh Sherman

When he could be moved, the army transferred Decker Brown to Chimborazo Hospital, placing him with the maimed and terminal patients. His first visitor came from the War Department a few weeks after the Battle of Spotsylvania. The major was old as a parchment scroll, with yellowed skin and eyes that could not be read. He stood at a distance, a telegram clutched in his hand, staring at Decker. After a few minutes of apparent contemplation, he stepped forward and began to speak.

"Major Alexander Pelham," he said by way of introduction. "And you are Private Decker Brown?"

Decker stared without speaking. When the major continued to wait, Decker nodded. *Get on with your business. Say your piece and go.*

"I've brought you a dispatch," he continued, "detailing your actions during the Battle of Spotsylvania Courthouse." He set the telegram on Decker's cot, next to his head. "You are the talk of the War Department, Private. One can scarcely believe the accounts." The major cleared phlegm from his throat before continuing. "When I heard they'd transferred you here, to Richmond, I offered to deliver this commendation personally. I wanted to meet you."

A nurse passed behind the major, glancing at Decker before moving on. "They say you killed a hundred men."

Decker groaned. "Round numbers lie."

"I would be grateful to hear an account from your lips."

Decker closed his eyes. "What does the dispatch say?"

"Without your efforts, the center of the line would have collapsed." Major Pelham paused. Despite his age, he stood ramrod straight, with a certain aristocratic bearing that matched both his solemn tone and the Roman slant of his nose. What hair he still possessed had been combed with precision. "Can you add substance to the dispatch?"

Decker licked his lips, trying to muster the energy to answer the major's question. The hospital staff had tucked him into the corner of the hospital barrack, far from the stove. The plank walls were whitewashed, leaving him little to keep his mind occupied. Part of him longed to talk to the major and tell him what he'd seen and done. "I kept moving. If I'd been a half second slower, I'd have died a dozen times."

The major blinked.

"I was lucky," Decker added.

The major couldn't help but look at the flat spots in the bed where healthy limbs should have been. "Lucky," he whispered. He drew a finger across his sparse mustache and leaned forward. "They have a name for you, by the way. The soldiers, the officers—they call you the *Courthouse Reaper*." He waited a moment. "And the place you fought is being called the *Bloody Angle*. That name has attached itself to other battles before, but now I think the stretch of logs in Spotsylvania will forever be remembered as the one and only Bloody Angle."

Decker didn't answer. A fly landed on his hand. The major frowned and brushed it away. "They told me the Yankee dead lay twenty deep in some spots," Major Pelham continued. "I cannot imagine such a thing."

"I cannot forget such a thing."

Major Pelham's voice dropped to a whisper. "If there is any consolation to be had, son, I would offer it now. You are a true son of the South."

"I'm a lieutenant in the Yankee army."

The major frowned and put a hand on Decker's forehead. "You're burning up." He turned and motioned to the matron, who was doing her best to appear busy with other wounded soldiers. After a brief conference, he returned to Decker's side, his hat in hand. "They will attend to you momentarily, Private Brown. Anything that can be done to make you comfortable will be done. I've seen to it." The major seemed ready to leave, but lingered, as if considering one last word.

Nodding to himself, he stepped close again. "A man who fought as hard as you did can't be expected to go to his death peacefully, whether on the field or in a bed. It's not in your nature. But I hope you do not suffer long, son. The Lord is ready to take you in."

"Begging the major's pardon, but it's you that's been taken in by the Lord."

Major Pelham stepped back, his wrinkled face a weary map of the miseries he'd seen.

Decker felt a moment of regret for his bad manners, and added, "Thank you for the dispatch, and for your efforts on my behalf." He closed his eyes, and when he reopened them, the major was gone.

He was still in bed when Richmond burned.

• • •

Before the Yankees arrived, the army evacuated the patients of Chimborazo that could be moved. Decker Brown stayed behind. His battlefield surgeon had made a mess of the amputations, and the doctors were forced to take more of the arm, leaving him little more than a nub below the shoulder. Surgery and the subsequent fevers left him bedridden, covered in sores, and unable to travel.

The Union army began filling the missing beds with their own wounded. Hospital volunteers stayed on, nursing men from both armies. A week after Richmond burned, news of Lee's surrender at Appomattox cheered the Yankee wounded and left the Confederate survivors in fits of despair.

Dori Curtis continued to work after the surrender. Her home on the north side of town had not burned, so she had a place to sleep. Paula's servant, Henry Lee, was long gone, and absent his carriage rides, she'd become used to the long, exhausting walk to and from the hospital.

In some ways, Dori was relieved by the end of the war. A semblance of order had arrived with the Union army. There was more to eat, and she could walk to and from her job without being accosted—the riffraff plaguing the streets for months had disappeared after the fire. And she was no longer a volunteer. The head nurse promised that tending to the Yankees meant she would be paid for her efforts at the hospital—forty cents a day—something that gave her hope for the future.

As for Lee's surrender, she could not think of it without crying.

Walking up Chimborazo Hill that morning might have been a blessing. The air was crisp and clean, and she'd eaten a biscuit and a strip of bacon for breakfast. More than a year had passed since she'd last had bacon! Birds sang from the trees lining the road. But she was not looking forward to her shift at the hospital.

Though she'd worked with the worst of the wounded, she'd never attended the *Reaper* before, and caring for him gave her pause. She'd heard terrible things from the other nurses. First, he *smelled*. She had never gotten used to the gangrenous stench of wounds, and her coworkers claimed his combination of infection, urine, and excrement was truly unbearable. Second, no one dared attend him at night. After a year on a cot, he hadn't died, which seemed *unnatural*. The colored girls were afraid and refused to go near him. One old Caribbean slave, who made herself useful mixing herbs and teas for patients when she wasn't scrubbing floors, called him a *brujo,* claiming he left his cot at night and flew through the air.

They'd tucked him into the corner of the ward reserved for the hopeless wounded.

Steeling her nerves, Dori put on her best plain-faced expression and began tending him as if he were any other wounded man. She changed his sheets, dumped his bedpan, and changed the bandage on his weeping arm stump. Several minutes passed before she took a good look at his face, which brought her first flicker of recognition. "Decker? Decker Brown?"

Thus far, he'd kept his eyes clamped shut. Now, he opened them, though he maintained his silence.

"Is that you, Decker? It's Dori. Dori Curtis. Paula's friend —" She stopped. She couldn't even be sure the man on the cot was Decker. He was a bundle of sticks — perhaps half a bundle. And he looked very old.

"Dori Curtis," he whispered. "I remember. You look much thinner, Dori."

"As do you," Dori said, blushing. "Why, we're both a pair of scarecrows, aren't we?" Decker stared, as if he couldn't quite focus. "You are a matron here?"

"Yes. I've been volunteering for more than two years."

Decker closed his eyes. "I should like to ask you something."

No, please don't. Dori returned to her care routine. Decker's condition was appalling. "When was the last time you were bathed?" she demanded.

He managed to shrug.

"Your skin is a mess. You have to move. You can't just lay in one position. If you're going to recover, you'll need sunshine and clean surroundings. And most of all, you'll need a bath." She spoke in quick bursts, not allowing him time to respond. "I'm going for a sponge and basin."

She left, in no hurry to return. Several other patients needed assistance, and she allowed them to distract her. One Union soldier — another double amputee — had spilled the pan collecting pus under his leg stump. The doctor would be angry. The pus was needed to salve the soldier's other wounds. She repositioned the pan and applied a cold cloth to his fevered brow, wondering how to respond to the inevitable questions when she returned to Decker Brown's cot.

Back at his side, sponge and basin in hand, she launched into an explanation of what he might expect. The bath would be painful. Decker spent more time apologizing for his state than trying to spark a conversation.

"Have they given you something for the diarrhea?"

"They tried."

"Calomel works wonders. Mercury is good for the intestines."

Decker shook his head. "Makes me salivate. I drool like an idiot."

Dori shook her head. "You are a stubborn man." She paused, squeezing out the sponge. "As I said, this will hurt."

"Nothing new."

"Normally, I would ask one of the other nurses to bathe you. It might not be proper to bathe someone I know personally."

"They won't do it." His lips pressed together in a grimace.

"Why is that?" she asked, though she knew the answer.

He took a deep breath. "I smell bad. And they're afraid of me."

She paused, sponge poised. After a long moment, she began to wash him. "Don't worry. I will do this. And you will feel better when it's over."

He nodded, though the grimace would not leave his face. Halfway through, she had two soldiers help her turn him over. The sight of his back and buttocks brought her to tears.

When she finished, one of the soldiers offered to remove the basin and its pink water. She covered Decker with a fresh blanket and stood to go.

"My father." The words were a statement, not a question, but she knew what was meant. "I've asked other nurses and doctors, but they don't have the time to check for me. I know my old house burned, or at least I think I do. Wherever he is, he's not there. You don't happen to know if he's all right, do you?"

Dori's shoulders slumped. "I'm so sorry."

He bit his lip. "Bad news, then?"

"Your father died at Gettysburg. We all saw his name on the lists. He was with Pickett's division. He likely died in that last, valiant charge."

Decker exhaled, sinking into his cot. For the second time, she was moved to tears. The tragedy of lives forever destroyed had become linked in her mind to General Lee's surrender. The death of nobility. The end of a way of life. She waited for a moment, and when he didn't speak, she saw a chance to turn and go.

Before she could take three steps, he called out to her. "And what of Paula?"

Dori stopped. *This* was the question she'd dreaded most. She turned back, facing him, her face drawn and pale. He lay back, his blue eyes watering, lips twisted in pain.

"Mrs. Hill is well."

"Mrs. Hill?"

"Mrs. Whitaker Hill."

At first, he did not move. Then his shoulders began to shake. She thought he was weeping at first, but his sputtering became a dark laugh. "Well," he said when he'd regained his composure, "everything turns out for the best."

"I'm sorry," she said, unable to think of anything that might comfort him.

He bit his lip, hard enough that she worried he'd draw blood. Then, as if remembering something forgotten, he turned his head and said, "Thank you, Dori. Thank you for your kindness." His voice was a strangled whisper.

• • •

Later, glancing back at his bed in the corner of the ward, she saw him talking to himself, as if engaged in a heated argument.

He pointed his finger at the ceiling and then went silent. Later still, she watched him sit up and lay back down, repeating the motion several times.

She approached the bed, alarmed at his pained expression. "Can I help you?" she asked.

He stopped, gasping for breath. When he'd regained his composure, he said, "Nothing's wrong. I'm fine."

"Are you uncomfortable?"

He gulped and waved her off. "I have been still, waiting for death, and it appears he's not coming. Perhaps the smell frightens him as well." He sat upright, pain from the effort etched in his face. After a deep breath, he continued. "Over the years, I've discovered that with practice, I can make the graceless appear graceful." He held her gaze for a moment. "There are things I must relearn now. Please don't let my efforts concern you."

CHAPTER TWENTY-ONE

New York City, New York
April 1867

"Americans are undoubtedly the most practical,
but they surely lack taste."
~Jules Verne

The Frenchman spent the morning wandering New York with his brother. The marble edifices lining Broadway reminded him of Europe, and the vehicle-cluttered streets displayed the best of industrious America. Horses pulled buggies, carts, taxis, and trolleys through crowds of pedestrians — men in hats and long coats, walking with a purpose. The Frenchman's brother strolled at a different pace, stopping every few moments to look around.

The bustle of the city was both heady and uncomfortable at the same time. "Paul, if I lived here," the Frenchman said, "I would be expected to write a book a month. Even Hetzel would be pleased."

"Your publisher is the *trou de cul*." Paul pointed at one man in a top hat, hand to the brim, bent forward at the waist, rushing along the sidewalk. "And that man there will rush to the grave without having glanced around him. Learn nothing from him."

Jules Verne snorted his appreciation.

Pausing at a lamppost, the brothers looked to the right, out over City Hall Park. "A fountain. Some trees and shrubs. A museum of the wild for those who live in boxes." Paul shook his head. "I hope the falls are not so disappointing."

"Cooper country," Jules said with a sigh. "You will not be disappointed." He longed to see the Hudson Valley and Niagara Falls, ancient home of the Mohawk. "But first, lunch with the American."

"He chose the diner. I hope the food is edible."

"He said the stew is good."

Paul frowned as another frenzied pedestrian brushed past him. "I wonder what he really wants from you."

"Just a short visit. His letter said he is an admirer of my novels. *De la Terre à la Lune* in particular."

"An admirer." Paul gave a loud sigh. "I fear that an unbearable ordeal awaits us, brother."

"Don't fret. A short lunch, and then Barnum's new museum." Jules pointed to a side street. "Shall we? The ordeal commences."

The diner was a glitzy affair, festooned with chandeliers, wall murals, and plaster columns. But the plank floor was more emblematic of the city. A thin veneer of dirt covered the walkways. The brothers sat at a table in advance of their visitor, speculating on his appearance. Paul spotted the man first, whispering, "Given our luck, brother, that poor soul over there is your admirer."

The man scuttled toward them like a spider missing most of its legs. One arm, one leg, a peg, and a cane worked furiously to weave a path through cloth-covered tables, arriving with a grim smile and a greeting, spoken in French. "*Monsieur* Verne? I am Decker Brown."

The Frenchman stood, pulling out a chair, a gesture the American accepted without comment. A glance to the side confirmed what Jules suspected. Paul sat, open-mouthed in dismay, his face pale.

The American wasted no time in niceties. "I must first apologize for my French. You don't speak English, is that correct?"

Jules nodded.

"Then we are at the mercy of my pronunciation. My understanding of your language comes from reading, rather than speech. Like many endeavors, practice is my pathway to excellence, and I have had no opportunity to practice your beautiful language."

"I understand you perfectly, sir. And since that is the purpose of language, we are as one."

The American nodded. "Have you eaten?"

The brothers glanced at each other and then shook their heads. "Wonderful. I am hungry but would not think to eat if you were not doing so as well." When the waiter arrived, all three men ordered stew. Jules and Paul ordered wine. The American ordered two ales. "Your food is good here," he told the waiter, "but it takes too long to get a second drink. Bring it at the outset."

Paul turned to Jules, frowning.

"And so," the American said when the waiter disappeared. "I am greatly interested in your novel, though I was dismayed to discover Mr. Lincoln was still President of the United States at the outset of the tale. His assassination must have come as a shock to you."

Jules winced. "Yes. Subsequent editions, including the American edition, feature the appropriate changes."

"I read the original French edition," the American said, pride evident in his voice.

"Well done." Jules looked around for the waiter, hoping for his wine. Paul stared as if their guest were an exhibit in a shop of curiosities.

"I did have questions," the American said.

"Please. I would love to discuss the novel."

"Why a giant cannon?" Rather than listen to an answer, the American continued. "A cannon has a single impulse of thrust. Surely you knew the amount of thrust necessary would crush any hollow projectile like your moon ship? Why not use continual thrust to escape the earth's gravitational pull? I have considered the possibility of liquid oxidation—"

"It's a story." Paul's declaration put a temporary halt to the conversation.

The waiter delivered drinks. The American was silent while the glasses were set on the tablecloth. As soon as the waiter was gone, he grabbed the mug and swallowed half in a single gulp. Wiping his mouth with his sleeve, he continued. "I'm intrigued by your selection of Florida as a launch point. Projecting out into the Atlantic . . . brilliant."

"Thank you."

"You also propose the use of guncotton as a propellant. As it happens, I myself explored the possibilities of that substance."

Paul's frown deepened. Jules maintained a straight face.

"Gentlemen, I was a lieutenant with the Union during the war. I worked with the Ordnance Department. My expertise was rocketry. Before the war, I crafted illuminations. I love. . ." He paused, scratching his chin. "I love all things to do with rockets."

Jules nodded. "Then you are well aware of the deceits in the novel, sir."

The American waved his one arm emphatically. "No, no! I found the novel to be extraordinary! Your processes for removing excess carbon dioxide within the capsule, for example. Inspired!"

Jules smiled, closing his eyes. *This is quite unbearable.*

The American finished the first ale and slammed the mug down on the table. "I have wondered something. I am consumed with the idea of—" He stopped, searching for a word. *"plausibilité?"*

"Yes, space flight is plausible." Verne gulped his wine—a nervous reaction to sitting in the presence of an evident madman. "Ruggieri is said to have launched a ram five hundred meters into the air and recovered the animal alive through the use of a parachute."

"Two hundred meters," said Paul.

The American sat back, stunned. He tapped his cane on the floor repeatedly, the body language equivalent to a stutter. Meanwhile, the waiter arrived with three bowls of stew and a loaf of fresh baked bread.

When the waiter left, Paul said, "The French are not strangers to exploration or the sciences."

"But this is extraordinary," the American said. He took a single bite from his stew and then returned to the second ale. "Someone has already launched a living creature?"

Jules and his brother tried to eat quickly. The stew portion was small. With luck, they would say their thanks and be on their way to the museum.

"Do you think it's possible, sir? To launch a sentient being?"

Jules blinked. He knew what the American meant, but the notion was pure fancy. "As my brother said, the idea of rocket flight serves a story, for the amusement of my readers. The science attending the novel is meant to help the reader achieve a level of belief. Nothing more."

The American dropped his spoon.

Paul shoveled the last of his stew from the bowl. "Jules, please remember that we have an appointment."

Jules glanced at Paul, failing to understand. "Our *appointment*," Paul repeated.

Jules nodded. "Oh, yes." He turned to the American. "We do have business to attend to, regrettably. I enjoyed our visit—"

"I fear I've been . . . overbearing. Forgive my enthusiasm."

Jules felt a sudden tug of sympathy for the man. He reached out and touched his sleeve, patting it. "Not at all, sir. I'm gratified that you enjoyed my story."

"I do wonder, sir, what became of the space travelers? Your book ends at the moment of launch. Do you have plans to write a second volume? If so, I have some ideas for you —"

"We must go," Paul said.

The American sat back, sighing, an unhappy look on his face. The Frenchman rose, suddenly regretting he'd not brought some small memento as a gift to compensate the man for his obvious disappointment. In that respect, Paul rescued them both by fishing a folded piece of paper from his pocket. "This is a drawing from a forthcoming edition. The artist is Henri de Montaut. We would like you to keep it as a remembrance of this most excellent lunch." The rudimentary pencil sketch showed a huge cannon, laid flat across a pastoral scene.

"Thank you," the American said, his voice barely a whisper. His eyes began to water, so both Jules and Paul made their way from the table without delay.

On the street again, Jules broke the silence. "That was a fine gesture. What made you think of it?"

"An admirer of your work? Worthy of a keepsake."

Jules stopped to stare at a passing trolley and then began to walk again. "Nice enough fellow."

Paul shrugged. "The man meant well. Passionate, but without restraint."

"I am pleased you thought to bring the drawing."

"One of the early sketches. I would not have parted with the finished work. But I suspect the drawing, poor as it was, will mean something to him. And in exchange, we received lunch and a glass of wine."

"You are a person of quality, Paul," Jules said.

. . .

After delaying dinner for more than an hour, Paula was relieved to hear the knock at the door. Her father-in-law had been invited to dinner for the first time since his wife's passing. Paula had planned the dining details with Millie, agonizing over the menu and decorations. Millie chose the entrée and found the ingredients. Paula chose the wine.

"Commissioner Hill," Whit said, greeting his father at the door. "It's late. I'd begun to worry."

"Son, so good to see you." Jubal Hill removed his hat and stepped through the threshold of Whitaker Hill's small home. Glancing around the foyer, he smiled. A chandelier overhead joined the candle sconces on the wall to give the entryway a warm glow. A vase filled with sunflowers on the marble table looked twice as large, thanks to the antique mirror on the wall behind the bouquet. Jubal turned to Paula and bowed. "You have a touch with décor, my dear."

"I hope our foyer seems welcoming, sir, for you will always be welcome in our home." Paula curtsied. Her pink hoop dress hung from her hips like a bell. The candles gave her skin a radiance that direct sunlight refused her.

Millie joined them at the door, taking Jubal's coat. When she left, he asked, "Isn't that your old house servant?"

Paula nodded. "Millie found us again about six months ago. Her husband is having difficulty finding work—"

"There are a lot of good men out of work. And more Yankees come rolling into town every day. It's a shame, and something I hope to address in the coming months." Jubal had been appointed to his position by the occupation troops. The elder Hill clearly relished his new position, from his attire— vest, jacket, and tie, ornamented with a tie pin and huge watch fob—to his complexion, flushed with renewed vigor.

Moving to the small dining room, Jubal took a seat at the head of the table. Whit sat to his left, and Paula at his right. They had not been seated for more than a few moments before Millie arrived, carrying plates filled with catfish and fried corn.

"Thank you, Millie," Paula said.

"Why, of course, Miss Paula," Millie said brightly. "You folks enjoy this."

Whit grabbed the decanter at the table's center and poured his father a glass of red wine. Jubal frowned. "You don't need to serve me, son. You have a servant."

"Millie does nearly everything around here," Paula said. "We're lucky to have her."

Millie disappeared into the kitchen. Jubal's gaze followed her exit, shaking his head.

"She's a sassy one, isn't she?" He took a sip of wine and winced.

"Is the wine acceptable?" Whit asked.

"It's fine, it's fine." Jubal sat back. "So, how do you find your job?"

"I'm happy enough," Whit said. His father had secured Whit a position with the city. It would take years to rebuild Richmond, and men used to organization and supervision were needed to oversee the work. For that reason, many of the men who ran the city before the war were still in office after the war.

"Well, if you've any concerns about General Schofield running the district, you can put your mind at ease. I spoke with him today." He shoveled a bite of catfish into his mouth, chewing and swallowing before continuing. "The man is wholly sympathetic with our views."

"Is it your opinion that the creation of the military district won't interfere with self-rule?" Whit asked. His voice took on a sharper edge.

"Oh, they will stick their noses in everything. They seem determined to repeal the *Punishment for Vagrants* act.

Foolishness. If the field hands won't work, they must be forced to work. How else will we solve the labor shortage?"

"Millie's husband can't find work at a decent wage," Paula said. "It seems he must choose between low wages or arrest, and if he's arrested, they'll make him work for low wages."

The men at the table stopped eating. After several long moments, Jubal began to chew again, and upon seeing his father chew, Whit took another bite.

"The fried corn is excellent, don't you think?" Paula asked.

"Of course, my dear," Whit said. He glared at her.

For dessert, Millie served plates of Confederate Pudding. Jubal stared at his portion, smiling. "Do I see whortleberries here?"

"Orange peel, too," Millie said.

Jubal glared at Millie and then turned back to Paula. "Whortleberries?"

"Orange peel, too," Paula answered, her face as plain as the white china the pudding had been served on.

Millie crept out of the room.

"This is a new world," Jubal said, his voice distant. "But the old world still matters. My wife would never have ventured an opinion on politics, for example." He finished his glass of wine and dabbed his chin with his napkin. Turning to Whit, he said, "Your mother was a saint, Whitaker. I miss her greatly."

"I know you do, father. But as you said, it's a new world. Our freedoms are being curtailed, one by one. I am relieved you found General Schofield so agreeable, but I am inclined to think that the Republicans will shove their plans down our throats unless we are willing to stand up to them."

Jubal began stroking his white beard. "Am I to assume our mutual friends persuaded you, then? I don't agree with all their methods, though their grievances — our grievances — are legitimate."

"It's a matter of resistance," Whit repeated. Without turning from his father's gaze, he reached across the table and took Paula's hand. "The night Richmond burned, I made a promise to my wife, and I intend to keep it. The Yankees won the war, but they will *not* win the peace. I will bend, but I will not break."

"Hear, hear!" Jubal clapped his hands. "Spoken like a true son of the South."

Paula sat still, trying to sort all that had been said. *Will the war never end? What was the purpose of so many dead and maimed if not to arrive at a lasting peace?* But one question sounded above all the others.

What has Whit gotten himself into?

CHAPTER TWENTY-TWO

Boston, Massachusetts
May 1867

"The real use of gunpowder is to make all men tall."
~Thomas Carlyle

Nicholas White tried to assume a casual air as the cripple entered the business office of the Oriental Powder Company. The poor man managed himself well, considering his missing limbs. Learning to walk again must have taken a great deal of practice. *Don't* stare, he thought. A glance showed no such restraint on the part of the company's owner, Gilbert Grafton Newhall. The hint of pink blushing the man's cheeks was normal for a man of his corpulence, but the smirk threatening the corners of his mouth was *not* normal. In the time White had spent with Newhall, he'd seen various degrees of scowl, but never a smile on the man's face. Now it seemed Newhall would have to swallow his mirth, or risk insulting the man he was about to interview.

The cripple balanced the efforts of his peg leg with a cane, steadied by his one arm. The war had caused such terrible damage. This poor fellow was, by all accounts, a hero for the Confederacy. In his prime, he must have been a fine physical specimen. Now, he was a pitiful sight.

"Mr. Brown," Newhall said, standing up and moving from behind his table. He extended a hand by way of greeting. The cripple was unable to respond, still depending on the cane to remain upright. "So sorry! Let's get you off your feet, shall we?" He pointed to a chair. The cripple hobbled across the carpet and spun in place, sitting in a single fluid motion. "Nicely done, sir," Newhall said.

Nicholas White turned away. *Newhall is a dung heap. The man's applying for a job. A job I've already secured . . . should I care to accept it.*

Back behind the polished wooden table, Newhall pointed at White. "This is Mr. White. He will be starting work here next week. Now, I understand you are hoping to secure a position?"

"I've been to Gambo Falls. Your operation is impressive—"

"You went to Gorham?" Newhall looked off to the side, staring at the small fireplace to his right. The morning fire had burned down to embers.

"Yes, sir. I wanted to see what I could bring to your company in the way of—"

Newhall coughed, a fist in front of his open mouth, his other hand extended to stop the conversation for a moment. He grabbed a water pitcher from his desktop and poured himself a glass. After clearing his throat, he nodded. "Where were we? Oh yes, you were wondering how you could help my company. That is an interesting point, sir. What do you offer us? Surely, you don't intend to run pallets?"

Decker Brown sat without answering. His Adam's apple bobbed for a moment, and then he launched into a monologue. "Your charcoal house was using maple. I understand you prefer alder, but none was available. I would prefer willow— Pacific willow—but your man there didn't seem to know the difference."

Newhall's gaze narrowed, and the hint of a smile disappeared.

"At any rate," Brown continued, "I made a series of notes on specific improvements to your operation."

"Where are these notes?"

Brown paused again, his face blank. "Mental notes, sir."

"Ah. I thought perhaps you had a list somewhere on your person."

"I can recite them to you. But you asked a specific question—what do I have to offer? I have suggestions that will increase your powder's quality, and your company's profitability. My suggestions originate from several years with Ordnance, exploring operations such as yours."

"Ah, the famous Confederate powder. Bat guano and horse urine. You did the best with what you had in hand, I suppose."

"I am intimately familiar with Northern works as well," Brown said. His forehead glistened with sweat.

Nicholas White bit his lip—an easy gesture, given his pronounced front teeth. "Gentlemen?" He stood as if to leave. "Please excuse my absence. Allow me—"

"Sit down," Newhall ordered. He turned back to his applicant. "You propose to revamp my operation, is that it?"

"More than that, sir," Decker said. "I have a new product in mind." Newhall sat back, his mouth open and wet. "I *must* hear this."

Brown closed his eyes as he began again, picturing a scene in his mind. "I fought at Spotsylvania. Both armies battled over a short stretch of parapet for sixteen hours. Thousands upon thousands of rounds fired. Barrels fouled, and muskets became nothing more than lances, worthless in the rain." He took another breath, opening his eyes again. "The problem of barrel residue will become worse and worse, with the advent of the Henry repeating rifle and the Sharps breechloader. Rifle design has moved ahead of available powder products—"

"I certainly hope you aren't going to tell me about guncotton. It's much too volatile for use with firearms."

Brown was silent again, this time for an uncomfortable length of time. He sat forward. His blond hair, run through with hints of gray, slipped down over his eyes, masking them. "Not guncotton," he said at last. "An incremental improvement. I've worked out much of the process. As your employee, any formula I develop would become yours, of course. My powder will be less volatile, with less residue. Lighter. Forty dead men becomes sixty."

Newhall squinted. "Forty dead men?"

Nicholas White cleared his throat. "Soldier slang for a box of cartridges. Lighter loads mean more shots for the same grain weight."

"Soldier slang." Newhall repeated the phrase as if touching spoiled meat to his lips. He stood up and walked to the bookcase just beyond the fireplace. He pivoted on his heels, pointing to the books at his fingertip. "Do you see these references, Mr. Brown? These are the finest books ever written on the subject of black powder—"

"Black powder will be outmoded within five years. Perhaps you'll be selling my powder. Perhaps the Hazard Powder Company."

Newhall snorted, shaking his head. He waggled a fat finger at Brown, his merry voice dripping with undisguised condescension. "Do you know why I agreed to this interview? I asked after you, of course. The famous *Courthouse Reaper*. Killed a division of Union soldiers with a pocketknife and a soup ladle. I was *curious*. I wanted to measure the extent of arrogance necessary to lead rebel scum like you to imagine that you could secure a position with my company. In Boston of all places!"

Decker Brown stood, his lips pressed into a thin line, and began to make his way across the office carpet.

"Yes, Mr. Brown, take your withered rebel bones out of my office. And—"

Quick as a breath, Brown slapped his cane against the tabletop, the sound like the crack of a rifle. Brown pointed the cane at Newhall, who backed up a step, hands upraised. "What is this?" he demanded.

"Hire me or not—that's your prerogative. And your loss since you've chosen the latter. But don't think you can insult me again without cost." The tip of the cane, pointed at Newhall's face, did not waver.

"Come now, gentlemen," White said, rising again from his chair.

Brown pivoted to face him. "I don't know about *you*. But Mr. Newhall is no gentleman." He lowered the cane and began moving across the carpet again, slower now, head held high, like a buck crossing the road in front of a wagon.

When he was gone, Newhall's habitual scowl had returned. "Can you believe it? I should call the authorities and have the man arrested. Why, he threatened me! What sort of interview is that, to threaten a man?" He wandered back to his table and took a sip from his water glass. His hand shook. "Clearly, the poor fellow is unbalanced." He paused, as if considering his words. "Unbalanced. To be expected from a man missing some of his limbs, I suppose." The smirk returned.

White turned away.

"Tell me then. What was your assessment of the interview? I wish to gauge your reaction. You will be supervising my employees, after all."

"I don't believe it matters. He won't be working here," White said. *Neither will I,* he added silently.

• • •

Because he was in Boston, Decker decided to visit his uncle. Despite his dwindling resources, he hired a carriage and made the trip up Beacon Hill. The weather was pleasantly warm, and he closed his eyes, concentrating on the sensation of fresh air on his face.

While soldiering for the Union, he'd kept his pay without spending more than was absolutely necessary. Once in Washington, he'd banked the money with a mind to eventually take the nest egg south to Richmond. Now, with his future uncertain, he'd invested the funds in travel, looking for employment. His savings dwindled. The Oriental Powder Company and the Hazard Powder Company had rejected him. Paquin Powder would not even respond to his inquiries for an interview. Only Laflin's Mill had shown him any courtesy, which came in the form of a polite rejection. He had gunpowder samples for a serious prospect, but no one seemed interested.

Why gunpowder? Had he not seen the consequences of that substance? The answer was simple. No one would hire half a man for a man's wages, not without good reason. The war had given him a level of expertise that might help him overcome his physical shortcomings. Though nightmares wrecked his slumber, dreams of war were not his only tormentor. He also dreamed of having to beg with a bowl.

The carriage rolled over cobblestone streets, along brick sidewalks that fronted the finer houses on the hill. Nearing his uncle's home, he began to feel uneasy. Oskar would not recognize him. Decker hardly recognized himself. He hoped Oskar would offer him the same gruff familiarity he had in the past. The last two years had taught him to expect otherwise.

Arriving at the address he'd given the driver, the carriage stopped. Decker pulled himself out and, leaning back against the carriage, brushed the front of his brown suit. After checking to see that the empty sleeve was properly pinned, he approached the entrance.

He rapped at the door with the head of his cane, tilting his body slightly to the side to facilitate his balance. The door swung open, and a man stepped forward. Bald, blinking, and peering into the street, he seemed like a mole emerging from a tunnel. "Yes?"

"I'm looking for Oskar Brown."

The man shook his head. "Not here."

He started to close the door, but Decker stuck his cane in the jamb. "This is his house, is it not?"

"Was. It's mine now. Been that way for a year. Who are you?"

"Decker Brown. I'm Oskar's nephew."

"Ahhh," the man said. "Well then, you should know your uncle died a year ago. The house is mine now."

Decker pivoted and walked back to the carriage. The man behind him kept talking, but the flow of words was drowned by the pounding inside Decker's head. *All dead. They're all dead. The war killed them all.*

"Where shall I take you?" the carriage driver asked.

"To the boardinghouse," Decker said. Slumping back against the padded seat, he closed his eyes, suffering a carriage ride on cobblestones. *Funny. Coming here, I hardly noticed the road. Now, every bump is a bruise.* The air seemed hotter, and the buildings crowded the streets, pinning him in.

• • •

His accommodations at the boardinghouse were affordable, thus cold and shabby. He had a small room, precise dining hours, and no one troubled him, nor did they engage in any fashion, as if he did not exist. He amused himself by speculating that he'd discovered the secret to invisibility. Wherever he went, people looked the other direction. He might become, should he care to, the greatest thief in all the world.

Lying on his cot, his leg began to cramp. Both limb stumps burned — the doctors called the malady *causalgia*. The hollow-Y peg leg hurt. More naturalistic prosthetics were expensive. Much of the time, he went without, relying on the cane instead. At the end of a strenuous day, the demands of his unusual gait left him tired and sore. He carried a bottle of laudanum in his duffle for nights when the pain of ghost limbs became too much. Most nights, he drank rye whiskey.

Rather than think about the unrelenting bad news, he lay on his cot, imagining a sky full of stars. His moon was full and pocked with craters. Meteors whizzed by, sounding like rockets firing. Earth was a blue disc growing smaller in the sky, sliding away like the pain in his leg.

A knock at the door awakened him.

He struggled up and, taking his cane from the side of the little nightstand, hobbled over to the door, calling "Yes? What do you want?" in a raw voice. He'd been asleep. Flying, he suspected. Sleep was a precious commodity, and probably would be for the remainder of his life. Thu, the interruption of sleep was a crime.

He opened the door, revealing a short, portly man, hand extended in greeting. Decker sighed and nodded down at his good arm. "The arm is presently engaged, sir. What do you want?"

"To whom do I have the pleasure of speaking?" the man asked.

"Decker Brown. And you?"

"Wilson Bennington, attorney-at-law."

Decker frowned. Had someone from the War Department traced him here? Was he to be arrested for desertion? No, they'd have sent soldiers, not a fat little attorney.

"May I come in?"

Decker shook his head to wake himself, and then pointed the cane. "I've only one chair, sir, but you are welcome to it."

Bennington waddled into the room, carrying a leather bag under his arm. He sat down, removed his glasses, and began cleaning them. "One moment, please," he said, focused on the lenses.

"I am at your disposal," Decker said, hobbling back to his cot.

"I'm quite glad to have found you," Bennington said. "One really had no idea where to look, or if you were even alive, for that matter." He returned the glasses to his face and gave Decker a thorough glance. "You gave much to the war, sir."

"Have you business to discuss with me?"

"Of course." He propped the leather case on his ample lap and began sorting papers. Glancing up, he asked, "Can you provide me with some proof of your identity?"

"Of course," Decker said. He stood and hopped over to his duffle, retrieving papers pertaining to his bank account in Washington.

"Very difficult getting from one place to another, isn't it? I suppose I should have offered to get your bag for you."

"Not at all," Decker said. "Now, as to the nature of your business?"

Bennington repositioned his glasses on his nose and studied Decker's papers. "Yes, you seem to be who you are."

"I'm glad of that."

"Yes, well." Bennington reached a hand into his case and paused. "You visited your uncle's old residence today, I believe."

"Yes, I did," Decker said, surprised.

"The gentleman who now owns your uncle's house was kind enough to let me know of your visit. And a few inquiries led me to you. Mystery solved." He removed a small stack of papers from the case. "Your uncle left everything to you, sir."

Decker stared.

"He was a man of means. Prior to his death, he sold his business. The dissolution of his house and personal belongings added to an already tidy sum. His will named you as his sole heir." He extracted a check, clipped to one of the papers. "If you would be so good as to sign these papers, we can conclude our business." He held out the check.

Decker sat at the edge of the bed, not moving. "Oh, yes, of course," Bennington said, blushing. He pulled himself from the chair, crossed the room, and handed his pile of papers to Decker. "The matron of the house has agreed to witness your signature, should you be agreeable."

"Of course," Decker said.

"I will be back in a moment, then. Don't worry, I've brought an ink pen."

Decker sat on the bed, staring at the papers. Curiosity having gotten the better of him, he turned the check over and looked at the number. Then he read the papers, one by one. When Bennington returned to the room, the matron in tow, Decker commenced to the necessary signatures. The matron, a woman in her later years, wiped her hands on her tomato-stained apron repeatedly before adding her delicate signature.

"Very good," Bennington said at last. "Congratulations, sir."

"Have your services been compensated?" Decker asked, his voice flat.

"Yes, my efforts were more than adequately rewarded. Your uncle was a generous man."

"You knew him, then?"

Bennington turned, as if to make certain the matron had returned to her kitchen work. "Your uncle and I shared an occasional distilled beverage. On such occasions, I found him to be an interesting fellow. An immigrant who made good on the American dream, sir. Turned his back on his family in the old country and made his way here."

"I am ashamed to admit I don't know much about Oskar's early years."

"The usual tale. The family wanted him to join his father and uncle in pursuing a military career, but he loathed the idea.

Instead, he and his brother came here to pursue their own versions of happiness. His pursuit was quite successful, and it yielded a tidy sum. May he rest in peace." Bennington closed the flap on his leather case. "And now, I must be off to attend to other obligations. Have you any questions?"

"No." Decker shook his head.

"Have a good life, Mr. Brown. Your uncle thought very highly of you. Said so, often. Though the money is no compensation for your losses . . ." He paused, blushing. "I believe that money makes everything easier, sir. And you have earned some measure of ease."

CHAPTER TWENTY-THREE

Boston, Massachusetts
June 1867

"Perfect partners don't exist. Perfect conditions exist for a limited time in which partnerships express themselves best."
~Wayne Rooney

The knock at the door was no less irritating than previous interruptions. Boardinghouse guests and a series of salesmen had been at Decker's door for days—ever since he'd deposited the check. His patience for fawning conversation had worn thin. *The Courthouse Reaper! You are notorious here in Boston, sir! And now, you are a person of means, is that not so?* When polite excuses failed, Decker feigned illness to be left alone.

This time, he opened the door to the house matron. She stood, hands together in front of her apron, fingers scrabbling over each other. "Sir?" she asked.

"You knocked on *my* door, Madam. Do you have business with me?"

"Yes, sir. Yes, I did. I do." She took a deep breath. "You were screaming again, sir. Frightens the others, it does."

"Sorry. Every bit as sorry as the last time."

The woman made no move to depart. She bit her lower lip. "Is there more?"

"It must stop, sir. You didn't use to scream. You were so quiet when you first got here. But something's changed. For the last few days, you've been . . . wild."

Decker took a deep breath. He stood on one leg, without his cane, gripping the doorjamb for balance. "Madam? Observe the room I've rented here." He glanced back at his cot and nightstand. "Threadbare, Madam. The very definition of threadbare. The nap of the cot is worn, so to speak. Indeed, I am unable to nap on it."

"You're drinking, I see." The matron's lips tightened. Her gaze locked on the half-empty bottle on Decker's nightstand.

"No, Madam. I was sleeping. But you've spied the bottle that fueled my previous endeavors — sharp eye. May I pour you a glass? No? The other patrons of your house certainly wouldn't turn down my offer. And *that*, Madam, is why I paid a week's room and board in advance. Establishments of this sort must be tolerant in lieu of amenities. Tolerant of alcohol. Tolerant of screaming." He leaned forward. "And tolerant of violent fits."

Lower lip trembling, the matron scurried off down the hall. Decker slammed the door closed and hopped back to his cot. *Idiot. Now you'll have to find another room. You'll have to move all of your things.*

Another knock at the door startled him. *Evicted so soon? Damnation!*

This time, the visitor seemed familiar, if only by virtue of his prominent front teeth. He stood, top hat in hand, smiling like a donkey.

"Yes?" His impending eviction apparently postponed, Decker's voice regained its edge. "What do you want?"

"I want to offer my services. May I come in?"

"No, you may not."

The visitor looked past Decker's shoulder. "I see a bottle in need of emptying. Perhaps you'll give a parched stranger a drink, and in the course of time, I'll either convince you of my sincerity, or you'll throw me out into the hall."

Decker stared at him for a long time. His squint, seemingly frozen, opened up, and he hopped back a step, nodding in the direction of the table. "I have but one chair, sir. We can share the bottle, but not the cot. I have a reputation to uphold."

"I've heard about your reputation," the visitor said. "You are a formidable man. I'm Nicholas White. We met once before. I was in the office when you applied to the Oriental Powder—"

"I thought so!" Decker said, sitting back on the cot. "I'd recognize those teeth of yours anywhere."

White frowned. "Yes, an unfortunate set. Still, when I see men without any teeth at all, I'm grateful."

"Very commendable," Decker said. "You may use the glass. When you're done, pass me the bottle."

White dragged the wooden chair closer to the nightstand, poured himself a tiny shot, and passed the whiskey. "You're a fine host."

Decker took a swallow directly from the bottle. Wincing, he tucked the bottle between his leg and thigh stump, wiped his mouth with his sleeve, and let out a sigh. "Well then, we've made small talk. What's your pitch? Did Newhall send you begging for my services? Did he have a change of heart?"

"No, regrettably for *him*."

"How so?"

"Because I think he made a mistake about you."

Decker took another drink.

"Rebel amputees don't apply to Union powder manufacturers to run a cheat." White tilted his head slightly to the side, a sly smile on his face, his gaze never straying from Decker. "You're not out to hornswoggle anyone."

Decker snorted.

"But why offer your services to those hoity-toity bastards? Why not start your own company?"

"That takes money."

"And you, sir, have money."

Decker scowled.

"My friends in the banking game tell me you recently deposited a healthy sum—"

"Mystery solved," Decker said, slapping his leg. "All right, you've had your drink. You can go."

"You haven't heard my proposition—"

"Here's *my* proposition," Decker said. "Get out of here now, or I'll beat you out of here with my cane."

White shifted the chair to face Decker directly. Leaning forward, he said, "Let me counter that offer. Give me two minutes, and if you are unmoved after hearing me out, I'll offer my back to your cane unhindered."

Decker gave a surprised laugh and took another swig from the bottle. He shook his head and waved for White to continue. "You are an entertainer, sir."

"Start your own company," White said, plunging ahead. "I know buildings in Boston that can be had for a song. We open shop, produce our formula, and bank our profits. Live like kings."

"You are curiously uninformed. Have you never seen a full-scale powder operation? The Oriental Powder Company, for one, has buildings on both sides of the Presumpscot, spread out over a mile of riverfront. My little inheritance can't purchase a charcoal house, wheel mills, press mills, kernelling mills—"

"It doesn't need to." White's eyes seemed to dance. He took a sip of whiskey and put the glass back on the nightstand. "You need one building, along with the necessities for a workshop."

"Again, you are an idiot. The various steps in gunpowder manufacture must be kept separate to avoid chain explosions."

"True. But we're not going to *manufacture* powder. We're going to perfect our process for smokeless powder and sell it to an established company."

Someone in the room next door thumped against the wall. "*Our* process?" Decker asked.

"Our process, perfected in *our* warehouse, funded by *our* money."

Decker glanced at White's top hat, sitting on the bed, and then down at White's feet. "Your duds are fine enough, but your shoes give you away, sir. You are either without means, or you perform honest, physical labor on a daily basis. I'll wager it's the former. I don't believe you have any money."

"I was referring to your money, sir. As partners, it will be *our* money." The thump from next door came again, louder this time.

White stared at the wall. "Your accommodations are surprising. I would have thought a man of your recently acquired wealth would have a nicer room."

Decker tapped the bottle. "I'll celebrate my inheritance in my own way. Let us return to the topic at hand. I will fund this project in order to develop my own process. What resources do *you* bring to the table?"

White smiled, presenting all his teeth at once. "Having perfected your process, how do you propose to sell it?"

Decker shrugged. "I had no intentions of starting a business, so it won't surprise you that I cannot answer your question."

White downed the last of his whiskey. "My mother married into the Paquin family, a happy circumstance that led me to an executive position with the company. I spent the duration of the war dealing with Washington. I have contacts, sir." He leaned closer. "I know the boss dogs."

"So *that's* your proposal," Decker said. He sat back, nearly spilling the bottle, snatching it from his lap at the last moment. He glanced again at White's shoes. "Your contacts have not yielded you any riches so far."

White's smile disappeared, and his face seemed to darken. He sat silent, glancing about the room, as if considering his next words. When he spoke again, his voice was a whisper. "Despite my best efforts, I was not appreciated by the Paquin family. I decided to pursue other employment."

"The Oriental."

"Yes."

"And they didn't want you either?"

White shook his head. "The job was mine."

"What are you doing here, then?"

"I would not work for that man." No longer the jovial fellow, White's voice took on a raw edge. "I left immediately after your interview."

Decker handed over the bottle. *I've had enough whiskey. My senses must be dulled . . . I believe this man.* He cleared his throat. "Go away now. I need to study on your idea. Come back tomorrow."

White stood, placing his top hat on his head, giving the brim a tap. "As you wish, *partner.*" He stood, walked to the door, and left without another word.

• • •

When White returned the following day, Decker was not alone. Wilson Bennington, attorney-at- law, sat on Decker's cot, taking up more than two-thirds of it with his ample bulk. In the day that had passed, Decker had acquired an additional wooden chair, and though the room was crowded, all three men could sit.

"The particulars of the agreement—" Bennington began.

White stopped him. "What agreement are you referring to?" he asked.

Decker sniffed. "It seemed to me that if we're to go into business together, we should put certain details in writing."

"So, you hired a lawyer?"

Decker smiled. "It seemed like a prudent use of *our* money. Don't you agree?"

Bennington coughed. The man was a smoker—the stench of tobacco clung to his vest. He rubbed his glasses on his vest and lifted a handful of papers. "The agreement is a standard business arrangement, but Mr. Brown wishes you to be aware of several important particulars."

White sat back, lips pursed in surprise.

Bennington glanced up. "No objections? I'll proceed then. First, the location of the business."

"Boston," White said.

"Richmond. Mr. Brown wishes to build a warehouse in Richmond."

Decker cleared his throat. "The war turned Richmond into a crater. If I'm going to put money into a business, I'll do it at home. Are you unwilling to relocate, sir?"

"But I've connections in Boston, and—"

"Your part of our project will involve travel either way. Are you in agreement?" Decker's voice had a hard edge, as if the question were a mere formality.

White frowned. "What on earth makes you think the First Military District will allow a powder company run by a Confederate war hero in Richmond?"

"You said you have contacts. Put them to use."

When White did not answer, Decker pointed to Bennington, who continued. "Secondly, your stake in the company being limited, you will own half of the proceeds of any process sold. In addition, you will receive half of any proceeds derived from consultations—"

"What consultations?"

Decker leaned forward, one hand pressed to his one knee. "Have you noticed, sir, that for most companies, powder is powder? You are familiar with Paquin products. You have military grade powder, which the company sold, admirably I might add, for just over cost to the government. Then, there's the coarser grind, used for blasting. Blasting powder is the most lucrative product for Paquin. The Oriental's products differ only in minutiae." Decker sat back again, shifting in his chair, struggling for a comfortable position. "During the war, I spoke with a rocket manufacturer. I asked him the formula for his rocket propellant. He used ordinary black powder. He said something foolish like, *if it's good enough for the troops, it's good enough for me.* The man was an idiot. Different applications demand different chemisms."

"Chemisms?"

"For example," Decker continued, "the amount of sulphur either speeds or retards oxidation."

"Consultations? You mentioned consultations."

Decker nodded. "All right, then. I will be brief. The war is long over, and the Union has warehouses full of powder. If we're going into business, we might well need to sell more than one product. Something that differs from what waits in surplus. Illuminations manufacturers may appreciate a mixture designed specifically for rockets. And certain European countries don't face the same prospects for peace that we do. Different formulations may benefit specific weapons."

White turned to Bennington, who sat waiting, one hand to his spectacles. "However," Bennington continued, "if the business fails to attract customers, you will not share in any of the hard assets."

White turned back to Decker, who smiled. "If your contacts don't pan out, you won't make a nickel."

"How am I to live, then?"

"I will pay you a small salary to cover expenses."

White shook his head. "This isn't what I envisioned at all."

"I imagine not," Decker said. "Mr. Bennington?"

Bennington scratched his jowls and said, "Finally, the business shall be called the *Brown and White Powder Company.*"

"No," White said. *"White and Brown.* If I am to perform the miracles you've laid out for me, I must be the face of the company. My contacts in Washington may help me establish ourselves in occupied Richmond. *White and Brown* it is, though the *Nicholas White Powder Company* would be better still."

"Better, perhaps, but inaccurate." Decker said. "You have my proposal. Will you sign?"

"Perhaps I might read the document first," White said.

"I encourage you to do so," Decker said, *"partner."*

Chapter Twenty-Four

Richmond, Virginia
August 1867

"Unfortunately, there was one thing that the white South feared more than Negro dishonesty, ignorance, and incompetency, and that was Negro honesty, knowledge, and efficiency."
~W.E.B. Du Bois

The pile of stone and brick was smaller than Decker expected. Bits of charred wood littered the area. Any surviving household items had been carted off. Bull thistle shoved its leaves and spines through the debris. The remnants of a fence, four feet long, stood untouched, white paint showing through the smoke-stained slats. Decker perched on one leg, hand on his cane. The bustle of city business lay to the north. Here, in the rubble of what had been his home, the only sounds were the buzz of flies and the occasional snort from the horse behind him.

"This is a poor place to build a warehouse," White called from the driver's seat of the carriage.

Decker ignored him. *Don't dwell on this,* he thought. *That's where the danger lies.* Recovering from his wounds, he'd discovered that he had the energy for only one path. He could regret his losses and try to wish away what had happened, or he could practice the tasks he needed to survive. *He could not do both*. The memory of happier times was an insidious foe, clothed in sepia and lilac. In Richmond, a city of memories, he would need to guard his thoughts and banish his emotions.

"I do have another warehouse location for you to consider," White called. "There are certain advantages. A building, for example."

Decker pivoted and made his way back to the carriage. He placed the cane on the carriage floor, turned, and sat down on the running board. Raising his knee, he tucked his heel under his thigh. Gripping the rail, he launched himself onto the seat.

"You're very quiet today."

Decker didn't answer.

"I said, you're very —"

"I heard you."

"You didn't answer."

Decker sighed, sitting back, his eyes closed. "I was affirming your observation."

The carriage headed west. "The warehouse is out of the way, and there's plenty of space. It's a bit cluttered, but we can clear it out easily enough." He turned and frowned. "Shall I credit your mood to this morning's news?"

Decker had asked White to use his connections to inquire after a Union soldier — Mike Kelly. White's inquiries yielded a telegram from the War Department. Lieutenant Michael Kelly of Buda, Illinois had died in the Battle of Franklin near the end of the war. White ventured that the name was common enough. Perhaps the Kelly that Decker sought was still alive. "Buda is too small to have two Mike Kellys," Decker said.

"Who was this Kelly?"

"He was a friend. That's all."

"How did you become friends with a Yankee lieutenant?" White asked.

"We were tent mates."

"Pardon?" White shook his head. "I don't understand."

"I spent the first half of the war fighting for the Union," Decker said. "After Gettysburg, it seemed clear the Confederacy would lose, so I switched sides."

"You're jesting, sir." White took his eyes from the road, trusting the horse to stay the course. "Your sense of humor is unusual—"

"I'm not joking," Decker said, his eyes still closed. "After Pittsburg Landing, I worked for the War Department. They had me chasing down proposals for various inventions, from rockets to new powder formulations. I worked under Admiral Dahlgren—"

"You're *serious*."

Decker popped open one glaring eye.

White drove south and west, while Decker stared at the passing piles of rubble and the skeletons of burned buildings Along the way, they encountered other wagons and carriages. One warehouse was already under renovation. A man in a felt jacket and top hat stood directing his workers. As they passed, the man took off his hat, revealing carefully shaped hair. He ran a finger under the scarf around his neck. "Damned rebels don't want to work," the man in the felt jacket said. "I'm half-tempted to bring a wagon full of Irish niggers down here to do the job." The man next to him nodded.

Rolling ahead, White shook his head. "That reminds me. We need to hire some men. I may have understated the amount of cleanup necessary." When Decker didn't answer, White bit his lip. "Tell me. How is it you fought for both sides? Assuming you did, that is."

Decker sighed. "Can we talk about something else? Assuming we must talk, that is."

"You're telling me you're a deserter from the Union army. Is that right? You worked for the War Department? Is that why I had to trace your friend for you, rather than you doing it yourself?" White's eyes were wide, and his mouth hung open.

"You understand what this means, don't you? The War Department won't do business with a deserter. They'll arrest you. They'll hang you—"

"They won't *know* me. My name is common. Like Kelly. And I look different than I did in a Yankee uniform." He shook his head, frowning. "Besides, there were plenty of deserters on both sides. No one is looking for me. *No one cares.*"

They drove on in silence. Clouds to the west covered the sun for a moment, and the air felt cooler. White nodded and looked away. After a few minutes, he said, "You're right. Besides, you're the *Courthouse Reaper*. That's how everyone knows you. Not by your name. By your reputation."

"I suppose."

"We're close now," White said, steering the carriage around a pile of rocks in the middle of the road. "If you wouldn't mind satisfying my curiosity, what exactly were you thinking when you decided to fight for both sides?"

"You are a bother."

"Please."

Decker scowled. He debated striking White with his cane but decided against it. "As a citizen of the Republic, I had a duty to defend the Union. As a citizen of Virginia, I had a duty to defend my home. I did my duty, both ways."

"You are crazy, sir."

"I've begun to suspect as much."

White's face sank into contemplation, his lips curling around two protruding front teeth. "When was the last time you were in Richmond, then?"

"Haven't been home since before the war."

White seemed incredulous, his eyes wide with surprise. "Why, this must be an ordeal for you."

Decker closed his eyes. He would not let his mind linger on the question.

"Do you have family here?" Silence. "I imagine some of your friends died in the war. Had any of the local women captured your heart?"

"Shut up," Decker said. His stomach clenched.

At last, White stopped the carriage in front of a small warehouse. The two-story, brick building was rectangular, with a sloped, shingled roof and a chimney at the west end. White hopped down and waited for Decker to follow.

The interior of the building was a wreck. The second story had torn loose, and lay in piles on the warehouse floor, leaving a rim of jagged wood beams around the inside perimeter of the building. "There's a hole in the roof," Decker said, looking up.

"I wonder if a shell hit," White said. "Perhaps that's why the building is such a bargain." He grinned. "Well, partner? What do you think? The price is right."

To be productive? To do meaningful work? Any price would be right. He took a deep breath. Practical considerations were still in order. "Will you get a finder's fee for the building?"

White stood quite still, staring at Decker. Then, the hint of a smile playing out beneath his teeth, he nodded. "Yes, I will."

Decker nodded. "Good. Having dipped your toes in the waters of honesty, tell me . . . is the building's price a bargain, or am I being taken?"

"Neither one. The price is fair. And the location fits your needs."

"All right, then. Make the arrangements."

• • •

Charles Smith spent the evening talking to his wife, Maddie. Hearing someone was opening up a warehouse on the west side, Maddie insisted he apply for a job. Charles had finished work on a building in Jackson Ward, and the influx of free Black craftsmen willing to work for low wages made it difficult to secure a new position. "You'll find something," she told him. "You have to." He lay face down on their makeshift bed, while she traced the striations on his back, as if sketching the roads of an exotic map with her finger. Her touch convinced him. "Something good will happen, Charles. Promise me you'll try."

True to his word, Charles arrived early on the following day, only to be joined by a yard full of ex-Confederate soldiers. He almost left, but something about the sullen glares cast his way made him want to stay, danger be damned. Besides, the warehouse was a calamity. Any employment would surely involve cleanup, and those white boys wouldn't want to haul rubble. It would take two men a long three months or more to clear the place. *By then, the baby will be born.*

Charles tried to hide himself in a corner of the old building, tucking his huge, calloused hands under his armpits. He watched the two owners—a cripple and a man with bad teeth—talk to the other applicants. The rebels were a thin, pale lot. Charles was thin, too, almost too thin at first glance, but he'd spent the war working in the flour mill, and he could outwork most anyone, given a reason.

And Maddie was with child—all the reason a man could need.

If he waited another few weeks, there would be field work, but no food at home before then. *I'll bet I'm wasting my time with this ol' white cripple,* he thought. *But I promised Maddie.*

The white man with the bad teeth called on the others first, and Charles nearly gave up the wait as pointless when the one-armed, one-legged white man pointed at him with his cane. Charles took a deep breath and walked across the room, careful not to trip on debris.

"My name is Charles Smith," he said, approaching the man's stool.

"Decker Brown."

"Uh-huh." Charles took off his felt hat and mopped his forehead with the back of his arm. "Well, Mr. Brown, is you still hiring?"

Brown looked up, surprised. "Why would I call you over if I wasn't?"

Charles considered the question. His gaze narrowed, and his jaw shut tight. If Mr. Brown had a good pair of ears, he'd hear teeth grinding.

Brown seemed to study Charles—first his shoes, and then his hands. "I'm looking for someone who knows how to work."

"I'm your man, then. I work *hard*—"

"I have more in mind for the job," Brown said. Beyond the fact that he was missing body parts, something about the man was not right. His eyes looked red, like he hadn't slept in a week.

"What else you lookin' for?"

Brown pointed up without breaking his gaze. "The second-floor caved in. I need the mess carted out, and the floor cleaned up. I will be purchasing machinery. I'll need it moved in and positioned—"

"I can do all of that."

"Not alone, you can't. I'm hiring a foreman. I want someone who can hire and direct other men." He squinted at Charles. "Part-time workers. Can't promise a steady job. I need someone who can round up good men and get things done."

"Then I'm your man," Charles said. He considered a lie and went ahead with it. "I was an overseer during the war. Nobody dared put in a half day's work when I was around."

Brown seemed exasperated, growling and shaking his head. "I don't need a whip hand. I want someone who's going to organize help and get specific jobs done. Someone who knows the right people to hire for two, maybe three days at a time. I don't need an *overseer*." He waved his one hand in dismissal.

Charles clutched his hat. *This crazy white fool might hire me!* He mustered his best smile. His teeth were good—not like what was in the other white fellah's mouth. "Wait," he said.

Brown looked up again, a frown on his round face. "What?"

Charles rolled his shoulders and eyes in a display of sheepish regret. When he spoke, he drawled, a marked difference from his earlier tone. "Ah lied a minute ago. Ah was *never* an overseer."

"Why'd you lie?"

"I needs the job, suh."

"You lie on a regular basis?" Brown's face was blank as a flagstone.

Charles tried not to be angry, but the crippled white fool was to blame. He could feel his teeth clamp tight. His forehead throbbed.

Brown pointed at him. "*There.*"

"There, what?"

"That face of yours. The face of a man with no time for nonsense." He nodded in the direction of the ex-soldiers who stood in a corner of the warehouse, glaring. "See those men? They came *expecting* a job. I'm looking for *workers*. It's not the same thing."

Charles held his breath.

"I give you that one lie," Brown said, turning back to a sheet of paper in his hands. "Know what happens if you lie again?"

"I guess so."

Brown shifted in his chair as if he couldn't get comfortable. "If you come in late and say you're sick, and I smell liquor on your breath, I'll fire you. I send you with money to buy supplies and you come back with a story about lost money, I'll fire you. You tell me your friend is a good worker and all he does is talk the day away? I'll fire you."

"You mean I have the job?"

"You do. Tomorrow. Be here before the sun."

Charles twisted the hat in his hand. "What's the pay?" Brown looked up, a sharp expression on his face. "My wife will want to know . . ." His voice trailed off.

"You don't want to know? Your wife is the curious one?"

Charles bit his lip.

"Before I answer, there's something *I* want to know. And don't lie to me. Can you drive a carriage?"

Charles nodded, perplexed. "Yes suh."

"Good," Brown said, pointing at his partner. "That man talks too damned much. I'll give you a try." He turned back to Charles. "And don't call me 'sir.' My name is Brown. That all right with you, Smith?"

Charles nodded, glancing back at the white men watching them. *This cripple has lost his damned mind.*

• • •

Decker watched as White fiddled with his drink without managing to take a swallow. The day's work well finished by early afternoon, they sat in the first open tavern they'd encountered, drinking at a table long enough to seat a dozen men. The stone walls were adorned with copper pans and woodcuts of pastoral scenes. The smell of baked bread filled the room. "Pleasant little tavern," White said. The barkeep, a paunchy man with dark patches in the underarms of his shirt, stood against the far wall, dusting a stack of glasses. White pointed. "That man came from the North."

"What makes you think so?"

"Richmond natives are all thin." White called out, "Sir? Indulge my curiosity. Where do you call home?"

"Philadelphia."

White gave Decker a triumphant smile. He lifted his glass, reconsidered, and set it back down. "I've been thinking about

what you said. About fighting for both sides. You said you were
attending to duty."

Decker nodded.

"How could you have a duty to both sides?"

"I thought it was possible." Decker took a swallow from his
glass. "Since then, I've had time—more than enough time—to
reconsider." He finished his drink and winced. "A weak lot,
that bunch this morning. The first man applying for the job told
me I ought to send the Negro away." He snorted as if nothing
else needed to be said. "The second one," Decker continued,
"was home guard. Spent the whole war stealing people's
property and shooting deserters. You can understand why I
didn't hire *him*." He paused to empty his glass. "The third one
started off shaking my hand. Softest skin I ever felt." He
frowned his disdain. "My uncle had great success hiring free
Negroes. That Smith has some horse sense, I think. The rest of
them weren't worth a goober."

White pushed his glass to the left, then pushed it back to the
right.

"Are you going to drink that whiskey or dance with it?"

White ignored him. "Every one of those men has already
told five friends that you hired a Black man over a white
Southerner. You made a mistake."

Decker snatched White's drink and downed it. "I'll run the
damned business. You worry about selling the process. Are we
agreed?"

"It's not so easy. You are required to fit in here. You need to
hobnob with government people—"

"I'm hobnobbing with you. That's as close as I plan to get."

"No, all you're doing is drinking," White said. "Which is
fine, as long as you're an agreeable drunk."

Decker stared and tilted his head. "What are you angling
at?"

White took a deep breath. "We've been invited to a ball."

"I'm not taking you to a ball."

"Then go alone. But you're going. We need to spread a little cheer and goodwill, especially after today. I'm *sure* you'll be fine on your own. You can introduce yourself to the officers of the military district —"

"All right, then," Decker said. "You can go along." He waved at the barkeep, trying to get his attention. Miraculously, the man managed to ignore him, despite the fact that aside from the partners, only two other men were drinking. Decker turned back to White, a grimace on his face. "I need another drink."

"Are you in pain?"

Decker bit his lip and nodded. "This has been a long day." White called out to the barkeep and pointed at Decker's glass.

"Thank you," Decker said. "Now, tell me again. Why do I have to go to a ball?"

"The locals need a glimpse of their war hero, and the provisional government needs assurances that you are harmless." Grinning, he added, "And since ladies will be present —"

"Stop smiling," Decker said. "You are ruining my whiskey."

CHAPTER TWENTY-FIVE

Richmond, Virginia
August 1867

*"No young lady should go to a ball, without the protection of a
married lady, or an elderly gentleman."*
~Florence Hartley, The Ladies' Book of Etiquette
and Manual of Politeness

Charles drove them to the ball in the carriage. Decker wanted
White to drive, but White insisted. "This is not business. This is
a social event. My realm, not yours. We need to attend as
partners with a driver."

Smith seemed to have no opinion either way, as he didn't
speak beyond asking for instructions.

When they arrived, Decker sent White ahead. "I have an
errand for Charles, and you need to scout our situation."

"Scout for what? What nonsense is this?"

Decker narrowed his gaze, frowning. "I have limitations, sir.
I need you to discover if I will be able to manage the walkways.
If there are stairs, note the railings. Now, if you please."

"As you wish," White said, a sulking expression on his face.

As soon as his partner was gone, Decker fished a piece of
folded paper from his pocket. "Smith?"

"Brown?"

"This is the drawing I mentioned. Take it to your woodworker. I will pay for materials, but I want him to see what I have in mind first."

Charles turned in the driver's seat and took the paper without comment. "You're certain that your man is right for the job?"

Charles ignored the question. "When it's done, should he bring the thing to the factory?"

"It's not a factory. And no, I'll want the finished product delivered to my residence. And Smith? Don't bother mentioning this to White."

Charles turned, suddenly interested. "What do I say if he asks me?"

"Why would he ask?" Decker felt his face flush hot, and he glared at his foreman.

"All right, all right. Just askin'."

"Mind your business and turn around. I'm getting out of this damned carriage." Decker maneuvered himself to the floor of the vehicle and slid to the ground. Once situated, he brushed off his clothes and reached back for his cane.

"Should I wait for you?" Charles asked.

"No. Take care of the errand." Without another word, Decker made his way into the building. White was nowhere in sight. *No matter,* he thought. *I'll find my way around well enough without him.*

His first few steps were painful. *I'll never get used to this peg leg.* Balanced on one leg, he tugged at the straps, trying to adjust the prosthesis. *If I'd had the sense to stay home, I'd have left this damned thing in the corner.*

The ball was held in one of the government buildings near the capitol. White met him in the hallway outside the main room. After fussing over Decker's clothing and making a nuisance of himself, White led the way into the main ballroom.

The wooden floor had been cleared, and new curtains hung in the tall windows along the south wall. Chairs lined the perimeter. At the far end, a dais had been erected with chairs for the guests of honor, including officers from the military district and officials from the city government. The officers were in uniform. The old guard—Southerners who'd fought and lost their war—were dressed in their Sunday best. Some of the faces were familiar—men who'd run the city before the war, and now sat shoulder to shoulder with their conquerors. At the other end of the room, an empty table awaited refreshments.

The late evening sun through the windows lit the room, though light from elaborate candle chandeliers overhead promised to finish the dance in the embrace of a soft glow. "This is all very fancy," Decker said, staring at the room's finery.

The curtains, in particular, caught Decker's eye. Three layers, including sub-curtains of sheer cotton, a middle set made of deep blue velvet, and a brightly colored tapestry on top. Each window ensemble was dressed across the top with pelmets and pulled into place with tasseled tiebacks. Balanced on one leg, he fingered the fabric. "These are quite nice, White," he said. "I didn't think anything so fine survived the war."

"I suppose they brought out their best for the ball. Besides, the war ended two years ago. The city is rebuilding."

Both young and old people filled the room. Women in long dresses glided across the floor. Men clustered together, talking and gesturing. At the entrance and near the dais, soldiers watched the crowd. An uncomfortable number of gazes followed Decker as he crossed the room. Some faces were curious, some respectful, while a few struck him as openly hostile. Decker recognized one of the applicants for his foreman job, leaning against a wall, arms folded to match his scowl.

White had insisted Decker replace his old brown suit, and Decker grudgingly agreed. He opted for a simple vest and jacket, though the gray outfit he first admired was passed over. "Looks too much like a rebel uniform, Brown. Use your head."

The advice proved sensible. Major General Schofield, the commander of the first military district, arrived with his staff. One shorter officer, a captain, spotted White and Brown lingering by the window and crossed the floor between dances to introduce himself.

"Gentlemen," he said with a curt bow. "Captain Thomas Wells, at your service." He eyed White for a moment. "Mr. White. I understand you've set up shop in the west end of the city."

White nodded. "Yes indeed, we have. Captain, let me introduce—"

"The *Courthouse Reaper*, I presume."

Decker sighed.

Captain Wells turned, facing Decker head-on, his body erect. "I served at Spotsylvania, sir. I understand you single-handedly killed a division or more of our men."

"You seem like a practical man, Captain. Stories are for children."

Wells frowned, deep furrows cutting across his forehead. An angry scar ran from his left ear, halfway to his chin. He had a diminutive build, but something in his stance and demeanor carried a warning. "Tell me. How is it that a Southern war hero is allowed to open a powder factory in occupied Richmond?"

Decker nodded in White's direction. "My partner is a magician."

"Hardly, sir," White said, stepping closer to Decker and grabbing his cane arm. "I served the War Department for Paquin Powder during the war. This is my company, really. Mr. Brown brings expertise in the field of research. And that, Captain, is the crux of the matter. We are not a manufacturing firm. We are researching products that will eventually be used—"

Captain Wells ignored White, addressing Decker directly. "Whatever arrangements you've made, I can certainly undo them. I don't want you supplying Southern sympathizers with weapons."

"Powder is readily available, sir. Even for Southerners."

"You aren't one of those ghosties riding around at night, terrorizing the darkies, are you?"

Decker snorted. "Riding is not a skill I've retained—"

"Because if I hear of a ghostie with one arm and one leg, I'll shut your factory down. Then, I'll show up with a rope, and I'll hang you myself."

Decker glanced at the dais, which was nearly filled with blue uniforms. Spotting one particularly portly major, he licked his lips and smiled. "Do you know how to spot a railroad brakeman who's been on the job for years?"

Wells didn't answer, a moment's confusion showing on his face.

"The experienced brakeman is the one with one or two fingers on each hand." Turning back, Decker stared at the scar on the captain's face. "Most of the men on that dais served behind a desk during the war. You and I are different."

"I have *nothing* in common with you," Captain Wells said, his face turning red.

"Experience, sir. We both survived the grinder. And while many of the men here tonight will prattle on about glory and such, we know better. Now, let me ask you a question. Do I really look dangerous to you?"

Wells frowned, his lower teeth showing. "You remind me of a cannonball with a faulty fuse. Harmless? Perhaps, but one does not get too close."

Decker laughed, despite himself. "You don't like me, Captain. It's a pity. I find much to admire in you."

From behind them, another voice joined the conversation. "Pardon me, Captain. I'd like to meet the two businessmen everyone is talking about." The voice was familiar. Decker pivoted in place.

Whit.

"Whitaker Hill, gentlemen. I'm with the Richmond city works." He smiled and bowed.

Decker stood silent. White offered a friendly hand, introducing himself. "And this is my partner—"

"The *Reaper*," Whit said. He stared into Decker's eyes, without any sign of recognition. "Hello, Whit." Decker's voice came out in a croak.

"Do I know you, sir?"

"Decker Brown."

Whit's face registered genuine shock. "Decker?" He stepped back. "I . . . I didn't recognize you."

Decker gave a single, slow nod. "I don't look the same."

"Of course not," Whit said. His voice regained its smooth composure. He tapped his arm stump with his good hand. "Few of us were untouched by the war. And yet, here we are." He glanced down at the wooden peg extending beneath Decker's pant leg. "So, *you* are the *Courthouse Reaper*?"

Captain Wells stepped away. White followed him, jabbering at his side as they crossed the floor.

"Well," Whit continued. "Since we are more than acquaintances, I will approach the subject at hand with a little more candor. I have nothing but respect for your service to the cause, sir. You are a hero. With that respect in mind, I ask you to reconsider your hiring decisions, as regards your new enterprise."

Decker stood silent.

"I'm speaking of your failure to hire a veteran of the cause for the position of foreman in your factory—"

"It's not a factory. And I'll hire whomever I please."

The band began to play, and the sounds of fiddle, banjo, guitar, and mandolin filled the room. Men hovering near their desired dance partners closed in on their targets. Bows and curtsies exchanged, couples moved to the center of the room, side-by-side in the open position, forming a large oval. The band's spirited rendition of *Hog-Eyed Man* put the room in motion. Whit turned to watch the dance, and Decker took the opportunity to hobble away.

Standing against the far wall, Decker searched the crowd, afraid of both whom he might see, and of whom he might *not* see. The dancers moved in a promenade, with the hops and slides prescribed by the dance master.

As Decker stared, an elderly gentleman approached, escorting a young woman. The man was a bulbous fellow sporting a top hat, walking with the aid of a cane. His cheeks hung from dark-ringed eyes. When he came close, Decker could smell whiskey on his breath. The woman, much younger than her escort, had a round, pretty face bracketed by blonde curls. Her small, red, upturned mouth seemed to Decker like a rosebud ready to bloom.

"Sir? My name is Alexandros Curtis. I would like to take this moment to introduce my daughter, Calista." The girl curtsied, her blue eyes glancing up at him through downy eyelashes.

Decker bowed. "You have a lovely name."

"It means *most beautiful*," Alexandros said, with a sonorous voice, worthy of a pulpit. "I understand you are recently returned to our fair city. We take this opportunity to greet you."

The song ended. Men escorted their partners to the chairs at the room's perimeter so pairings for the following dance could commence. "I noticed you have not entertained a single dance partner," Calista said. Her voice seemed shy and unchallenging, but her eyes held a hint of amusement.

"I lack the necessary equipment." He tapped his peg leg with his cane.

"Nonsense, sir," she said. "I've watched you move about the room with as much grace as any man here. You are very good with your cane." Alexandros started to speak, an apologetic expression on his face, but Calista silenced him with a glance. Turning back to Decker, she said, "I should like very much to dance with you."

The request was scandalous. Gentlemen did the asking, not young ladies. The rule was inviolate. Decker smiled. "If I were to dance, I believe I would dance with you." He had no love of convention. Convention was just another means of ordering people about.

Clearly, the girl shared his disdain for society's practices. She was delightful.

The music began again, a waltz this time. "I know this one," she said, her mouth drawn up in a pretty smile. "It's called the *Charming Waltz*. You must join me." On the floor behind her, another oval formed in open position. The song was a *redowa* waltz, a lively tune that allowed the dancers both spring steps and a sprightly pace.

"I'm afraid I'd be run over by the other dancers," Decker said.

"Then I shall dance with you right here, sir." Calista began to dance in front of him, not at his side — more scandalous still. Alexandros stepped away, giving them space, or perhaps trapping Decker with his daughter. Decker stared as the girl danced around him. Unable to think of what else he might do, he began to move his cane in time with the music, placing it to the left and then to the right. She responded to the movement with tiny leaps to the direction of the cane, as if their dance had been choreographed in advance. While most couples on the floor continued to move to the music, some peeled away and stood watching, so that by the end of the song, much of the room had focused on Decker and the girl. When the music stopped, there was a brief silence, followed by applause that began to build as the moments passed. Cheers came from some of the city officials on the dais, though the soldiers in uniform either clapped politely or not at all.

Calista's cheeks flushed red, and she smiled knowingly. "You are a success, sir." She curtsied. He bowed, and the applause redoubled, as if to say *yes, we have lost the great war, but we are undaunted.* Decker spotted Calista's father, seated at the edge of the room. He offered his arm to the girl. "Allow me to escort you to your seat. Your father is not far away, thankfully."

She put her hand on his elbow, moving with him as he used the cane to walk to her seat. He took time to glance at the crowd. A cluster of old women—the wives of the old guard—stood scowling. But the rest of the crowd continued to clap, smiles on their faces. Nearby, White stood nodding, a ridiculous grin pasted to his face, perhaps mirroring Decker's own involuntary smile. *There, Mr. White. I've done all you asked and more.*

Glancing toward the dais, he saw Whit—and his wife. He knew her at once, though her face was far thinner than he remembered, and older as well. She wore a dark green bustle gown that filled out her figure, perhaps hiding just how much weight she'd lost since he'd seen her last. She stood, both hands locked around Whit's elbow. Decker looked away, afraid that his face would give away the anguish he felt.

" —quite the sensation," Calista said.

"I'm sorry," Decker said. "The noise was a distraction."

"No matter, sir. You have given me a most wonderful moment. Thank you."

Look at this girl, he thought. *Don't look back.*

Calista leaned back in her chair, her chin raised and a smile on her rosebud lips. "Don't think for a moment I'm going to let you get away," she said.

CHAPTER TWENTY-SIX

Richmond, Virginia
September 1867

"War was easy. The hard part was cleaning up afterward."
~Evan Meekins, *The Black Banner*

When Paula arrived at his residence, there was no surprise. The visit was inevitable, like the change of seasons. Fall had arrived in Richmond, painting the maples and dogwoods with the colors of pumpkins, butter, and blood. Paula had arrived with a new carriage and driver. "Mrs. Hill," he said. "How nice of you to visit."

"May I come in?" she asked. He stood aside, door open, and waited for her to pass. She moved with the slow tread of a condemned prisoner — ironic, given the condition of his room, which more resembled a cell than a home. A cot, a wooden table, and a pair of chairs were the full extent of his furnishings.

"Please, take a seat. I recently added a second chair to my room, as my partner is fond of bothering me at home." He grabbed his correspondence with the Prussians from the table, setting the stack of papers on the floor. As soon as she was seated, Decker slid the remaining chair back a few feet and sat down some distance from the table. "I would offer you refreshments, but I have none."

"Your accommodations are threadbare, sir."

"During the war, I became used to the Spartan tradition. Since then, I find I'm more comfortable in simple settings." He would not meet her gaze. He gestured to the wall as if conversing with the paint. "You look well."

She waited a moment before answering. "How would you know, sir? You haven't looked at me once."

Decker turned to face her. His turn, now, to play the part of the condemned—he feared the impact of seeing her. The lines of her face, always fine, were sharper now. Her eyes seemed even larger than before, and dark with whatever sorrow she carried. He found her beautiful beyond words.

"It was a shock to see you at the ball." Her voice was solemn. "I am married now—"

"Yes."

"—to Whit."

"Fine choice."

She closed her eyes. "I thought you were dead." When he did not answer, she continued. "So many men died. It was very easy to imagine you were one of them."

"I nearly was," he said, his voice a whisper. "What kept me alive was the thought of you." She sat still as a painting. He could not be sure she was breathing. "Why are you here?" he asked.

"To give you your due."

"What do you mean?"

She took a breath, as if to steady her voice. "When you left Richmond, we had an arrangement. I broke that arrangement. I've come to let you have your say."

He snorted. She seemed startled by the sound. "Nonsense," he said. "You've already said that you thought I was dead. No blame will attach itself to you."

"I received letters at first, but they stopped—"

"I wrote you every week."

"I did not receive them after the first year. I didn't know if you were still with the western army, or if you were in a grave somewhere. I did not know you'd crossed over . . . that you'd joined the cause." She looked away. He searched her face for tears and saw none. "What made you change your mind?"

"I didn't change my mind. The war was well won after Gettysburg. I underestimated the tenacity of the Confederacy. . . and the stupidity of the Yankee generals. But the war was exactly what I said it would be." He could hear the sharp edges in his voice, but he felt powerless to change them. "Once my duty to the Republic was fulfilled, I came back. I still had an obligation to Virginia." After a pause, he added, "and to you."

"You owe me nothing, sir. But the South owes you its thanks —"

He laughed, and the sound was so out of place that she shuddered, shrinking in her seat. "Let me tell you a story," he said. "I've told *no one* about this. Let it be our secret." His hand jumped as he spoke, and his cane tumbled to the floor. He paused to retrieve it, resting it against his thigh. "Once I made the decision to cross over, I headed through the wilderness, just before battle. Along the way, I crossed paths with a group of Yankee scouts. I crept around them and headed into a clearing, no more than a few seconds ahead of them. Imagine my surprise when I found General Lee and his staff on horseback, sitting out in the open. I realized the danger and chased them back into the trees just as the scouts began firing." He paused again for effect. "I saved General Lee's life."

Her expression had gone from one of rapt attention to one of some reservation, as if not quite certain of his veracity. "If that's true, sir, then the South owes you even more —"

"Do you think so?" The edge in his voice had become derisive. "Perhaps you are right. I am celebrated for the slaughter of my fellow man at Spotsylvania, but saving General Lee was a far greater act of violence. If a Yankee sniper had killed him . . . if I hadn't warned him . . . then the war would have ended within *weeks*. And a hundred thousand men—more!—would be alive today, instead of rotting in their graves. Now, perhaps you consider that a service—"

Her face seemed to draw into itself, and her eyelids closed, squeezing out a single tear. She stood and said in a garbled voice, "Please excuse me. I must—"

Panicked, he said, "You promised me my due!"

She wiped her eyes, trying to compose herself. When she had control again, she sat back down.

He pressed his lips together, wondering what he should say next. He'd tried to make her cry, to elicit a response, and having done so, found the sight unbearable. He ticked off the possibilities, things he might tell her, and dismissed them one by one. He would not share the despair of amputation—of being incomplete. He would not tell her of his humiliating efforts to secure meaningful employment. He would not complain about the endless practice necessary to accomplish even the simplest tasks. Only the impossible—starting the last few minutes over—would suffice.

At last, he said, "That was terribly unkind of me. I find I'm no longer able to control my words. I wish to express my gratitude for your visit. You came on an errand of justice. I failed to rise to the moment." Standing, cane in hand, he began hobbling across the room. He looked over his shoulder and said, "I will walk you to the door."

She paused at his front step before heading for the carriage. "I am told you are to be married."

"Yes. This Friday is the happy day." His voice had the tenor of a eulogy.

"My congratulations to you and your bride. I saw her at the ball. She's quite lovely."

The second most beautiful woman in the ballroom. He cleared his throat. "She has an independent mind." He studied her face.

Does that bother you? Have I struck a chord? Or is there nothing I can do to shake your newfound happiness with Whit?

Paula reached out, nearly touching his face, but stopped, blushing. "Was your story true? About saving the general?"

"You're the only one I've told."

. . .

Hiring Charles proved to be a smart decision. Once headed in the right direction, his bullheaded nature guaranteed he would finish a task exactly as required. To begin, he'd assembled a team of six men to haul debris from the warehouse. White was concerned that so many free Negroes could not muster the necessary discipline for a group effort, but Charles seemed more than up to the task of supervision. He directed and organized the effort, establishing a firm hand when the work slowed. Within two weeks, he'd cleared the warehouse from end to end.

The next step in their enterprise involved roof repairs. Decker stood watching the work from the inside of the building. The sun shone through the hole, casting a circle of light on the warehouse floor. White joined him, his notes in hand. "How much will this cost?" he asked.

"We can't work in the rain. I need dry conditions."

"We're running out of money."

"I know. I have reserves, should the matter become critical."

"The matter is critical now."

Decker nodded. "All right, then."

"Smith appears to be quite knowledgeable."

"It's not as important to know how to do things as it is to know whom to ask," Decker said, still looking up. "When he doesn't know something, he finds out."

Outside, a carriage pulled to the double doors, and Captain Wells disembarked. He came in without announcement and began looking around the building, his lips pursed. As he walked, he moved from the waist down, holding the upper half of his body at rigid attention. His scar looked redder in the sunlight than it had at the ball.

"Captain Wells?" White said. "A pleasure to see you, sir. How can I be of service?" White slid effortlessly to the captain's side, latching onto the officer like a wagon hitch. "What do you think of our little endeavor?"

Captain Wells continued to survey the room, staring at Decker's workbench, cluttered with correspondence—the only part of the warehouse to show any evidence of production. "I don't understand how you intend to produce powder here," he said. "This building is too close to other buildings."

"Ah, I understand your confusion," White said. "We don't intend to manufacture powder here—"

"This is not a factory," Decker said. "I told you that before."

The captain glared at Decker. "Yes, you did. What is it you intend to do?"

Decker pointed at the captain's holster. "Colt Navy revolver? Fine weapon. How often do you clean it?"

"What difference does—"

"How many rounds can you fire before the barrel is fouled?" Captain Wells shook his head. "I'm not here to socialize. I'm—"

"You asked me what my intentions were. I intend to develop powder that won't foul the barrel of your fine pistol."

The captain pointed at Decker. "I'd do well to foul the barrel now, sir!" he said, biting the words off as he spoke. "My brother died at Sharpsburg."

"My father died at Gettysburg."

"Captain Wells," White said, his voice smooth and even. "Is it your intention to fight the war again here in our warehouse?"

Captain Wells shook his head. "I'm here on business. This morning—"

Charles dropped a crate on the floor near Decker's workbench. The sound shot through the building. The captain turned, annoyed at the sound. "What is your man doing?"

"That's my foreman," Decker said.

"Foreman?" Wells snorted again. "A fine title indeed."

"Smith!" Decker called.

"Brown?" Charles answered, his hands on his hips.

"How long until your men finish my roof?"

"They'll finish when they finish." He turned back to the box, bending to unpack the contents.

Decker turned back to the captain. "He's cantankerous, but he earns his pay." Captain Wells stared at Decker for a long time without speaking, clearly perplexed.

"We have nothing but good intentions here," White said, gesturing with open hands. "Mr. Brown is a chemist, and he is working with me to provide the Republic with a formula for a superior gunpowder. And our door is open to you, sir. But I would remind you that my partner is no more a threat to you or the Republic than the men who currently hold public office both in the city and the district. The vast majority of whom were Confederate soldiers."

Wells snorted. "Am I to understand you don't consider four years of war a *threat*, Mr. White? Well, I have a *threat* for you, gentlemen —"

"White, shut up," Decker said. "You're making things worse."

"I'm only pointing out —"

"Nicholas!"

White's mouth dropped open at the sound of his Christian name. He stood gaping while Decker turned back to the captain. "We are at loggerheads, sir. Let me try to undo the damage." He stepped back and called out, "Smith!"

"Brown?"

"Captain Wells is to be a frequent visitor. He is welcome at all hours. Try to show him more courtesy than you show to me."

"Yes suh."

Decker turned back. "Our doors are open to you. This is all I can do, sir."

Captain Wells nodded, frowning. He pointed at Charles. "I suppose he minds his tongue when your rebel friends are about?"

"I have surprisingly few friends," Decker said.

The captain crossed his arms. "I came here for a reason. We cut a former slave down from a sumac this morning, just a few blocks from here. They say ghosts did the hanging. You wouldn't know anything about that, would you?"

"Is that what this is about?" White asked.

The captain stepped closer to Decker. "There are those who won't accept the new way of things, no matter what. Murder means nothing to them."

Decker's voice dropped to a whisper. "This business of ours *is* the new way of things. I'm a Virginian, doing research that may well benefit the Republic. White is from Delaware. He supplied powder to Washington for Paquin Powder during the war. And Mr. Smith was a slave. Now, he's my foreman."

"We are done here," Captain Wells said.

As the captain walked away, back straight, hat in hand, White slid next to Decker and whispered, "You did very well, sir. You have the makings of a—"

"Shut up, White."

• • •

After their visitor was gone, Decker called Charles over. "I understand that some folks dressed like ghosts have been causing mischief. Do you know anything about that?"

Charles stood silent, his face impossible to read.

"Has anyone threatened you?" White asked.

Charles shrugged.

"Why didn't you say anything?" White seemed incredulous.

"What you gonna do, Mr. White? You gonna change the world for me?"

Decker tapped his cane on the ground. "If I ask you to do something, and it puts you in danger, let me know. I'll find another way. Understood?" He looked up at the hole in the roof. "If something happens to you, we'll never get the damned roof fixed."

• • •

The day before the wedding, Alexandros showed up at Decker's door, carpetbag in hand. "Calista informs me you insisted that we all live under the same roof."

"I'd not heard of it," Decker said. "At any rate, I have just the one room here."

His future father-in-law glanced about, one eyebrow raised, his mouth twisted to the side. "We will surely need a larger residence. Shall I set about finding us one?"

"I hadn't considered it." Thinking quickly, Decker decided the quickest solution had already been proposed. "Yes, please do. Something small with two bedrooms would be ideal."

Alexandros set his bag down and bowed. "I will find something worthy of you, sir."

"No, I want something small. Two bedrooms. Nothing ostentatious."

"Of course, of course."

"The ceremony is tomorrow. Have you vacated your own room?" Decker asked.

"Alas, I've already checked out —"

Decker sighed. "No matter. You may stay here until we find other circumstances. I secured a room at the Spotswood for our wedding night. I thought Calista might enjoy the amenities."

"At Eighth and Main? Marvelous hotel! First rate. I considered it myself when first I came to town. Perhaps that's the proper residence for you—"

"No, sir. I repeat—something small. Two bedrooms." Decker hopped to the table and took a chair. Even after sitting, his leg continued to tremble. Cramps and tremors were normal at the end of a day, but he'd taxed the leg a great deal over the last month. The limb seemed determined to make its complaints known earlier in the day. Decker grabbed the small stack of letters on the table and turned them over. Leaning back, he tried to stretch before continuing the conversation. "May I be frank with you, sir? We are going to be family, are we not?"

"Yes, of course."

"I think perhaps my resources are more modest than you've imagined. And my inquiries lead me to believe you have little or no resources of your own."

"My name is my legacy." He pulled at his beard, striking a pose, his belly pulled in for as long as he could hold his breath. "As for your resources—"

"Limited at best."

"That can't be so! You own a factory—"

"I own half of a warehouse. I allowed your daughter to spend more on our wedding than was prudent."

"Are our accounts empty?"

Decker chuckled, shaking his head.

White had insisted on hiring the Pinkerton Agency out of Chicago to learn what they could about Decker's fiancée and her father. Alexandros—Alexander Kenzie Curtis—was no more Greek than Decker was. The man seemed to have a genuine affection for the Greek culture, as evidenced by his daughter's name (if that, indeed, was her name), but their family came from England. His foray into patent medicines led to a brief incarceration in Philadelphia. During the war, he was a sutler, until an unspecified accident left him with a damaged knee. Thereafter, he depended on his daughter's contacts for his livelihood. He'd arrived in Richmond, daughter in tow, just weeks before Decker returned.

White had argued against the marriage. "Now that you know the kind of woman Calista is, what can you still see in her?"

"My prospects are limited," he said, "and living alone is a burden. But there's more to the matter. It's true that Calista doesn't act according to convention. Men seem to require the yolk of servitude from one another. The demands of society are yet another form of bondage. She does not comply. I find that admirable." More, there was something exciting, something deliciously wicked in a woman who insisted on doing as she wished.

Her father, however, was a different matter. "We are not destitute," Decker told Alexandros. "And I intend to keep our finances in order." He looked around his little room. "I am used to a simple life. I would provide Calista with something more. But we all must live within our means." He looked up. "Hopefully, the promise of a roof and consistent meals will be satisfactory for you, sir."

"Of course, of course." He was still smiling, but the enthusiasm had clearly left his eyes.

• • •

The room at the Spotswood was small, but luxurious, with tall ceilings, mullion windows, and thick velvet curtains. The bed, piled high with pillows, sat on a platform. Decker eyed the bed, wondering in advance how he would negotiate the climb. The lamp on the nightstand would have to be dimmed or turned off. Calista sat in a chair at the window, sprawled out in a most immodest way. "I'm so glad you took a room on the second floor. Thank you—I know it was a bother. I should have liked the top floor, but that would be too much to ask."

Decker peered out the window. The streetlamps below were a pretty sight. Looking up, he glimpsed the half-moon slipping behind the clouds. The stars weren't visible. He bit his lip and put a hand on her shoulder. "It's late."

"This place is magnificent. How much did you say the room cost?"

"Three dollars a night. Quite extravagant."

She glanced back at him, her pretty mouth drawn up in a knowing smile. "You are ready for me, then?"

Decker considered the question. "Actually—no. I'm not." He crossed the room and began removing his clothes, folding each item and placing it on the chair next to the nightstand. He continued to speak with his back to her. "I manage the necessities of living through practice. Even things most often taken for granted must be practiced. Things like walking and bending. Some things are beyond me. I cannot grip a cane and shake hands gracefully, for example."

I should have thought this through. He cleared his throat. "Until I met you, I had not considered the possibility that I might end up married . . . in my condition. You were a surprise, a gift, and I am grateful for you. But I am unprepared. The mechanisms of love are not something I've practiced."

He took a deep breath and dropped his trousers. Eyes closed, he hopped out of them by leaning on the cane. *Now,* he thought. He pivoted and faced her.

"Oh my," she said. She made an effort to smile. "They chopped you to pieces."

"You've made a bad bargain."

For a moment, he saw something new in her eyes. Something both serious and sad. Then she smiled and shook her head. "Don't be silly. Get in bed. Do you need help?"

Blushing furiously, he placed his palm on the mattress and, using the cane for leverage, hoisted himself up. Setting the cane against the wall, he leaned back into the pile of pillows. As she began to disrobe—a painstaking process, given the layers women were required to wear—he reached out to dim the lamp.

"No need, sir," she said. Her smile was all dimples and blush. "No one from the street can see us. And I want you to see everything." She was a study in soft curves, from her chin to her feet. Her porcelain skin glowed in the lamplight. "Do you like what you see?"

As she came to him, he began to panic. "I have not thought this through," he said, a stricken expression on his face. "There is the question of balance—"

She put a finger to his lips, silencing him. "No need, Decker Brown. Lay back, and I will do the rest."

CHAPTER TWENTY-SEVEN

Richmond, Virginia
October 1867

*"Eighteenth-century doctors prescribed sugar pills for nearly
everything: heart problems, headache, consumption, labor pains,
insanity, old age, and blindness. Hence, the French expression
'like an apothecary without sugar' meant someone in an utterly
hopeless situation."*
~Tom Reiss

As promised, Alexandros found two properties to consider for
their new home. Decker secured the more modest of the two,
though Calista weighed in heavily for the more expensive
location. "By taking the more sensible property, you'll have
more money available for making the house a home," he told
her.

Within days, she'd ordered twice the furnishings he could
afford, and he was forced to return some of the items, an
unhappy circumstance that led to a day of chilly silence,
followed by her apology. "I've spent a portion of my life with
an empty cup, and now that it overflows, I find myself anxious
for a larger cup. Please forgive me."

Next was the matter of gambling debts. Alexandros was a
gamer, and the men to whom he owed money were the
disreputable sort. A week after the wedding, Calista came to

him in tears, begging him to vouchsafe her father's safety. "They will kill him. I *know* it. I know their type of men. Please help him." The debts were paid.

Days later, he spotted his father-in-law outside of a tavern. He had Charles pull the carriage over to admonish him. Grim-lipped and hardly contrite, Alexandros explained, "I am thirsty. Hardly your realm of concern." Thereafter, Decker kept a bottle in the house for the man's thirst, that being the more fiscally practical option.

Having done her marital duty on the evening of their wedding, Calista had shown no interest in sharing his bed again. He expected nothing else, being less than whole, but the disappointment made him melancholy.

Soon after moving into their new home, she began staying out well past dark, coming home after he'd gone to bed. "I'm visiting friends," she explained in a tone of voice that made it clear that her whereabouts were none of his concern. Her father, ever present and willing to chime in, waited until she was out of earshot to explain, "She's always been this way. She is a free spirit. Be patient."

His admonition made sense. Calista's refusal to be bound by convention lay at the heart of his feelings for her. How, then, could he hold her accountable now that she was his wife?

When she spent the evening at home, she was charming company, though a bit distant. Her patience with the practical side of his wounds included helping him with salves and gauze when the stumps rebelled against his rigorous schedule. When he awoke screaming, she soothed him back to sleep with quiet words and a soft hand. This side of her always surprised him. Under different circumstances, she might have been a nurse.

Still, he was uneasy in his new life. By marrying him, she'd made a bargain to help her and her father's circumstances. He'd known that much from the start. He'd married her anyway, but her presence had not banished the ghosts that haunted him or filled the hole in his heart.

Decker continued to rent his previous apartment for use as a private workshop. Charles had the contraption he'd ordered delivered there so Decker could inspect it away from prying eyes. Every inch of the piece had been sanded and sealed. The sheer weight bothered him, but the trade-off between strength and mass was a critical element of craftsmanship. In the end, the value of the contraption owed more to the sense of calm it gave him—a feeling he could not match at home or at his warehouse. The mere sight of the glass portal near the apex of the contraption calmed his soul and summoned waking dreams that did not include blood and body parts.

In all of Richmond, his private workshop was the only place he could bear to be in his own skin.

• • •

Decker watched as Charles panted, sweat running down his face. The roller press had been heavier than anticipated. The two men he'd hired leaned back against the wall, shaking their heads.

Decker pointed at Charles and waved him over. "Did you pay them yet?" he asked.

"Not yet. I thought we might use them for a few other—"

"No." He peeled off a few paper bills and handed them to Charles. "Pay them and get them out of here."

Charles scowled at him. "They was hopin' you might—"

"I said no, Goddamn it."

Charles snatched the bills. "No reason to holler." He walked to the men, paid them, and then ordered them out of the warehouse. Shoulders slumped, downcast, they left in short order. Once they were gone, Charles turned back and called, "Is that what you wanted, Boss?"

Decker ignored him. White, who had a way of hovering when he was about to take issue with something said or done, followed behind Decker, his hands clasped behind his back and his head down. When Decker stopped, White bumped into him, nearly knocking him to the floor.

"Oh! So sorry, Brown!"

Decker stabilized himself, whipping the cane in an arc, causing White to jump back. "*That far.* Stay that far away from me. Do I make myself clear?"

Too stunned to speak, White watched as Decker hobbled away.

At the warehouse, he'd finished tiny batches of his smokeless powder but had yet to see if the work he'd done would translate to larger sample sizes. If not, his work would be for naught.

As for his correspondence with Europe, he'd received rejections from France and Italy. Only Prussia remained as a possibility.

With so much failure in mind, he battled himself from morning to night. He had not abandoned his stretches and exercises, designed to help day-to-day functions. But by the middle of the day, he was loath to do anything at all, and minor irritations became major obstacles. "And that is why I snapped at you," he told Charles at the end of the day, an hour after White had gone.

Charles seemed unimpressed. "Those men might have helped us, and they needed more than half a day's pay, that's for damned sure."

Decker's stomach knotted like a rope. "We are running low on funds," he said, tight-lipped.

"Am I next? Next out the door?"

"Long as you do your job, you get paid. That's the deal. You work. I pay."

"That's not right. Folks need help."

Decker tried to keep a calm expression, but the pain in his hip made it difficult. "I gave you a job because you're a good worker. That was enough for you when you started. Now, I'm supposed to take care of you *and* your friends?"

"You a cranky old grayback."

"Yes, I am. But understand this, Smith. *I'm not your daddy.* You wanted to be free? This is what it looks like."

"Looks a whole lot like the same old, to me."

"One difference. You can walk out any time."

"Fine. You drive yourself home tonight," Charles said, stomping off.

In a moment, Decker was alone in the warehouse. The sun had set, and the room was chilly. The lamp in the corner provided the only light. He hobbled over to the workbench and shuffled papers. "Fine, then. Fine. I'll keep working."

There was a time, before the war, when he'd kept his opinions to himself. These days, his mouth had its own rules, and there were too few of them. Because of that, he would have to hobble home alone. *Serves me right.*

• • •

Driving away in the carriage, Charles fumed. He'd battled Brown before. Deferential at first, in keeping with his behavior toward most white men, Charles soon discovered that Brown treated everyone around him the same—with a surly sort of honesty. Though he was not a partner, Charles was an important part of the operation. *Without me, those two fools would be lost. What's more, they know it.* Having discovered Brown needed him, Charles set about testing his new boundaries at every turn.

When Brown proposed new flooring for the warehouse, Charles disagreed. "No, don't put in a floor. That would be *stupid.* I'll put down some pallet wood. I thought you wanted to save money."

Brown stared at him, a half-smile on his face. "Well, I wouldn't want to be *stupid.*"

On another occasion, Brown asked about his work at the flour mill during the war. Feeling tired and angry after another day of breaking his back, Charles was in no mood to talk. Brown insisted. "Not much to say 'bout that. I spent most of my time hauling sacks, but sometimes they let me work on the water wheel if the flow was blocked. I'd have to climb up on it to clear the debris. I set traps for the rats and cleaned up the shit to keep it out of the flour. Mister Crane never let me touch the grain, though. That was for the miller."

"William Crane, the owner of the mill?"

Charles shrugged.

"I wonder, is he still alive?"

"He dead," Charles said with certainty.

A frown crossed Brown's face. "How do you know?"

"I was there when he died."

Brown had a questioning look on his round, white face, and Charles decided to test the man again. He would tell the truth. If there was a touch of threat in the story, so be it. *In the end, there are more workers than bosses.*

"The night they burned Richmond, Mister Crane came to the mill all full of vinegar about this and that. He had a string of niggers chained together. Pretty soon, he figures out there's one of him, and a dozen of us, and his voice gets real low and calm, and he starts backtrackin'. That was a mistake. Those men would have left him alone out of habit if he hadn't shown his pigeon heart. The next thing you know, they were on him. Kicked him to death.

"Just about then, rebel soldiers showed up and shot a few of us. I wasn't shackled, so I took off running and kept running until I come upon the Yankees west of town." He pursed his lips. "They had hot biscuits, and they were damned good."

"You killed William Crane?" Brown's stricken expression was almost comical.

"Not me." Smith narrowed his gaze. "Well, I put my foot to use once or twice, but by that time, the man was already gone."

Brown turned away, silent, and for a moment, Charles feared he'd gone too far. You could only be so honest with a white man. Then, Brown turned back and said, "You probably shouldn't tell your story to anyone else."

"Probably not," Charles agreed.

Now, driving the carriage in a circle around the buildings in the warehouse district, the whole matter made less and less sense to him. *That crippled old man 'bout to drive me crazy.* He stopped the carriage, halting in the middle of the road. *Stubborn fool likely to try to walk home.*

· · ·

Decker worked into the night. Because the guncotton samples he'd purchased still had traces of acid, Decker had taken a chance and manufactured his own. The hanks of spun cotton were soaked in potash and then spun to dry. The resulting strands, washed free of grease, were satisfactory. The next step involved the preparation of an acid mixture, however, and he was unable to obtain the proper results. The earthenware pots and the cast-iron, three-compartment dripping pans he'd designed proved useless. In the end, he had to purchase an outside supply, acid and all, which would make the finished product more volatile than he liked. *Perhaps I'll blow myself up tonight and finish the job.*

Just as well. Why on earth was he trying to create a more efficient powder? Wasn't there enough death in the world? He shook his head. He couldn't think about that, now. *If I had it to do over, I'd have lived on the inheritance. But now I've sunk my fortunes, and I've no other choice.* Like his decision to fight for both sides during the war, his pursuit of smokeless powder had become hopelessly tangled in his mind. He'd wanted a vocation, one that would keep him from being an object of charity, something that frightened him. And he'd nurtured hopes of being part of his beloved Richmond's recovery from the war. Instead, he'd built himself a trap, made enemies, and provided one job for a surly ex-slave who hated him.

Much later, his hip on fire, he decided it was time to go home. He'd been in no hurry—his wife would likely be arriving now. *Let her come home to an empty house and wonder.*

The thought stopped him. *I am a fool.*

He hobbled to the door and stepped into the night air. The walk home would be nearly impossible. He didn't care. *I do wish I had my peg* he thought. He'd left the prosthesis at home, preferring to do without it at the warehouse. He locked the doors and headed down the street, hopping as he went.

One block away, he knew he'd made a mistake. *I can keep this up for a while. Then I'll have to stop.*

Two blocks later, he encountered a group of three men, sharing a bottle behind the fence of an empty lot. The building across the way was still lit on the inside. He passed the men, moving closer to the building than to the drinkers, when one of them called out, "Brown? Decker Brown?"

He stopped and turned. The three men were walking his way. It wasn't until they came within a few yards that he recognized one of them—older, thinner, and uglier than he recalled.

Edgar Cully—the Hill's old overseer.

"Well, well, well," Cully said, his voice slurring. "Here's the great war hero, boys. This man won the war single-handed, and that's why Robert Lee is the President of the Confederacy today. What are you doing out alone, Mr. Brown?"

Decker shook his head and struggled on.

Cully slipped ahead and stepped in front of Decker, cutting him off. The other two men followed but kept a little distance.

"Step aside, Mr. Cully."

"*Mr. Cully?* I like the sound of *that*. I'm wondering, Decker Brown. Do you call your nigger foreman *Mister*?" He stuck his chest out and folded his arms in front. He wore a rebel cap, turned slightly to the side, either because he thought it the fashion, or because the ill-fitting cap would not sit properly. Even in the dim light from the building's windows, Decker could see that Cully's pockmarked face had aged more than the passage of six years could explain.

"I gonna ask you something, Mr. Brown, and I want you to give it some thought before you answer. I got a bottle here. Would you like to share a drink with an old friend?"

Decker tried to hobble around Cully, but the man turned and reached for him. In a motion almost too fast to track, Decker slashed Cully with the tip of his cane, laying open the man's cheek. Cully staggered back and fell to the street. Decker scrambled forward and placed the tip of the cane in the hollow spot under Cully's throat. Pressing down, he pinned Cully in place. "Don't move," he said. He glanced up at Cully's two friends. The men didn't back up, but they stopped advancing. Decker looked down at Cully. "You are a bad egg, sir."

Cully tried to wiggle away, but Decker pushed down harder with the cane, nearly drawing blood. Cully, bug-eyed, lay still.

"Gentlemen?" Decker said, addressing the two men behind him. "If I push any harder, your friend will die, choking on his own blood. I've done such a thing before. It won't bother me to do it again. If you care about him, you'll skedaddle. *Now*."

Neither man moved.

The sound of a carriage interrupted the impasse. Charles drove up behind them and stopped, silent.

"Hello, Smith."

Charles smiled. "Hello, Brown. Is you all right?"

Decker snorted. "Ever go eel fishing, Smith?"

"No suh. Don't like eel."

"You stick them, Smith. Run them through." He pushed harder with the cane, and Cully moaned. Decker looked down. "My ride is here, Mr. Cully. I'm going to go home. You are going to stay on the ground until I'm gone." He glanced back at Cully's two friends. "And your friends will be able to escort you home, unharmed."

Cully gurgled. Blood ran from the slash in his cheek.

"The next time I see you, Mr. Cully, you're going to cross to the far side of the street. You're going to keep your distance. And if you don't—" He pushed again, and Cully choked. "If you don't stay clear, I'm going to kill you."

So saying, he hopped his way to the carriage and hoisted himself inside. Charles did not wait for him to climb into his seat to drive on.

From behind them, Cully was up on his feet, shouting. "I know about you, Brown! I know something, and soon, everybody is going to know!"

From the driver's seat, Charles said, "See? Everybody knows you're a sour, old cracker."

"True enough." Decker's leg trembled beneath him. "Thank you for coming back for me." He sat back, suddenly short of breath. "You still peeved? I know you wanted more work for your friends." Charles didn't answer.

How to explain? It had taken him months in bed, weighing the right and wrong of things, to come to his present mind. Elucidating his thoughts was another matter entirely.

"When we first met, you came offering work in exchange for wages. *That exchange made us equals.* Two men, agreeing on the circumstances of trade."

Charles shrugged.

"Would it help if I told you that I've come to abhor slavery in all of its forms?" Decker leaned forward, his hand on the back of the driver's seat. "The world has no shortage of overseers. Priests and old biddies tell you how to live. Politicians and generals tell you how to die. And the rest? They're in line for a piece of you, too. *An open hand can be another whip hand.* Do you understand?"

"No, Brown. I surely don't."

Decker sighed.

• • •

"I need you to wait for me," Decker said when they arrived. Before his foreman could answer, Decker lumbered from the carriage and checked inside the house. Calista was not home. Returning to the carriage, he said, "Please stay. I may need to leave again." When Charles started to protest, Decker reached up to the driver's seat and patted his knee. "Do this for me, Smith."

Inside, he lit a candle and sat at the table, waiting. Anticipating a confrontation, he took a sip from her father's bottle and sat back, waiting.

When she came in, the sight of him still awake startled her. She started to smile, and then her face became stern. "You are up late, sir."

"Where were you?" He'd avoided insisting on an answer before this, dreading the truth. Now, he'd asked her anyway.

"With friends."

"I am your husband. I should like to be acquainted with your friends. Perhaps rather than staying out, you might bring them here. I will be a jolly host."

Her lips tightened, turning down. Her eyelids drooped, and her voice took on the temperature of ice. "I find that highly unlikely, as you've been a tepid host at best to my own father.

He was the man in my life long before I met you, and he is treated like a boardinghouse customer, rather than an honored guest."

Decker considered this, and long moments passed before he spoke again. The silence angered her, and she seemed ready to storm off, so he answered. "Your father is a swindler who sold faulty potions and spent time in prison."

Her eyes grew wide and her mouth dropped open. She stopped still, her hands clasped in front of her. "That is . . . completely untrue—"

"I ask you again—will I be introduced to your friends?"

Her face transformed a second time, this time accompanied by tears. All aspects of her expression drew down, and her lips trembled. "What are you accusing me of, husband?"

"I've made no accusation. I've asked to meet your friends."

"You've implied much more—"

"Let's not pretend. You've been unhappy since your father related our financial situation to you."

She cried harder. "That is so unfair—"

He waved his arm, cutting her off. "You are clearly dissatisfied with our marriage. Perhaps you misunderstood my situation. Perhaps I have been unsatisfactory in other ways. I wonder what I might do to take a step in your direction, madam."

She stopped crying and rubbed at her nose. Something in her eyes told him to expect another attack. "You require me to be home every evening, but the fact is, you've been absent as well. I am not a servant, standing at the door to wait for your arrival."

"I work."

"Are all of your hours away spent at the factory?"

"It's not a factory."

"You avoid an answer."

He sat back. *She's very good at this.* "What do you want?"

"I know nothing of your time away from home, and yet you accuse me. Do you not think that odd?"

He smiled. "You are right." He stood. "I believe Charles is still outside. Come with me, please."

"It's late—"

"And you were out until minutes ago. We will go out again." He made his way to the door, his glance demanding she follow him.

Outside, Charles sat shivering on the carriage seat.

"Take us to my old place," Decker said as he gave Calista a hand into the carriage. They traveled in silence. The wheels of the carriage and the sound of horse hooves echoed off the houses, tumbling down the street into the darkness. Calista sat pressed against the far side of the seat, staring into her lap.

When they arrived, Decker slid from the carriage and waited for his wife to disembark. Once inside, he pointed at an object in the center of the room. "This is what I've been working on."

She stared at the thing, scrunching her nose and forehead. "What is this? It looks like a statue."

"No, it's functional." Decker moved to the conical object's side. "Watch this," he said, pressing on a small wooden panel. The panel sank at his touch and then dropped to the side. "Springs," he explained. "Marvelous engineering."

The object resembled a wooden replica of a Minié ball, more than a yard tall. The wood had been varnished to a high sheen. He pointed to a small portal of glass near the top of the cone. "It's a window," he said. "A parachute will invert the capsule on descent, and the window will open a view to the ground below." He tapped the open panel. "And this is a door."

"What on earth is it for?"

"I told you that I built illuminations before the war. Imagine, if you will, a rocket big enough to lift this wooden compartment. Inside, a person—"

Her mouth dropped open in apparent disbelief. "You would put a child on one of your rockets?"

"Oh, no," he said, laughing. His eyes were on the object, not on his wife's reaction. "Watch this!" He bent down to the open panel. Folding up, he tucked himself neatly inside. "Ironic, isn't it? I have discovered the one true advantage to having lost an arm and leg. I'm able to fit inside—"

Calista screamed.

Decker shuddered and hastened to climb back out of the cone. Panicked, he made a mess of the maneuver, tumbling out onto the floor. He stood as quickly as he could, brushing at his clothing.

"You are *insane!*" she cried. He stared into her wide eyes and realized with horror that he was seeing a genuine reaction from her for the first time that evening.

"Let me explain," he said, blushing. "I have always believed . . . that is, my father taught me . . . the thing you need to be happy, that is, the pursuit of happiness, is to have three . . ." He stopped, gulping. She backed up a step, her hand to her chest. "You need three things. You need work, you need something to hope for, and someone to love. My work is my research. The thing to hope for is . . . this. This bit of whimsy. I understand that this might seem strange to you—"

"You intend to fly up in the sky on a rocket?"

"Please, Calista, listen to me. This is a dream. If you have a dream, you can go on living, no matter what the war did, no matter the nights spent bleeding in bed. No matter that my father died and everything I hoped for burned to ash. A dream is still worth living for. I *believe* that." He paused, searching her face. "And the third thing you need is someone to love. That's you, dearest." He stopped short, his mouth hanging open. *Lies. She's a substitute. A changeling. You lied to her, and you lied to yourself. Here is your payback. You deserve her.*

"You belong in an asylum," she said, her voice shaking.

Decker sat down on the floor next to his capsule. He'd imagined her reaction to seeing the capsule. The delight or admiration he'd hoped for was absent. *Perhaps she's right. Perhaps I belong in an asylum.* He glanced up at her. She stared back, a look of disgust on her face.

I was a fool, fool, fool. I've put all my hopes into this hollow piece of wood and this ridiculous marriage.

Long minutes passed. He waited until he could speak without his voice breaking. "I want you to understand something. The war took nearly everything from me. My limbs. My family. My friends." He paused. "I had this contraption built to make my very last dream physical, so that I could hold it. Touch it. So that it would not slip away like everything else. Not that I could ever really follow this to a conclusion." He stopped. Another lie.

Her breathing slowed, and the fear in her eyes diminished. She looked at the capsule, then at him. "I think I understand," she said, though it was clear that she didn't fully understand, and probably never would. "You gave me quite a start."

Her late arrival, her long nights out forgotten, she was pretending to forgive him.

"Charles is outside," Decker answered. "He will take you home. I will be staying here tonight."

CHAPTER TWENTY-EIGHT

Richmond, Virginia
November 1867

"Reconstruction is the great black hole that remains to be filled. Even experts on the Civil War don't really understand its full significance."
~Ron Chernow

White found him sitting outside of the warehouse. Snow had begun to fall at daybreak, and a half inch had accumulated on his shoulders. He sat on a wooden barrel, leaning back against the building, his one leg outstretched. His breathing seemed shallow—so much so that White wondered if his partner had passed away sitting up. "Are you all right, Mr. Brown?" he asked, his voice soft as the white flakes sifting over them.

Decker glanced at him and then turned back to his empty stare. "Time for you to saddle up, Mr. White," he said.

White frowned. *The man is breaking down in front of my eyes. We are ruined.*

Decker fished a folded piece of paper from his jacket pocket. "The news is not all good."

"Not all good?"

"The process is a success. I've a small barrel of our powder sitting next to the roller press. Time to see if your contacts yield us anything."

"You've finished? The process is complete?"

"Yes," Decker said. "But there's *this* matter to attend to." He handed the paper to White.

White scanned the letter. He gripped tight, crumpling the paper in trembling hands. "But this is wonderful," he said. "They want our new powder?"

"No." Decker shivered. "They want black powder."

"The correspondence mentions *your formula —* "

"They mean my custom blend of black powder." Decker noticed the snow on his shoulders, seemingly for the first time, but he did nothing to brush it away. "I explained this to you before. Weapons have specific needs. If the bulk of your army is armed with a certain model rifle, for example, you can alter the formula for powder to maximize the capabilities of that particular model. The Prussians use the *Dreyse* needle-gun. The bolt action allows a much faster rate of fire. Imagine a firing line able to deliver volley after volley." He shivered again. "Smokeless gunpowder is what they need. In the meantime, they're interested in a black powder blend specifically designed for the needle-gun. By altering the formula, I've provided them with an optimum composition. Unfortunately, my grasp of the German language appears to have been less satisfactory than my French and Italian. Those countries rejected my offer, by the way. Their loss — the *Chassepot* rifle would have benefitted from a custom formula. As for the Prussians, they've placed an order, as you can see. I've tried to make it clear that we are *not* a manufacturing concern — "

"But this is wonderful," White repeated. "Powder companies are struggling now. The army has tons of powder in storage, a holdover from the war, and with the exception of Paquin's blasting powder, no one is producing anything." He shook the letter. "This is an order for a sizable amount of powder. This order is an asset. This is . . . bait." Decker laughed. The sound warmed White's heart. "How did you accomplish this?"

"My uncle and father came from the old country years ago. My uncle's uncle works for the war department in Prussia. Relations with France are not good, and I imagined that they might be interested in an arms advantage. They were. My family connections were a suitable introduction."

White tucked the letter into his vest, a satisfied smile on his face. "I will gather my provisions and be on my way."

"Hurry," Decker said, his face gone blank again.

Any good feelings White had dissipated as he watched Decker lean back against the warehouse wall. "You are not well, sir," he said.

"I am staying in my old room."

"Charles said as much."

"Hmm. I am surrounded by old women, whispering camp canard."

"We worry over you."

Decker shot him a glance, suddenly furious. Then, just as quickly, his blank expression returned. "I am trying to come to grips with the essential facts of my life."

"Your marriage—"

He closed his eyes. "My wife is not what society would demand of a woman. To be honest, that was much of the attraction. I've come to regard social mores as a form of bondage." He shook his head. "Her behavior led me to believe that she was a free thinker. I wish I'd done more thinking on the matter myself. My marriage was a terrible, terrible mistake, but it was *my* mistake, not hers."

"Your wounds—"

"I've overcome them, to the extent that such a thing is possible."

"What then? I don't understand—"

"Nor could you. I've not been candid about my past. The failure of my marriage rests not on who she is, but on who she is *not*. I married her under false pretenses. My heart belonged to another." He nodded toward the warehouse door. "You'll find some papers stacked on the sample barrel, outlining the process. I basically take guncotton—"

"Guncotton? That's quite volatile, isn't it?"

"Yes. If I had more time, I'd experiment with something less so. Perhaps something based on wood cellulose."

"You had guncotton on the premises?"

Decker shrugged. "I tried to make my own, but that was a waste of time and money."

"Good God, man, are you *insane*?"

Decker stood slowly, brushing the snow from his shoulders. "That possibility has been suggested. Rest assured, the sample barrel I'm sending you with is benign. I've reduced the combustion rate—something similar to adding sulphur to the black powder ratio—and with alcohol and ether, I changed the structure of the cotton to a gelatin. Then, I stabilized the paste and rolled it into a sheet that could be dried and flaked." His voice gave out for a moment, and he held up a hand to keep White standing still.

A cold wind came blasting down the street, sending both men into another fit of shivers. "We should go inside, sir."

"No. I'm headed home." He fixed his gaze on White. "There are more refinements needed in the process, but we are out of funds." He paused to lick his lips. "The guncotton must be free of acids, for one thing. That's why I tried to make my own. Residual acids make the finished product a bit more unstable than I'd like."

"Will I blow up on my way?" White asked, his eyes open wide.

"Don't be an idiot. I've already said that the sample is benign." He stopped, eyes closed, to regain his composure. "I've sketched the basic process in the papers. Familiarize yourself with them on your way. We have enough to file for a patent. The rest will wait."

"Shall I have Charles drive you . . . home?"

Decker nodded. "Now, I think."

White started to leave and turned back. "May I ask you something?" Decker waited.

"Why did you switch sides? In the war, I mean. I've never really quite understood."

"I am befuddled on that point myself," Decker said.

• • •

Charles drove him home. Decker was silent, wondering how to broach a delicate subject. Charles was a touchy sort. *Not unlike myself,* he thought. When the carriage pulled in front of his home, he tapped Charles on the shoulder. "I won't need you for several days," he said. "We await Mr. White's return. In the meantime, I have a question for you. Do you carry a knife?"

Charles nodded, momentarily confused. He fished a small pocketknife from his trouser pockets.

"The codes restrict you from owning a firearm," Decker said.

Charles shrugged. "Black Codes."

"And that knife won't help you in a tussle."

Charles scowled. "I know how to use a knife —"

Decker pulled out a cloth-wrapped bundle and handed it to him. Charles opened the cloth and stared at the contents.

"It's a Bowie. I had this custom-made for you in a shop near the Capitol. Knife fighting is too unpredictable to rely on for defense. But if you pull out a Bowie, the fight may never happen, and the blade will have done its job in the most efficient way."

Charles pulled the knife from its leather sheath and stared at the cutting edge. "I can see that. How much a thing like this cost?"

Decker ignored the question. "These are perilous times for a man of your color," he said. "You need to protect yourself. The government won't allow you a gun, and they'll do nothing to help you if the worst happens."

"I been thinkin' on that," Charles said. "I saw what you did to that man with your cane."

Decker snorted. "I practiced two moves over and over until I could do them in my sleep. That is the extent of my expertise. If Cully had pursued the altercation, he'd have beaten me to a pulp." He pointed at the knife. "Keep that hidden. Don't flash it around, pretty as it is. Part of its value lies in surprise."

Decker slipped out of the carriage and made his way to the door. Charles called out his thanks. Decker stopped to wave his cane in answer.

• • •

Over the following week, Decker spent his mornings walking the nearby streets, thinking. The cold, crisp air seemed to help. One festering wound remained unresolved. Paula had married Whit—the source of his worst anguish. He loved her still, and that bit of unfinished business consumed him. Chopped down as he was, he was not fit for marriage. His union with Calista proved that. Whit was an amputee as well, but he wore his pinned sleeve like a badge of honor, and he had two good legs.

Decker did not regret the impulse to fight for the Union. Liberty was something worth dying for. He'd done what he could. He was at peace with that part of the past.

He kept returning to his father's advice. Pops had always said the pursuit of happiness meant three things—work to do, something to hope for, and someone to love. Loving Paula should have been enough, but it wasn't. Not nearly enough. She'd put her eggs in Whit's basket, and that made the rest of his life seem pointless and absurd.

What do you want? The question was like a mating ball of snakes — a writhing mass of tangle and teeth. Nothing so simple as wanting her back. She was Whit's now. And she would never leave him — to do so would violate her own sensibilities. She'd believed Decker to be dead. *Damn that useless war!* As for marriage, he'd entered into one of his own — a grievous error.

What do you want, then?

He stopped in the street, staring straight ahead, while people rushed past, some brushing against him. On the far side of the street, he watched an old couple walk hand in hand, headed in the opposite direction. *I want my love to have mattered. To both of us. I want my love to mean something beyond mistakes and regrets.*

As he stood thinking, a man raced past him, nearly crashing into him. Something about the man's gait caught his eye. His height was right, and his posture was the same as someone he knew. He hurried after him, hopping with the help of the cane, but two legs would always be faster than one. The man soon outdistanced him. On reflection, he realized the man could *not* be Sergeant McHenry — the fellow he'd seen had two arms.

Still, the encounter left him shaken. *I am a haunted man,* he decided. *Not by ghosts, but by memories.*

As for ghosts — real ones — they were terrorizing Negros in Richmond. Men in sheets were making themselves known. Some blamed the violence on the Republicans, who pushed for repeal of the Black Codes and the vagrant laws used to control former slaves, believing that if the Republicans would just leave well enough alone, the transition to freedom would be less violent.

An element of the Black population had turned to crime, something the old guard used as a justification for their tactics. And all of Richmond chaffed at the invasion of carpetbaggers — opportunistic scallywags from the North who saw the First

District as a way to cash in. In a way, Nicholas White was a carpetbagger. As were Calista and her father.

And perhaps, so was Decker.

Resistance took the form of night attacks and lynchings. How hanging a Black man from a tree addressed the inequities of postwar military rule, Decker couldn't imagine. The violence only convinced Northerners that leniency had been a mistake. The idea that understanding could be accomplished through conciliatory policies was being disproved in the streets of Richmond. A sea change was coming, and *everyone* would be the worse for it.

Beyond sorting his thoughts, the morning's walk gave Decker a glimpse of what the new Richmond might become. He passed buildings being reconstructed from the rubble, noting the number of free Black men accomplishing and directing the work. With so many white men dead, they filled the need for craftsmen, laborers, and artisans. They moved with purpose, their laughter and good natures as integral to their industry as their hard work.

The sight of them made him long for his missing limbs.

The local government, on the other hand, was more interested in recreating the past with their restrictions and regulations. The Richmond they'd known was gone—burned away and rebuilt, while the bitter city fathers clutched at old, dead straws.

Decker had no place here. This was no longer home.

Exhausted, he returned to his apartment workshop to find White standing at the door, waiting. "Why didn't you go inside?" he called as he hobbled up the street.

"I thought you might be asleep or . . . I kept knocking."

Decker reached the door and opened it. "You are an idiot. What news?"

"I have an offer."

Decker ushered White in, saying, "Please forgive the mess. A bachelor makes a miserable housekeeper."

White stopped halfway in, staring at the bullet-shaped object in the middle of the room. "What is this?"

"A muse," Decker said. "Research."

White smiled, shaking his head. "You have an amazing mind." He ran a hand across the polished surface and then took a chair.

"Tell me about the offer. The government wants the formula?"

"The government? No. Paquin Powder."

"What?" Decker said, sitting down in the other chair. "I thought you hated the Paquin family. Didn't respect you, and all."

"I don't *hate* them. I simply couldn't work for them." He removed his top hat and set it on the table, next to the nearly full whiskey bottle. "They treated me abysmally. Worse, even, than you."

Decker laughed. He pushed the bottle closer to White. "Will you have a drink? If you want a glass, they're over there."

White waved him off. "You are the drinker, sir."

Decker tapped the bottle. "Not so much of one, these days. The offer?"

"They want both the process and the Prussian order."

White mentioned a tidy sum, which caused Decker to sit back, eyebrows up and mouth open. "Really? So much?"

"Divided in two, you'll have more than your initial inheritance by a considerable margin."

"Did you agree?"

White frowned. "No. I needed your approval."

"That seems like a fair deal —"

"You need to understand the Paquin family," White said. "Are you familiar with graphite glossing?"

"Of course. The coating inhibits the absorption of moisture. Wet gunpowder won't fire."

"Two methods existed for solving the same problem. One involved tumbling the powder with graphite for twelve hours at a time. The other involved the use of sodium nitrate, mined in Peru. Gerrard Paquin patented *both* processes in a single patent, using language that laid claim to both processes, neither of which really belonged to him."

"And your point is?"

White leaned in closer, his teeth projecting his smile. "Gerrard is a clever man. He knows how to use patents, and how *not* to use them." He sat back, stared at the bottle, and then at Decker. "He will purchase your work, and then he will bury it."

"Get to the point, White."

"Paquin Powder is all too happy to supply the Prussians. Think of all the buildings and workers, inactive. Paquin still sells plenty of coarse grain powder for blasting, but your order is a welcome bit of business. As for your process, embracing it would make those buildings obsolete. Paquin is not ready to retool the entire company. A competitor, however, might be."

"What's to stop someone else from applying for the patent?" Decker asked.

"A matter of timing. Gerrard Paquin has informants in the patent office. The moment he is warned, he'll submit your patent himself, expedited, and prevent any other company from producing your powder."

"If I agree to their proposal, my powder may never be produced?"

"Perhaps not in your lifetime."

Decker sat back and grinned. His expression seemed to surprise White. "That is for the best," Decker told him. "The idea of men firing repeating rifles without smoke has begun to trouble me. I have been focused on the main chance since we came here. When you focus, you risk ignoring the wider scope of ideas." White's brow furrowed. "I am confusing you for no reason," Decker continued. "Suffice it to say that I'm pleased with this development. How soon can you finalize the deal?"

White sat back, somewhat relieved. "I worried you would not agree."

"I wonder that you even asked."

"It is a matter of *ethics*, sir." White paused. "I have been observing the way you conduct yourself. You are insane. But you are honest."

"Perhaps they go hand-in-hand," Decker said.

. . .

White arranged to sell the warehouse and the machinery. Though the proceeds were nowhere near the original costs, the additional money, when paired with the Paquin check, made a welcome total. Decker took his half gratefully. "You have been a most clever businessman, Mr. White. We did good work here."

White gazed at the interior of the warehouse, emptied now, save for Decker's workbench and crated equipment. His face was twisted with some unnamed emotion. He did not speak.

"I have a few days more work for Mr. Smith," Decker continued. "Personal arrangements, so I will pay him. But I ask you to consider a suggestion." He made his proposal. White nodded with great vigor and then turned away.

"You seem concerned, White. What worries you?"

White cleared his throat and tried to speak, stopping before a single word escaped his lips. When, after deep breaths, he spoke, his voice was thick with emotion. "Working here has been an experience out of context with the rest of my life." He stared at Decker. "I will be working for the Paquin family again."

Decker smiled. "I'm glad. Perhaps they have a newfound understanding of your abilities."

"And what will you do?"

Decker's expression sank. "I have an unpleasant task ahead of me. Your Pinkerton friend did me one last service. My wife keeps the company of a certain officer with the First District."

"Not Captain Wells!" White said, aghast.

"No, not Captain Wells. A major. Calista tends to aim high." He tried to smile but could not. His voice was even, as if he were relating another fact about gunpowder. In truth, the detective's revelations had stung him. Admitting the truth to White was nearly as bad. "I've called on my lawyer in Boston to make arrangements for an annulment."

"For the best," White said. "I'm sorry."

"Don't be. The mistake was mine. Your Pinkerton gave me reason to know exactly who she was before we were married. I chose to ignore him, or rather, I understood I was making a mistake, and chose to ignore my better senses." Decker's leg shook, and he adjusted his cane for better balance. "Early in the day for cramps," he muttered.

"Do you need to sit down?"

"No. I need to get on with things. I will take care of Charles. And you, sir? You will take care of yourself?"

White tilted his head, his teeth protruding from between his lips. "This is the end, then?"

Decker pursed his lips. "Do we have additional business?"

"I suppose not."

"Well, then. You will take care of yourself, partner."

"I will," White said, gulping.

"Goodbye, Nicholas."

"Goodbye, friend." White stepped closer.

"I can't shake hands with this cane —"

White wrapped his arms around Decker in a hug. "Oh, shut up," he said.

• • •

The news that his wife had betrayed him stung Decker more than he admitted, even to himself. When the detective made his report, Decker took the news calmly. There had been no mystery. He'd engaged the Pinkerton out of due diligence.

After the detective left, Decker sat alone, imagining the worst of events. He understood that a woman had needs, just as a man had. And he was hardly able to satisfy those needs. Still, the news worked on his feelings of inadequacy. A plan was generated, and he found himself looking forward to a satisfying denouement.

After visiting the bank, Charles drove the carriage to Calista's home. Alexandros greeted Decker at the door with a relieved smile. "You've come home! I'm so glad! You must not blame her, that headstrong girl of mine. I'm certain you can work things out—"

"Is she here?" he asked.

"Yes, indeed."

"A miracle of wonder," Decker said, stepping inside. Calista stood in the hallway, her hands clasped in front of her, eyes downcast. Decker asked Alexandros to excuse himself, and he did so with haste. Calista followed Decker into the parlor. Neither one sat.

"I've come to say goodbye," Decker said. "In the coming weeks, my lawyer will bring papers for you to sign. I'm having our marriage annulled."

Calista's face turned sour. "What makes you think I'll agree to any such arrangement?"

Decker's face was a sheet of slate. "Let's not waste time. Perhaps you can muster a touch of grace. Let honesty guide our parting." He had several items in his hands, and he extended the first to her. "This is a Pinkerton report. I believe the officer's name is Major Dunham."

A dark blush colored her cheeks.

"Under the circumstances, our marriage is voidable. You have my permission to tell friends I was unable to consummate the marriage. That will help you save face, if such a thing matters to you."

She turned back, surprise on her face. "Why would I say such a thing?"

"I won't be here to deny it," Decker said. "As for me, there is some advantage to being thought impotent rather than being thought a fool." She began to huff, and he scowled. "Calm down. I'm not finished." He extended a check. "I've sold the business. This represents your half of my half of the proceeds."

"What?"

"Half. Half of a half, that is. My partner has the other half. Still, the amount is substantial. As my wife, you shall receive half of what is mine."

She took the check by the corner, holding it aloft as if it might bite her. "You're paying me off?"

"Among those who ply your trade, this check is proof of your ascendency."

When the force of his words struck her, she moved to slap him. He blocked her with his cane. She stepped back, massaging her palm as if she'd sustained great injury, though he knew she had not. "Careful," he said. "If I cared to, I could void the marriage and put you and your father in the street without a penny."

She considered his words, gripping the check tighter. "Is this real?" she asked.

"Yes. Our marriage was *my* mistake, not yours. For your part, you are getting what you married me for. You may eventually regard our marriage as a smashing success." He took a deep breath and let it out in a sigh. "Our business is done.

When the lawyer comes, sign the papers. Don't spend the money all at once. Put some aside. And *don't* tell your father how much you have. He will go through that check like he goes through whiskey."

He pivoted—a practiced maneuver—and made ready to leave.

"Wait, please."

He turned back. Her expression hovered midway between confusion and regret. It was not the response he'd expected.

"Why are you doing this?" She placed the check face down on the end table and sat in the rosewood chair. "I am not conventional, sir. I am my own woman. You are not a fool. You knew who I was *before* you married me. Why are you so angry?"

He stared. He'd anticipated a brief, angry parting. This sudden turn left him confused. "A husband should not have to share the affections of his wife. She belongs to him."

She tilted her head, the hint of a wry smile on her lips. "I've heard you speak with great passion against the institution of slavery. You argue that liberty is the natural state of man. Will you not extend that privilege to the fairer sex?"

Decker stood still, his mouth hanging open.

"Sir? You said a wife belongs to a husband. Do women yearn for and deserve a fair measure of liberty, or are they a belonging?"

"I am unable to answer you," he said, "because you are irrevocably correct."

What had been her sin against him, he wondered? That she'd failed to conform to the expectations of a wife? No, he'd been *attracted* to her lack of convention. The embarrassment that she'd caused him? Beyond White, who'd thought far too much of him, he did not give a damn what others thought. Did her obvious machinations to secure financial security for her and her father offend him? No. What other recourse did women have but a safe marriage? Her crime was her failure to love him, and him alone.

And did I love her and her alone?

"Who will care for you?" she asked. She shook her head, as if he were behaving like a stubborn child. "You are an amazement, sir, but that cannot last forever. Your health will fail. I watch after my father and I would watch after you." Her voice grew quiet, and her eyes acquired the sadness he'd seen on their wedding night. "I've grown genuinely fond of you, Decker, whether you believe that or not."

He stared at her. She'd surprised him again. "May I sit down?" he asked. His leg trembled, and he thought he might topple.

She stood and pulled a chair to him. He thanked her and sat.

"You are right," he said at last. "I came here angry. I hope that you'll believe me when I say that the anger is gone, entirely. Thank you for your kind offer, but I must decline. We should never have married in the first place." The expression on her face told him that she could not disagree. "There is much to admire about you, Calista. Your loyalty to your father, and now your offer to . . . care for me. I came here with insults and you answered with kindness. I will remember that until the day I die."

She looked down. "Is that all you'll remember?"

He tried to keep his voice even and failed. "I'll remember our wedding night. And most of all, I will remember our dance."

This last seemed to shake her. Her eyes became misty.

He pulled himself up and stood waiting until she met his gaze. "You are not suited to marriage, Calista," he said, regaining control of his voice. "But with these funds, you become a woman of means, answering to no one save yourself and your secret heart. You can chart your own course, for however long you manage to maintain the money."

She stepped close and kissed his cheek.

"I will remember you," he said.

. . .

"Here is where we part ways," Decker told Charles. The carriage sat in front of his small residence. "We've sold the warehouse and the equipment inside. The new owners are well satisfied with the state of the building. You did well with the roof. He mentioned the roof specifically."

Charles stared straight ahead, his hands on the reins. "I know. I went by yesterday, expecting the worst, and that's what I got."

"Ah," Decker said. "We tried to convince the buyer to obtain your services, and he pretended some interest, but he's old money and he's white. I don't expect anything to come of it."

Charles slumped in the seat. "Well, I got me a knife."

Decker snorted. "More than that, I think." He reached over the driver's seat and placed a pouch on the cushion next to his foreman. "White and I both put a portion of the sale toward your bonus. Without you, we would not have succeeded in our endeavors."

Charles opened the pouch and stared inside. "Damn."

"Like the knife, I suggest you keep the money out of sight. Tell only your wife. Best to find a hiding place, and never speak of this, lest you make a target of yourself. Don't trust your friends and don't trust the authorities."

"This a *lot* of money."

"Be smart with it." Decker started to slide out of the carriage. "I'm leaving Richmond. White and I both felt you could make use of the carriage. It's yours now."

Charles glanced up, his expression soft, and then something seemed to occur to him, and his mouth turned down. "What about the men I hired? They getting anything?"

Decker smiled, his gaze narrowing. "What about them indeed? You have money. What will you do? Are you going to take care of them?"

Charles frowned, wrinkles creasing his forehead.

"The war is over. *Nobody owns anybody.* You own yourself. But the idea of slavery dies hard." He bit his lip. "The preacher and the taxman will tell you why that money doesn't belong to you. Your friends will say the same. Where were they when you hauled rubble at the warehouse? What gives them a right to your sweat and muscle? Half a million men died so you could cast your chains aside. Don't let someone talk you into putting them back on."

Decker saw the confused look on his foreman's face. "Let me make it simple for you. You worked. We paid you. It was *clean.* No one forced anyone to do anything. That is how free men live in the world." He turned and shuffled to the door.

"Brown?" Charles called.

"Mr. Smith."

Charles shook his head, frowning. "I don't understand you."

"I know," Decker said. "But we got on well, regardless."

He stepped into the house, closing the door behind him. Saying goodbye to so many had drained him. The last fifteen feet between him and his chair seemed like a mile. He stood still, marshalling his energy. The sound of steps came too fast for him to react. When the club struck him from behind, he dropped forward without a sound.

Chapter Twenty-Nine

Richmond, Virginia
November 1867

"Here, in the dread tribunal of last resort, valor contended against valor. Here brave men struggled and died for the right as God gave them to see the right."
~Adlai E. Stevenson

Paula sat at the breakfast table, her hands in her lap. Whit had a bite of biscuit in his mouth and a spoon in the gravy. He glanced up and stopped chewing. "What's wrong?" he asked, his voice muffled with food.

"I would like you to tell me where you've been going at night."

He began chewing slowly, never taking his eyes off her. "My job requires several evenings a week —"

"I did not say I wanted to *know* where you were. I said I wanted you to *tell* me. I wanted to hear it from your lips."

Whit set the spoon down on the china plate. "I just told you."

"You told me a lie." She sat, hands folded in her lap, her hair drawn back into a severe chignon that rested at the nape of her neck. Her dress was plain. Her chin jutted forward in a most unusual fashion.

He blushed. He pulled at his goatee once and then rubbed his nose. "If you wish to accuse me of some dalliance —"

"Who are these people you're involved with, Whit?"

His face went blank.

"If you are going to pursue something illegal, I should be forewarned."

"I will tell you what I want to tell you, and not a word more." He pointed at her plate. "Do you enjoy having a meal when you're hungry? I provide that." He pointed at the ceiling. "Do you enjoy having a roof over your head? I provide that, too."

She glanced around the room. Her home. Her things. "Yes, you've been a good husband. I'm wondering though. Are you a good man?"

Whit shoved his chair back from the table. He glowered. "How *dare* you?" He stood, thrusting out his chest. "All right. Two can play this game of yours. I want to hear you tell me about your friend, Decker Brown. Notice, I did not ask you about his service in the war. I know *everything*. I want to hear it from *your* lips." He smiled in grim triumph and waited for her response.

Paula did not flinch.

"I wonder how you come by the knowledge of my activities. Is it perhaps because we meet not two blocks from Mr. Brown's warehouse? Have you been seeing your friend when I'm away?"

"How dare *you*?" she asked, her face flushed crimson. "I have *never* given you cause for doubt, sir. What an infamous accusation!"

Whit ignored her. "You'll be interested to learn that your friend will be called to accounts this very day. Traitors must be dealt with."

Paula shook her head. "The war divided families. Some fought for the Union, and some for the South —"

"How many fought for both sides? I'll wager *both* sides would consider him a traitor if the truth were known." He leaned forward. "And you knew all along, didn't you? I took you for a patriot." The knuckles of his good arm braced on the breakfast table. "You've always cared for him, haven't you?"

"You have destroyed us," she said. The plain language seemed to stagger him. He stood straight, took a tentative step away, and then looked back. Shaking his head, he frowned, showing his lower teeth. He strode out of the room. Moments later, the door slammed.

Paula sat alone, silent and in shock. Millie called her name twice before Paula blinked and turned to face her. Millie stood in the doorway to the kitchen, her hand on the frame. "Are you all right, Miss Paula?"

"I need a carriage," she answered.

• • •

She visited Decker's small home and found it empty. She had not visited his warehouse before and had some difficulty locating it, though she knew very well where her husband and his friends met. By chance, she met Decker's partner, whom she'd seen at the ball several months past. She introduced herself, and after his initial surprise, Mr. White told her he not seen Decker either. He seemed quite disturbed to learn of his absence. She began to fear the worst.

Uncertain of how to proceed, she asked the driver to take her home.

Halfway there, an idea occurred to her. She instructed the driver to change direction, heading instead to East Franklin Street. When the carriage arrived at what was by now a well-known address, she sat for a moment, staring at the three-story, three-bay brick home. Columns at the entrance reminded her of her home before and during the war. Four chimneys bracketed the low-hipped roof. A simple home for a complex man.

She left the carriage, asking her driver to wait. Her knock at the door was answered immediately by the man she'd come to see. He stared at her, casting a baleful eye at her intrusion. "I've come to ask for a moment of your time," she said.

He shook his head. "Pardon my refusal, but I've suffered *constant* callers. While I am in Richmond, I wish to be left alone."

"I'm certain it's more peaceful in Lexington, sir. But I am here on a matter of life and death and must press my request."

The old gentleman closed his eyes, a grim frown visible beneath his white beard. He stepped back, holding the door for her.

The interior of the home was much the same as the exterior. Simple, with hints of Greek tradition in the molding and the wall coverings. He led her to a parlor and sat her by the fire, which felt like heaven after the carriage ride. Small touches, like the landscape painting on the far wall and the small statuette over the mantel, made the room cozy indeed. But she had no time for comfort.

"All right, Madam, how can I be of service?" His voice seemed tired, his face grave, and his manner stiff.

"I am going to tell you a story," she began. "Perhaps the story is true. Perhaps it is apocryphal." She took a deep breath. "But if the story is true, I'm going to ask a favor of you, and you will be obliged to help me."

• • •

Decker ached, from his bruised ankle to his throbbing head. He sat tied to a chair. The interior of the building was much the same as the interior of his own warehouse, with the exception of a second-floor loft that ran the perimeter of the building. The open area above him extended to the rafters, where a rope had been fixed. The noose dangled nearly to the ground floor, leaving a space of no more than eight feet—enough to hang someone easily enough.

A table had been set in front of him, and though no one had spoken, he understood he was to be given some sort of trial.

Decker didn't fear death. Indeed, he'd longed for it ever since Spotsylvania. But the prospect of hanging frightened him, and having suffered enough pain for a lifetime, he didn't relish the thought of more. Worse, hanging robbed a man of control. If they hanged him, he would shit himself.

I wonder if I weigh enough to hang properly? The thought gave him a start—something closely akin to a laugh, but more painful.

The room was silent, save for someone's whispers behind him. He tried to turn his head, but the ropes prevented him from looking back. At length, he heard footsteps. A procession passed him on the way to the front table. Five men, dressed in white sheet robes, sat at the table. He knew the one on the far left—Whitaker Hill.

"Where are your ghost hats, gentlemen?" he asked.

"The prisoner will be silent unless asked to speak," Whit said.

The man in the middle seemed familiar. Decker was certain he'd seen him at the ball. Some sort of city official. The others were unfamiliar. Whit was the youngest man at the table.

"You stand accused of high treason," the one in the middle said. His voice was solemn as a preacher's. "How do you plead?"

Decker closed his eyes. The room smelled musty, reminding him of rotting fruit and dust. He listened for a moment, wondering if rescue might save him from this ordeal. Perhaps

Charles would burst in with his Bowie. The thought made him laugh, this time out loud.

"You think this is funny?"

Decker shook his head, an action that sent bells crashing through his skull. He'd been struck, or perhaps kicked. He licked his lips. A sour taste flooded his mouth.

"The prisoner refuses to enter a plea. Let us proceed. Bring out the witness."

Another man in a robe stepped forward — a banty rooster with a strut. Edgar Cully. *The man keeps showing up in my life. I should have killed him.*

"Tell the court what you know," the man in the middle commanded.

Cully walked to the table and folded his arms across his chest. "Well," Cully said, and then paused, smiling at Decker. "When the war started, I headed west to fight in Tennessee. That's where my people are from, and that's where I planned to make a stand. Just before Shiloh, I was out on guard duty on the mighty Mississippi River, and I seen this Yankee standing on the riverbank, beggin' for supplies. He traded a few trinkets to another sentry downriver. I knowed it was him, but he went on and *confirmed* it. The other sentry must'a asked him his name because he shouted out, *I'm Decker by-God Brown, and I'm proud to be fighting for the Yankee army!* I never thought much of Brown anyway, so it didn't surprise me a lick that he'd turned traitor. After the war, I come back here to see what was left of Richmond, and there he was, all proud, like a chicken that's been half-plucked and don't know it. War hero? I don't think so."

Decker stared, a half-smile on his face.

"What do you say to Mr. Cully's accusation?" Whit asked.

"Sounds like the unvarnished, hand-to-Bible truth," Decker said.

The judge in the middle snorted. Cully looked around, as if suspecting he'd been made fun of. "That's all right, Brown," he said. "I'm gonna watch you dance on the end of that rope right there."

Whit pressed on. "Do you deny that you fought for the Union?" he asked.

"No, I don't," Decker said.

"Well, that's about it, isn't it?" the man in the middle asked.

"You men are going to be busy," Decker said. "As many men as wore blue during the war, you're going to need more rope."

Whit smiled. "Not all of them claimed to be a war hero for the Confederacy."

"You lost one arm, Whit. Seems like I sacrificed twice as much as you to this war." Whit started to speak, but Decker talked over him, his throbbing headache driving him. "Ironic. A Southerner took my leg, and a Northerner took my arm. Both sides already have a piece of me. But this trial isn't about the war, is it?" Decker said. The silence that followed made his words sound like an accusation.

Another sheeted man rushed past Decker, glancing back over his shoulder. "You ain't gonna believe this," he said, pointing to the back of the room. "I can't believe it myself—"

The commotion was accompanied by murmurs and gasps. Someone walked up behind him, and Decker waited for another blow to the back of the head. When it didn't come, he looked up at his judges. Their astonished expressions confused him. Then, the person behind him spoke. "I would like to address your court," he said. Decker didn't recognize the voice.

"General," the man in the middle said, gasping. "What brings you—"

The man stepped in front of Decker, never looking at him. He wore a simple suit, vest, and tie. His white hair and beard were well kept, and his voice carried a measure of dignity. "I've come to speak on this man's behalf."

General Lee! I am dreaming? Decker was incredulous. Of all the coincidences in his life, this was surely the most improbable.

"By all means, General. Please, proceed."

Lee turned and glanced at Decker. "You do not look like the man I recall."

"I've changed some."

"So have we all." He turned, shivering. "I am cold, gentlemen. I will be brief. Before Grant's wilderness campaign, I was conferring with my staff at the edge of a meadow. This man warned us of the approach of a Yankee patrol, and I moved to safety just before shots were fired." He glanced back at Decker before continuing. "In short, this man saved my life. And now, I've come to argue for *his*."

Cully shouted, "He's a traitor, General—"

"Shut that man up," the middle judge said. Whit pointed at Cully, and Cully closed his mouth tight.

Lee continued. "I have argued for patience and reconciliation. The war has been over for more than two years. Continued antagonism can't further the South's interests. We must move ahead and leave the war behind.

"This is not how gentlemen conduct themselves," Lee continued. "We are Christians, and we must accept what has happened. Our failure may yet prove to be a blessing, if we are able to call upon wisdom and prudence." He stared, perhaps by chance, at Whit. "And this proceeding is neither wise, nor prudent."

Whit sat, his mouth open, staring down at the table. He looked as if he'd been punched.

General Lee turned back to Decker. "I've done what I could." He gestured to the men at the table. "The South is grateful for your service, gentlemen. But the war is over. Haven't enough fallen men been plowed under? Can we not dispense with passion and give full scope to reason and to every kind feeling?"

The judge in the middle stood, bowed, and walked around the table, fishing a knife from his trousers. He bent down and cut Decker's bonds. Lee waited and watched.

"My cane?" Decker asked.

"I will wait outside," Lee said. "I think you might need a ride."

Whit approached with Decker's cane. He held it out, but when Decker grabbed for it, Whit held on tight, leaning close. "Don't bother going to the authorities—"

"Yes, I know where your meetinghouse is," Decker said. "But you'll move now. Ghosts disappear, don't they?"

Whit let go of the cane. "No one will speak of you," he said. "No one will ever speak of the *Courthouse Reaper*. You'll disappear, as if you'd never existed."

"Thank you," Decker answered.

CHAPTER THIRTY

Richmond, Virginia
December 1867

"Oi chusoi Dios aei enpiptousi, (The dice of God are always loaded.)
~Ralph Waldo Emerson

The general's driver dropped him at his residence, a kindness Decker appreciated. In return, he rode in silence, something Lee seemed to desire. When they arrived, Lee cut any thanks short. "I am cold, and I want to go home," he said.

Decker bowed and turned to his door. He was not entirely surprised to find Paula waiting for him.

Inside, he lit candles and sat down at the table, placing one candle next to the whiskey bottle. She joined him, her hands clasped in her lap, a solemn expression on her face. The telegram detailing his part in the battle of Spotsylvania sat atop the drawing of Jules Verne's space cannon. They were the last of his mementos — the only things left in the room that he would take with him when he went.

"I knew it was you," Decker said, his heart pounding. "It had to be you."

She nodded. She sat bundled in a coat and fur hat. The room was freezing — no one had tended the fireplace since morning. The flickering light of the candle softened the angles of her face. Her chestnut eyes watched him without blinking.

"Did I tell you I saved Lincoln's life as well?"

"Let's not joke," Paula said. "Are you all right? Did they hurt you?"

"They thumped me a little. Nothing lasting. How about you?"

"I am fine," she said, her lips pressed thin.

"Highly doubtful."

Her gaze rested on the whiskey bottle at the edge of the table.

"It may not seem so, but I've quit drinking. Haven't touched that in a week."

"I'm glad," she said. Her face sank. "My carriage is down the street. I suppose I should go now." Her expression belied her words.

"Not just yet," he said. "Talk to me for a moment." He could not hide the tremor in his voice.

"All right. What will you do now?"

"I will go west," he said.

"Always west."

He nodded. "Much farther, this time. I already sold my business, purchased a wagon, and loaded it with supplies." He rubbed his sore head. "I'll leave town in the morning. Staying on might be foolish. And you?"

"I will go home to my husband."

"Good. He's going to need you. Someone he cared for very deeply held up a mirror tonight, and Whit didn't like his own reflection."

Paula turned away, her face an austere mask. "I don't think he will be pleased to see me. He will know I interfered." After a moment, she added, "If he doesn't, I will tell him."

"He'll get over it. At any rate, he needs you. You are the better part of him."

Her shoulders began to tremble, and she wiped at her cheek. "I let you down, Decker. I betrayed you."

"Nonsense."

"I married Whit."

"Perhaps I am the one who betrayed *you*." His voice was clear and kind. She stopped crying for a moment. "You are the person I valued most in the world, but instead of attending to our shared future, I let duty get in the way. If I had it to do over, if I'd known how badly this would end, I might have taken you west when the war started. We'd have kept going until we were out of reach. We'd have had children—"

"Two boys and two girls," she said with the hint of a smile.

He sighed. "I love the idea of liberty. It's an idea worth fighting for. But the fight is over, and the outcome is murky. I fear my efforts were wasted. I love this Virginia of ours, too, but I abhor slavery in all its guises. How can you have a duty to something you don't believe in? That's just another form of slavery."

He waved his hand, as if to dismiss the subject. "History ran over us like a train. I believe most people want to live and work and love without the fingers of the world jabbing them in the eyes, blinding them to what's important. A pox on them all. They are more to blame than you or I."

She shook her head. "You make excuses for me, Decker."

"You are mistaken. Do you remember what you told me when I returned from Boston, just before the war? I asked if you were mine. You said *until the mountains crumble and the seas boil*." He smiled. "Well, the mountains crumbled, and the seas boiled, and you were here to save me. You've written a fine ending to our story, and I thank you for that with all my heart."

She stared at him. "I'd forgotten."

"Your heart remembered." He stood. "I will walk you to your carriage now."

When they arrived, she whispered, "I will never see you again." She grasped the lapels of his jacket, pulling him close.

"I will see you in my thoughts every day until I die. You are the love of my life." She tried to smile and failed.

"Stop, now. It's cold enough to freeze those tears to your face."

"Don't joke."

"I won't. I love you, Paula Crane."

"I love you, Decker Brown. I always did, and I always will."

He stepped back. "Go now," he said. "Or I won't be able to let you go at all."

When she'd left for the last time, he went inside the house and sat at the table. Tears running down his cheeks, he considered taking a drink. His limbs ached, and the lump on his head throbbed, but he'd told her he was done with the bottle, and so it would be.

For now.

• • •

Territory of Utah
April 1869

The crazy man pulled on the reins, and the wagon stopped. The boy gazed out of the back, staring at the white, alien landscape. Salt, from the wagon all the way to the mountains in the distance. "We're here," the man called.

The boy, barely thirteen, jumped out. "This is the Great Salt Lake?"

"The Salt Lake is some ways back," the crazy man said. He pulled at his beard with his one good arm, smiling. "This is a salt flat. And it's perfect."

Quentin shook his head. He'd been with Decker Brown for nearly a year. His previous owner had dragged him across the western territories, but nothing he'd seen looked like this. Flat and white as Decker Brown himself.

Brown had crossed paths with Mulvaney, the boy's owner, at a small trading store. Mulvaney was drunk, as he often was, ordering Quentin here and there, as he *always* did. Brown sat in the corner, sipping water, which cost more than whiskey in some places. At least, that's what Mulvaney said.

Brown stared at them, a curious look on his face. After a while, Brown asked Mulvaney if Quentin was his *slave*, and Mulvaney said, "Hell yes, he is." He cuffed the boy. "Ain't worth two shits, but he's my property."

Brown didn't bat an eye. He asked, "How much for the boy?"

Mulvaney wanted gold. There was never quite enough for the old miner. But the price he quoted was too high. Brown suggested a more reasonable sum, and after a few more shots, he offered to kick in a bottle of laudanum. "It'll put your whiskey to shame," he promised.

Mulvaney was the sort of man who bathed once a year. His beard was a shameful tangle, and his mustache, wet with whiskey, slipped between his lips when he talked. "That an officer's pistol on your hip?"

Brown glanced down at the Remington.

"How 'bout you throw in that there pistol?"

"How about I keep the pistol and shoot your stupid ass with it?"

Mulvaney frowned.

"Or keep the boy and say goodbye to the gold and the laudanum."

"Bought yourself a fine young buck," Mulvaney said.

The first night, Quentin planned on slitting the cripple's throat and getting away. There was no way he'd let a one-armed, one-legged man get on him like Mulvaney did. But the man surprised him. "I cannot stand slavery in any form," he said, handing over a bedroll. So saying, he trudged off to his own spot, away from the fire. He sat with his pistol in hand, awake throughout the night.

The next day, Quentin asked why he hadn't gone to sleep.

"Wanted to make sure that old pederast didn't have second thoughts." Quentin didn't understand the words, but he got the gist. Since he was hungry, and the man had plenty of supplies, he decided to stay with Brown for a while, and the while turned into near a year.

Over the long months, he'd formed a clear opinion of the man's mental stability. Brown cried often, laughed at the wrong time, and spent way too much time poking at his *rocket things*.

He stopped in towns along the way, asking for weird supplies they'd never need and certainly didn't have room for. Silk sheets? "It's for a *parachute*," he said. Paraffin? "Gonna light up the desert!"

When he showed Quentin the *capsule*, it gave him pause. Did the crazy man expect him to get inside? It only calmed him a little to see how Brown could fit his own self into the thing.

Over time, though, he came to appreciate Brown, crazy or not. He was a good cook. He didn't get drunk often, and he never laid a hand on Quentin, violent or otherwise. And the conversations they had, sitting near the fire at night, were enjoyable. Sometimes, Quentin triggered the discussion with a question. Once, he'd asked, "How come I never see you pray?"

"You never see me take a piss, either," Brown had answered. When that answer didn't seem quite enough, he added, "I pray in my own way. Back east, people made a lot of noise. Couldn't really hear God speaking. Out here?" He looked around, staring at the night sky. "I hear the whispers just fine." He poked at the fire, stirring up sparks. "Me and that old man still have some mending to do, but it'll come."

On occasion, Brown would ask what Quentin intended to do with himself, a question which made no sense at all to the boy. "I intend to go to sleep, and in the morning, I intend to wake up."

"That's not enough," Brown told him. He schooled him from a few books, and though Quentin couldn't read as well as Brown hoped, he could listen. Brown taught him about liberty and happiness, and a bunch of other things that seemed very important to him. Probably what drove him crazy in the first place.

"What do you hope for?" he asked once.

"I hope you'll get where you're going," Quentin answered. He didn't say, "soon."

"We're going to the salt flats," Brown explained. "Salt won't burn. It will be safe for all concerned." Like a lot of what Brown said, there was no sense in the answer.

On another occasion, Brown again asked, "What do you hope for?"

"I don't know what you mean. You always talk like this, and it's like that other language—"

"French."

"—it don't make sense."

Brown sat back against the wheel of the wagon. He liked to sit there, because when he needed to stand, he could grab the spokes and hoist himself up. "Hope is a wish, put into action. If you could wish for anything, and the wish would come true, what would you wish for?"

Quentin considered the question. Money? No, being with Mulvaney cured him of that. Money was for supplies, and not much else. What then? "Anything?"

"Yes. Anything."

"I guess I'd wish I could fly."

Brown laughed, and the sound bounced over the prairie like a manic echo. "Myself as well! We share the same wish!"

Traveling west through the Utah Territory, they encountered various Indian tribes. Brown picked up languages easily, and that seemed to make the Indians more amenable. Sometimes, the encounters weren't so friendly. One Ute raiding party cornered them in a small ravine in the Rocky Mountains. Rather than fight, Brown gave them the spare horse in exchange for one warrior's felt hat, as if that were a fair trade. Then, he sat up all night with his pistol and a Henry rifle, away from the wagon behind an outcropping of rocks.

In the morning, Quentin asked, "That hat looks stupid. It don't even fit your big head. If you're so ready to fight, why give up a horse?"

"Trading is better than killing."

"Then why'd you sit up all night?"

"Not everyone is so peaceable as myself."

Every time Brown taught him something, he'd finish by saying, "When you're on your own, you might need to know what plants you can eat when there's no water," or "When you're on your own, you might have to find your way using the constellations." To Quentin, it seemed like Brown wanted to send him on his way, though he couldn't imagine a one-armed, one-legged man alone on the prairie.

"When the time comes, you'll want to set out on your own," Brown repeated one night, just a week before they arrived at the salt flat. "I'll send you off proper, with some money to start you on your path."

"I don't want to go anywhere," Quentin had said. "I like it here with you."

Brown smiled in the firelight. It was a sad sort of smile, which was the best the crazy man could usually muster. "You can stay as long as you like. But someday, you'll move on."

Now, standing in the whitest flatland he'd ever seen, Quentin thought the time might be approaching. If this was the crazy man's stopping point, then he surely did not want to stay. No water. No town. "Damn," he whispered.

Sound carried in the flat. "Don't curse," Brown said, though he had a smile on his face.

"Seemed like the right thing to do," Quentin answered, and Brown laughed, because Brown said the very same phrase over and over, especially when following one of those rules of his. *Ethics*, he called it. He'd tried to explain the idea to Quentin, but the subject bored him.

Lessons on the stars, on the other hand, fired his imagination. He saw the patterns Brown pointed out—animals and people. His favorite was *Orion*. Part of him couldn't wait for the sun to set, so he could study the sky from this place, fifty miles from anywhere sensible. He was certain the sight would take his breath away.

Sure enough, after dinner, the sun crept behind the mountain, splashing the heavens with bands of color, disappearing in a pink glow. There were no clouds, and the new moon let the stars come out in all their *splendor*. That was a word Brown used for the sky.

The flat grew cold at night. Winter wasn't far behind them, and Quentin had to wrap himself in blankets to keep from shivering. The crazy man didn't seem to mind the cold. Same cold night air for both of them, but only Quentin felt the chill.

The band of white that bisected the sky—the Milky Way—was beautiful. Late in the evening, a star shot across the sky, headed for the mountains, leaving a green trail. "Damn!"

Brown chuckled. "I was about to curse, myself."

"What will you do out here?" Quentin asked. "Something with the wooden thing?"

It was getting too dark to see Brown clearly, but Quentin felt sure he'd shrugged. "I don't know it will ever come to that. But I am going to test a rocket powered with paraffin and a liquid oxidizer. I will take great pleasure in researching something for myself, and myself alone." After a moment of silence, Brown said, "What about you? What will you do with your life?"

This time, Quentin felt a kind of finality in the question. It made him sad. "I don't know. I guess I'll end up in a town somewhere. You've taught me things. Maybe someone will hire me."

Brown murmured something. He poured coffee on the fire, putting it out. "Let's do without fire, tonight," he said. "Tomorrow, we'll talk about things you might do on your own."

"Are you sick of me, then?"

"No, Quentin. I've enjoyed your company. But you're growing up. Time to make your way. Find a girl. Settle down."

Quentin felt himself blush. "Don't have use for no girl."

"You will change your mind, son."

"What about you? Did you have a girl?"

Brown didn't answer. Instead, he hopped to the wagon and began moving boxes in the back. Tired of waiting for an answer, Quentin joined him. "What are you looking for?"

"This," Brown said, removing a small bundle. He unwrapped paper and twine, revealing a small tube-shaped object. "Have you seen an illumination before, Quentin?"

"No."

"This is my last one. I've been saving it for a special night, and I believe this is the one. Have a seat. I'm going to take this out on the flat. Keep your eyes open."

Quentin did as he was told, sitting by the extinguished fire. Brown was a shadow hobbling off into the distance. A tiny flash of light signaled the striking of a match. A few seconds later, a whoosh sent the tiny rocket skyward, trailed by a stream of white fire. Quentin sat, open-mouthed. *Amazing!*

Then an explosion announced an eruption of blue sparks that filled the sky, followed by three smaller bursts of crimson. Flecks of color glimmered and then winked out, leaving puffs of smoke hanging like tiny clouds.

When Brown returned, he asked, "Did you like it?"

Quentin started to answer, but his throat was too tight to speak. After a moment, he was able to croak, "It was splendor," and that seemed to satisfy the old man.

Brown sat down and said, "Let's look at the sky for a while." Pinpoints of starlight cast a gray sheen across the salt flats. "The heavens are beautiful, aren't they? God did a fine job with the night." Brown asked. Then he said, "Men can be cruel, so it's easy to forget that they are capable of beauty as well."

Later, when the chill turned their breath to vapor, Brown stood, wobbling on one leg. "Good night."

"Good night."

Brown's hopping step, aided by the cane, stopped halfway to the wagon. He looked back. "You asked me a question, earlier. I'll answer you now. I did have a girl. I loved her with all my heart. I love her still. I wish that for you, son."

Quentin didn't answer, sensing that the crazy man would prefer the silence.

-END-

ACKNOWLEDGEMENTS

This book is a revised edition of the original (published by Cengage/Five Star in a beautiful little hardback book). Unfortunately, the Five Star division was being phased out, and no soft cover, Kindle, or audiobook version ever reached the market. The original hardback ended up in a lot of libraries, but the general reading public missed out on more affordable purchase options. I want to thank Black Rose Writing for giving the book a second life by publishing the new edition.

ABOUT THE AUTHOR

Brian Kaufman is the author of nine novels, five textbooks, multiple study guides, and a collection of novellas. He lives with his wife and dog in the Colorado mountains. Kaufman divides his time between his various passions, including blues guitar, weightlifting, hiking, and book hoarding. Most of all, he writes.

NOTE FROM BRIAN KAUFMAN

Word-of-mouth is crucial for any author to succeed. If you enjoyed *Dread Tribunal of Last Resort*, please leave a review online—anywhere you are able. Even if it's just a sentence or two. It would make all the difference and would be very much appreciated.

Thanks!
Brian Kaufman

We hope you enjoyed reading this title from:

BLACK ROSE
writing™

www.blackrosewriting.com

Subscribe to our mailing list – *The Rosevine* – and receive **FREE** books, daily deals, and stay current with news about upcoming releases and our hottest authors.
Scan the QR code below to sign up.

Already a subscriber? Please accept a sincere thank you for being a fan of Black Rose Writing authors.

View other Black Rose Writing titles at
www.blackrosewriting.com/books and use promo code
PRINT to receive a **20% discount** when purchasing.

Made in United States
Orlando, FL
13 September 2024

51461203R00207